TITLES BY MABEL SEELEY

The Listening House
The Chuckling Fingers
The Crying Sisters
The Whispering Cup
Eleven Came Back
The Beckoning Door
The Whistling Shadow

Praise for

THE LISTENING HOUSE

"Miss Seeley is to be welcomed as a very promising author of detective fiction." *—The Times Literary Supplement*

"Miss Seeley, with a good story to tell, ingenious plot and counter-plot, characters diverse and clearly seen, lifts her book into the first class." *—The Observer*

"Bloodcurdling. . . . Especially good." *—Saturday Review of Literature*

"The Crime Club have discovered a genius in Mabel Seeley. The author's style is unusual: she tells her story in natural everyday language, but she puts it 'right over'—and what a climax!" *—Manchester Evening News*

"So packed with weird thrills that it grips from first page to last. . . . Should take its place as one of the best thrillers of the season." *—National Newsagent*

"First-rate whodunit, with enough of romance to give it a Mary Roberts Rinehart appeal. . . . This is a newcomer in the field—a good 'un." *—Kirkus Reviews* (starred review, September 1938)

Praise for the novels of Mabel Seeley

"Beautifully told by a writer who is expert at finding horror in commonplace settings. Recommended for highest honors."
—*The New Yorker*

"*The Crying Sisters* is the Crime Club selection for this month, and it is an excellent mystery novel of the 'atmospheric' type. . . . It holds its interest from the beginning as it rises in crescendo toward climax."
—*The New York Times*

"Satin-smooth mystery novel in a family fracas which starts with acts of malignant mischief and leads to murder. . . . Ingenuous manner for some ingenious matter—expert timing and mechanics and pleasant romantic asides. Velvet."
—*Kirkus Reviews* (starred reviewed)

"Another superior job of atmosphere, character, and suspense."
—*Kirkus Reviews*

THE
LISTENING
HOUSE

Mabel Seeley

BERKLEY PRIME CRIME
NEW YORK

BERKLEY PRIME CRIME
Published by Berkley
An imprint of Penguin Random House LLC
penguinrandomhouse.com

Library of Congress Cataloging-in-Publication Data

Names: Seeley, Mabel, 1903-1991, author.
Title: The listening house / Mabel Seeley.
Description: Berkley Prime Crime trade paperback edition. |
New York: Berkley Prime Crime, 2021.
Identifiers: LCCN 2021007363 (print) | LCCN 2021007364 (ebook) |
ISBN 9780593334546 (trade paperback) | ISBN 9780593334553 (ebook)
Subjects: GSAFD: Mystery fiction.
Classification: LCC PS3537.E2826 L57 2021 (print) | LCC PS3537.E2826 (ebook) |
DDC 813/.52—dc23
LC record available at https://lccn.loc.gov/2021007363
LC ebook record available at https://lccn.loc.gov/2021007364

Doubleday, Doran hardcover edition / January 1938
Pyramid mass-market edition / January 1973
Berkley Prime Crime trade paperback edition / June 2021

Printed in the United States of America
1st Printing

Book design by Alison Cnockaert

To Gregory
With Love

DRAMATIS PERSONAE

GWYNNE DACRES, *copywriter out of a job, lodger.*

HARRIET LUELLA GARR, *whose business is and has been the taking in of lodgers.*

HODGE KISTLER, *ex-reporter but not retired, lodger.*

MR. JOSEPH WALLER, *retired, lodger.*

AGNES WALLER, *wife of Joseph Waller.*

MYRTLE SANDS, *salesgirl, lodger.*

CHARLES BUFFINGHAM, *soda jerker, lodger.*

JOHN GRANT, *retired accountant, lodger.*

MRS. HALLORAN, *Mrs. Garr's niece, mother of seven.*

MR. HALLORAN, *veteran of the World War.*

MRS. TEWMAN, *maid, resident in Mrs. Garr's basement.*

MR. TEWMAN, *co-owner of a hamburger castle.*

SAMUEL ZEITMAN, *whose time is short.*

ROVER, CECILIA, RICHARD, AND GEORGE, *pets of Mrs. Garr.*

LIEUTENANT PETER STROM, *in charge of the homicide squad, Gilling City police.*

RED AND JERRY, *officers of patrol car 22, whose territory covers the state capitol section.*

Reporters, additional police officers, a coroner, a ticket seller, doctors, nurses, etc.

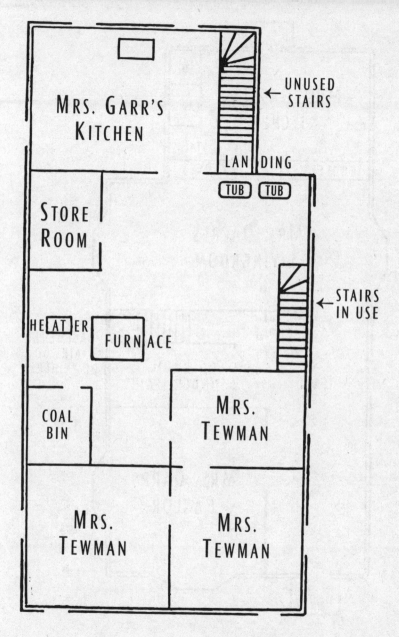

MRS. DACRES' ROUGH SKETCH OF THE BASEMENT IN
MRS. GARR'S HOUSE

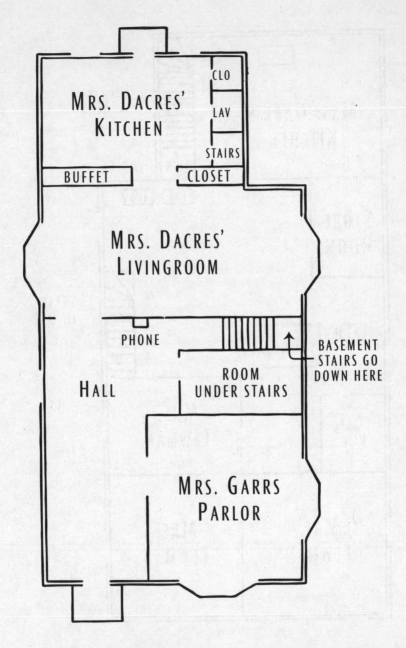

MRS. DACRES' ROUGH SKETCH OF THE GROUND FLOOR IN
MRS. GARR'S HOUSE

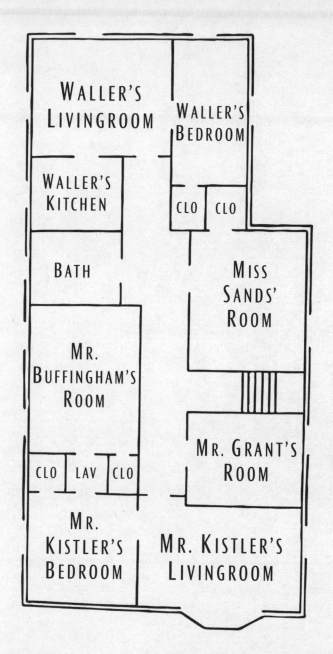

MRS. DACRES' ROUGH SKETCH OF THE FIRST FLOOR IN
MRS. GARR'S HOUSE

1

I AM NOT SURE, myself, that I should open the door of Mrs. Garr's house and let you in. I'm not at all sure that the truth about what happened there is tellable. People keep saying to me that the rumors going around are simply ghoulish, and ought to be laid to rest. But I've heard those rumors, some of them at least, and they're not a bit more nightmarish than the truth. Finally, of course, I gave in to pressure.

"Okay, I'll do it," I said.

Because, after all, I'm the one that not only knows almost everything that went on in Mrs. Garr's house in April, May, and June of this year, but also why a lot of it went on. And, unless Hodge Kistler wrote it, no one else could get the ending anywhere near right.

Since agreeing, I have made seventeen entirely separate and different beginnings.

I have begun with the cat's swift sneak and hunch under the bookcase of that dark hall. I have begun with my first sight of

Hodge Kistler chinning himself on the bar. I have begun with those terrifying hands reaching for my throat. I have begun with the opening of a door that led to an unimaginable hell.

But with any of those I have to stop too often for explanations. Mrs. Garr's house, I've found, isn't a house into which I can just plump you down. You need introductions. And so, at last, I have come around to begin at the beginning, giving you all the detail first, telling you, first, the little incidents which were to grow into such heart-shaking happenings. For the seeds of the mystery lay either in happenings which seemed at the time to bear no relationship to each other or to life in Mrs. Garr's house, or else in very small things, in incidents which might easily have meant nothing at all; incidents which, at the time, I considered myself silly for noting and wondering over.

First of all, as long as I'm telling this, and the only way you can go back in time and get into Mrs. Garr's house during those event-crammed weeks is by living there through me, I'm afraid you'll have to know, first, who and what I am and how I got to Mrs. Garr's house.

The whole thing began, for me, with a lost job.

I'm Gwynne Dacres, Mrs. Dacres. I'm twenty-six and divorced; I was married for six months when I was twenty-two—it took only that long for Carl Dacres to decide I was more of a wife and less of a nurse than he wanted. The last I heard of him, he was blissfully coddling his hypochondriac's soul with a day nurse and a night nurse, hired, down in South Carolina somewhere. The only thing I got out of my marriage was a bunch of complexes; I didn't ask alimony.

At Easter, this spring, I had been working in the advertising department at Tellier's for three years. Then, suddenly, I wasn't working at all.

There was drama, if you like that kind.

People as unimportant as advertising copywriters in a store as big as Tellier's aren't invited into the office of Mr. William Tellier, the president, very often. But I was bidden there at three o'clock of the Monday after Easter. I walked in to face Mr. Gangan, the advertising manager who was my boss, five vice presidents, and Mr. Tellier himself, all standing, all steel. On Mr. Tellier's desk was spread my own check sheet—I read the proofs of fashion ads—for that day's ad. Mr. Tellier bent toward it silkily.

"You recognize this proof, Mrs. Dacres?"

"Yes, it's my noon check sheet."

"You see this?"

The ad was a full-page ad for the big after-Easter sales, and across the top ran a big headline in 60 point caps and lower case:

Tellier's—
Where People Save!

What he was pointing at was my own scribbled notation at the side: "Change to 60 point caps."

"Certainly," I said. "The order to change the type came out on Mr. Gangan's revised proof this morning."

"Exactly. Then perhaps," he said, and his voice was awful, "perhaps you also recognize this?"

He picked up the check sheet, and under it was spread the first edition of that night's Gilling City *Comet,* opened to our ad, with the proof the paper had sent that noon right beside it. And on them both, on them *both,* blaring in 60 point capitals, was:

TELLIER'S—
WHERE PEOPLE SLAVE!

It didn't take even a split second to get it. I raised my eyes to Mr. Gangan's, opened my mouth to say what my instinct for self-preservation shouted to me to say.

But I shut my mouth again.

Only ruthlessness can raise a man to executive power at Tellier's. If I said what I had to say, I'd never again get a job in advertising in any department store in the United States. Mr. Gangan would see to that.

When I walked out of Tellier's big swinging doors, jobless, I fastened my mind, to keep its balance, on the laughter that must be rocking the town. For once a Tellier's ad had told the truth whole.

At the *Comet* offices, I knew that a printer and a proofreader were losing their jobs, too.

What I hadn't said in my defense was that Mr. Gangan had ordered me to shop a rival store's showing of new fabrics that noon, saying that he would have someone else check the noon proofs.

He'd forgotten, of course. Easy to forget. But he'd have taken hell if I'd told, and he'd have made it hell for me, and I'd have lost my job anyway. Now, at least, he'd recommend me—secretly.

Well, I knew, going through those swinging doors, exactly where I stood. It was almost April. The slow summer season was right ahead. The other stores would be suspicious of a recently fired Tellier's copywriter after this riot—even if they didn't want one to read proof. I had no earthly chance of getting another steady job before heavy advertising began again in August and September; perhaps not then.

I had exactly $278.32 in the bank.

NO JOB. TWO HUNDRED and seventy-eight dollars and thirty-two cents in the bank. I supposed I should be glad I had that much.

But if you've ever been on your own and out of a job—it's an experience plenty of people have shared with me—you'll know how I did feel, and glad wasn't any part of it.

I tried to shake it off, going home in the streetcar; tried to think instead of things I could do: look over the Help Wanteds, apply at all the other stores in town, do something about the way I lived. How could I afford thirty-five dollars a month for an apartment, on nothing a week?

But when I stood in my living room with the door locked behind me, I didn't think I could give the apartment up. It had been my harbor and refuge for two years; I'd created it myself; I loved it. I looked at my blue rug, my blue window hangings, my white lamps; looked at the sofa I'd had reupholstered gorgeously in blue satin on the strength of a raise the year before, looked at my clear, light salmon walls, so delectably lovely; looked at my grandmother's old rug on the wall, handwoven of dark blue wool as faded as smoke.

I didn't think I could give it up. But I had to. Firmly I sat down on the sofa and opened the *Comet* I'd abstracted from the advertising file on my way out of the office.

There weren't many Help Wanteds. They ran, mostly, "Girl wanting good home more than wages, help mother with 6 chil., $2 wk." Or, "Sell on sight, knitted sports frocks."

Nothing there.

I did the Unfurnished Apartments next, went on through Unfurnished Rooms, and started on Housekeeping Rooms.

There, on the third ad, my eyes stopped.

It seems queer, looking back, to think how casually I came across that ad. Queer, how inevitable that sequence of events was, that led from that lost job to Mrs. Garr's house.

> *Clean, lt, airy dng rm and kit of old mansion, gas, lt,*
> *and ht furn. $4.50 wk, 593 Trent.*

That was what the ad said. Words, I suppose, can't carry an aura. What I thought was, *Glory, that's cheap.* If I can't get a job by November, I'll go and be a mother's help, wants home more than wages. What awful hooey—could anyone? About twenty dollars a month for rent, gas, light, and heat. Two hundred and seventy-eight dollars and thirty-two cents divided by—well, divided by eight. Eight into $278.32 is about thirty-five dollars. Thirty-five dollars a month. Thirty-five dollars minus twenty dollars leaves fifteen dollars a month to eat on. Baby, you'll eat oatmeal and like it. But can you do it? Absolutely!

I KNEW JUST ABOUT where 593 Trent Street would be. Gilling City is the state capital; the capitol building is on the side of our biggest hill, and Trent Street runs along one side of the capitol. Five ninety-three should be pretty close to the top of Capitol Hill.

It was misting a little when I got off the streetcar at Sixteenth and Buller, to walk the three blocks up Sixteenth to Trent. Cold, too; just cold enough for the sleety mist to stick to the brown fuzz of my sports coat and make me look like a walking fog. My face prickled with the mist; when I stuck my tongue out at it, it bit like a hundred needles, and my ears were filled with the soft *spit, spit* it made everywhere it hit. Sixteenth is steep; the four-plexes lining it are all built on the bias, with one long side showing most of the basement wall, and one short side hitting the hill too soon.

As I walked the last block up Sixteenth I had, on my right, the old Elliott House that was built by one of the state's early governors; it's a huge square of red stone, boxlike except for the porte cochere on the Trent Street side, and with a red brick wall circling its grounds. Across Sixteenth was a pink ice-cream four-plex, brand new. Across Trent was a gray wooden monstrosity dripping wood lace. Kitty-corner, on the one remaining corner, was a big red brick shoebox broken by three-window bays. Even across the corner, I could see the scrolled gold numbers on the old-fashioned fanlight above the door.

Five ninety-three.

That, then, was my first look at 593 Trent Street. At Mrs. Garr's house.

I crossed over. I often like old houses; this one was dignified, not too ornate, not bad at all if it hadn't been so dirty.

Mist was sticking to its red-black brick, but instead of looking foggy and clean, it looked foggy and dirty, grimy with a dirt unbelievable in a city as young as ours. Against its sniffling background of air indistinguishable from sky, all one thick, damp, even gray, it was drenched but still dirty, with black soot washing in little runnels down the walls, runnels that were still red-black after the soot had washed.

I walked along Sixteenth Street, down the side of the house, until I got to the railing. Sixteenth Street ends there, not ten feet behind the house, because the hill there drops sixty feet, straight down, to the huddled gray houses on Water Street, below. The drop has been cemented, smooth and straight, the entire dizzy height.

Right then, standing there, I had a moment of doubt. I'd read *Les Misérables* once, and laughed at the frequency with which its characters hung on the brink of an abyss. But 593 Trent Street hovered too closely to an abyss for comfort. Who could say, if a wind should come, that its bricks wouldn't waver like cards in a card house, clatter and rattle down that concrete cliff, shatter and stun and kill and heap in a gigantic trash pile on that huddle of houses below, so far below?

Mr. Gangan once said I had "too God damn much imagination."

I shook myself, walked around to the front of the house, up

the steps, and twisted the decorated iron triangle that stood out from the door casing.

A jangle sounded inside, but almost before it had begun the door opened.

I USED TO THINK, afterward, that I'd never depend on my judgment of people again.

Because my first impression of Mrs. Garr, as she stood there blocking her open door, was pleasant.

It was her hair.

Her hair was white, and the first time I saw her I saw nothing beyond it. It was beautiful hair. She talked, I answered, but instead of watching mouth and eyes as I usually do, I looked at her hair.

White.

If you've seen cleaned white goose feathers, sleek and shining, you know something of the color and the texture, too; it looked that soft. Her way of wearing it was old-fashioned: a curled pompadour in front, like a fluff of soap bubbles, and a soft knot of the back hair on top of her head.

"Didn't I just see you walking around the house, miss?" was what she said.

I didn't pick up on the suspicion, or the fact that she must have been watching me through a window. I was looking at her hair.

"Yes," I said in my pleasantest voice. "I walked back to see the drop. It's steep, isn't it?"

"Did you ring my bell to say it was steep?"

"Oh no." I laughed and hurried to say it. "I rang your bell because I saw your ad in the paper. About the rooms. Could I see them?"

"Oh, cer'n'y, cer'n'y, you can see the rooms." She stepped

back. Her voice was slurred; not a Southern speech, more a careless speech, eliding sounds.

I stepped into the hall. And thought I should step out again.

The hall wasn't inviting. It smelled of old gas. It smelled of animals confined to cellars. The ghosts of long-fried dinners, the acridity of long-burned cigarettes haunted the air, which was a thicker, foggier dark than the gray day outside; a murk that might have been the grime of the outside walls floated loose and suspended in the hall.

Ahead a rectangle of lighter gray outlined the door of a room on the right; farther ahead on the right glowered a doorway into pitch-blackness. The only window, shrouded in musty red curtains, was far ahead on the left.

"Oh," I gasped, turning. "I'm afraid I made a mistake. I—"

"No, no, miss." The woman took the sleeve of my coat in a light grasp. "This is the house. And the rooms are right down the hall. First-floor rooms. Very fine rooms. Very clean rooms."

There was urgency in her voice.

"Well . . ." I said uncertainly, thinking: She's poor, she needs the money.

She limped a little as she went down the hall. It seemed heartless not even to look at her rooms. She was a big woman; heavy bones showed through her sagging flesh, but from the back she looked very old, her head hunched forward so that her black crepe shoulders rose above her neck. She limped straight down the hall, stopping at the blackened double doors at the end, lifted a key from the casing, threw the doors open, and stood there in the opening, nodding, smiling, beckoning, in some odd way furtive.

The hall, as I went toward her, didn't improve.

The walls were hung with thick red paper. Red? It was again the red-brick black of the walls outside. Against the left wall stood a davenport and chair upholstered in black leather; huge things, such as you still see sometimes in old hotel lobbies. A bookcase of grimed golden oak stood next; behind its dirty glass I could *see* book agents' sets of unreadable authors, shelves of cheaply bound novels.

As I stepped past the door on the left I had an even stronger whiff of cellars. Suddenly a slack gray female alley cat shot out from that door, across my feet, flattened herself, and crawled under the bookcase.

"What the . . . ?"

"Kitty, kitty?" asked the woman fondly. "That's my puss. I'm very fond of cats."

"I've never known any intimately."

"You'd like 'em. Show me a person likes animals, and I show you a good person."

Stairs rose beyond the room from which the cat had come; then I was at the doors to which the woman beckoned me.

I had a surprise.

The room into which I looked was nice.

The woman—she hadn't told me her name yet—had sense enough to close the double doors behind me quickly. And this room didn't smell. Not after the hall, anyway. It ran the entire width of the house and was extended at each side by bays of three windows. The back wall, opposite the doors, was filled with shelves and drawers; it was an old-fashioned built-in buffet, but it was exquisitely done. It, and the rest of the woodwork, had been ivoried; the paper was soft *rose;* the rug had been a deeper rose, its flowers long stepped into their background. A new brown studio couch, a good one, along the wall beside the doors. White curtains. Gateleg table and dining chairs in one bay; green upholstered chair, table, and lamp in the other.

More astounding—it was almost clean.

"This is really nice." I hoped I didn't sound as surprised as I was.

"Oh yes, yes, indeed. Very nice. And you have to think about the neighborhood. An exclusive neighborhood. Only the best people live in this part of town. It's a privilege to live in this neighborhood. And walking distance. You could walk downtown, a healthy young girl like you."

She laughed ingratiatingly, a high, sharp, old woman's laugh.

"And the other room?"

"Yes, yes, indeed! The other room!" She limped toward a door beside the buffet, swung it open.

The kitchen made me forget the hall.

The good old American kitchen, celebrated in song and story, reminiscent of pumpkin pies, stuffed chickens, applesauce, and gingerbread. Cupboards around the walls, bright linoleum on the floor, a big table against the back window, green rag rug in front of the table, a family-size gas stove, a cavernous icebox. This was a kitchen still holding the furnishings of its heyday, when a dexterous cook had ruled over the feasts of some early great.

It was no dirtier than a little scrubbing would remedy.

"Where do the three doors on this west wall lead to?"

"This middle one, that's a lavatory."

I hadn't expected that. Chalk one up for a private toilet and washbowl.

"The first door's locked. It goes down cellar. We don't ever use these back cellar stairs anymore."

"I see."

"You wouldn't ever use that. And this here door . . ." She paused, and her eyes seemed to focus on a point three inches east of my face. "This here is a closet I keep some of my things in. There ain't any closets in the front of the house, and seeing the back has so many, it seems like the people back here don't need it. I used to live in this part myself. I used to live on this whole floor, but now I rent out the back, except I always keep this closet."

It was true I wouldn't need that closet; the short passageway from the kitchen to the other room had drawers on one side, a deep, narrow closet on the other.

I stood uncertain. The place was surely better than I could have expected, from the price. But that hall!

"I'd like to think about it—" I began.

"There's a many comes and looks at this place." The woman stood beside but a little behind me again, her soft voice urging me over my shoulder. She never seemed to stand where I could look at her. "But there's a many I don't want. Chillern, now, I can't stand chillern around. I'm a middle-aged woman, and my nerves ain't as good as they were."

She was sixty-five if she was out of the cradle.

"You any chillern?"

"No. There's only myself. I'm divorced."

"Oh. You give parties?"

"Not very many."

"One or two quiet men friends, now, I don't object to. I know how girls are; they got to have men friends. But I don't like my furniture broke."

"I've never had any furniture broken."

"You a working girl?"

"Yes," I said, "but I shan't be working all the time. I'm taking most of the summer off."

"Oh." I'd expected suspicion there, and got it. "I like my rent paid in advance. A week advance. And them as don't pay up, I only give a day notice to vacate. I'm an old woman alone in the world and I got to pertect myself."

"I have money in the bank . . ." I tried, again, to face her, but she again edged around so she kept her view of my half face.

"That's fine, that's fine," she said. "But you oughtn't to trust banks. I'd never keep a penny—" She stopped there, seemed to come to a decision; she came closer, took her light grasp of my sleeve. "You're a nice girl, I can see; it would be lovely to have a nice girl in the house, almost like a companion to me. I don't get so much chance to rent over summer, so many goes to the lake. For a nice girl like you, dearie, having a little trouble with her job and all, I could maybe let you have it for four dollars a week for the summer. Till September, maybe."

Four dollars a week! That would leave me almost eighteen dollars a month to eat on. Heavens! I could almost go to movies! I took a breath.

"I'll take it," I said.

We went back to her parlor for the receipt for the first week's rent. As we passed the stairs I chanced to look up. On the wall of the landing was a shadow cast by some hall light upstairs, a shadow with a head on it, perfectly still.

Someone was standing there, listening.

Curious, I thought, and thought no more about it.

2

IT WAS MARCH TWENTY-NINTH when I lost my job, when I paid my first visit to Mrs. Garr's house; it was April fifteenth that I moved. I'd picked up a couple of days' work as a salesgirl at Chapman's, so it was eight o'clock in the evening before I loaded my suitcases, my steamer trunk, my cedar chest with the china packed in it, my sewing cabinet, my aluminum kettles and copper frying pans into a taxi. My precious furniture was safely in storage. As it was, the taxi was so full I sat on top of a suitcase with my feet on the box of kitchenware, and the driver had my trunk upended on the seat beside him.

"Why don't you put the steamer trunk in back and let me sit with you?" I asked him, with an eye to his own comfort.

"Lady, that's against the rules," he reproved me. "You stay in back."

We started off. I looked in my handbag mirror to see if I looked like a seducer of taxi drivers, but I didn't, so I just took my foot out of the teakettle every time it jounced in, resigned.

The driver evidently felt sorry for me when he saw what I'd come to. In front of 593 Trent Street, he helped me out of the kitchenware with a flourish. He even carried things into the house.

"You leave these boxes to me, miss; I'll take 'em in."

Mrs. Garr—Harriet Luella Garr was the name she'd signed to that first rent receipt—opened the door quickly; she must have been watching again. She hovered near the double doors, taking a good look at everything that went in. I tipped the driver three dollars, which made cheap moving, and he said, "Thank you, miss," as if he meant it.

Mrs. Garr said approvingly to me before he was halfway down the hall, "I like to see a body be generous to servants," and I saw him hesitate at the door as if he wanted to come back and kick her in the shins. But he winked at me instead and went back to his sacred front seat.

Mrs. Garr trailed me, back and forth, as I began pushing the kitchen boxes toward the room where they were to go.

"I've got some rules for this house all the people in it have to go by," she said. "A young girl like you don't realize, now, the expense you can run up in gas bills, running a lot of hot water. The gas heater, that's terrible dear to run. If you want to take a bath, you let me know, and I'll be respons'ble for turning it off. I don't want any more turning on the hot-water heater and then forgetting it, like I've had happen. And if you want any water for washing dishes or such, I'd thank you to heat it on the gas stove in your kitchen. The big gas heater is more expensive. That's your sheets and cases I got laid out on the table there. They go in a place in the studio couch if you want, but I can see you're going to have plenty of drawer room to keep 'em in the buffet. You going to unpack that trunk?"

"Not now. That's mostly filled with summer clothes I won't need for some weeks yet."

"I could help you move that. That's heavy for a young girl like you."

I'm short and stocky, as a girl with Scotch peasant ancestry has a right to be; I'm perfectly capable of pushing around my own steamer trunk. I'd just been lugging to the kitchen boxes that were twice as heavy as it was. If she was going to be Mother's little helper, why hadn't she volunteered before?

I looked around at her and had a shock. It was the first time I'd had a good look into her eyes. They were black and little and hard and hot, set deep in puffy eyelids like little lumps of hot coal pushed deep into bread dough. Evil eyes. Evil eyes under that lovely white hair.

"Why, certainly," I said, to cover my own startled recognition. "That's kind of you. I wonder where——"

"In that closet is a place this trunk would fit. You take that end."

She breathed with gasps, carrying her side. I hadn't been into the closet before; it had no light, but a way back at the far end was a raised platform perhaps six inches high that the trunk just fit on.

"They's stairs under here." She looked at the trunk with satisfaction. "That's a good place for a trunk. Most apartments, you'd have to keep it in a basement."

After that she just watched me again, her eyes like spyglasses on every movement.

F' heaven's sake, I asked myself, *is she going to stick like the old man of the sea?*

I asked: "Are there many other people in the house?" I hoped I wouldn't have quite all her time.

"I got only high-class people in my house. Except them Tewmans. I let them live in the basement for helping around. In front upstairs, I got Mr. Kistler; he's a newspaperman, a fine young man, two rooms. And back of him I got Mr. Buff'nim, one room, and Mr. Grant, one room, and the bath on one side, and Miss Sands on the other, and the Wallers in back. Mr. Buff'nim is a drugstore man; he gets me my med'cine. Mrs. Hall'ran, that's my niece, keeps on at me I should go to a heart specialist—"

"Oh, I'm sorry! You shouldn't have lifted that trunk if your heart bothers you."

She said short and sharp, "It's no matter," then went quickly to a new tack. "Mr. Grant's a gentleman, a retired old gentleman. So's Mr. Waller. He's a policeman, retired. Nice people," she lipped to herself. "All nice people. Gentlemen."

I hinted. "I haven't the keys yet, do I? I'm so tired, I won't unpack tonight."

She limped out to the dark room in the hall, came back with a new Yale key.

"I had a new lock put on my house," she said impressively and lowered her voice. "I tell you, I didn't like the people who used to have this apartment. I had my suspicions of those people. They went nosing around in my things. So I said to them . . ." Her eyes licked at me. "So I asked those people to get right out of my house. I won't stand for any nosing around my things. That's why I was glad to get a nice girl like you, dearie. I knew you'd never go snooping in my things."

"It's nice to know there's a good lock on the front door." I ignored the last of her remarks. Water Street, below the drop-off, has a bad reputation, and there's a flight of stairs coming up from there, a block nearer the capitol, where the drop is less steep. I went on about the doors.

"What about the back doors, and the double door to the hall?"

"That back door bolts inside. There ain't no key to it. And the door to the back cellar stairs, it's never used, like I told you. See, the bolt's on your side, all rusted in; you can't even move it. On the other side it's nailed shut. You don't need to worry about anybody comin' in there."

"And the double doors?"

"Well, those double doors, now, dearie, I like to have the key of the double doors hanging on the outside on that nail in the casing when you ain't here. In case you would be gone and there would happen to be a fire, and I'd have to get my things in the closet."

"But I couldn't do that! Why, then anyone in the house could walk in!"

"There ain't anybody in the house would hurt anything."

I felt it was time to make a stand. "I'm sorry," I said firmly. "But I'll want to keep the key to the double doors, too."

She handed it over.

For a minute or two more she stood there, and I did, too, obviously waiting for her to go. She finally mumbled something and limped slowly out.

Of all the tiresome old women! Had I moved in with a deranged old semi-lunatic with delusions of persecution that might make her throw me out any minute under suspicion of snooping?

If the old woman could have known the amount of snooping I was actually to do in that house, and what I was to find—well . . .

But I didn't know that then, either.

THE LOCK ON THE double door didn't look difficult enough to me, and the key looked too much like the old-fashioned skeleton key that would unlock any door. But by experimenting, I found I could hook the dinette chairs under the knobs; the doors couldn't open then without heavy pressure and a lot of clatter. The two doors in the kitchen seemed as tight as Mrs. Garr said they were. I wanted to be barricaded until I had the lay of the land.

With that settled, I went to sleep.

I slept hard.

It must have been nearly midnight when I woke, with cramped muscles, to stretch lightly and turn over.

Seeping in came the thought of strangeness. Strange bed. Strange house. I must have been lying there for fifteen minutes, listening.

Not hearing for anything specific, just listening. A creak here. A drip there.

My room wasn't dark at all; there's a streetlight at the corner of Sixteenth and Trent, so the place was filled with that vision-less yellow light streetlamps make in a room at a distance. I lay staring up through the yellow haze at the just-visible stains on the ceiling.

Creak . . . crack . . . stir. Not a single active sound. Just tiny noises such as a house makes at night. Not even that much. Less noise than a house makes at night. As little noise as a house might make if it were holding itself tensely awake in the dark, listening.

"Cut it out," I said to myself. "You'll be going utsnay, too."

Creak . . . crack . . . settle . . . stir. A whole house lying awake in stealth, waiting, listening. Listening, waiting.

For what? For stealthy feet creeping, for stealthy hands groping . . .

I sat up with a jerk and pushed the light button by the head of the studio couch I slept on. Of all the silly nonsense! I'd never gone in for ideas such as this before.

I'd left a pile of magazines on the floor; I padded over for one on my bare feet, padded back to bed, pulled my bathrobe around my April-chilled shoulders.

I hadn't any more than begun on a story than there were three little ghost raps on my door. That had me sitting up, breathless.

"Who is it?" I asked hoarsely.

"It's me, Mrs. Garr," the whisper came back. "You sick or anything?"

My breath came back with such a rush it knocked me limp. This really was the limit.

"No, I'm not," I said loudly and clearly. "I woke up, couldn't sleep, felt like reading. Isn't that all right?"

"It's near two o'clock," she muttered, receding. I heard her slithering back into the room under the stairs where she slept; I'd seen a cot there.

I was so jumpy, I read down into the middle of the story without knowing who the characters were or what they were doing. I started over and was maybe three paragraphs along when I heard the house front door open and heavy steps in the hall.

"It's me, Mrs. Garr," a man's voice said thickly. He wasn't steering well, because he bumped against the wall before stumbling upstairs.

Just a good old-fashioned drunk, but even that was reassuring. I got up, reinspected my doors, and said to myself, "No one can get in here. And if the house is listening, let it listen. There's no harm in a house listening if it wants to. You're going to think this damn silly in the morning."

I calmed down finally and went to sleep.

But I was sure the house or *something* was listening to every breath I took.

I WOKE UP EXPECTING to laugh, but all I got out was a feeble grin.

After I was up and about, my imaginings of the night before did seem a bit ridiculous, but while I was still in bed, with the house quiet and the sunlight streaming in, I could still feel the house listening. Walter de la Mare, who wrote that poem called "The Listeners," should have slept in that house once. He'd have had something to write about.

I heard, finally, sounds of people stirring above me. Perhaps it was a house so well, so heavily built that it deadened sound, but even now, thinking back, I can't remember ever having heard a loud, sharp sound in that house; I can't remember anyone or anything that succeeded in filling that house with sound. It was a subduing house; it muffled steps and voices, it muffled even the roaring voices of policemen.

But on that morning, I still did not know any policemen.

I got out of bed as quickly as everyone else in the house seemed to be getting out of bed, unhooked my chairs, flung open my doors. There wasn't a soul in the hall.

After I'd had toast and coffee I kept close to those double doors while I worked about the living room. I was going to look over the inhabitants of that house. If they were suspicious, I'd move. I didn't want to get into anything.

I saw all the boarders through the morning.

My first catch was a thin woman with dyed black hair and a thin, rouged face; a woman with the pitifully well-pressed afternoon dress, the tired, artificial sprightliness of a saleswoman straining at her job.

It was easy to place her as Miss Sands. I knew that type well enough, at Tellier's.

She hurried past me without nodding, although I said, "Good morning," at her pleasantly and clearly.

Sounds in the room under the stairs announced that Mrs. Garr was rising. Barks and cat cries below announced that she was joining pets in the cellar. Mrs. Garr's voice soon rose from there, too. She was berating someone soundly as a lazy good-for-nothing. *She could get up early in the morning, but not Mrs. Tew-man, oh no, not Mrs. Tewman; Mrs. Tewman had to lie abed while the gentlemen didn't get their rooms done. Mrs. Tewman, oh no, not Mrs. Tewman; Mrs. Tewman had stayed dirty; here it was Friday with all the halls to be done, and all the stairs to be done, and what was Mrs. Tewman doing? She was looking at pitchers in the paper.* The shrill old voice went on and on.

Well, toward nine a mousey old gentleman in a gray suit slipped quietly down from upstairs.

"Good morning," I said.

He stopped, as if startled.

"Good morning, good morning," he replied in a dry, brisk voice before hurrying on as if I were chasing him out.

I couldn't imagine a policeman being that small; that would have to be the other retired gentleman: Mr. Grant. Heaven knew, he looked innocuous enough.

At midmorning a sullen, black-haired woman—French Canadian, I guessed—slumped up the cellar stairs and on to the second floor, a pail, scouring powder, brushes, and very dirty cleaning rags in tow; that, I guessed, was Mrs. Tewman, finally released to her work from the scolding below.

She stared straight at me but, like Miss Sands, did not reply to my greeting. On the stairs she passed another woman who was coming down; a dark woman with a faint, silky black mustache, a woman so fat she lunged a little from side to side as she moved, so fat her sides and thighs were pendulous, as well as her breasts.

The fat woman was dressed decently in black.

She answered, "Good morning," shortly.

Mrs. Waller, without doubt. She hung around in the hall until she was joined by a man in his early forties, ponderous, slow-moving, red-faced. That must be the ex-policeman, then. I wondered a little at his age. Were policemen retired so young?

It wasn't until nearly noon that the other two men came along. They came downstairs one behind the other, but they weren't, I thought, together. I wondered which one had come in drunk the night before, or if that had been Mr. Waller. The man ahead came down quickly and lightly; he wore a slouch hat pulled down over his eyes and a light topcoat; he was heavily, stockily built. He looked me over with funny round brown eyes over a nose that was just slightly pug.

"Hello and welcome!" he said before I'd said anything; the first one who'd done so.

The man behind just grunted; all I could see of him as he hurried past was that he was older, tall, and dark, with a strongly featured face almost as sullen as Mrs. Tewman's.

It wasn't until a week later that I knew which one was Mr. Buff'nim and which one Mr. Kistler.

AFTER A DAY SPENT scrubbing, I treated myself to a dinner in one of the small restaurants below the capitol. It was dusk when I'd fumbled with the unfamiliar lock and landed in the dim hall; the minute I was inside a dark body pelted at me.

"Get down!" I said, making it good and loud.

What had come at me was a dog. If rooming-house keepers are going to have dogs, they should introduce them to their paying guests before the paying guests are jumped on.

The surly dog got down, but he growled, backing away from me and showing his teeth as I pushed down the hall. There was a flurry in the dark room under the stairs, a light snapped on there, and Mrs. Garr rushed out, panting.

"Rover, Rover, nice Rover, don't growl at the nice lady. That's my dog, Mis' Dacres. Rover, his name is. I was down cellar. I usually keep 'em locked in, but I guess the door got left open."

"I guess it must have." I didn't like Rover much better seen than unseen. He was a big, hulking brute of a dog; he was about the size of a police dog, but built to be heavier if he hadn't been so thin. He was covered with short black hair that was a coarse imitation of sealskin.

I immediately recalled a nightmare I'd had at the age of eleven after reading a tale about werewolves. He had that narrow, grinning muzzle.

He stood at bay, staring at me still, when two big black-and-white tomcats, followed by the gray female cat, came slinking out of the room, too, to flatten against the wall and look me over with tilted eyes.

"My gracious, you have a family!" I couldn't say I liked it.

"They're the best friends I got," Mrs. Garr snapped. She stooped, picked up one of the tomcats, held him awkwardly dangling against her bosom. Her voice pitched higher, as if she wanted someone at a distance to hear. "You don't catch *them* coming around asking for money, money, money all the time, asking for help all the time, always this, always that, bad times, can't get work—"

The door of the front parlor jerked open.

"Did I hear you speaking, Auntie?" asked a saccharine voice.

The owner of the voice teetered into the hall.

"Mis' Dacres, I make you acquainted with Mis' Hall'ran. She's my niece." Mrs. Garr's voice was heavy with contempt.

Looking at Mrs. Halloran, I thought immediately of Dickens' Mrs. Micawber as she would be if played by ZaSu Pitts. Mrs. Halloran wore a yellow-green felt hat, pushed far back on a frazzled finger wave; her dress was blue-green rayon crepe with a white lace collar, limp and long unwashed. Her rayon stockings were twisted, her black patent heels tipped to the side, but overall she was dreamily elegant.

"So pleased to meet ya." She smiled impressively.

"I was tellin' Mis' Dacres," Mrs. Garr repeated for emphasis, "how a man's best friend is his dog. And his cats. They don't come asking for money, money. All the time money, money, money."

Mrs. Halloran's fingers twitched at a crystal bead necklace.

"Oh, but not like your own kith and kin, wouldn't you say, Mis' Dacres? Not like your own flesh and blood." She bore heavily on the kith, the kin, the flesh, and the blood.

"Some kiths and kins is worse than gangsters. Oh, I could tell you about kiths and kins," Mrs. Garr pursued bitterly. "Especially when they marry themselves to no-good drunken bums, that's who they get married to, and get a pack of bawling chillern, that's what they get."

I excused myself and escaped. Unnoticed, I think.

As I made up my studio couch for the night I could not help learning, through the double doors, that Mr. Halloran was a bum, and *where was the ten thousand dollars he got on his completely disabled insurance from the gov'ment? Where was the bonus money he got from the gov'ment? So, she had to come to her poor old auntie, working her fingers to the bone, while they lived high, they lived handsome, they went to movies, they went to taverns, they bought a Packard, that's what they bought, and went out and wrecked it drunk, and where was it now?*

At this point the argument must have adjourned behind a closed door, thank goodness.

I inspected my barricades, put out my light, and went to bed.

I thought that after a whole day spent in the house, after seeing how commonplace it was, I'd spend a quiet night.

But the same thing happened as the night before. At midnight, or shortly after, I woke again feeling tense, not of my own ears hearing sounds, but of other ears listening, of the house listening. Again I lay awake, staring upward through the misty dark, not afraid so much as waiting, waiting for something that did not happen that night, nor the next, nor the next. For I did the same thing every night: woke at least enough to recognize the awareness, to know it was there again, before increasing familiarity allowed me to sleep in spite of it.

It wasn't long before I knew the routine of the house, by day. Mrs. Garr rotated from the davenport in her parlor at the front of the house, where she was seldom, to the black chair in the hall, where she was slightly more often, to the basement, where she spent most of her time. After I had been down there with my boxes of wrappings, I knew she had a table and rocking chair down there by the furnace.

She didn't read, didn't knit, didn't sew; I could sometimes hear her rocker creaking on the cement floor an entire afternoon. That's how I came to picture her, as an evil-eyed old woman with lovely white hair, sitting there doing nothing, with the three big cats sitting on her lap or rubbing against her chair, and the black dog parked alongside.

But the rest of the household was reasonably respectable. If that gentlemanly Mr. Grant, for instance, lived here by choice, then I should be able to stand it, considering that I'd have to pay almost twice for what I was getting, anywhere else.

That, I remember, was my attitude the first week. The Friday I had been there a week I woke early; the April morning was lovely, and the air streaming in my windows smelled sunny and as fresh as Easter tulips. I wandered outdoors, after I'd dressed, to get more of that air. The house I left behind me was still quiet, but the morning outside crackled with spring growth. I walked across the paved court at the back of the house to stand at the railing and look down.

It had rained in the night and, as happens once in almost every April, the twelve hours since yesterday seemed to have brought us suddenly into spring. The plots of earth between the houses below were green for sure now: that lovely, sunny, tender green of spring.

Green even showed beneath the straggly brown stalks of last year's weeds at the foot of the concrete drop. The inhabitants of Water Street threw refuse there: paper, tins, boxes, rusted iron.

Someone had even thrown a heap of old clothes out there.

A heap of clothes.

I found myself leaning perilously far out over the guardrail.

Not a heap of old clothes. For a moment I clung dizzily to the rail.

A head with dark hair, arms outflung, feet . . .

A man, a man twisted and motionless in a position that could only mean death, lay facedown in the weeds of Water Street, straight below where I stood.

3

A MAN, A DEAD man, sixty feet below me!

As if the rail had pushed at me, I jumped for the house.

"Mrs. Garr," I cried, speeding through my rooms. "There's someone lying at the foot of the drop! In the weeds! He looks dead. We've got to call a doctor, call the police! How do you get 'em? How do you get the police?"

I fumbled dazedly with the phone book, trying to get the operator. Mrs. Garr stumbled out of her room in a short white nightgown, just as she had come from her bed.

"You can't call without a nickel!" she screamed at my incompetence.

I sped back for a nickel; it seemed minutes before my fingers could pick one from the inside pocket of my handbag.

The operator switched me quickly to the police.

"There's someone lying in the weeds, the weeds down below on Water Street," I babbled. "He looks dead. It's a man."

"Who is it?" the big voice at the other end of the wire asked calmly.

"I don't know. I just saw it lying there."

"Where is it? Where you calling from?"

"Five ninety-three Trent Street. Oh, hurry, hurry!"

"Right there!"

The receiver clicked.

"What should we do?" I continued into the unhearing phone. "What should we do now?"

"We could go on down there." There was a greedy light in Mrs. Garr's eyes. She turned back into the room under the stairs for a bathrobe, then, still in her bare feet, padded through my rooms and across the back court to the guardrail, to peer avidly over.

The scene below was just as it had been. Heap of clothes in last year's weeds.

"It's a sure thing it's a man lyin' down there," Mrs. Garr cried back to me. "There's been illegal dealings down below in one of them houses; I'll bet that's what it is. Some fella stuck a knife in him and dumped him—Here they come!"

It was no longer than that before the siren wailed, far off, then near. I ran around the house to intercept the two policemen at the front door.

"Did you call up about a—"

"Yes, I did," I said breathlessly. "Come around the back. You can see—"

I ran back; the two officers walked after, their longer legs keeping pace.

"Right down there, Off'cer, right down there," Mrs. Garr screamed, pointing.

The two men looked once, then ran back to their car. The car

slung off, leaving Mrs. Garr and me at the rail alone, but not for
long. People began popping out of my back door. First the man I
had guessed was Mr. Waller, elbowing into a bathrobe, his slippers flapping.

"What's all the racket?"

We told him what I'd found. He leaned excitedly beside us.

"That's right. That's right, all right. That's a man there!"

He and Mrs. Garr repeated that, over and over. The police car
came hurtling up the street below; as it did so, two more men ran
down my back steps to be greeted with explanations. They were
the two men I'd seen together that first morning. I paid them
little attention; all my interest was riveted on the scene below.
The police car stopped at the street's edge, not four feet from the
body. The two officers burst from the car at its instant of pause,
bent over the heap of clothes.

They straightened quickly, conferred briefly. Then one man
dashed off in the car again; the other stayed by the body. The
man on guard waved up at us, as if in affirmation.

"I'm going on down," the youngest of the men beside me said.
The other two went after him with alacrity, cutting across Sixteenth Street and the backyards of the houses in the next block
to reach the stairs that go down to Water Street near the capitol.
I turned, and there was Mrs. Garr paddling after.

"Mrs. Garr!" I called, running to catch her. "You can't go
down like that! Not in your nightgown! Not in your bare feet!"

She halted at the edge of the yard, with my hand on her arm.

"Why, I hain't got my clothes on," she grumbled in bewildered discovery. Her white hair was whipping about her face;
long streamers of it were loose from the tumbled knot on top of
her head. She scuttled for the house.

"Wait'll I get my clothes on! Don't you go on down before I
get my clothes on!" she commanded.

I wasn't anxious to go down; the rail was close enough for me. In the short interval I had spent running after Mrs. Garr, the policeman below quickly had his hands full; people were streaming out of the Water Street houses to crowd the scene, fall back, crowd forward again as he ran back and forth, pushing them away.

"Stand back there, stand back!" I could hear his shouts, rebounding against the concrete wall.

Up Water Street, running, came the three men from Mrs. Garr's house. As they neared the group below new sirens cried. An ambulance and two more police cars sped ruthlessly through the crowd; people scattered back momentarily, pressed forward again. Uniformed men spilled from the cars.

"What is it? What were the sirens for? Where's my husband—where's Mr. Waller?" the fat woman's breathless voice asked beside me.

"There's a man down there, dead," I answered, looking up only to see that the other inmates of the house were there, too, now: the department store clerk, Mr. Grant, Mrs. Tewman. "Your husband went down there with the others."

The men below turned the body over. There was a moment of quiet, then hubbub again. Faces lifted, looking upward at us. I moved back from the rail.

The fat woman screamed. "Joe! They're taking him!"

"Your husband? Why, that's—" I began. It was true. "But look! The other men, too. They're all getting in one of the cars."

The car holding the men from Mrs. Garr's house sped back toward the capitol.

"Wait! Watch where the car's going. It's coming up here!"

"Joe!" the woman wailed.

In the crowd below there was active movement now; I saw photographers' tripods, the body being lifted to a stretcher.

A car screamed to a stop beside the house. The three men from the house and as many policemen came out of it, walked in a group toward us. Mr. Waller cried:

"It's a dead man all right. He was shot. But he fell down that hill, too. And they figure he must have fell or been pushed down that concrete drop from just about here!"

THE DEAD MAN HAD fallen from up here! Involuntarily I looked over the rail again, shuddering at the drop.

"Stand back from the rail there!" one of the policemen ordered peremptorily. He waved us away as the other two officers began examining the concrete paving and the rail. "Go on back to the house, all of you. Get in that house, there! I'm going to want some statements, and I don't want to miss anybody."

We crowded through my rooms into the hall. Mrs. Garr, fully clothed now, was just emerging from her cubbyhole.

"What you comin' in here for?" she asked the officer angrily.

"Man fell or got pushed over that rail right in back of this house," the man explained impatiently. "You run this joint?"

"I'm the owner of this prop'ty."

"Good. Tell me who all lives here."

"All nice, respectable people."

"I don't care what the heck they are; I'll find that out. Their names I want."

Mrs. Garr listed us, one by one.

"Okay. Now, which one raised the alarm?"

"Mrs. Dacres—that's my new lodger—called it in. That's Mrs. Dacres. She lives right there in the back."

"All right, Mrs. Dacres, how'd you come to discover this body?"

"After I'd been up a little while I went outdoors because it was such a nice morning," I explained. "I walked as far as the rail and looked over; at first I thought that was just a heap of clothes thrown out there, but then I saw it wasn't a heap of clothes."

"Uh-huh. You know anything about this guy getting thrown over?"

"No, I don't."

"Hear anything out back last night?"

"No."

"Any shots?"

"No."

"Any cars backfiring?"

"No, I can't remember any."

"Where was you from seven o'clock last night until this morning?"

I detailed my commonplace activities.

He merely grunted at the end, and left me.

One by one he questioned the others. Everywhere the answers were the same. No one had heard anything unusual or seen anything unusual. The three men who had seen the body up close claimed that they had never seen the man before, and signed statements to that effect. Mr. Tewman came in the front door as the inquisition was in full swing; he was a rabbity little blond man in his forties, who said he had been working in his hamburger castle all night, had just come home to sleep. He was completely at sea as to what had happened, but was enlightened by eight voices at once.

The policeman finally snapped his notebook shut.

"I'm not gettin' anywhere with this," he said. "Looks like a gang killing to me, anyhow. All of you that didn't see the body this morning will need to report down at the morgue sometime during the day and see if you recognize the guy in any connection. And don't run your mouths to reporters too much."

That last was easy for me, harder for Mrs. Garr and Mrs. Tewman, who answered the doorbell. The others scattered to their rooms, to work, or elsewhere; the house seemed unusually empty that day, perhaps in contrast to the constantly going and coming crowds outside the house. People hung around the sidewalks and the backyard, leaned over the railing. Every now and then throughout the day I saw policemen emerging from other houses in the neighborhood, too; they must have been canvassing the whole vicinity for any clues to the man's identity or death.

It wasn't until the *Comet* extras were cried on the streets around noon that we began to know anything about the slain man; a radio flash on a midmorning news program gave only the briefest details of the discovery. The *Comet* extra played the story up big:

MYSTERY MAN SLAIN

STRANGER FOUND SHOT;
MAY BE NEW YORK MAN

The body of a man who had been shot and then dumped down the cliff side of Capitol Hill, to fall sixty feet to Water Street, below, was discovered this morning by a young woman resident of one of the houses on upper Trent Street. Police were immediately called to the scene and arrived within ten minutes of the discovery. The only clue to the identity of the slain man was in a New York State driver's license, issued to Samuel Zeitman, 37, New York City. As 37 is the dead man's approximate age, Gilling City police are already in touch with New York City police in an effort to discover if the slain man is the Samuel Zeitman to whom the license was issued.

CITY RESIDENCE UNKNOWN

*An investigation is now underway of hotels and lodgings to
ascertain the Gilling City residence, the activities, and the
acquaintances of the dead man. Any Gilling City residents
having information that might concern the dead man are
asked to bring such information to the police. The deceased
was about 37 years of age, had dark hair, a swarthy com-
plexion, was five feet six and one-half inches tall, wore a
large diamond ring on his left little finger, had a dark mole
on the left temple. He had been shot through the heart with
a .38-caliber pistol, at a time estimated by Police Surgeon
Thomley as approximately midnight. A pistol, which is now
being tested to ascertain if it fired the fatal shot, was found
beside the body. Fingerprints on the gun are all those of the
dead man, indicating that he was shot with his own gun.
However, the fact that, according to Dr. Thomley, the man
was thrown over the cliff at least fifteen minutes after death
does away with the probability of suicide.*

The rest of the account I won't give; it repeated the story of
the discovery. A picture of the man lying facedown in the weeds
accompanied the story; one of those sickening pictures the papers are going in for nowadays under the guise of honest realism.

Mrs. Waller knocked at my door early in the afternoon to ask
if I'd go to the morgue with her. Mrs. Garr had already gone with
Mrs. Halloran, both all agog. Mr. Waller went with us, although
he didn't have to go; he agreed with our questioner of the morning that it was a gangster killing. He elaborated on his theory all
the way downtown.

The morgue is down by the river; it is a yellow brick building
that looks like a factory but smells vilely of disinfectants. I tried

to see and feel as little as I could on that trip; heaven knows, it wasn't enjoyable. We told our errand to a gray, toothy young man in a glassed-in cubicle, were led down a scrubbed, hospital-like corridor to a small scrubbed room with one operating table in it, and a mound on the table.

The rubber-soled attendant silently pulled a cloth back from the face; it was a thin face, mean even in death, the hair dark and oily, the forehead bumpy, the eye sockets close to the fleshy nose, the chin too narrow. I turned away after the briefest possible glance, hurried out into the corridor again, Mrs. Waller right on my heels. I stood there for a moment until my stomach subsided; we went, tiptoeing, I remember, back to the cubicle, where we signed statements as to our ignorance of the dead man, and that we possessed no information whatsoever concerning his death.

Getting out of there was like getting out of a—well, like getting out of a morgue. We hurried three blocks as fast as we could walk, then had to stop to breathe, because we were still trying to breathe as little as possible. That is, I was, and I think Mrs. Waller was; Mr. Waller was stodgily matter-of-fact about the whole thing.

The regular evening edition of the *Comet* came out with a story that corroborated Mr. Waller. It ran:

SLAIN MAN IDENTIFIED

IS SAM ZEITMAN, N.Y. GANGSTER.
GANG WAR HINTED

New York police this afternoon identified photographs of the man found shot on Water Street this morning as Samuel Zeitman, suspected of connection with the New York restaurant racket ring, which was broken this last winter by the vigorous persecution of rackets now being conducted in New York City. Sam Zeitman, the New York police indicated, fled the city this spring to evade the roundup of racketeers; the discovery of his body this morning was the first news they had of his subsequent whereabouts.

POLICE HINT GANG FLARE-UP

Lieutenant Peter Strom, in charge of the Gilling City homicide squad, said that the death was in all probability due to an attempt to muscle in on some of the small local gangs who have been attempting to establish rackets in Gilling City. Although such activities are well under control, police indicated, sporadic attempts are made to extort revenue by such means, or through the use of slot machines and similar gambling devices.

It may have been fear of Zeitman's big-city methods which led to his death.

RESIDENCE IN CITY LOCATED

The proprietress of a small loop hotel testified to police this afternoon that a Samuel Zeitman had registered at her hotel on the seventeenth of March, this year, and had since resided there. She later identified the body as that of her lodger. She was unable, however, to tell anything of the man's activities. He was very quiet, even secretive, she says. She could remember no men visitors to his room. A search of the dead man's room revealed a second gun, several cartridges, and a blackjack, but no clue as to his activities. Every effort will be made, however, to seek out the killer, police stated.

The rest was repetition.

In the days that followed, not one new thing was discovered about that death. I watched for the case every day in the papers,

of course; it was played up on page one for a couple of days, then
slipped rapidly into newspaper oblivion.

It was some days before I ventured again to look over that
railing. From that time until I left Mrs. Garr's house I never did
stand there without expecting to see another heap of clothes in
the weeds below. Sometimes I'd feel pushed to look—and I'd see
Water Street, dirty but innocent, with children playing in the
rubbish heaps where a dead man had lain a few days before.

One thing I certainly took for granted: that the killing of Sam
Zeitman had nothing to do with Mrs. Garr's house or the people
in it. It never entered my mind that it had, any more than it concerned the other people in the houses up and down Trent Street.
Some gangster had had reason to shoot Sam Zeitman, had done
so, and had quietly and efficiently slung the body over the rail at
Sixteenth Street because it was a handy, quiet spot. That it could
have been me that caused Sam Zeitman's death—well, that would
have been as incomprehensible as that it was me that caused the
moon to shine.

Life in Mrs. Garr's house went on as usual. I was jumpy for a
while, but it wore off. Mrs. Garr kept to her orbit. Mrs. Tewman
cleaned. The lodgers came and went. My apartment was settled.
I liked my two rooms; on bright days they were extremely pleasant. Mrs. Garr was the fly in the ointment, of course. I was putting away my winter clothes one day, shaking them on the back
porch to air, dragging the steamer trunk out to the kitchen floor,
unpacking my summer clothes, when the sharp rap I'd come to
know so well sounded on my door.

"You're running my hot water in your kitchen," Mrs. Garr
burst at me, her eyes hard and hot.

"Why, no, I haven't been using any water."

"It's no use your talking that way to me. I can tell." She
pushed past me, halted a moment to stare at my clothes and the

trunk in the kitchen, limped on to the sink. Her fingers closed over the hot-water faucet.

"No, you didn't," she grunted. "I can tell if anybody's been using my hot water in their kitchen, because then their faucet's hot." She switched subjects quickly. "You doing something with your clo'es?"

"I'm putting away my winter things."

"My, you got a lot o' clo'es. I cer'n'ly admire to see pretty clo'es." She plumped herself down on the kitchen chair.

She stuck like a limpet, sitting there while I shook out and hung my summer dresses, folded and packed the winter things. She sat hunched forward, her arms folded across her knees.

"We're going to have another change in this house," she told me importantly. "Them Wallers, they're going. I don't trust that man. I don't trust her, either."

"Why, I thought he was an ex-policeman," I said. "Certainly you can trust an ex-policeman."

"No, I don't trust 'em. He snoops. Oh, they don't think I know what's going on, but I can tell. Coming down into my basement, says he's looking for nails. She comes right into the kitchen, asks can she borrow an egg. Oh, they're looking, all right."

I forbore saying that the only person I had known to do any snooping in that house was Mrs. Garr. I couldn't move a table without having her turn up, her black eyes inquiring and suspicious.

"But what could he be looking for?" I argued, instead.

She shot me a glinty look. "They like to snoop. They just like to snoop, people like them."

"Oh, you're just imagining it. You're here too much. Cooped up. Now it's getting to be so nice outdoors, you ought to get away once in a while. Go somewhere. See a movie. Why, you never go out!"

"I ain't a hand for going. Not now no more. Oh, in my young days, then I was a goer. I could put many a young girl now'days in the shade."

"I'm sure of it. Your hair's still so lovely."

I'd reached her pride, of course.

"Yes, I always had a handsome head o' hair. Many's the people remarked about my hair. A handsome head o' hair . . . I could help you get that trunk back, now."

"Oh, don't bother. I got it out myself. It's too hard on you."

"No, 'tain't. I ain't so old as you think."

She took one end of the trunk again, and again, gasping, helped me get it back in place before she'd leave.

OF COURSE, I WAS certain her talk of people rummaging through her possessions was imagination.

Certain, that is, until the day in late April when Mrs. Halloran finally persuaded Mrs. Garr out to see *Three Little Maids*, which was playing at the second-run movie house below the capitol that week.

They left in a flurry of argument; at the last moment Mrs. Garr, with all an old person's reluctance to change from settled habit, sat stubbornly down in the chair in the hall to say no, she wasn't going. Mrs. Halloran knocked at my door to get my seconding opinion that it would be good for Mrs. Garr to get out for a change. They went finally; I've seen less fuss made over plane trips to New York.

I was out that afternoon, too, on the eternal job hunting that took most of my daylight hours. I returned around four thirty, and as I came past Mrs. Garr's living room I heard a drawer closing softly. I stopped to ask how Mrs. Garr had liked the movie.

Mrs. Garr wasn't there. Only the mousey little gentleman from upstairs, Mr. Grant, was sitting on the davenport.

"I wonder if Mrs. Garr won't be in soon; I'm waiting for her to pay my rent." His speech was as dry and brisk as he was.

But his hand on his knee shook so it moved the knee.

"She went to a movie with Mrs. Halloran. She should be back any minute."

"Oh, thank you. I won't wait, then."

He hurried out past me and upstairs.

I stared after him in unbelief.

So there was a rummager! So there was some foundation for Mrs. Garr's imaginings! And that foundation was in Mr. Grant; little, blue-eyed Mr. Grant!

Thoughtfully I left my doors open and sat in the upholstered chair in my left bay window, where I could watch the hall while I read the paper I'd brought home.

I'd only just settled down when a man I'd never seen before crept silently out of the room under the stairs, came to a dead stop on seeing me, then shot down the hall and out the front door.

4

"WELL, WHAT THE . . . !" I said, jumping up.

What was going on in this house?

Should I call the police?

I went to the head of the basement stairs, but I could hear nothing down there except dark silence—the type of silence that's so much more frightening than any understandable sound. My nerves weren't what they had been before the discovery of Sam Zeitman.

Hurriedly I got away from there, hastening toward the upstairs; I wanted company. Who else was in the house?

I knew Mr. Grant was, but I couldn't very well speak to him about the prowler, not when I'd almost caught him rummaging among Mrs. Garr's possessions, too. If anything queer was going on, he probably was in on it. The watch, perhaps.

I knew, by this time, just about who lived where in the upstairs. Miss Sands wouldn't be home yet. I walked back toward the Wallers' door, but stopped with my hand lifted to knock. Mrs. Garr suspected the Wallers.

If she was right, they might be in on it, too.

I left there for the front of the house. The bath was empty. The room ahead of that was quiet, too. But in the rooms at the front, thank goodness, I heard a steady *thump, thump.*

I knocked.

"Come in," yelled a man's voice.

The *thump, thump* went on, slowly and steadily, but nothing else happened. So I turned the knob and went in.

I almost forgot what I'd come for, because I walked in on a man with nothing on but a pair of shorts, chinning himself on a bar which had been put in at the top of the doorway between that room and the next. It was the stocky man with the brown eyes, Mr. Kistler. With his clothes off, he looked like nothing so much as a buff gorilla; his arms were long for his height and obviously powerful; he pulled himself up until his head bumped the casing—that was the thump I'd heard—and counted.

"Twenty-six . . . twenty-seven . . . twenty-eight . . . Oh, hello!"

He dropped to the floor, and again I thought of a gorilla; he took the jar so easily on bent knees.

"Hello again!" He disappeared in the other room, came back shouldering into a bathrobe. He smiled ingratiatingly.

"I wasn't expecting a lady, but one's always welcome."

I stuck right by the door.

"You took my breath away. I don't usually walk in on exactly this scene."

"You never can tell what opportunities will develop," he said cheerfully.

"Oh," I said. "I didn't—I came up because a strange man that acted like a burglar or something came out of the cellar. Mrs. Garr's out. He came up the cellar stairs tiptoeing; he must have because I didn't hear him at all. Then when he saw me through my open door he dashed out the front as if he expected me to yell for the police."

"What interesting adventures you have! Weren't you the one that found the slain gangster, too? We'll look into this." He left for the other room again; when he came back he had added slippers to his costume.

He ran ahead down the stairs, but I went, too.

The basement, as far as we could see, was empty now. Mrs. Tewman's rooms in the front were locked and seemed undisturbed. Mrs. Garr's kitchen in the back was locked and seemed undisturbed, too; I was sure of that last because as we came near the door the dog barked and the cats cried. She always locked her pets in there when she went out on errands, leaving the key on a nail on the casing. The key hung there now. Those animals would have shot out of there if anyone had opened the door.

"Not much evidence of prowling here," my fellow detective said.

I took another look around the furnace room. One thing you could say for Mrs. Garr was that she didn't keep a mess in her cellar; she was too much enamored with the idea that every scrap of paper burned saved on the coal bill. The furnace room was bare except for a pile of newspapers on a box near the storage-room door. That pile of papers . . .

"Look! Some of the papers have been knocked down."

"You mean you think we have a newspaper fiend in our midst? What depravity! What vice!"

"They might have been knocked off by someone hurrying into or out of the storeroom."

The young man walked toward the storage-room door, tried the knob gently. It turned.

"Whoever's in there come out," he yelled, standing back.

No one came.

The young man opened the door then, and we both went in.

Obviously someone had been prowling there. Boxes were pulled down, papers and musty old clothes strewn over the floor.

"Well, what the hell do you know! So you weren't thinking up fairy tales!"

"Do you think we should call the police?"

"Police? He's gone, isn't he? You saw him scoot out, didn't you?"

"Yes, but—"

He shook his head.

"We don't even know if anything's missing. If anything valuable was stolen, Mrs. Garr can tell the police. That'd be the only way they could catch him now—by nabbing him when he tried to sell what he got. How would you go about catching the guy? If he's as far away as you'd go if you were him? No, no, lady, you've always got to think, in moments like this, that police are just as human as we are, and not any brighter. If as."

"Thanks," I said.

There didn't seem to be much more we could do in the cellar. Nothing else that we could see looked as if it had been touched. In fact there wasn't much else there, just gray cement walls, gray cement ceiling, a swept but grimy gray cement floor, the big hot-water furnace, pipes, laundry tubs, Mrs. Garr's table and chair. What could there be that a thief would want?

Unless, of course, she had something valuable hidden in that storage room.

In that case, it was probably gone.

I trailed upstairs again. The room at the head of the basement stairs, and under the second-story stairs, looked in only its normal mess; a rather unclean old lady's room, with faded tapestry curtains hiding the dresses on a rod at one end, one cot with a matching tapestry cover, one many-times-varnished chest of drawers, one chair, no window. I didn't see how Mrs. Garr could sleep in that airless place, with the peculiar overhanging ceiling made by the stairs above.

The young man, right at my heels, paused when I did to look at Mrs. Garr's room, then followed me confidently into my living room.

"I'll stay by until you're safe and sound with Mrs. Garr back," he offered debonairly. He dropped onto my studio couch before I'd sat down myself, and examined the room.

"My, my, how clean we are."

"My personal imprint."

"She brags about herself."

I was still standing. He wasn't a particularly polite young man, and it disturbed me to think how few clothes he had on. I wished he'd go upstairs for more. He triangled an eyebrow at me and patted the couch by his side.

"Come sit by Papa?"

"No, thanks. I like this chair." I stood by the armchair.

"Oh well, I always try," he philosophized. "Why don't you sit in it then, instead of emphasizing how impolite I am? Didn't you ever hear about George Washington drinking coffee out of his saucer so as not to embarrass the congressmen, who were just as elite in his day as in ours? Now, my motto is, if at first you don't succeed, try, try again. Sit down or come here."

He was impudent. I sat down.

"You're Mr. Kistler, aren't you?"

"Yes, I am. Mr. Kistler. Hodge Kistler."

"I was sure you couldn't be Mr. Buff'nim."

"Mr. Who?"

"Buff'nim. Mrs. Garr said—"

"Oh, Mr. Buffingham. Spelled B-u-f-f-i-n-g-h-a-m. What those English don't think up!"

"I'm Mrs. Dacres."

"Always formal and a lady?"

"Names are good dresser-uppers."

"Alas, aren't they? Do you like this weather, Mrs. Dacres?"

"Very much."

"Lovely April day."

"Very."

"Don't think it might be coming on to rain?"

"Not a chance."

"I'm so relieved. These damp nights . . ."

I stood up again. "I suspect I shall never know you again after Mrs. Garr gets home."

"Slapped again. But, ah, you got it. That was all I wanted to know." He was grinning at me fiendishly. "Is there any approach you do like?"

"I'm sorry, but I'd like it just as well if I waited here alone."

"Oh, sit down, baby. You know how newspapermen are. We have to live up to the reputations the movies give us, don't we?"

"Not with me."

"The trouble with you is that you should be introduced to yourself sometime."

"I shan't go to a reporter for the introduction."

"Reporter? If by that name you mean me, Mrs. Dacres, you belittle me. Once I may have been a reporter, but no more. I have left that infancy behind. In me, you behold a publisher."

I stared at him. Mrs. Garr had said newspaperman, and I'd filled in the reporter without thinking.

"Then what are you doing living in a—a place like this?" I blurted out.

"Dear lady, why not?" he asked largely. "I get two rooms for six dollars a week, big ones with plenty of light and air. I've got practically a private bath. I've got maid service, such as it is. How much'd I have to pay in an apartment hotel? Or would you suggest I rent a house? Me, a bachelor?"

"William Randolph Hearst in disguise, I suppose."

"Just like all women, always expecting too much. Very silly of Mr. Hearst, squandering himself on all those papers. Spreads himself out too thin."

"Have you telegraphed Mr. Hearst your opinion?"

"I am too big a character to write anonymous telegrams. Now me, I devote all my talent to one paper, and what a paper. Fastest-growing paper in Gilling City. Most ads. Brightest columns. Most wit. Best movie reviews. I handle most of it personally." He waved a grandiose arm.

I stared again. Gilling City has only one big newspaper.

"Do you mean to sit there and try to make me believe you're the publisher of the *Comet*?" I began furiously.

"That tradition-bound, blind, earmuffed rich man's rag? No, no, lady. I wouldn't touch the *Comet*. I haven't touched it since I said good-bye to it forever in 1933."

"You were fired, I bet."

"Bull's-eye in one shot." He grinned again.

"Then what?"

"Now, Mrs. Dacres, haven't you heard of the paper everyone in town reads? The paper at every door? Haven't you heard of that illustrious, that incandescent, that blisteringly brilliant publication, the *Buyers' Guide*?"

Comprehension flooded in on me.

The *Buyers' Guide* is interesting. When I first saw a copy, two years ago, it was a small, four-page sheet of local ads for the north side. But it's been growing. Its ads cover the whole town now; it comes out in full newspaper size, sometimes even in two sections. It's delivered at every door in town once a week; I always go through it on Thursdays myself.

The radical thing about it is that it's free. It's full of ads, grocery, meat market, small shop; it's completely an advertiser's paper, without the perfunctory bows to the news made by regular newspapers. But it carries several features so good, people read and talk about them every week.

"You're the *Buyers' Guide*!"

He rose, bowed. "The same."

"I can believe it, too. The 'Sh-sh-sh-sh' column. The movie reviews. How do you get away with 'em?"

"I don't. Theater owners lurk at the doors with blackjacks when rumor has it I approach. I go disguised. Why, I even have to pay my way in!"

"Brace yourself. I never go to a movie unless it's on the 'Morons Keep Away' list."

"Be still, my heart. You mean you think you're not a moron?"

"Not so much I don't think your *Guide* a good idea."

"You grow on me."

"Not literally, I hope. Does it make money?"

"Money? You mention a thing like money when I'm bent on expressing my soul?"

"You're running enough ads to make money."

"Money, she says. That's all I hear. That's what that superannuated, supercolossal old press we've got wants, too. *Les*—that's my partner—says we've got to make money! Pooey!"

"How about the city council?"

He gave me a black look.

"That's where our money for our next twenty new presses went."

I knew, from the *Guide*'s own vitriolic columns, what it had been up against. Chain stores were cutting down their ads in the *Comet* to run full pages in the inexpensive *Guide*. The *Comet* had tried to push through a city ordinance making it illegal to leave broadsides (broadsides were defined as all unpaid-for printed matter) at doors. That would have put the *Guide* where the *Comet* wished it was.

But it hadn't gone through. I could only guess the cost.

Mr. Kistler stood up, stretched, and began prowling my room: thumbing through my magazines, opening the buffet's glass doors to look over the china appreciatively, pulling out the linen and silver drawers for brief glances.

"Nice," he said.

"I'm beginning to think Mrs. Garr is right and it applies to everyone in the house."

"Mrs. Garr *is* never right. About what?"

"She says people snoop."

"Oh, she does, does she? Me?" He stood wide-legged in front of me, pointing a finger at his chest.

"She never mentioned you."

"You?"

"Oh no."

"Who, then?"

"The people who were in this apartment before me."

"Aw nuts. They were a respectable middle-aged couple, and they couldn't take it. Not when I brought that—Skip it. Who else?"

"The Wallers."

"The bulky ones? No, they're no threat."

"Maybe. Maybe not. I saw something myself."

"Little Bright Eyes."

"All right, laugh. But when I came home this afternoon I am sure I heard a drawer closing in the living room. I looked in, and there was Mr. Grant sitting on the davenport. His hands shook."

"Him? That innocent little twerp? Oh, now, sister!"

"I said you could laugh. And right after that the man came out of the cellar."

"Well, I'll concede you the man in the cellar." He sat down on the couch again and observed me solemnly. "Let's figure it out. Mrs. Garr, unbeknown to all, has the Hope diamond. It was given to her in her youth by a lover—ah, the gay and dashing Grant. Spent, burned out, and impoverished, Grant comes to steal the diamond from his erstwhile love—"

"But, ah, the villain enters," I said. "Peering through a crack in the basement shutters, he sees Mrs. Garr fondling her incredible jewel by the furnace. She keeps it there, in a chink in the furnace. A bold plan enters the villain's mind. No sooner is he . . ."

We were having quite a good time when Mrs. Garr came home.

MRS. GARR CAME HOME, tenderly escorted by Mrs. Halloran, around six o'clock. The black eyes took in Mr. Kistler pretty fast.

"I didn't know you knew Mr. Kistler." The voice suggested I had made the acquaintance for no good purpose.

"Oh, but she does know me now, Mrs. Garr." Mr. Kistler stood up, beaming like a father.

"Mr. Kistler came in to—to stay with me because I had been a little startled," I explained hastily. "You see, a man—a strange man—ran up out of the cellar. At least I saw him dash out of your bedroom—"

Mrs. Garr turned yellow and swayed. I cried: "Catch her!"

Mrs. Halloran and Mr. Kistler were close enough to ease her into the black leather chair before she toppled. Mrs. Halloran started fanning her with her handbag, which wasn't much use; I ran for water while Mr. Kistler undid her dress at the neck.

Mrs. Garr came around quickly. But her eyes were sick with terror when she opened them.

"He go in your rooms?" she asked thickly.

"Oh no. No, indeed. No one's been in my rooms. He came tiptoeing out of that room under the stairs and saw me, then dashed out the front door."

"Up the cellar stairs," she said, thickly still. She looked around at us, heavy and tired, her white hair slipping in back, only her eyes alive, with their ominous black heat.

"You stay here. You all stay here."

She was out of the chair with surprising quickness, darting away from us into the room under the stairs. She shut the door; we heard the click of a key, the snap of a light switch.

Mr. Kistler looked at me, eyebrows more triangular than ever; then we both looked at Mrs. Halloran.

"She acts as if she had something she was frightened to death might get stolen," I offered. "What could it be?"

Mrs. Halloran tittered and shrugged her shoulders; she looked frightened but swaggering, as if she were carrying something off with bravado. "Well, she don't believe in banks," she said.

"But surely she wouldn't keep money around the house," I began slowly. "I remember, she said something to me one day about not liking banks, too. I wonder if she could—"

Mr. Kistler pinched my arm. "Don't wonder too much."

We stood there in a hesitant group, waiting for Mrs. Garr to come back. Mrs. Halloran's nervousness obviously doubled every minute of the six or seven it took before the door clicked again and Mrs. Garr came out.

"The storeroom, that's where he was," she said. She was stronger now, angry instead of terror-stricken. She stood thinking a moment, then turned to Mr. Kistler.

"You see him?"

"No. No one saw him except Mrs. Dacres, as far as I know."

"Mr. Grant might have," I remembered. "Mr. Grant was waiting in your parlor to pay his rent when I came in." Should I say more? After all . . .

"Mr. Grant? He paid his rent yesterday."

"Oh, look here," Mr. Kistler broke in. "Don't get suspicious about that poor old guy. I'll ask him if he saw anything."

He bounded upstairs. Mrs. Garr turned to me.

"*You* saw him." It was almost an accusation.

"Yes, I—"

"Wha'd he look like?"

"He wasn't a tall man, just about medium. He looked sneaking and furtive. He was wearing a gray cap and a gray topcoat, open but belted in back. I think there was a sweater under the coat, no suit coat. His face was thin and red; a big nose; I'd say he had brownish-gray hair. And when he ran down the hall I thought what a funny countrified haircut he had in back, cut straight across. I'll describe him to the police if you—"

"No, you don't have to. I ain't calling no police."

Mrs. Garr had quit looking at me. She was looking at Mrs. Halloran. Mrs. Halloran was standing pinched and trembling, with a terrified look on her face.

"You *had* to stop for ice cream," Mrs. Garr spat at her. She shoved Mrs. Halloran ahead of her into the parlor and slammed the door.

I was standing alone in the hall when Mr. Kistler came leaping down the stairs again, calling out:

"He says he didn't see any—Well, where's the party gone?"

"It looks as if it's over as far as we're concerned," I said. "But I'd like to know what the heck it means."

5

FOR ONCE, WHAT WENT on in that front parlor was too low to reach my ears. It was a good two hours before the parlor door opened again; I heard Mrs. Halloran rush out of the house. After that I didn't see her for two weeks.

I had a streak of luck. One of the copywriters at Benson's got sick; they took me on until she could return. During that time I was at Mrs. Garr's house only through the evenings and at night, so I heard only the night activities of the house.

And I heard plenty of those. If that house had seemed to stay tensely awake, listening, before, it seemed to do so doubly then, when I knew it only at night. I'd wake up, not once, but five or six times a night. I even told Mr. Kistler about it; he took me out to dinner or to a movie a few times, and once I asked him for Sunday dinner. He was hard to keep down, but he was fun when he wasn't being too obstreperous.

He laughed about the listening, but the next morning before I went to work he knocked at my door and swore at me.

"Now you've got me started. I heard the damn thing listen last night. You're going to have to come up and stay with me nights; I'm afraid to sleep alone."

"You might ask Mrs. Garr to let you borrow Rover."

"No heart."

"Good ears, though. I can tell you everything that happened last night from midnight to dawn. You came in at midnight, reeling."

"Weariness, that was. The *Buyers' Guide* is distributed to its waiting public today."

"Around one thirty Mr. Buffingham and another man came in. At two Mrs. Garr got up and began prowling again . . ."

I was there when the doorbell rang, when Mrs. Tewman went to answer it.

"You got a guy named Buffingham living here?" asked a big voice, held low.

Mrs. Tewman made only a frightened squeak.

"What the . . . !" began Mr. Kistler. "Say your prayers, baby, it's cops."

He left me for the newcomers.

"Good morning, Officer. Anything I can do?"

"Yeah. Guy named Buffingham in this joint?"

"Yes, sir. Upstairs."

The bluecoat came in, and behind him five more like him. They came into the hall with revolvers drawn, tense, watchful. Mrs. Tewman squeaked again, dashed for the cellar stairs. Mrs. Garr popped out, cowered back when she saw the police. I stood startled in my doorway as they came on, Mr. Kistler pointing the way.

"First door to your right toward the front of the house," he told the leader.

The policeman in charge reconnoitered at the foot of the stairs, ran lightly up, leaving his men below. A moment, and he was down again, arranging two men on the stairs, going ahead with the other three. They were unbelievably quiet in motion; there was quiet above, too.

Then a sudden knock, loud but muffled, as sounds were in that house.

The big voice yelled, "Put down the gun, Buffingham, and come on out here!"

A shot answered, two shots, splintering wood. The house was no longer quiet; the two shots seemed to echo, and heavy breathing stirred.

"You can't get us that way! We've got you, Buffingham, six to two, even if your father's fool enough to stick with you. We aren't dumb enough to stand in front of that door. Come on out!"

I don't know why it made me turn. The sound was so very small.

It was the first window of the bay at the left side of my living room that drew my eyes.

Two legs dangled outside the upper sash.

I screamed.

Even as I screamed the man dropped. I saw him for an instant, falling, his face distorted.

But even in that time I could see that it wasn't Mr. Buffingham. It was a younger man, heavier, shorter.

"He's out the window!" I cried.

I think the policemen came down the stairs without hitting more than two or three steps; they surged through my room, pushed the lower sash up, went right through the screen.

More shots outside now, to the rear of the house. I ran to my kitchen door; the fugitive crouched at the back near the corner of the house, supporting himself on one hand. He fired around the house the way he had come, but the police were on him from the other side of the house, too; there must have been some of them stationed outside. I'd no more than got my door open a crack than the hunted man threw his gun to the ground, crying: "You've got me! You've got me!"

He tried to haul himself upright, but one leg dragged; the police were on him in a smothering heap; I saw a fist crash his chin, and he went down, limp.

The tangle broke then. Three policemen emerged, carrying the unconscious man; they disappeared around the Sixteenth Street side of the house.

Breathless, I went back to the hall. Mr. Buffingham, the one I knew, was there, handcuffed to another policeman. Hodge Kistler, alongside, was rapt and intent, his eyes shining. He was practically wagging his tail.

The three of them disappeared out the front door as the sirens began to cry.

IT WASN'T THIRTY SECONDS before Mrs. Garr and Mrs. Tewman, Miss Sands and Mr. Grant, Mr. and Mrs. Waller and I were all there in the hall in a knot. Mr. Waller was sent off posthaste to find out what it was all about.

Mrs. Garr was quivering with excitement.

"It's that no-good boy of his, that's who it is. Oh, he's got his hands into some dirty work now. I always said to him, 'That boy'll come to no good,' I said, ever since he got his first job driving trucks for those dirty bootleggers."

"Herc! How did he get here?" Mrs. Waller was still breathing hard from hurtling her weight downstairs.

"Brought him in, that's what he did," snapped Mrs. Garr. "No respect for a decent house. You mark my words."

My mind leaped to another possibility.

"Sam Zeitman—that gangster—do you think that's what he could have done? Do you think he was the one that shot him?"

Four tongues spoke at once as they considered the possibility. I had to leave for work while the talk still raged.

When I came home, that session—or another one—was still in progress. By that time, Mr. Waller had long been home with the story. But the papers were full of it, too; I read the account coming home on the streetcar.

The gist of it was this. The younger Mr. Buffingham—his given name was Reginald, of all impossible names—had driven out to Elsinore the day before with three other men, and the four of them had robbed the little Elsinore bank. They'd shot and killed a schoolteacher, waiting at the wicket for the money from her paycheck, because she didn't get out of the way fast enough. Reginald Buffingham, bending to push her aside, had lost his hat. The cashier had a good look at him; he was shot for that, but he lived long enough to give the police the description. The Buffingham boy had fled, with all other hands against him, to his father for hiding, but the police had rounded up all his known associates, and they'd squealed.

"He robbed a bank," Mrs. Garr screamed at me when I walked in. "Killed a lady! Killed a cashier!"

"I saw it in the paper," I said. "Do you think Mr. Buffingham, the one that lived here, had anything to do with it?"

"Oh no, he didn't have nothing to do with it," spat Mrs. Garr. "He wouldn't have the nerve. I know *him*."

"Will he be sent to prison, too? He must have known about it when his son came here last night."

"Get sent up for harboring?" Mr. Waller's bulk was quick with excitement. "Maybe he will. You can't tell, though. Mostly they jug people for harboring when they can't get hold of the big shots, or don't want to get hold of 'em. Do it to stop the public hollering."

"They certainly caught young Buffingham, if you could call

him a big shot." I shuddered, thinking of the exhausted, desperate boy who had cried so truly that morning, "You've got me!"

"Was he hurt much?"

"Broke a leg when he fell out that window. Lucky you saw him. If he could have made his father's car parked alongside on Sixteenth Street he could have made the start of a getaway anyway, and they'd have been shooting up the whole town. Can't tell who'd of been killed."

"I notice it didn't say anything about the possibility of his having shot Sam Zeitman," I said. "I wonder if the police didn't think of that. I should think they would."

"I should think they would, too," Mr. Waller agreed. "He's been here with his father before; he knows about that drop. They'll bring it up yet, see if they don't."

I left the four of them to their pleasant conversation for the greater pleasure of eating. But I waited up until Hodge Kistler came in just after midnight.

"Poor Mr. Buffingham," I said when I had supplied coffee and a sandwich. "Imagine having children and having them turn out like that."

"Yeah. But don't let it keep you awake. This isn't the first job Reggie pulled. He had it coming."

"That doesn't make it any easier for his father."

"They all have fathers."

"Yes, but we know this one. I mean, I've seen him around. Couldn't we do something?"

"Sure. Maybe we could take up a collection for bail. It wouldn't take much—a couple grand here, ten grand there—"

"But the father's in jail, too, isn't he? If he gets out, we could go out of our way to show sympathy. Ask him for dinner or something."

"Say, are you nuts?" Mr. Kistler's lips pressed tightly together, and his eyebrows almost hit his nose. "You let me see you talking, just talking, to that guy, and I'll take your pants down and spank you with a table leg. Get that?"

"But just because the son—you don't know the father isn't all right. Look at Dillinger's father. Look at all the other fathers."

"No, I don't know, but I'll take it on trust. And you keep your funny nose out. You hook your little chairsy-wairsies under the doorknobs and beat it to bed."

He stood in the hall until I did it.

THE BOARDERS OF THE house were still excited the next morning, of course. I learned that Mr. Buffingham's hours in the drugstore were from twelve noon to six p.m. one day, from twelve noon to twelve midnight the next day, a regular drugstore schedule. But of course he wasn't on that now. That didn't keep Mrs. Garr, Mrs. Tewman, and the Wallers from lurking in the hall at likely hours in the hope they'd see him come home.

Mr. Waller was right about the police. The papers that second day screamed:

BANK SLAYER SUSPECTED OF
ZEITMAN MURDER

POLICE TRY TO PIN THIRD SLAYING ON KILLER

Reggie Buffingham today faced a third murder charge, as police worked to force a confession that he had shot and killed Sam Zeitman. Zeitman was found dead a few weeks ago at the foot of the Capitol Hill cliff directly behind the Trent Street house in which Buffingham was taken. Although no connection between the New York gangster and Buffingham's gang has been found, police hope to uncover some clue that will solve the Zeitman killing.

It went on for columns, but it was all review.

The police weren't successful. A more modest account some days later announced:

POLICE UNABLE TO TRACE ZEITMAN KILLING TO BUFFINGHAM

So the fate of the dead man I had found was still unknown.

The elder Mr. Buffingham was held an entire week before he was released on bail. Even after all that time Mrs. Garr and Mrs. Tewman were close enough at hand to the hall to see him when he came in. It was early morning; I was just getting ready to leave for work.

I heard the outside door open, heavy steps in the hall and upstairs, a hush, and then Mrs. Tewman's voice: "My, he looks terrible."

I expected, of course, to hear Mrs. Garr tramp up the stairs immediately to ask Mr. Buffingham to move. Day came and day passed, with Mr. Buffingham's hours more irregular than ever. I saw him only once, during that period, but that was enough to know Mrs. Tewman's opinion was justified.

"I suppose Mr. Buffingham will be moving soon," I said to Mrs. Garr one evening.

"He can't get that boy in here again. He's in jail." She avoided my eyes.

"I suppose you hate to ask him to leave when he's having so much trouble."

She looked at me then, expressionlessly, with her coaly little black eyes.

"My, yes, I wouldn't want to do a thing like that. Kicking a man out of his home, that's an awful thing to do. I always say about my house, I want people to feel it's their home. I wouldn't kick a man out of his home."

However that was, it didn't seem to apply to the Wallers, because as the days went by, instead of her gossiping threesomes with the Wallers in the hall, I came to know they were quarreling. I came home one night to hear three heated tongues going in the parlor; as I went past I heard Mr. Waller roaring:

"You can't turn us out like that!"

Well, well. I wondered if Mrs. Garr had brought up the snooping.

Later on that evening, to my surprise, I heard Mrs. Garr at the phone. I'd heard her use it very seldom—it was a pay phone.

The telephone was right outside my doors, on the wall at the foot of the stairs. I got all the conversations in the house—they came right through the wall.

The person Mrs. Garr called was Mrs. Halloran. *So, that feud is over,* I thought amusedly, thinking how much gossip about the Wallers and Mr. Buffingham must be spoiling in Mrs. Garr's breast.

After that Mrs. Halloran was in the house often again. She and Mrs. Garr were mulling something over; I wasn't interested enough to listen to what it was. Mrs. Garr was just an annoyance to me. She hovered through the house more than ever; I started moving my furniture around one evening for sweet variety's sake, and she was there like a shot, staying until I had things rearranged, though I couldn't imagine why she'd think I wanted to hurt her precious furniture.

She was that way with the other lodgers, too. Hodge Kistler ran down to light the hot-water heater for a bath, one night, just to save her old legs. She ran out of her parlor, screaming at him.

"What you doin' down there? What you doin' in my basement?"

She began letting the dog run through the house, too; if I cooked dinner in the evening he'd snuffle under my door, breathing hard and emitting plaintive woofs.

I think she starved those animals of hers, in spite of her incessant talk about her fondness for them, because I gave the cat that was about to have kittens a sausage one day, and she swallowed it whole, in one gulp. After that the cat was always mewing at my door; she was so thin her back sank in along her backbone. I fed her quite often, although she was completely unfriendly outside of her anxiety for food.

I said to Mrs. Garr one day, "All animals care about is getting fed. They're the great original moochers."

It was nasty, but all four animals had been howling in that cellar kitchen all evening, unfed, I was sure, and I was cross.

She was as full of delusions about animals as a sixteen-year-old girl is about love.

"A dog is man's best friend," she said stiffly. "Cats, too. They're true friends. True friends."

She was so moved she actually went down and fed the beasts, and they shut up.

That next evening Mrs. Halloran was over again; this time she had two uncombed little girls with her. After dinner, Mrs. Garr knocked at my door and invited me to sit a spell in her parlor.

I sat there for as short a spell as I politely could. It was a cluttered room, overawed by the biggest grand piano I ever saw; you had to edge past the piano bench to get to the front of the room where the tables and chairs were.

"Me and Mrs. Garr, we're taking us a trip!" Mrs. Halloran told me grandly the news I had been called in to hear. "We're going to Chicago for the excursion on Memor'yal Day!"

I said that was lovely. The two girls went out into the hall, where they sat on the black chair whispering to each other and furtively sniggering; I wondered if everyone attached to Mrs. Garr was as unpleasant as the Hallorans.

Mrs. Halloran was full of excited plans, but Mrs. Garr, I noticed, mostly kept silent, looking at me, looking at Mrs. Halloran. She nodded, now and again. That was all the cooperation Mrs. Halloran's conversation needed.

During that evening and the next day I heard either Mrs. Halloran or Mrs. Garr telling everyone in the house about the trip, in detail.

I wondered about it, mildly. Except for that one movie, which had had such burglarious results, and for quick trips to the grocer's when she couldn't get someone to go for her, I had never known Mrs. Garr to leave the house. She brooded over that house, I'd thought, like a hen over chickens. And now she was calmly leaving it for four days.

"That shows you," I said to myself. "You're a hot psychologist, you are."

Mrs. Garr and Mrs. Halloran were leaving Friday night. I went down cellar early Thursday morning, to pay my rent.

Even at eight thirty Mrs. Garr was already established in her rocker near the furnace. The five-dollar bill I gave her was badly worn, I remember; it had been torn almost an inch at one end, in the lateral crease. Mrs. Garr said something about people not having decent respect for money. She went limping off to her kitchen to get the change, said:

"Don't you plan too wild parties for when I'm gone, now."

That was all. Nothing unusual, nothing strange.

We worked until almost seven o'clock at Benson's that Friday night; they were right in the middle of their Anniversary Sale. Hilda Crosley and I—Hilda was the other copywriter—stayed downtown for dinner because it was so late, then went to see *After the Dark Man* for fifteen cents at the Lido, which is about a tenth-run movie house, but gets all the good pictures in the end.

The hall at Mrs. Garr's house was as dark as usual when I stepped into it about ten o'clock that evening. I'd no sooner stepped in than something light and small came hurtling down the stairs from the second floor.

I turned the light switch and bent to peer under the bookcase. Sure enough, the green eyes of the gray cat stared out at me; it was her favorite hideout. A minute later, someone ran downstairs. Mr. Buffingham.

"Good evening," I said. I was particularly nice to him now, whenever I saw him.

"Hello," he said.

"One of the cats is loose," I told him. "Mrs. Garr must have forgotten to lock her in the kitchen before she went. She told me she was going to lock them in with food enough to last until she got back."

Mr. Buffingham shrugged. "I guess she couldn't have caught this one. I nearly fell over her upstairs."

"But this is the one that—my goodness, I should think she'd be especially careful to get this one in, because she may have kittens anytime, and you know how cats are about picking the best sofa. Do you think we ought to try to get her in the basement room?"

"Why should we worry? Mrs. Tewman'll feed her."

"Well . . ." I said; then, "Of course it isn't any of my business, either," and went on into my rooms.

I was dead tired and had another hard day coming; I was going to have eight pages of proofs to read next day. I went to bed right away but was too dead tired to sleep.

With Mrs. Garr gone the house felt different. Almost empty, in spite of the people I knew were upstairs. It seemed to me there were more noises than usual, too. Someone stayed an unconscionable time in the bathroom, right over my head. Later on I thought I heard footsteps too stealthy to be real, first coming down from upstairs, then going on to the cellar, footsteps so slow they took twenty minutes for the trip.

But there were always noises in the cellar, of course; the animals were down there. Occasionally the dog would grumble, and once he barked quite sharply for a while.

After that, I was just dropping off to sleep when I suddenly found myself lying tense with my eyes staring wide.

This time I knew I had heard unusual sounds. Quiet, furtive sounds at the back of the house.

Then, almost as if it were directly under me, a sharp *plink!*

It was a late May night, clear and quiet. No wind. My windows were open from the top. There wasn't any doubt of it. Someone was fiddling around at the back of the house.

That was getting to be too much.

If anyone was really prowling around Mrs. Garr's house— well, I was going to find out if my imagination was working overtime or what.

I wrapped my negligee around me, clicked on my light, slipped quietly to my back door. The bolt made a tiny whine when I pushed it back.

There were basement windows below the back porch both to the right and to the left; it was from one of those that I thought the sound must have come. I leaned to the right over the rail to peer at that window.

What happened next was incredibly quick.

I tried to scream but couldn't. The hands were too soon on my throat.

I hadn't heard a sound. I'd had no feeling of a body approaching.

Just hands coming out of the air and grabbing at my neck.

Powerful hands that closed around my windpipe, squeezing breath out of me, squeezing life out of me.

I fought desperately, but it was a short fight, I know; I was overpowered at the beginning.

The bottom fell out of the world and I went whirling down into the black dark.

6

IT WAS AN AWFULLY long, dark way to climb up again.

I knew I had to climb, though, because there was such a loud, imperative calling for me at the top.

I climbed and climbed, fell back into the dark, climbed again. Even when I was up over the brink, I could just lie still for a while, staring at night over me.

Then I came to with a jump.

I was lying in a heap on the kitchen floor, as if I'd been thrown there. The door to the back porch was closed now; I could see it in the light that came through from my living room.

On the doors in my living room a fist was pounding. There was a voice, too.

"Mrs. Dacres! Mrs. Dacres!" it yelled. "Gwynne, what's the matter? Gwynne!"

I picked myself up from the floor. The floor wavered when I stepped on it; the ceiling tipped drunkenly. But my feet moved me falteringly toward the other room and the noise.

"Who is it?" I croaked. My throat felt frightfully sore; I could hardly push words up through it.

"By God! What've you been doing? It's me, Hodge Kistler. Let us in!"

I pulled the chairs out from under the knobs and unlocked the doors. They almost hit me in the face, opening; Mr. Kistler was pushing them so hard from the other side. When the doors were open he stood glaring at me; behind him I could see Miss Sands, Mr. Buffingham, Mr. Grant, Mr. and Mrs. Waller, all peculiarly dressed in rumpled pajamas and robes.

"I . . . I . . ." I said.

I threw my arms around Mr. Kistler's neck and began weeping on his chest. He picked me up and sat down in the big chair with me on his lap; I pushed my face into his neck and kept on crying. It was confusing; people kept patting me here and there and saying: "What happened? What is it?"

And there was a murmurous buzz.

Mr. Kistler said, "Cut it out, drizzle-puss, and tell us what happened."

I pulled my face out of his neck to wipe it on the handkerchief he was kindly holding in front of me. Crying had softened my throat.

"A man choked me."

"Go on, you're foolin'."

"No, I'm not. My neck's still sore."

People crowded around to look at my neck.

"My God, look at the bruises!" Mr. Kistler said. "She did get choked! Who did you have in here?"

Miss Sands and Mrs. Waller screamed; everyone but Mr. Kistler stood off a little to stare at me and the room.

"It wasn't anyone I knew. I heard a noise in back—near the basement window I thought it was—so I went back to look—"

Mr. Kistler stood up, dumping me unceremoniously on my feet.

"You heard a noise so you went back to look."

"Yes."

"Why, you little rattlebrained piece of goof! Opened the door, I suppose, just waiting for whoever it was to get his hands on your neck!"

"No, I didn't. I leaned over the railing and looked. But I guess he must have been on the other side."

"Oh, you guess he must have been on the other side." This time his eyebrows did hit his nose. He pushed me into the chair with one hand and then opened his arms wide to the others.

"No brain," he said.

"It was someone—"

I looked at the people in my rooms then. Every person who lived in the house, except the Tewmans and Mrs. Garr. Mr. Grant little and shivering in a blue bathrobe. Mr. Waller, burly and pompous even in red-stripe pajamas. Miss Sands, eager and nervous in aluminum curlers and a Japanese kimono. Mr. Buffingham, in rumpled white pajamas, with his eyes quick and dark flickering over both the room and me. Mrs. Waller, hovering near the door as if she thought what was going on was not quite decent, perhaps, and she ought to leave.

What I had started to say was that I thought the choker was someone from the house.

Because now, I thought the stealthy steps I had heard coming from the second floor were real.

I decided not to say it right then.

"I think I'll call the police," I said.

Mr. Kistler was the only one who answered.

"Okay, baby; it's your party," he said slowly. "First, though, I'll take a look around the back of the house myself."

The three other men went out with him. They all came back very quickly.

"Couldn't see a thing," they reported.

"All there is out there is a door, an empty porch, two railings, cement, and untouched windows." Mr. Kistler amplified it. "I'll call the police for you. A lot of good they're going to do."

The others stood hesitantly around the room while he phoned.

"You can just as well stay here," he told them when he came back. "You'd get called down again anyway."

The four men again wandered out to the back porch while we waited. Mr. Grant returned first; he sat down in a chair to look vacantly about the room; he wore thick-lens glasses and bent his head to look over the tops of them with his round, popping little blue eyes. Miss Sands asked me breathless questions: *what did the man look like, and wasn't you terribly scared, dearie?*

The police came quickly.

Two of them. They were both very young policemen, so young they bristled with importance and assumed boredom. One of them knew Mr. Kistler.

"Hi, Hodge," he said.

"Hi, Jerry! So you got put on. That's swell!"

"Yeah, thanks. What's the trouble here?"

"This young lady got choked by a strange man."

"You shouldn't let strange men in, lady."

"I didn't."

"Who was it?"

"I don't know," I said, but I braced myself and let go my bombshell theory. "I think it was someone from the house."

They all froze at that.

Then there was a burst of excited voices.

"All right, all right, calm down. Let the little lady tell her story. Spill it."

I did, beginning with the footsteps I thought I'd heard on the stairs.

"Any of the rest of you hear anything?" Jerry turned to the people who lived upstairs.

They all talked at once, but he weeded them out one by one.

Not one of them would admit that he had either seen or done anything unusual.

Miss Sands reported having been in bed and asleep since nine thirty, after a particularly tiring sale day in her store.

Mr. Grant had gone to bed a little after ten, had been asleep.

The Wallers had been at a movie at the little house below the capitol, had come home just after eleven, gone to bed and to sleep.

Mr. Buffingham had been on his way out for a package of cigarettes when he passed me in the hall; had come back, read for a while, slept.

Mr. Kistler had stayed downtown until after midnight, had stopped at my door to say hello when he saw the thread of light under my doors, and had been disturbed when I didn't answer. The other people had appeared from upstairs, one by one, when they were awakened by his pounding on my door and calling my name. They'd gone to their doors to see what was up, then out into the halls, and finally been lured downstairs, pretty much as they slept.

Except for Mr. Kistler, *they had all come down together.*

Unless they were all lying, there couldn't be any doubt of that. They all verified it.

"Of course," speculated Jerry gloomily, "we can't tell how long before you was found that the choking took place. Whoever it was might have had time to get upstairs and undressed. Or he might just have gone around the front again, come in, and started pounding on your door."

"That wasn't what happened." Mr. Kistler was elaborately calm.

"Oh hell." Jerry abandoned that track and tried another. "Who runs this joint?"

They explained to him about Mrs. Garr's going to Chicago. He was interested in that. He asked them over, one by one, if each one had been aware that Mrs. Garr was to be gone that night.

They all knew. Mr. Buffingham said, at first, that he didn't know, but then he recollected it.

"Oh yeah, I guess she did say somethin'. I didn't pay much attention."

When it was Mr. Grant's turn he said, "Oh yes, I knew," vaguely.

"What time'd she go?"

"It was that excursion on the Great Western," I said.

"Pulled out at 8:05 p.m., Jerry," the quiet second officer said.

"I wonder who else knew the old lady was gone?"

"The Hallorans would—" I started.

"But Mrs. Garr didn't go, then." It was said absently, as if the speaker were thinking aloud.

It was Mr. Grant. He blinked at us over his thick lenses when we stared at him, fidgeting as if he wished he hadn't spoken.

"What do you mean she didn't go? She's gone, ain't she?"

"Oh, it's nothing, nothing at all."

"I'll decide that. You talk."

"It was just that I saw her after that. After eight-five, I mean."

"Oh, you did! Where at?"

"I saw her across the street, walking up Sixteenth Street. I was in my room, looking out the window, and I *saw* her crossing over from the other corner, from the Elliott House corner, you know. I remember I wondered about it because I knew she was going away. Then I thought she must have come back for some-thing. She started across Trent Street just as a car came along; she went back to the sidewalk again until it went past. I looked at my watch pretty soon after that because I wondered if I should go for a walk until bedtime. It was after eight thirty-five then, al-most eight forty."

"Why, I suppose she might have come back for some reason," Mr. Kistler said. "Funny she didn't turn up with all this racket going on, though. She's usually Johnny-on-the-spot. I'll call her."

He went into the hall. "Mrs. Garr! Mrs. Garr!" he called loudly.

His voice echoed, but there was no other answer. He came back.

"Sure about the time that excursion left, Red?" asked Jerry.

Red went into the hall, made a telephone call, came back.

"Eight-five. Checked it," he reported laconically.

Jerry took Mr. Grant in hand.

"Mr. Grant, there's a lot of old ladies around."

"It's not likely I would mistake Mrs. Garr." Mr. Grant was quiet but stubborn.

"Yeah. Maybe. And the time, now. How long before you looked at your watch?"

"Not more than five, ten minutes."

Jerry laughed. "That's what you think. If you'd listened to evidence in court a couple times, mister, you'd know how right people are about time."

He stood up impatiently.

"This ain't getting us anyplace, anyhow. You don't think the old lady came back and choked her, do you? Time for you to speak up, lady. I mean you, Mrs. Dacres. Think it could have been the old lady choked you?"

I thought back. "Oh no. No, it couldn't have been. Whoever it was was strong. Mrs. Garr had a bad heart. It made her breathless to do anything taking strength. Breathless to walk upstairs, even. I didn't hear the—the person breathe at all, until he grabbed my neck."

"Get any look at him at all?"

"No, I didn't. But I have a feeling it was a man. That was my impression."

Jerry grunted. "A lot of good that's going to do us. Couldn't tell was he short, fat, tall, thin?"

Again I tried to think, desperately. It was important, I could see that. If it were someone from the house. Short—that would be Hodge Kistler or Mr. Grant. Tall—Mr. Buffingham or Mr. Waller. Fat—Mr. Waller. Thin—Mr. Buffingham or Mr. Grant.

But try as I might, I couldn't give the figure that had attacked me any bulk at all.

Just hands, coming out of the darkness. Arms. Steel strength in clenching fingers.

I shook my head.

The looks Mr. Waller, Miss Sands, and Mrs. Waller directed at me now were resentful. Mr. Grant merely looked mild. Mr. Buffingham sullen. Mr. Kistler alert. I looked from one to the other, hoping for a telltale sign.

Jerry gave signs of new impatience.

"You keep an eye on 'em, Red," he said. "I'm going to take a look around."

He pulled a flashlight from his pocket, strode toward the kitchen. After a minute or two Mr. Kistler followed him out. We were quiet while they were gone. When I turned to look at one of the others, now, his eyes would slide from mine.

Jerry was back shortly. "It don't look like anything's been sprung," he announced.

He tramped through my rooms, into the hall; we heard him running down the cellar stairs. He was down there a much longer time. When he came back he stood thoughtfully in the center of the room, swinging his flashlight.

"Them steps you thought you heard stealin' down the stairs, that's all you got to go on, to think it was someone in the house?"

"Yes, that's all."

"Now listen, sister. This is how I dope it out. Some small-time guy is around trying his luck, see. Some poor sod from down on Water Street, maybe. There's a basement window back there that's open about an inch. It's nailed there or something; anyway, it sticks; I can't move it. He tries to jimmy it open, can't make it. You hear him. Then you open your door and scare him so he jumps on you to keep you from yelling, and beats it. You come with me if you want to rest your mind. I'll show you."

He started for my back door, beckoning us after him.

I've often thought what a theatrical procession we must have made, if anyone had passed to see us at two o'clock of that moon-less night. The policeman ahead, flashing his light low at the basement windows, the night-clad parade after him. We toured the entire house that way, the light playing on each basement window in turn.

All those basement windows were of frosted glass, made dou-bly obscure by dust and dirt. They were all locked tight, too, except for the one to the left of my back porch, which was open an inch or so from the bottom. It seemed nailed there, as Jerry had said: I guessed that Mrs. Garr knew her pets needed air, but didn't want burglars.

The policeman played his light on that window longest.

"See that window? That's where some guy thinks maybe he can squeeze through and pick up whatever's loose inside. But he don't make it. He don't get through. I'll show you if you're still scared."

We all trooped back through my kitchen door; Mr. Kistler, last, bolted it. In the cellar Jerry continued his assurances.

"See? I'll go through everything here. Rooms in front empty, and not even locked."

The Tewmans hadn't been around all evening. I guessed they were taking advantage of Mrs. Garr's absence.

"Not a soul in there. Nothing touched that I can see. Now look at this furnace room. Nobody in the furnace. Nobody under the washtubs. Nobody in the storage room."

He darted his light briefly in there; the room was now orderly again. There was something, though. Mrs. Garr's chair, with some clothes left on it in a dark heap.

"Mrs. Garr's chair's in there. She usually keeps it near the furnace."

Jerry snorted. "Well, she wasn't going to sit on it for a while, was she? Why shouldn't she stick it away in there?"

I subsided. Jerry took up the march.

The dog barked as we drew near the back kitchen.

"And this here room, see? The door's safely locked."

We all looked at the kitchen door. The dog barked again, and for some reason I didn't know a shiver shook me. I tried to explain it, seizing on the only reason I could see.

"That's funny, the key's gone. Mrs. Garr always left that key hanging on the casing. She must have taken it with her."

"Well, you got a right to think things is funny," Jerry said paternally. "But now you've seen for yourself there ain't a thing wrong down here." He turned, stalked toward the stairs. "The next time you get to thinking, don't go opening your back door to see what noises is in the middle of the night. Wasn't it near here that Zeitman guy was picked up? Yeah, I thought it was. You keep that in mind, lady. What if you'd run into something like that? You could have been knocked over that railing, just as well as left on that kitchen floor. You're lucky, that's all."

"All right," I said meekly. It would have been a longer, darker drop, that real one over the rail.

"Why don't you come on up and sleep on my couch in my living room the rest of the night?" Mrs. Waller suddenly offered. Now that the attack had been pinned on an outsider, there was forgiveness and a sort of amused condescension at my weakness in the air.

"That's fine, that's fine," Jerry said.

Mr. Kistler had been at my elbow during the entire tour of the house; when we stood once more in the hall on the main floor he spoke up thoughtfully.

"There's one more reassurance we might make, Mrs. Dacres. We might glance over the rest of the house to make sure no one's in hiding. And there's one thing more we might look at. The way I figure it, if it was anybody in the house, that person must have gone around in his stocking feet. And those stockings would be pretty dusty—show they'd been walked on, anyway. I suggest we look over all the socks in this outfit. We can begin on mine."

He sat down on the black leather chair to pull his shoes off. He hadn't been walking outdoors in those socks.

I looked at the other slippered feet. The policeman laughed.

"Okay, buddy." He was bored now.

One by one the others showed socks or bare feet, guiltless of dust.

They looked briefly into Mrs. Garr's parlor before going upstairs. Mrs. Garr's house has no attic; it's a flat-roof house. So we just went around to all the rooms.

It was a comedy by that time.

No one in the bath.

We crowded into Miss Sands' room, peered at the limp mended stockings across the chair by the rumpled bed, peered into her laundry bag, all of us looking at the pitiful, bare, uncomfortable room—gas plate, varnished dresser, brass bed—half ashamed and half suspicious.

The Waller apartment was next; it had three tiny rooms at the back: bedroom, living room, kitchen; it wasn't as poverty-stricken as Miss Sands' room, but it, too, had a pathetic bareness, few pictures, no knickknacks, none of the loved impedimenta that clutter up a happy life. Just the walls, the furniture, the rugs. Clean, undisturbed, barren with the barrenness of people who are childless in their middle age. Their stockings lay over their shoes, hers at the right of the bed, his at the left, clean.

Mr. Grant's room was next. There was a difference here. The room's essential cheapness was overlaid with luxury. A good reading lamp by a comfortable, down-cushioned blue chair. An expensive set of brushes on the dresser top; a bookshelf crowded with well-bound books. He was wearing his socks.

Mr. Buffingham's. His room was like Miss Sands' but more cluttered; unwashed kettles and a frying pan with grease congealed in it stood on the gas plate; unwashed dishes on the table. The story was the same here: bedding thrown back and clothes on chairs. He dug out all the soiled socks from the heap of laundry on the closet floor, all dustless.

Mr. Kistler's rooms, the last, were locked before he opened them; the air was stale as if they had been closed all day. He made a ceremony of hunting up soiled socks.

Not one single clue in the whole house.

The men stood about in the hall after that, talking with that insufferably superior indulgence men often use when some woman has exhibited weakness. Jerry and Red, leaving, flung back:

"Good night, all. We're goin'. Ring us up when you really get murdered."

Mr. Kistler helped me carry sheets and blankets up to the

Wallers' couch. He took all the bedding in one load; I looked at his hands and thought of the strong hands on my throat. Certainly he had the strongest hands in the house.

"You said you stopped at my door because you saw light under it?" I asked.

"I didn't think you'd be asleep with the light on. I thought I'd say good night. I rapped lightly and you didn't answer, so I rapped louder and you didn't answer, and pretty soon I was giving it the works."

"Lucky for me," I said.

But I was wondering.

IN THE WALLER APARTMENT, I felt perfectly safe and dropped right off to sleep. In spite of Mrs. Garr I wasn't particularly suspicious of the Wallers then; I thought that even if Mr. Waller had been the one who attacked me, he wouldn't be likely to throttle me again in his own apartment. It would be a dead giveaway.

So I slept the sleep of the unthrottled, and when I woke in the morning, both Mr. and Mrs. Waller came out to look at me in bed, more wistfully and jocosely than anything else, it seemed to me. Mrs. Waller asked me how I was and said I could just as well eat breakfast with them; Mr. Waller kidded me and treated me altogether as if I were a great big wonderful joke.

I did eat breakfast with them, too; first going downstairs to dress and bring up bacon and cream for my share. We became so friendly Mr. Waller put on his hat to walk down Sixteenth to the car line with me, after breakfast. To see, he explained, that no one choked me on the way.

"Don't let this thing get you." He was grandly paternal. "That sort of thing happens often in a town this size. Always some guy around trying to see what he can pick up. But it isn't dangerous, not if you keep your doors and windows locked."

"You must have had a lot of experience with people like that," I said. "Mrs. Garr told me about your being a retired policeman. You're awfully young to be retired, though."

His geniality changed to sudden storm.

"That old bitch! I could tell you things about her that would empty that house in a hurry and keep it empty!"

That left me at half-mast. I tried to pass it over and be friendly again, but it was hard going. He shut up like a trap; I couldn't get anything except a glower out of him, and when the car came he lifted his hat and stalked away without having said one more word.

I was bewildered by the change. What had brought it on? My reference to his having retired so young? Why should he be infuriated by that? I began to wonder what could be the hidden story behind his retirement—had there been one of those police scandals that break out in newspaper rashes?

I was still puzzling over Mr. Waller when I reached the office.

I had a heck of a day there. Of course I had to begin by telling my dramatic experience to the girls in the office; being a copywriter, I detailed the attack in full. By ten o'clock, when I was swimming in a sea of proofs, the buyers began coming up with corrections so important they couldn't possibly be sent up with the office girl as usual, and demanding with their second breaths, had I really been attacked by a man, and how far had it gone?

The advertising manager didn't like it; at six o'clock, I was told the girl I was replacing would be back next week, and thanks for helping out.

Well, that job had lasted longer than I'd thought it would.

Unemployed again, I took my week's pay in its envelope and went home to bed, stopping only for a sandwich. Once home, I printed GONE TO BED in big black letters on a sheet of paper, pinned it to the outside of my doors, and did a sound job of barricading myself. That last included pulling the overstuffed chair over to reinforce the two dinette chairs under the doorknobs, pulling the kitchen table against the bolted back door, and hooking a chair under the doorknob of the door in my kitchen that led to the unused basement stairs.

I slept well, too.

If there was any prowling that night I didn't hear it.

Memorial Day, Sunday, dawned rainy and gray, as Memorial Days have a habit of dawning. I had, at breakfast, almost a reception. Even Mrs. Tewman came in, more sullen than ever because the disturbance Friday night had shown up her absence from the house, and she was afraid Mrs. Garr would hear of it when she came back. She stared at me as if I were a victim in a wax museum. Mrs. Waller had told her the story.

"You missed out on it," I condoled.

"Jim and I went out on a party. We don't get much chance to go out on a party when *she's* here."

"I'll bet you don't," I said. "Sit down and have a cookie?"

She took the cookie, but she wouldn't sit down; she munched grimly, standing up.

"It was a beer party," she said defiantly, and left.

Mr. Kistler came down at eleven to eat everything left on the table.

"I suppose you know your publicity by heart?" he started.

"Whose publicity? You mean I got in the papers?"

"Don't tell me you don't know a whole reporter stormed the house yesterday! He telephoned."

"He missed me. I was a working girl."

"Didn't even read last night's *Comet*?"

"Too tired."

"These people who can't read and then try to alibi," he said.

He left, taking his slice of toast with him, and came back, still chewing, with a paper.

"See? Page eleven."

The item he pointed at was a brief notice at the obscure bottom of page eleven.

PROWLER ATTACKS WOMAN

Mrs. Gwynne Dacres, 26, lodger at 593 Trent Street, was set upon by an unknown assailant who attempted to choke her, early this morning. Mrs. Dacres told police she was wakened by a slight noise at the back of the house and went to investigate it. The moment she stepped outside her door, the man sprang upon her and, she says, attempted to throttle her. She found herself lying on the floor of her kitchen when she recovered consciousness a short time later. Police believe she probably surprised a prowler who was trying to break into a basement window. No clues were found. Mrs. Dacres recovered promptly without medical assistance.

"Short and sweet! 'Recovered promptly'? What about my nerves?"

"Copywriters don't have 'em in the plural. Only in the singular."

"Sir! No gentleman is insulting to a lady at her own table!"

"But it's a breakfast table. How do you know what goes on at breakfast tables—or do you?"

Miss Sands and the Wallers came in then. After they had been there awhile, the breakfast things were all pushed to one end of the table so we could play put-and-take with matches for chips. Mr. Grant came down to chirp around the table, too, although he refused to play. Mr. Buffingham poked his head in at the door just before noon.

"How're you doin'?" he asked awkwardly.

"Fine," I said. "I have almost all Mr. Kistler's matches. Come in and take a hand?"

"No, thanks, I'm a workin' man."

After he left we played without interruption. At three o'clock we were still sitting there; the rumpled tablecloth still held the toaster and the empty dishes at one end of the table. At three o'clock Mr Kistler had all the matches. The Wallers and Miss Sands gave up and went upstairs.

"Unlucky in love." Mr. Kistler aggrievedly piled the matches back into their box. "I'll pay you back in dinner for that breakfast I ate."

He did better than that. We dined and danced, and the next morning he got me up early to go fishing in a woolly gray drizzle. We spent all that holiday sitting in a boat on Slater Lake, pulling flat little sunfish up on drop lines, screwing hooks out of their gelatinous mouths, and then throwing them back into the lake again, because they were too little to keep. He thought it was fun. We didn't have licenses, either.

I rose late on Tuesday morning because of the long day before, and because I wasn't working. In fact I was just getting out of bed when the telephone rang, about ten o'clock. Mrs. Tewman didn't answer, so I did.

The high voice at the other end of the wire was Mrs. Halloran's.

"Could I speak to Mrs. Garr, please?"

"Why, hello, Mrs. Halloran, welcome home. I haven't seen her, but I'll call."

With my hand over the mouthpiece I called, "Mrs. Garr! Mrs. Garr!" I waited, but there wasn't any answer.

"I haven't seen her yet, and she doesn't answer," I said to the phone. "When did you get in? Did you have a nice time?"

"About a hour ago. I just got home. Oh, swell, I had a swell time. I saw four movies and Lincoln Park and Michigan Avenue and I bought me a hat in the Boston Store and I saw the house where that girl shot her friend in the back; you know, you saw it in the papers?"

"It must have been lovely."

"Oh, it was, just *lovely*, my, I had a *swell* time."

"Shall I take any message for Mrs. Garr when I see her?"

"No, you just tell her I called up and it was just *lovely*, my, I had a *swell* time."

I don't see how I could have had an inkling of the truth from that conversation.

The only thing that struck me, as I went back to dress, was that Mrs. Halloran's message didn't sound grateful, it sounded vindictive, and that it was odd of her to call before Mrs. Garr had even had time to get home from the station.

I went downtown that morning to proposition different companies, letting them know that I was a good experienced copywriter they might call in while regular people were on vacations. It was a surprise, though, when I bumped into something immediate. The third place I hit was Hibbard's, and they were wild because their advertising man—they have just one—had obviously gone on a holiday bat; at any rate he hadn't returned that morning, and they couldn't reach him. Hibbard's had a half-page sale ad all full of little items—a big ad for them—running Wednesday night. The ads were set up, but buyers were yipping for proofs and corrections, and no one knew anything. They hired me on the spot, and I waded in.

That night I went home late, slept, left early; I saw no one in the house. The next day I did the same. It wasn't until Thursday morning that the Hibbard advertising man stole sheepishly into his office. I stayed until closing time to show him what I'd done and help him get back in step, so I got paid for three whole days.

That was Thursday, June third.

7

THAT WAS THE NIGHT.

Even now, looking back, I get tense when I think of it.

I went straight home from Hibbard's, cooked dinner, ate.

It must have been around seven o'clock that I opened my door after a gentle knock to see Mr. Grant standing in the hallway blinking.

"I haven't seen you around these last few days," he said as mildly as always. "I thought I'd inquire."

"I'm awfully glad you did. Come in and sit down. I've been in luck; I had three days of temporary work again; eighteen fine lovely dollars' worth."

"That's fine. I'm very glad to hear it. Very glad to see you aren't having more of your—er—experiences." He cleared his throat, as if now the preliminaries were over. "I have also been wondering a little about Mrs. Garr. Wasn't she going to come back soon?"

I stared at him with my mouth open.

"Isn't she back? Why, she was supposed to be back Tuesday morning!"

"I haven't seen her." He was as quietly positive as he had been about his statements Friday night.

"Why, that's right, I haven't, either. But I've been gone until so late—I thought she'd be in her room sleeping."

"Well, I have been about a good deal in the daytime, and I haven't seen her." He said it still mildly, but with interest, too.

"Oh, she must be back. She must be around here somewhere. Have you called her?"

"No, I—not exactly. But I am positive she is not here."

"Well, we'll soon find out. I'll call."

As Mr. Kistler had on Friday night, I went out into the hall to cry toward her quarters, "Mrs. Garr! Mrs. Garr!"

As on Friday, there was no answer. I went to the head of the basement stairs; the cellar was dark, but I called down there, too.

Again no answer. I went back to Mr. Grant.

"She's certainly not in the house now. And that's odd. You wouldn't expect her to go away again when she had just been gone over the weekend. She may have decided to stay longer in Chicago, of course; we wouldn't know. But in that case you'd think Mrs. Halloran might—"

I stopped. Because I'd no sooner said Mrs. Halloran's name aloud than the memory of having talked to her on Tuesday morning came to me.

"Wait, let me think. Mrs. Halloran's back! She came back from Chicago. She called up Tuesday morning just before I left for downtown. And she asked to talk to Mrs. Garr."

Mr. Grant glimmered at me for a long time, his eyes bewildered behind their glasses.

"Then Mrs. Garr must have come back. You'd think she'd come here. But I haven't seen her around at all, and I was looking for her. My rent was due. You know, it was queer, very queer, about my seeing her Friday night. After the train had left, you know. I could have sworn it was Mrs. Garr. After all, it's light at eight thirty now. You don't believe in—er—ghosts, do you?"

I laughed. "No, and I don't think you saw any. But I agree it's queer. Perhaps she did go somewhere else after she came in on the train Tuesday morning. Or she might have been hurt, run over—be in a hospital somewhere."

"You think we should do nothing, then?"

"Oh no, I think we should find out where she is, in case we should be doing something. But what could we do? Call the hospitals? I know; we could call Mrs. Halloran."

We decided to do that. There were plenty of Hallorans in the phone book, but none on South Dunlop, where Mrs. Garr had told me the Hallorans lived.

The Hallorans had no telephone, then. But the more names I looked through the less I thought I could let the matter drop.

"Just the same, I don't want to go out all that way to see the Hallorans," I admitted. "Who else is home?"

"The Wallers, I think. Miss Sands."

"Let's go up to see the Wallers. We'll ask them what should be done."

We both went up.

Mr. Waller, with his shoes comfortably off, was reading; Mrs. Waller was busy with paste, sheets of paper, and cut-out newspaper photographs of children, matching twins for the *Comet* contest. They weren't much interested at first in our worries over Mrs. Garr.

"That old bitch," Mr. Waller interrupted testily. "The longer she stops away the better I like it."

"She might have got hit by a hit-run driver, though," Mrs. Waller speculated with the indecent hope people seem to have that some other person will have come to harm.

Mr. Waller grew more alert.

"That's so, that's so. Might even be dead. Where did you say this Halloran fella lived?"

"It's on South Dunlop Street. The city directory's probably the only place you could find the number. It isn't in the phone book. You don't think we should call the hospitals first? Or maybe the police?"

Mr. Waller turned that over slowly.

"Oh, she'd have had this address on her somewhere if the hospitals or the police had her. We'd of heard. You're sure nobody ain't heard? Mrs. Tewman might of—"

"Mrs. Tewman's been gone ever since Monday," Mrs. Waller put in thoughtfully. "I been lookin' for her. The bathroom's a mess. I cleaned it up once myself. I been lookin' for her."

Mrs. Tewman gone, too! It quickened Mr. Waller's interest, as it did mine.

"Okay, I'll go huntin' the old so-and-so." There was a gleam in his eye as he turned to his wife. "Never thought I'd go huntin' *her*, did you, Agnes?"

"No, I never did." Mrs. Waller was increasingly excited. "I can't think what can have happened to her, now I think about it. I've never known her to go off like this before."

"Before we start off on any wild-goose chase, though"—Mr. Waller turned back—"we ought to look through the house for sure. You say you called her?"

"Yes, I did. Thoroughly."

"Well, we can soon look."

The looking was quickly done. Upstairs rooms, parlor, stair room, cellar. The Tewmans' rooms in the front were again unlocked and vacant, the furnace room empty.

Mr. Waller bellowed, "Mrs. Garr!" before the basement kitchen, but except for an answering bark from the dog, all was quiet.

"She ain't here, that's a cinch," he concluded.

He left with Mr. Grant. I invited Mrs. Waller to stay downstairs with me until they came back. We stopped at Miss Sands' door to ask her to come, too; *she* came with alacrity when she heard what was afoot.

There were only the three of us in the house.

Our wonder grew as we talked, hashing over Mrs. Garr's non-appearance from every angle.

"Perhaps she's lost her mind and is wandering around somewhere, not knowing who she is," was my best solution. "She's old, you know. She's been acting queerly all along; I've thought she was queer ever since I moved here. Did she ever tell you she thought people went snooping around the house at night? People who live here, I mean?"

"No, she never said to me." Miss Sands shot a furtive look from me to Mrs. Waller.

Both the women were anxious to speculate about Mrs. Garr's peculiar behavior in this one instance of not coming home; they were avid to talk about it. But every time I switched to Mrs. Garr's general peculiarities and to her life in the past, they were both queerly reluctant. I couldn't get any gossip out of them at all, in spite of an admission wrung from Miss Sands that she had lived in that house with Mrs. Garr for twelve years.

"It's handy," she excused herself. "You know, walking distance and all."

"Has Mrs. Garr always been like she is now?"

"Well, she was different when I first knew her."

That was all I could get.

A thought hit me.

"I'll bet it will turn out she went somewhere. She must have known she was going to be away for a long time because—think of those animals in the basement. They'd be crazy for food by this time if *she* hadn't left a lot. And the dog hasn't been barking much—I've just heard a growl once in a while. By this time, though . . . Do you think we should go down and let them out?"

"They'd be awful hard to get back in," Mrs. Waller objected.

We decided to wait to see what the men found out.

Mr. Waller and Mr. Grant did not return to the house until nearly ten o'clock. They both looked stirred up and alert when they walked into my living room, and they were not alone. Mrs. Halloran was with them.

Mrs. Halloran was drunk with excitement.

"Oh, Aunt Harriet! Oh, Aunt Hattie! Oh, she must have been killed! I can't think whatever happened! There I was, thinking she did it a-purpose, and getting mad, and going on about how I'd show her I could have a good time anyway, and she may be kidnapped!"

"It's funny, it's pretty funny, all right." Mr. Waller looked quickly from one to the other of us. "I guess we better call the hospitals, all right."

"What are you talking about?" I asked Mrs. Halloran. "She was all right when she came home with you from Chicago on Tuesday, wasn't she?"

"That's it! That's it! She never went to Chicago!" Mrs. Halloran screamed at me, twisting her hands. "Right up at the gate we was, Aunt Hattie and me, and I kep' a-saying, 'Better get out your ticket, Auntie, better get out your ticket, Auntie'—I had mine all ready in my hand—but she kep' a-saying, 'I got plen'y o' time,' until right when the man says, 'See your ticket, lady,' and she opened her purse and hunted, couldn't find it. She says to me, 'You go ahead save me a seat,' she says to me, so I go ahead on down to the train; I get on and pick a good seat right in the middle of the car, and she never come! I kep' lookin' out the window and up the aisle, and there was lots of other people wanted to sit by me, sayin', 'This half took, lady?' And I kep' sayin', 'Yes, I got a friend comin',' but she never come. So then the train started, and I thought she must-a been lookin' for me in some of the other coaches. The conductor come and took my ticket, and I says, 'You see a lady lookin' for a lady?' I says to him, but he says, 'There's a awful lot of ladies on this train, madam,' so after a while, I got another lady across the aisle to keep my seat for me while I went through all the train lookin', and she wasn't there. So the other lady, she stayed, and she said maybe they run two trains. So then in Chicago I went to the Clinton Hotel. I went in a taxi where she said we was goin' to stop in that hotel, but she never come there, neither. So I was mad and said nobody was goin' to leave *me* like that, so I went to four movies and saw the house where the girl killed her boyfriend and all—she shot him in the back—and here maybe all the time poor Aunt Hattie lost her ticket and got murdered!"

Mrs. Halloran stopped there because she had to blow her nose.

Her narrative style was the kind that needs close following. She'd had it. She rolled her eyes around at us as a finale, thrilled horror added to her excitement.

"You don't think somebody could-a murdered her for her ticket and stuck her dead body someplace in that station, do you?"

"We better get in touch with the hospitals, we better get in touch with the hospitals, all right." Mr. Waller was all action. "They do it from the Missing Persons."

For the third time since I had moved there a call to the police department was put in from Mrs. Garr's house.

FROM MR. WALLER'S EFFORTS at our end of the line I gathered that the police department wasn't much interested in the unexplained absence of Mrs. Garr.

"Yes, she is a missing person," Mr. Waller reiterated. "She's been missin' since last Friday night . . . No, she ain't a young lady. She's a old lady. Maybe sixty, sixty-five . . . No, she didn't go visitin' relatives. She ain't got but one relative, and she's right here havin' fits now. This Mrs. Garr was goin' to Chicago on Friday, see, but she never got on the train . . . No, she didn't get lost in Chicago. She never got on the train . . . No, I don't know how many trains there was."

He wiped perspiration from his face when he was done.

"Dumbheads. What do they think, I think it's fun to report missing persons? Maybe there was two trains run on that excursion, though."

"I wonder if that could be it. It would be more likely for her to get lost in Chicago than in Gilling City."

"Except that I saw her on the corner after train time Friday," put in Mr. Grant obstinately.

If ever a situation was well talked over, that one was. We were still at it when Mr. Kistler came home at midnight. Mr. Buffingham came home around one. They both added themselves to the party, but we couldn't rouse them to our pitch of interest. They just weren't worried.

The two policemen came almost on Mr. Buffingham's heels. They were the same two men we'd had the Friday before: Jerry and Red; I felt we were practically friends, but they tramped into my living room sourly.

"Now what've you got going on around here? More monkey business?"

Mrs. Halloran appointed herself spokesman.

By that time, she had worked herself close to hysterics. I didn't see how the policemen could make much sense out of her recital, but they'd probably had the outline of the story from the officer Mr. Waller had talked to on the telephone. They were definitely bored.

"Aw, she'll turn up. Maybe she does miss the train, but she's all set for a visit, so she goes somewheres else, see? She's of age, ain't she? She's on her own, ain't she? There isn't any reason why she should report to you where she goes, is there?"

Mr. Grant trained his blinks on the policemen.

"I have lived in this house for four years, and I have never known her to leave it overnight before."

"Well, she did now. She *said* she was goin' to Chicago, didn't she? I bet she went. Her excursion ticket wasn't any good because she missed the train, so she gets another and takes a reg'lar train."

"Then there wasn't a second section?" Mr. Kistler had arrived at the thoughtful-interest stage.

"Naw, there was only one section. These excursions ain't as popular as they was."

Miss Sands had a word to put in. "Then she never went. She was awful close."

"Okay, lady, then you tell us where she is." Jerry was still bored. "She ain't in a hospital; there ain't been an unknown lady in a hospital this week. She ain't in the morgue. She ain't in jail."

"She may have been hit by a car, picked up by the driver, and cared for in his home," contributed Mr. Kistler with quickening eyes, "or else dumped, dead, out in the country somewhere."

Mrs. Halloran shrieked and fell over backward in her chair. She came to very quickly, though. She hadn't had any attention for almost two minutes, but on the other hand she didn't want to miss anything.

"Well, we'll keep an eye out," Jerry promised us largely as he rose to go.

"Wait a minute, Jerry," asked Mr. Kistler, still contemplative. "There doesn't seem much use in going over the house again; that's been done since she left, thanks to Mrs. Dacres. But there's one place we didn't look, remember? That kitchen downstairs."

"Aw nuts."

"But the key *is* gone," I said, picking up Mr. Kistler's idea. "Suppose she'd left her ticket there, come back for it, and fallen or become ill—she might be lying there sick—or dead, even!"

"Then how did it get locked again?" asked Jerry reasonably.

"Did you try to see if it was locked?" asked Mr. Kistler quickly.

"Hell, sure I did. Sure. Anyhow, I think I did." Jerry's voice, certain at first, grew a trifle less certain. "Okay, I'll take another look."

Once more nine people trailed down the cellar stairs in disorder, the policeman, ahead, switching on the cellar light from the head of the stairs.

The coldness of the basement, in contrast to the June warmth above, struck our flesh with chill. The far reaches of the furnace room, with only one bulb to light them, were shadowed. The place smelled worse than ever. Mrs. Tewman, I thought, had certainly been doing as little cleaning as Mrs. Waller said she had. And then, of course, those animals.

Jerry's hand closed on the knob of the kitchen door.

Inside the room, the dog growled.

The door didn't open.

Jerry turned triumphantly to us.

"Okay? It's locked, all right. Satisfied now?"

"No. No, I'm not satisfied." Mr. Kistler had the nose-to-the-trail look he'd worn the morning Mr. Buffingham's son was taken. "I think you should break that door in."

"Aw, listen, buddy."

"We'll vote on it. If Mrs. Garr comes home and kicks up a fuss, we'll chalk it up to our interest in her welfare. All those in favor?"

"Aye," several voices replied. I don't know how many, but at least no one said, "No."

Jerry said, "Okay," crossly.

He, Red, and Mr. Waller pushed against the door. It was a strong door; when Jerry had his shoulder against it, it gave a little, but the lock held.

"Wait," Mr. Kistler suggested. "There's a hatchet around here somewhere. I've seen Lady Garr herself chopping kindling."

They hunted until they found the toolbox under a laundry tub. Jerry took a small ax out of it and soon splintered the lock out of the door; when it came free the door swung inward.

Instantly the three cats shot out and scattered from under our feet. The dog came, too, standing at bay for a moment in the door, then slinking fast around the group of us.

"God! It's a zoo!" Jerry said. "Smells like one, too." He pushed the door farther open, purposefully. The room ahead was completely dark; he slid his flashlight from his pocket and played the light ahead. He took two steps forward; his light seemed to draw us; we all moved forward, too.

"See, there ain't anybody in—" he began confidently. Then his voice stopped, as if it had been pushed back into his throat, and there was an odd, electric instant of silence.

"Jesus Christ!" he whispered. "Get out of here! Get—"

His arm went up in front of his eyes, as if he were warding something off; the beam of the flashlight accompanied the gesture with a wild parabola of light. He came backward, staggering; he turned on us blindly.

"Red! You—where—you—"

His face was pea-green in the light from the one bulb in the furnace room. Again we gave way as he lurched away from the kitchen door, leaving it ajar as it was; he reached the furnace, caught at that.

"Jesus Christ! I—God!"

He gagged, turned frantically, and was thoroughly sick in the ash barrel.

The furnace room was suddenly full of movement then. Red wheeled, grabbed Jerry's flashlight from his limp hand, whirled toward the kitchen. Mr. Kistler and Mr. Waller, too, leaped to look over his shoulder. They didn't go in; they just peered around the edge of that quarter-open door, then backed away quickly.

Their faces were pea-green, too, when they turned to us again.

Mr. Kistler looked as if he wanted to be sick but wouldn't be. The rest of us stared back at them. I don't think we thought much; it was as if something in the air suspended both time and thought. Somewhere inside my head a ticker tape began running of its own volition, a tape that repeated incessantly: "What is it? What is it? What is it?"

Then Mrs. Halloran began screaming steadily, one shrill shriek after the other. I went over to her, slapped her, pulled her away from the group to the foot of the stairs, where I pushed her down until she sat on a step. She began panting then, and the screams subsided into little blubbering noises: "Oh-hu. Oh-hu. Oh-hu."

Scared, I can remember thinking. I looked around to see what the others were doing. Red had gone over to Jerry and stood clapping him on the back. Miss Sands and Mrs. Waller walked over to stand near me at the foot of the steps. Mr. Grant and Mr. Buffingham were looking uncertainly from the door to Mr. Waller and Mr. Kistler.

"My God almighty," Mr. Waller was whispering over and over to himself, reverently.

His wife whispered back, from beside me, "What is it, Joe? What is it?"

"Her." Mr. Waller's voice answered tonelessly. "My God. Even her. Jesus."

"You mean she's *dead*?" I whispered, too.

For a moment there wasn't any answer. Then Mr. Kistler said shortly:

"Yeah. She's dead. She's dead, all right."

Mr. Waller came over to the stairs to sit beside Mrs. Halloran. Mrs. Waller held on to his shoulder.

No longer sick, Jerry leaned against the furnace, glaring at Red.

"If you ever let a peep out of you . . ."

"Hell no." Red avoided looking at him.

"What a hell of a mess that was to walk in on. Well, I guess I know what a cop gets in for now, all right." Jerry grinned around at us wryly. He stood a moment longer, hesitating as if he didn't know what to do; then he squared his shoulders for action.

"What do you say, Red? Gosh, we gotta put in a call! I'll do it—you stay here by them."

He walked heavily toward the group of us at the foot of the stairs. Mr. Waller stood up to let him by; Mrs. Halloran was still weakly sobbing.

Mr. Kistler handed Jerry his flashlight, and he started up the stairs, flashing it ahead of himself as he went, although it was half light in the room ahead, from the light in the hall. Halfway up he stumbled, fell back a couple of steps and stood there, lurching.

"Get out!" he yelled. "Get out! Beat it!"

We looked up. One of the cats was crouching at the top of the stairs, looking down, its eyes catching and reflecting the light from the flashlight. When Jerry yelled, it backed away, and he went up again, cursing steadily under his breath.

We could hear his voice at the telephone above, but not what he said. We just stayed where we were, not saying anything, as if all our normal actions were stopped, as if on the outsides of ourselves a thick layer had been frozen by the horror in the air, and only a little warm life trickled through inside.

"What is it? What is it? What is it?" My mind continued ticking from down in my stomach somewhere, where it had retreated for safety.

Jerry had again regained his pose of imperturbable policeman when he returned to us.

"They'll be here in a minute. You folks go on upstairs now," he ordered. "Red—"

"Yeah."

"Think anybody ought to . . . ?"

"Naw. What's the use now?"

Both policemen came upstairs with us. Right at our heels.

We were all herded into my living room; we stood apart there, as if we might contaminate each other in that frozen silence. Mr. Kistler stood in the west bay, staring out the window. I walked over to him.

"What is it? What's so awful?" I whispered to him. "Was she—murdered?"

"I don't know," he whispered back.

"Then what is it? What is it?"

"She must have been dead a long time," he whispered, not looking at me. "You know. Cats."

8

I SCREAMED THEN.

Even telling about it, having to remember it, makes me feel sick. Most of the time, now, I can keep it pushed so far back in my mind that I'm safe against stumbling into it accidentally. But it was new then. For the first time in my life, I knew how deep horror could go.

It's a lot different—the horror you feel from just hearing about something loathsome or reading something horrifying, like *Dracula*. But this was horror that was right in my own life. It was right in the house with me. I wanted to cry and shriek and push away with my hands the pictures that jumped into my head. Hodge Kistler's face was whirling in front of me like a pinwheel, and it seemed half an hour before the world got props under itself again and steadied down.

Hodge Kistler was shaking me, and I just let myself be shaken, limp. There was a chair under me; I don't know when that got there. For a while all I could do was wipe my forehead and the palms of my hands with my handkerchief; I never knew emotion could squeeze so much moisture out of me.

It was a while before I got around to being interested in the other people. By that time Mr. Kistler was pounding me on the back. I don't know why it is that men think pounding on the back is such a cure-all.

I looked, then, to see if the others knew what I knew.

No. Except for Mr. Waller and the two policemen, they stood as wondering and separate as before, staring now at me; people of a different world, staring across the ocean of my knowledge. Only Mrs. Halloran was living in herself instead of in that outside fear and awe; her face was twisted into a whimper, a whimper that grew steadily stronger.

"What is it?" Mrs. Waller whispered again dully, this time asking me.

Mrs. Halloran burst into a scream.

"Nobody tells me anything! It's my aunt Hattie! She's been murdered! That's what she's been! Nobody tells me anything!"

Mr. Grant appealed soberly to Mr. Kistler.

"Surely if Mrs. Dacres can be told, then the rest of us . . ."

Mr. Kistler turned to where Jerry and Red stood at the door as if on guard. Jerry's head nodded, almost imperceptibly; he was giving permission, but he didn't want to be responsible for having given it. He was watching me; I had the impression he'd been cataloging every emotion I'd had when Hodge Kistler had told me.

"You tell 'em, Jerry."

"Not me."

"Well," Hodge Kistler said, "I don't know why it should be me, but here goes."

He stood now at the side of my chair, hands in coat pockets, legs braced wide; only the two of us in the west bay; the others were halfway across the room or farther, as if we were speakers and they an audience. I could feel rising from them a wave of self-defense that still held eagerness, and fear. Mrs. Halloran, arrested in midwhisper, Mrs. Waller and Miss Sands, with faces frozen still, Mr. Grant, blinking, Mr. Buffingham, eyes alive in a dead face.

Mr. Kistler's voice came slow and low.

"Prepare yourselves to be shocked. You especially, Mrs. Halloran. It's worse than that she's dead. It's uglier than murder. It's that the—the animals didn't wait to be fed."

Even with the preparation they'd had, even with some of them, surely, guessing even if they didn't want to acknowledge the guess, it hit them like a strong blow. Mr. Buffingham's head jerked back; his face turned as red as fire. Mr. Grant's face whitened; he sagged as he reached behind him toward the buffet for support. Miss Sands sucked in a long, wheezing breath before she seemed to stop breathing altogether; she stood as stiffly and blankly as if she were stone. Mrs. Waller turned yellow; her husband had had his arm at her back from the moment Mr. Kistler's voice began; she crumpled, and Red kicked a chair toward her as he leaped to help Mr. Waller hold her; they got the chair under her as she came down. She didn't faint, though; she moaned, turned her face to bury it in her husband's coat.

Mrs. Halloran was slow. She stupidly watched the others take it; when Mrs. Waller moaned the idea must finally have seeped into her mind, too, because she screamed once, a high-pitched, senseless cry, before her feet slipped out from under her. She went down so fast her head hit the floor, hard, before Jerry or Mr. Kistler could reach her.

Jerry, I noticed, had been watching as much as I had, his eyes flickering quickly from one face to another.

The two men lifted Mrs. Halloran to my studio couch,

stretched her out flat. When Jerry began slapping her face I staggered out to the kitchen for a glass of water; the men gladly left her to me when I came back with it, Miss Sands stepping quietly forward to help me.

Mrs. Halloran was less of a nuisance out than in; we should have left her alone. Conscious, she began the oh-hu business again, varied with little cries and gulping sobs. She was a stringy, scrawny woman—nothing describes her as well as those old-fashioned words—and frightfully unlovely lying there flat on my couch, with her pointed shoes sticking up in the air and her face blue under the cheap makeup.

It wasn't long after Mrs. Halloran revived that more police began turning up. We heard the first siren, a thin faraway whine crescendoing to a scream, abruptly stopped. Then another . . . another. Men in uniform stood around in groups to glare at us. Men not in uniform did the same. They stalked through my two rooms, which suddenly looked denuded of everything but people, and there were too many of them. Heavy feet pounded the stairs going down; heavy feet stamped in the furnace room below.

But we heard no loud walking in that room under my kitchen. There, when it stepped, no foot was proud.

Now so allied, the seven lodgers of that house and Mrs. Halloran, niece of that house, stood or sat, waiting. Mr. Kistler and Mr. Waller disappeared, reappeared again. Mrs. Waller kept to her dinette chair, her eyes glassy, her lips moving without expressing sound. Mr. Buffingham smoked steadily, leaning against the buffet and tapping ashes off on my floor. At one time I picked up a smoking stand, walked across the room to plank it squarely in front of him, but he didn't seem to notice it, beyond jumping when I appeared before him. He was more haggard than ever; a damp forelock hung over his forehead; his lips puckered and un-puckered as if he were going to whistle, but changed his mind. Miss Sands and Mr. Grant cowered in corners.

At one time a commotion began in the house, upstairs, downstairs. The dog barked loudly, and we looked at each other, sick.

Suddenly a cat, with two policemen after her, darted from the hall into the room; it was the gray she-cat, now very heavy with her kittens, running fast and low, almost brushing along the floor.

The women screamed; Miss Sands leaped on the gateleg table and stood yelling with her skirts tight around her knees; Mrs. Halloran sat up, crouching back against the wall, a hand protectively over her throat. I turned my back, but I knew when the men caught the snarling beast and took her away.

After that there was just the previous disorder. The doorbell rang, was silent awhile, rang again. Mr. Kistler grinned wryly at the roomful of us.

"Reporters," he said.

"Oh, my goodness," I said. "Will the papers . . . will they tell . . . ?"

"Don't worry, Mrs. Dacres," he said grimly. "It won't make more than a three-inch obituary on page seven. How'd you like to come across the details of this delectable little yarn in the *Comet,* say at the breakfast table?"

We looked sicker.

"The chance of a lifetime," he mourned. "In on the inside. Think what I could have made out of it as a freelance! And this is the sort of story it is! Phooey!"

He turned his back on us abruptly to stare out the window.

On the face of the white electric clock on my buffet, the hands slid leadenly past three o'clock, four o'clock.

Night, I told myself. In other houses, people slept. Night, with a little moon shining down, still and white, on a dim, normal world just outside the windows of Mrs. Garr's house.

Shortly after four o'clock a tall man with thinning blond hair and a disillusioned face stepped back into the room. He was dressed in civilian clothes but carried an air of official authority.

"I'm Lieutenant Strom. I'll see you one at a time, please. In the room at the front of the house." He glanced once around the room. "Who was it made the call to the office? Mr. Waller? Okay, you first, Waller."

Mr. Waller went out with him.

Seven of us left now, with Red sitting by the door, on guard. Mr. Kistler once walked toward me, but Red stopped him.

"No talkin' in private."

Mrs. Halloran sobbed herself to sleep. The rest of us looked at her with envy; I was dead tired.

Mr. Waller stayed in that front room until after five o'clock.

Then Red took Mrs. Waller in. She stayed only ten or fifteen minutes; I heard her come out, join Mr. Waller in the hall, and the two of them go upstairs.

Mr. Buffingham was the next called. It was well after six before he went upstairs. Mrs. Halloran was called then. We woke her up, wiped her face with a damp cloth, sent her in trembling so she could scarcely walk, supported as she was by Red.

The rest of us began prowling then, too nervous to be quiet longer. My mind was too numb from the shocks of the night to work well. I wondered dully what the policemen were finding out.

What had happened in that room below the stairs? When had Mrs. Garr died? Could Mr. Grant be right—had he seen Mrs. Garr coming home at eight thirty that Friday night? Now that we had Mrs. Halloran's story, it seemed quite possible that he might have seen her. And what then? What had happened in that listening house?

Had Mrs. Garr walked into her house, walked down the stairs

to her dark kitchen, fallen there or had a heart attack, lain on that cement floor calling weakly for help, and slowly died?

Or was there deeper terror in it? Friday was the night an assailant had leaped upon me. Had she come home, been seized in the dark and killed—choked—by the very hands that closed on my throat? But why? Was there some strange mystery in the house that killed . . .

I didn't think I could stand not knowing. I said loudly to Red at his doorway post:

"Did she die naturally? Was she murdered? Can't you tell us that much?"

He shrugged.

"No talkin'."

What did that mean? Did the police know, and not want us to know? Or didn't they know themselves? Were they trying to break someone down? What was going on in the room at the front of the house? When one of us went in, would there be a break—a cry—a confession?

I listened tensely, my ears quick, but I could distinguish no words, only the rumble of voices in their differing rhythms.

It was daylight by that time; had long since been. Our faces looked unslept and indecent in clean morning light. A stubble came out on Mr. Kistler's cheeks and chin; one minute, it seemed, it wasn't there, the next it was.

Jerry brought Mrs. Halloran back.

"You're next, Kistler."

Mr. Kistler went.

Mrs. Halloran was sobbing wildly. Jerry eased her into the armchair and turned to me.

"Okay if she stays here? She can't go home, not in the state she's in. Besides, she might get wanted again."

"It's all right," I said. "Let her stay."

In a few minutes Mrs. Halloran was asleep; her head lolled back like a limp rag doll's.

Mr. Kistler's interview lasted a scant half hour. Mr. Grant went next, Miss Sands after him.

So they were leaving me for the last. What did that mean? That I knew least, of course. I'd been in Mrs. Garr's house such a short time, compared to the others. I couldn't be expected to know much of Mrs. Garr's affairs.

When I finally was called I stumbled with weariness as I got to my feet. Since Miss Sands had left I had been lying on the couch, and I'd dropped into a stiff, half-awake sleep. Jerry took me in; Red stayed with Mrs. Halloran. In passing, I took a look at the clock: almost eight.

I squeezed past men and the grand piano to get before Lieutenant Strom. He sat in the middle of the davenport, which stood with its back to the bay of the front windows; there was a card table in front of him, and a chair in front of the table. Seven or eight other men stood about the room, smoking, writing in little books, or just watching. The lieutenant had a fountain pen in his hand and two piles of paper on the table before him, one pile written on, one not. He made notations as I answered.

I was put in the chair facing him. The light from the windows struck me full in the eyes; I was blinded and numb with tiredness.

The lieutenant's heavy eyelids drooped a little lower over his eyes. He spoke quietly, but his first words shook the exhaustion right out of me.

"No use stalling, Mrs. Dacres. Who helped you out on this job?" My tongue stuck to the top of my mouth, paralyzed.

Abruptly he lunged forward over the table, yelled: "Come on, talk!"

"But I don't know what you're talking about! You can't mean you think I—"

"Yeah, I mean I think you! And you don't even have to answer. We know who was in with you on it—Kistler!"

"Mr. Kistler?" I vainly tried to piece sense out of it.

"Oh, so it wasn't Kistler! So it was someone else! Talk
fast, now."

He bellowed at me, and it reminded me so much of Mr. Gangan that what he was doing suddenly made sense—and not in
the way he wanted it to. A quick glance at the other men in the
room—all poker faces—clinched it.

Lieutenant Strom was putting on a loud bluff to shake me into
admitting something, anything, that would involve me in Mrs.
Garr's death.

I became angry then, and anger pulled me together. I shifted
my chair enough so the sun hit me from the side instead of
squarely in the eyes. It was a relief to see without weeping.

"Nonsense." I put decision into it. "I didn't have a thing to do
with Mrs. Garr's death."

"You can take care of yourself, can't you? Good control, too.
And you didn't have a thing to do with it. Perhaps you can tell
us who did?"

"Haven't you found that out yet?"

"I'm asking, not answering."

"Isn't it possible that she may have died naturally? She wasn't
young—over sixty-five, I'm sure. Her heart was bad, too. She
told me so."

"So that's your story, eh?"

"I haven't any story. I'm completely in the dark."

His manner became silkily insinuatory.

"Odd, isn't it, how many disturbances began after you
moved in?"

"Did they? I don't know what happened here before I
moved in."

"Well, it was a decent, quiet house before then."

"Perhaps you'd like to suggest I got Mr. Buffingham's son to rob a bank? Or tried to throttle myself? If that's what you mean by disturbances."

"Was that what you meant when you talked about disturbances in this house to Mr. Kistler?"

"Oh, you mean about the house listening at night?" It sounded silly when I put it into words in that roomful of stolid men.

"Yeah, what did you mean by that?"

I took a moment to think it over. "Just that I often wake in the night and feel a tension, an exaggerated stillness, as if the house or people in it were lying tensely awake, listening."

"Uh," he grunted. "Now listen, lady, does that make sense?"

"No, it doesn't," I admitted. "I can't get away from it, though. I feel it every time I wake at night."

"Well, no one else hears the house listen." He ended that subject grimly. "No one heard anything and nothing happened in this house before you came. It was a respectable, quiet—"

"Perhaps it was," I broke in on him. "Perhaps it still is. But I don't think so, myself. I think there was something going on here long before I came. I don't think Mrs. Garr died naturally. I think she was killed. It seems more—reasonable."

There, it was out. I hadn't known I believed those things before I said them, but as the words came out, I knew those were my convictions.

"Now we're getting somewhere." Strom was sitting forward, his eyes following my lips. "Keep on."

"Mrs. Garr told me she asked the people who had my rooms before me to leave because she caught them snooping."

"Caught them what?"

"She thought they were searching through her things."

"For what?"

"She didn't say. I asked that, too. She passed it off as curiosity about her possessions."

"Nuts. Those people been back since?"

"Not that I know of. But someone was."

I told him then, two or three times over, to every detail, the story of the prowler I had seen run out on that afternoon, weeks before, when Mrs. Halloran and Mrs. Garr had gone to the movie.

Lieutenant Strom, finally satisfied, said, "M-m-m-m," still watching me intently from under his heavy eyelids.

"What's your first name, Mrs. Dacres?"

"Gwynne."

"Maiden name?"

"MacGowan."

"Husband?"

"Divorced."

"In jail?"

"In hospital."

"M-m-m-m. You a record?"

"No." Indignantly.

"Why'd you move here?"

I told about my lost job, my finances, the ad in the paper.

"Ever know Mrs. Garr before?"

"Never saw her before."

"Know anyone else in the house before?"

"No."

"You're pretty friendly with Hodge Kistler, I hear."

"He's amusing, I think."

He grinned at me suddenly, a kidding grin.

"Watch your step there, sister. You may wake up surprised someday."

"Thanks. He handles nicely."

"How he'd love you for that!" He grinned once more before reverting abruptly to his former manner.

"Okay, now. Notice anything else peculiar after you moved in?"

"Well, there was that man we found dead at the foot of the drop in back of the house. That made quite a stir. You know, that gangster. But, of course, that didn't have anything to do with this house."

"That what you think?"

"Of course."

"Okay again. What about inside the house?"

"Mrs. Garr. Mrs. Garr always seemed peculiar."

"Any fights with her?"

"No."

"Like her?"

"I can't say I did."

"Why not?" Like a shot.

"She was old and seemed—somehow unclean and evil. I sometimes thought she suffered from hallucinations or delusions."

"What do you mean on that last?"

"About that snooping, for instance. She seemed to suspect everyone in the house of it."

"Begin when you first moved in, and tell every instance."

I did. I told that, and practically every word ever spoken to me by Mrs. Garr, or by me to Mrs. Garr, as far as I could remember at the time. I told how she had knocked at my door the night I'd turned my light on late. How she'd bawled Mr. Kistler out for lighting the gas heater. How she suspected the Wallers. Lieutenant Strom listened with careful attention to every word.

"Loony," one of the men at the side contributed when I stopped.

"That's what I thought, until I saw that prowler."

"Any actual evidence after that?"

"Not until last Friday, when Mrs. Garr went to Chicago. I mean when she was supposed to—"

"Okay, now we're down to Friday. Where were you Friday?"

"Working. I had a temporary job that lasted until Saturday night."

"Um. Worked until when Friday?"

"Almost seven."

"Then where'd you go?"

"To dinner with Hilda Crosley; she's a regular copywriter at Benson's, where I was working. You can ask her. We saw a movie, too."

"When'd you get back here?"

"About ten, I think."

"Tell me every move you made from then on, Friday night."

"Why, I just walked in, and—"

"See anybody?"

"No. I—Wait a minute!" The scene flashed back into my mind. "Yes, I did see something. When I came into the hall, a cat ran downstairs and under the bookcase. She—that's funny! The cat. Because she was back in there with the others when the door was opened tonight. Back in that kitchen downstairs. It was the one with the kittens."

A stir went over the room. A man spoke up from the side-lines.

"If that's the dope, then the old lady must have croaked after ten p.m., Strom. That's what they all said—all three cats came out of there hell-bent when the door opened."

I was shivering with the idea I'd caught.

"No, that may not be the dope," I said, my teeth practically chattering. "Because, think. If Mrs. Garr didn't die of her own accord—if she was . . . helped to die—there wasn't anything to keep the murderer from catching the cat and putting it back in the kitchen with the others. He'd do that if he . . . wanted it to be the way it was."

They didn't answer right away. Then Lieutenant Strom spoke, softly.

"You're a smart girl, sister, or else. If the old lady died naturally, why, the cat makes it pretty sure she went into that kitchen after ten o'clock Friday. But if she didn't, somebody used his head pretty fast. Maybe this isn't the first time you had that idea?"

9

THERE WE WERE, BACK on the old ground of suspicion.

I took a look at the men around the room again, and it seemed to me every face swam in suspicion. All the tiredness came back to me; my head felt so heavy I didn't think I could possibly go on using it for a fighting weapon. But I had to.

"I haven't even thought of that cat from that day to this minute," I said wearily. "I didn't even think about it when I saw her run out of that kitchen tonight. What do you think I did—go down and strangle the old woman with my bare hands?"

"You could have had a fight with her and given her a push so she fell over, and her heart did the rest."

"Well, I didn't."

"Or you could have let someone else in the house."

"For heaven's sake, can you tell me one single, solitary reason why I should have wanted that poor old woman killed?"

Lieutenant Strom sighed, and I thought that, after all, he was probably almost as tired as I was. He hadn't had any sleep, either.

And while I'd sat waiting he'd been struggling with seven other people as he had with me, trying to get some clue to possible guilt.

"You've got me there, sister. Why the hell should anyone want the old woman killed? You ever hear of her having any money?"

"No, I haven't."

"Ever mention money to you?"

"Well, she said once that she didn't believe in banks."

"Oh, she did, eh? When'd she say that?"

"When I was looking at the apartment. I said I wasn't working but had a little money in the bank. She said she would never keep a penny in a bank."

"Um. Ever hear any other reference to this?"

"That day I saw the prowler. When I wondered what frightened Mrs. Garr so, Mrs. Halloran said, rather significantly, that Mrs. Garr didn't believe in banks."

"Who all was in on this conversation?"

"Only Mr. Kistler, Mrs. Halloran, and I."

"Mr. Kistler. Mrs. Halloran. You. Any more relatives around besides Mrs. Halloran?"

"Not that I've seen."

"She says she's the one and only." He took out his watch, looked at it, turned to one of the other men.

"Nearly nine, Hitchcock. The bank'll be openin' pretty soon. Don't forget what I said about keepin' your eye peeled for anything that looks like a will."

"Yes, sir."

Two men left.

Lieutenant Strom stretched, yawned, and turned back to me.

"Now let's get down to this attack on you last Friday night."

I told that tale, too. He took down so little of it that I ended

lamely; evidently, he'd heard it over and over from the other witnesses. I got down to the part where we'd all gone down into the
basement and seen there was no one there.

"No one there," I repeated. "No one—" The words themselves caught me up. "Why, if Mrs. Garr had been around the
house we'd certainly have seen her then! We went through every
room. Unless she was—unless—oh, my goodness, you don't
think she was lying there in that kitchen then, do you?"

Lieutenant Strom turned on young Jerry one of the nastiest
looks I have ever seen on the face of man.

"That possibility has entered our minds," he said.

"She might still have been living."

"That also has crossed our minds. Knowing what you know
now, can you remember any evidence that she might have been
in the basement kitchen when you searched the house Friday
night? Any sound? Any clothing seen? Any gesture on the part
of anyone in the searching party?"

I thought desperately.

But I could not think of one bit of evidence that could have
told me, that Friday night, of Mrs. Garr's presence in the house,
alive or dead.

"Just like the others," groaned my questioner when I had
admitted my defeat. "All as blind as bats. See what you expect to
see, and that's all. Now I want you to turn to something else. I
want you to tell me, as well as you can remember, exactly what
each person in this house said as to his or her activities that Friday night."

Slowly, piece by piece, I did that, too. The activities given by
the various people in the house that Friday night had been so
simple that they were easily remembered. As I checked over each
person in turn, Lieutenant Strom checked his sheets.

"Well, they all told the same story to me as they told Friday night," he sighed at the end. "Not a decent alibi in the lot, except maybe Kistler's. 'Went to a movie.' 'Asleep in bed.' Hooey! Who can prove it isn't so? They might all have been slinking around the house, as far as those alibis go."

The rest of my questioning went quickly.

I was asked to tell briefly what I had done since Friday night, how Mr. Grant had come last evening with his questions about Mrs. Garr, how we had approached the Wallers, our wait, the coming of the police, the finding of Mrs. Garr.

No, no one had looked to me as if they had expected what we'd found. Everyone had been horrified, to all appearances.

"Do you know where the Tewmans might be?"

"Mrs. Tewman said Sunday she had visited Friday night at her brother-in-law's house. Mr. Tewman and his brother have a hamburger house somewhere."

"M-m-m-m. That'll be all now. Keep your eyes open and your mouth shut."

I was dismissed.

GETTING OUT OF THERE, I had just one thought: sleep.

Opposite the stairs, I looked up at the sound of feet. Miss Sands was coming down, her eyes sunken, her mouth drawn, but as neatly waved, as rouged, as pressed as ever. She had her hat on.

"You're going out?" It seemed incredible.

She gave me a bitter glance.

"Work."

"F'heaven's sake! Call 'em up. Tell 'em you can't work. Tell 'em someone died—someone did die! You can't work today!"

"There's plenty waiting to grab a job." She went on out.

For the first time I was glad I didn't have a job. Not today, anyway. I was sorry for Miss Sands, but the pity couldn't come up far through the tiredness. Mrs. Halloran was still sleeping unbeautifully in my armchair; I thanked goodness she wasn't on the studio couch, and didn't even feel ashamed of my selfishness.

The house should be safe with all those policemen littering the hall. I left the double doors wide open. Every movement like a slow-motion picture's drag, I got out the softest blanket and a pillow, took off my shoes, and rolled onto the studio couch.

Sleep is very wonderful.

IT WAS MIDAFTERNOON BEFORE I woke up.

Whatever went on in the house that day is still unknown to me; I slept through it all.

When I woke, though, the events of last night were right there in my mind; I didn't have to have it spring out afresh at me at all. I looked around for Mrs. Halloran. She was gone.

Still heavy with sleep, I stumbled out into the hall. The house was completely quiet; one policeman sat in the black leather chair in the hall.

"Hello, miss." He greeted me with a grin. "Have some sleep? I seen you sleepin'."

He was a young policeman, I saw when my eyes got focused so they could see anything as small as features; an Irishman with blue-black eyes, lashes, and hair, and very red cheeks.

"Looking at defenseless girls sleep is small potatoes around here," I said. "Are you the only policeman left?"

"Yep, I'm all alone." He grinned more widely. "If you want to bump anybody else off, all you've got to do is bump me first."

"Oh, forget it." I was sick of death. Policemen, too.

In my kitchen, I drank tomato juice and discovered I was ravenous. The only time I have any use for skipping meals is when I'm sick, and now I hadn't eaten since dinner last night— nearly twenty hours ago!

When I came up for air, my icebox was as bare as a striptease artist at the end of her act. But I felt better.

It was a good thing I waited until after I'd eaten to take a good look at my rooms. They were an awful blow. The kitchen linoleum was gray with ground-in grime and ashes; I picked cigarette and cigar butts out of the sink, off the stove, off the floor, out of the cupboards, off the washbowl, off the toilet rim, off the buffet, the rug, the chairs. There were even a few in the ashtrays.

Violently I went to work. Cleaning. That's what my intentions were: to clean. I pushed away to the back of my mind all wonder as to how Mrs. Garr had died, naturally or otherwise, and if otherwise, who had done it and why. Questions such as that, I said to myself, were for the police. All I had to do was wait. Sooner or later all the mysteries would be solved, and I, like the rest, would know the truth. It wasn't any of my business anyway. All I had to do was keep my nose at home, and they'd see how innocent I was, forget suspicion of me, concentrate on the real criminal.

If there was a criminal.

That was what I *thought* I thought.

But you'll notice I didn't think of getting away, of moving out of Mrs. Garr's house.

I couldn't have, of course; the police wouldn't have let me.

But I didn't even think of moving.

That shows you how a girl who thinks she is completely honest with herself can be an awful liar.

Because I hadn't any more than started scrubbing the kitchen floor when my mind was biting into the mystery around me as if it was a steam shovel. By the time I had finished, I was already so intent on digging out the answers to some of my questions that you couldn't have deflected me with guns.

Weeks afterward, when this whole thing was over, I began reading about homicides in the newspapers closely; murder stories in books, too. The big difference I noticed was how understandable the work of the police was in those other stories. The reporters in the newspapers and the characters in the fiction always seemed to comprehend what the police were working toward.

I don't see how they do it. From beginning to end, in the case of Mrs. Garr, I never knew what the police were going to do or think, and when I did find out, afterward, I usually disagreed strenuously. Every time they jumped on anyone, it was a complete surprise to me. I learned a lot about the case from them, because they did all the routine work, and we usually heard the results sooner or later.

On the whole, though, they didn't seem nearly as keen, as pushing, as intuitive, as *right* as they should have been. Not nearly as much so as detectives in stories, for instance.

I suppose it's discouraging to work on a case when you haven't even a decent corpse to go on, and the details are so gruesome, the papers won't print them and you can't get any publicity.

By nine p.m. of that Friday, June fourth, my rooms were shining clean again. The Irish policeman had stuck his head in a couple of times and grinned to see me go at it, but no one else had been near me.

I didn't know if the Tewmans had come back or not; I hadn't heard a sound below. I'd heard the Wallers move about overhead, seen Miss Sands drag herself in at six o'clock; she must have been dead to the world by the time I finished cleaning. Mr. Grant had slid quietly out at the dinner hour, and as quietly back again.

Had Mr. Grant killed Mrs. Garr? He alone had admitted seeing her that Friday night. Had he been quietly opening, closing things in her kitchen there below when she came in; had he sprung at her . . . ? Blinking little old Mr. Grant.

Or the Wallers. They'd been having trouble with Mrs. Garr. She'd asked them to leave. Funny, I'd forgotten to tell that to Lieutenant Strom.

Miss Sands. She had lived in the house with Mrs. Garr for twelve years. You can work up a lot of hate in twelve years.

Or Mr. Buffingham. Bad blood. His son was already engaged with criminals, was in jail. Mr. Buffingham himself had been held by the police for a week. But then, criminals' parents were usually innocent, though some, like Ma Barker . . . Lawyers and trials were costly, too; he must be hard-pressed for money. He might have been hunting money, the pitiful little worn bills a poor old lodging-house keeper might have hidden . . .

"I don't believe in banks . . ." A ghost was whispering it in my ears. Was that why she'd listened, was that why she'd suspected people of snooping, because she had poor little heaps of savings hidden here and there around the house?

I was practically shaking with excitement, like a dog at a gopher hole, by the time I'd thought that out.

I tried to calm myself; after all, I didn't want to spend my time at the wrong gopher hole. I needed someone to talk it over with; I needed to talk to someone who had been in the house longer than I had.

I wished Mr. Kistler were home.

Mr. Kistler.

I was pretty sure, wasn't I, that he wasn't the one?

Of course I was sure.

Was I?

It might be well, before I allied myself with Mr. Kistler, to think a little about it.

Mr. Kistler.

He had awfully strong hands.

I walked over to the west bay of my living room, where Mr. Kistler had stood so much of the time during the night before. I stared out of the middle window.

What I saw wasn't the windy June night outside, the one scraggly tree, the light of the streetlight; what I saw was Mr. Kistler chinning himself on the bar that first night I talked to him, pulling himself up and up by those heavily muscled arms.

He'd held my hand, once or twice since then. His hands had calluses across the palms. From the chinning bar, he said.

Fancy a printer, a publisher, with calluses on his palms!

I tried to picture those hands as the hands on my neck, choking me that night. But I couldn't make myself believe it.

Mrs. Garr, the police obviously believed, had died on Friday night, exactly a week ago. Hodge Kistler had been working that Friday night. So he'd said. He hadn't come home until after midnight, when he'd seen the light under my door and roused the house.

Nice, wouldn't it have been, if he'd been the one to dump me on my kitchen floor, half strangled, just a few minutes earlier?

All right, let's suppose he had.

Mrs. Halloran had made that telltale remark about banks to him, too. He was hard up for money; he'd said that repeatedly. The city council had taken all the money he had, and all he could beg or borrow. He'd had to overbid the *Comet*, with plenty of money behind it. He needed new presses badly. Maybe he wanted money to take me out to dinner.

That last was a nice possibility.

So when he knew Mrs. Garr was going to be away, he might have come to the house after train time to start looking. His quick, strong hands opening dresser drawers in the room under the stairs, flicking through the contents. His sure fingers prodding into sugar bowls and cream pitchers in the cellar kitchen. Mrs. Garr coming upon him, screaming:

"Thief!"

He'd jump to silence her.

He might not have thought how strong his hands were. Then quick, to hide it, to save himself . . . The cats . . .

I thought of his sick face the night before.

Impossible. But go on supposing. Suppose he had. What could I find out by?

Money.

If he'd found any, it might be around his rooms somewhere. He couldn't put it in a bank; wouldn't dare, so soon. Couldn't give it to friends to keep; they knew he never had any.

He'd had very little money with him on Memorial Day.

The key.

Mrs. Garr's key to the cellar kitchen. Where was that? If that could be found in anyone's room . . .

My fingers itched.

Right before my eyes, I could see Hodge Kistler's right hand unlocking his own door on that tour of inspection a week ago. See the key in his hand. It was as identical to the key that opened my own double doors as two Hollywood eyebrows. My grandmother had a big old house, and I know how her inside locks were—the same skeleton key opened them all.

I decided I'd look through Hodge Kistler's rooms. If I found anything, that would be that. If I didn't, I'd propose that he join me in hunting down Mrs. Garr's killer.

I knew that if Mr. Kistler came home and caught me—well, I didn't intend to be caught. A look at my clock told me it still wasn't much past nine o'clock. If Mr. Kistler had had to work until midnight last Friday he should do so tonight, too; he seldom came home much before then. It wouldn't take more than twenty minutes—thirty at the most—for what I wanted to do.

The Irish policeman was gone from the hall; the stranger in his place looked at me apathetically when I locked my double doors behind me and stood before him, jiggling my key in my hand.

"Is it all right, Officer, if I go up to gossip with the Wallers?" I asked brightly.

He waved a listless hand.

"Sure, go ahead."

I went up, walking as heavily as I could, knocked on the Wallers' door. Mrs. Waller answered and I went in.

We talked about Mrs. Garr, of course: had she been murdered or hadn't she? They weren't very communicative. They said they hadn't slept much that day; they'd been talking instead. They seemed nervous, discouraged, uneasy. Mrs. Waller once called me "ma'am." After their friendliness before, it was a change to be treated as a superior, and a superior under suspicion, at that. But I had too much else on my mind to worry about it.

I said good-bye inside their door, waited for them to answer, then opened and closed their door softly.

I stood outside their door, but I believed I had been so quiet the detective below would think I was still in the Wallers' rooms.

Lightly I stole down the long, sparsely lit hall. If my key didn't fit Mr. Kistler's door . . .

But it did fit. The lock turned as smoothly as if my key and no other had been made for it.

That showed me how wise I had been to keep chairs under my doorknobs!

Rapidly I flicked down Mr. Kistler's curtains, clicked on his lights. I remembered the layout of the rooms: the big room you walked into, used as a living room, the smaller room to the left used as a bedroom. In the bedroom, I opened the two doors in the back wall. The first one led to a closet, the other, bolted on the bedroom side, to a lavatory connecting with Mr. Buffingham's room.

I bolted that door again.

Having to leave things as they were slowed me down. But I did a thorough job. Fortunately Mr. Kistler's closet and drawers were those of a masculine man: neat, uninteresting, bare of clutter. Two hats on the closet shelf. A row of shoes beside them. Shoe trees to take out so I could feel in the toes. Nothing there. Suits and overcoats hanging from the rod; I went into every pocket, patted every inch of lining. Chest of drawers next. Shirts. Underwear. I squeezed all the socks. Looked under the pillows, the mattress, the rugs.

The bedroom netted me nothing.

In the living room, I took a look around for hiding places before I tackled the table with the typewriter and the stacks of papers that stood in the front bay. It would take a long time to go through those thoroughly. I lifted the cushion of the overstuffed chair, felt along the cracks. I shook out the books and magazines on the table by the chair. That reminded me there had been a couple of books on the table by the bed; I returned to the other room to shake those out.

Nothing there.

Walking back toward the living room past the chest of drawers, I stopped to look at it again: brushes, combs, and bottles on its top. An ecru linen cover.

Under that dresser cover is where it was. Mottled green paper with black printing. A railroad ticket.

A Memorial Day excursion ticket to Chicago on the Great Western.

I just gaped at it.

I didn't even have strength enough to scream when the voice spoke from the doorway.

"Don't tell me I've lived all these years to be mistaken at my age," it said.

The words were light, but the brown eyes I whirled to see were intent.

"Oh, I didn't think you'd be home yet," I gasped weakly, like a fool.

"So I gather." Mr. Kistler walked toward me, still intent. "How'd you get in here?"

"My key fits—Keep away! I'm going downstairs!"

"That's what you think."

I tried to dart past him, but he lunged and caught me by the shoulders; I opened my mouth to scream, but his hand closed over it. He sat down on the edge of the bed and pulled me down beside him, his hand still over my mouth.

"Feel that hand? Well, I'm going to clap it right back if you start to yell. Now talk fast, baby. You've got some explaining to do."

He lifted his hand from my mouth, holding it ready about a foot in front of my face; he held my left arm captive against his side; his arm across my back held my right.

"I was trying to—" I opened my mouth again, to scream.

He promptly clamped the hand down.

"See? It doesn't work. When you're ready to talk and not yell, nod so I'll know."

I nodded, gasping for air. His hand covered most of my nose, too; I could just as well be killed as smothered to death. I wasn't too frightened to think that out.

"Well, I was looking for clues."

"I see. The lady detective."

"Yes. I thought over who it might be if she was killed. If she was murdered, I mean. And you seemed the least likely."

"I seem the least likely, so you come in my room looking for clues."

"That was to eliminate you."

"I see."

"I wanted to make sure there wasn't anything against you; we could work together on finding out who did the murder, if she was murdered."

"Articulate, aren't you?"

"Certainly."

"Too damn much so. And what did you find?"

"I—nothing."

"Nothing?"

"Yes."

"Look at me."

I looked at him as innocently as it is possible for me to look, but I was sweating inside.

"Aw, baby," he said, his grimness dissolving a little, "is this a nice way to behave?"

"Now may I go?"

The grimness came back.

"No, you don't. Wait a minute. What were you looking at when I came in?"

"There wasn't anything."

"Under that cover on the chest you were looking."

"No. I was just going to look under there." I was panic-stricken now, and I must have shown it. If he knew I'd found . . .

"Liar. I'm always sticking junk under there. Okay, let's see what's under there now."

He carried me along with him, one arm around my neck with its hand on my mouth. I couldn't stop him.

He lifted the cover with his free hand.

There it was before us both.

The hand dropped from my mouth.

I opened my mouth for screaming. This time it wasn't a hand that stopped me; it was the dumbfounded look on his face.

"Whew!" he said unextravagantly. He turned, stared at me.

He began laughing, went back to the bed, sat weakly down, laughed until his face was dark red.

"Oh, baby, that's funny. Oh, God, that's funny. The sins of the transgressor come home to roost. Oh, God!"

"I don't think it's funny." It was my turn to be grim. "The police won't, either."

He stopped in the middle of a laugh, his mouth still open.

"No. I guess they won't, will they?"

"No, I guess they won't."

"Ye gods and little brass fishes. Here—sit down."

"No, I'll go downstairs, I think."

"I think not. You sit right here on the bed."

He pushed me onto it, stood in front of me, his hands jammed in his pockets.

"I suppose I've got to tell you." His eyebrows were crowding his nose again. I could almost see his mind working, fast, behind his eyes.

"Don't bother to use your imagination. I know fiction when I hear it. A copywriter writes so much of it."

"This isn't going to be fiction. It's going to be a lot worse. Truth."

"Your turn to talk."

"Friday. That Friday night. A week ago. I wasn't working."

"That'll be a big help to you."

"I've already told Strom. He could see why I'd twisted the truth a little Friday night, and I knew he'd check on my alibi. I didn't expect you to."

"Oh."

"Yes. You see, the paper goes out on Thursdays. So by Friday afternoon we're all cleaned up, and we usually celebrate. A couple fellows and I went into a bar for a drink, and we met a couple girls. They said they were getting set to start on a long hard journey, so we helped 'em to get set. One thing led to another— Say, you're a big help, you are."

"Yes, indeed."

"Well, the hell with it. These girls didn't go to Chicago— that's where they were headed for—that same Memorial Day excursion. Sometime during the evening, this one girl hauled a ticket out of her handbag and gave it to me. Said she wanted me to keep it in memory of a big evening."

"I can imagine," I said.

"So when I emptied my pockets after I finally got to bed that night, there the damn thing was. I stuck it under the dresser cover where I always stick things. I forgot it."

"And all this happened on the evening just before you came home and rescued me."

"That was it."

"How early you left your lady friend!"

"The hell with her. I wasn't interested in her anymore."

"And the next day you ate my breakfast and played put-and-take . . . and danced . . ."

I didn't have the slightest intention of sniffling, but that was what I did. Like many women, I cry when I'm mad.

"Aw, baby, don't go all misty-eyed!"

For the second time that evening, a voice spoke from the door. It was the policeman.

"I thought I heard talkin' up here," he said.

10

MR. KISTLER SETTLED BACK on his heels so fast you could hear them click down.

"Why, hello, Officer," he said agreeably. "Didn't hear you come in. Have a cigarette?"

He offered the packet, but the policeman just grunted and pushed it aside.

"What's going on here?" That seemed to be a set opening line for policemen.

Mr. Kistler waved an explanatory hand at me.

"Oh, you know, Officer. Just a little lovers' quarrel."

If I could have bitten the hand, I would.

"Yeah?"

"You know how women are, Officer. I got home a little late."

I was too mad to speak for myself, and besides, what could I say? The policeman looked at me. "I thought you was comin' up to visit the Wallers. I didn't hear you come in here."

"I—I happened to notice Mr. Kistler's door open, when I left the Wallers."

"Awful quiet, you walk around."

He quit looking at me; his glance began sliding around the room. My eyes slid after his, and then I froze stiff.

The cover on the chest of drawers had fallen in a fold when Hodge Kistler dropped it. A corner of the ticket showed.

We didn't have time to do anything about it. The policeman pounced first.

"Well, I'll be everlastingly hornswoggled," he swore, whipped about, dropped his right hand to his holster. "Don't move, you!".

We didn't.

"Which one of you—?"

"I'm responsible for that ticket getting there, Officer, if that's what you mean." Mr. Kistler spoke calmly.

"Golly! Of all the goldarn good luck!" Enthusiasm irradiated the police officer's lean face. "I'm not handling this myself. I'm sending you in. Come along. You, too, lady. Go on ahead there."

He shooed us on ahead of him, made us sit on the black leather davenport in the hall while he called headquarters.

The siren answered quickly. Two strange policemen came to hustle us off; I argued that I had to have a hat, gloves, and handbag; they gave in to that, but it was the only thing I had my way in for some time.

We were bundled unceremoniously into a police car, one officer explaining, obviously for technical reasons only, that we weren't being arrested; we were merely going to Lieutenant Strom's office of our own volition to bring in new evidence we had brought to light. One of those little crowds of human buzzards had collected in front of the house. Knots of people stood along the sidewalk, gaping, and I had a confused impression of more people across the street, and even clustered along the wall of Elliott House, across the corner. It was the first time I had been outside the house since the discovery of Mrs. Garr's death.

I felt silly. When I looked at Mr. Kistler, I saw his face had the same sort of half grin on it that I felt on mine, so I judged he felt the same way I did. I've never been driven so fast; we streaked through the night, with the siren a whistling scream in our ears, and swung to a stop before a building that looked, from the outside, like a fire station.

Rapidly the hand under my elbow propelled me through a crowded big room, down a corridor into a bare waiting room with scarred golden oak armchairs. I sat in one, Hodge Kistler in another; our guides lounged near the door. I'd gotten over feeling silly; my heart was thudding, and I was wondering what was going to happen next.

We waited quite a while. Now and then I'd hear a door closing somewhere else in the building, heavy feet would tramp by, or someone would come into the room, and my heart would thud louder.

Finally the door ahead of us, the door with the ground-glass top, leading to the inner office outside of which we waited, opened. Two people came out, a man and a woman, ushered by a police officer.

The woman was Mrs. Halloran. The man was . . .

There was a similarity in the expressions on the faces of the man and woman. They both looked bedraggled, worn, inexpressibly tired. Underneath was a curious elation.

It wasn't Mrs. Halloran's face my eyes settled on; it was the man's. As if he felt my gaze, his eyes traveled over Mr. Kistler, over the other men, fastened on me. The elation fled his face as if it had been wiped off; it was replaced by a furtive fright; he dodged behind Mrs. Halloran and began edging toward the exit.

"Why, stop!" I cried. "That's the man who ran out of the cellar!"

Stupidly, the man began running. The officer who had ushered him through the door made an easy reach to catch him by the arm; he struggled and pulled like a fish on a line, but the officer had him firmly.

"What's this?" the captor barked at me.

"Why, I saw a man run out of the cellar one day at Mrs. Garr's house. He acted like a prowler. And this is the man. It's the same haircut. I had a good look at it from the back. He even has the same cap on!"

"She's a liar! She's a-lyin'! It's a low-down lie!" the prowler howled, still struggling to get away, his eyes darting from me to Mrs. Halloran.

Mrs. Halloran favored me with a venomous look, too.

"That's what she's a-doin'! She's a-lyin'!"

"I'm certainly not!"

"Oh, for Chrissakes! Here, you, come along back in here!" The police officer jerked the prowler back toward the room from which he had just come, motioned with his head at me.

"You come along, too."

No one had to invite Mrs. Halloran. The three of us stood very quickly in the inner room. It, too, was bare, except for a desk and more of the armchairs; behind the desk sat Lieutenant Strom.

"What's the idea of bringing them back in?" The lieutenant scowled at the man holding the prowler.

"This lady has a little story, sir. Says Mr. Halloran here is the guy she saw hotfooting it out of Mrs. Garr's cellar one day."

So the man was Mr. Halloran; I should have guessed. Half cringing, half defiant, he was a fit mate for his wife.

Lieutenant Strom swung toward me.

"You say Mr. Halloran is the prowler you saw?"

"Yes, I'm sure of it."

"Wait a minute." He thumbed rapidly through a pile of typed papers. "Here's the description you gave me this morning. Um. Fits, all right." His eyes went to Mr. Halloran.

"What've you got to say, Halloran?"

"She's a-lyin'!"

"Sure, she's a-lyin'. I bet she was stealin' herself!" bleated Mrs. Halloran.

"Stealing, eh? So that's what you were doing, Halloran?"

"She's a-lyin'!"

Lieutenant Strom lifted himself from his chair, leaning forward over his desk to tower above the cringing little man.

"Shut up! No one needs to tell me you're a thief. I know you're a thief. How many times were you up for theft when you were bellhoppin'? Now, come across! What were you lookin' for in that cellar?"

Mr. Halloran cowered back. "What if I was?" he whined. "What if I was? I got a wife, ain't I? I got to feed a pack o' children, don't I? I'm a poor, disabled veter'n, lost my health fightin' for democ'ercy. While you guys at home was cleanin' up big, livin' on the fat o' the land—"

"Aw, tripe."

Mr. Halloran began sniveling. "That's what they say to the soldier boys now. They didn't say that when we was—"

"You get around to Mrs. Garr's cellar!"

"I couldn't see my wife and chillern starvin' to death before my eyes, could I?"

"Hell, your wife was at a movie."

"Our last cent, that took. So I knew the old lady had a lot of dough and she wouldn't give us a cent, wouldn't give a cent to the poor out of her riches. All I wanted was one dollar. Fifty cents even, so my wife and chillern—"

"Oh, for God's sake, shut up." The lieutenant fell back into his chair, weariness and disgust on his face. He turned to me.

"How long ago since you saw this man come out of the cellar?"

"Quite a while. Several weeks."

"Um. Then the question is, did he try it again when he thought the coast was clear Friday night?"

He picked up a phone on his desk, called an extension, barked, "Check those Halloran alibis again with a fine-tooth comb. Especially his. But get a man on checking if she really went to Chicago."

He brooded over the Hallorans a moment after that, made up his mind.

"Lock him up for the night. Send her home to those blasted kids. They may be president someday."

The Hallorans were cleared out quickly. Lieutenant Strom, one other policeman, and I were alone in the room.

"Bring Kistler in," the lieutenant ordered.

Mr. Kistler came in stepping as blithely as if he were here on a social call. Lieutenant Strom swung back in his swivel chair, his eyes lurking behind the heavy lids.

"So you two have an excursion ticket to Chicago for Memorial Day. Well, well, isn't life interesting? I suppose the old lady gave it to you for a valentine?"

"That's almost the story," I said coldly.

"Your story?"

"No."

"Then I'll get it from the source, thanks. Okay, Kistler."

"Well, sir, when I told you where I was Friday night I left out a few bits. You know, unimportant."

"Yeah, unimportant." The lieutenant lifted his receiver again to call another extension.

"Any more reports on the Kistler alibi?" He listened impassively, said, "Okay," hung up, swung back to Mr. Kistler.

"Unimportant. Yeah. So we found out."

They were checking alibis, then. I had a vision of the flurry there'd been at the advertising department at Benson's, with a plainclothes man questioning Hilda Crosley and schoolmarmish Miss Caddy, the advertising manager. I'd bet I was washed up in that office.

Hodge Kistler was looking at the lieutenant with his face very red.

"How about some privacy?"

Lieutenant Strom looked at me, and for an instant, I saw a grin: on the inside of his face.

"Nope. Talk."

"Well, in general, Lieutenant Strom, it was like I told you this morning. Les Trowbridge and Brown and I got through at the *Guide* around five o'clock, which is late as our Fridays go. We circulate on Thursdays, you know. We all dropped in for a couple quick ones in the West Street bar, because Brown is married; he had to go on home.

"A couple of girls were putting 'em down in the next booth. They looked approachable so we joined 'em. They said they were going on this excursion so they needed some fortifying. They took it. After a while Brown went home—that was about six o'clock. About seven the girls began talking about going to the station, but Trowbridge and I had a couple other ideas." He slid a glance at me.

"Yeah," said Lieutenant Strom dryly. "Unimportant ideas."

"God, yes. Well, the girls didn't go to Chicago. They were

only going there to meet a couple men anyway. We left the bar. And sometime or another during the evening this one gal dragged this ticket out and said, 'See what I've given up for your sake.' So she wanted me to keep it to remember her by."

Lieutenant Strom turned sober eyes on me.

"You believe this story, Mrs. Dacres?"

"Oh yes, I believe it." I made it bitter.

"Why?"

"Because it makes me so mad."

The lieutenant leaned far back in his chair, the better to roar. The other policeman helped him out. I didn't think it was so frightfully humorous.

"Oh, God, why is sudden death so funny?" The lieutenant wiped his face. "You're a God damn good storyteller, Kistler, but you've got to admit it looks suspicious. What was this girl's name?"

"Uh—Toots."

The lieutenant chortled again.

"Toots what?"

"Hell, I don't know and I don't want to know."

"It's bad for your story you don't. Where did you go after you left the bar?"

"Here." Mr. Kistler reached forward, picked up the pen on the desk, wrote briefly on a slip of paper, pushed it at the lieutenant.

"We've had a hint or two about that joint," the lieutenant said. "Bill, take this down to Thwaite and give him the background. I'm going to hold you, Kistler."

"Aw, Lieutenant, have a heart! I've got a date to see an important chain-store guy about a contract tomorrow. Do you know what that means? Money! And gosh, how we need it!"

"Got a partner, haven't you?"

"Yes, but—"

"Let him go. That was a tall tale, Kistler. We'll start checking on it right away, and if we can get any circumstantiating evidence, why, good for you. But it's a lot more likely you were in a fracas with the old lady and grabbed that ticket off her. And you don't need telling what happened to old lady Garr. If we can't get any proof on your story you may be sitting on an awful hot seat one of these days. Think that over tonight, and see if you can't think up a little more embroidery for your story."

Bill came back; Mr. Kistler gave me a last brown glance and went with him.

"Now you can see what you got me into," the glance said. "You got me into this."

Lieutenant Strom favored me with a brooding look.

"Now I get around to you, young lady. Why'd you go into Kistler's rooms?"

I gave him the explanation I had given Mr. Kistler.

"When curiosity was being passed around you took over a God damn big piece, Mrs. Dacres, or else."

"I admit the first. It isn't the 'or else.'"

"I'm not sure about you. I suspect you of being smart."

"I don't. Very stupid is what I feel." I meant it, too.

"Yes? Well, don't forget this. We'll find out. And remember this, too. If there's one thing that gets a murderer caught surer and sooner than anything else, that's what it is. Smartness. You can go on home now."

AN OFFICER DID ME the honor of escorting me home in a police car. After this, I was going to find an ordinary car tame. I told my escort with elaborate politeness that it was gallant of him to take me home, but he didn't rise. He left me with, "That's okay, lady," and swung away into the cool June night.

When I unlocked the front door of Mrs. Garr's house, there were two men in the front hall, but one ducked fast into the room under the stairs. I'd quit wondering why policemen did things. The other was the same policeman from earlier that day, the voice that spoke from Mr. Kistler's door. He had the evening *Comet* in his hands.

"You back?" he asked.

"No," I said.

"Where's Kistler?"

"I'm him."

"Okay, lady, I'll find out in good time."

He buried his face in the paper again. I looked at the headline of the front page; it was about a strike. The light in the hall isn't much for reading a paper, even your own; I had to get close to read the smaller headlines. There wasn't one about Mrs. Garr.

"So we didn't even make the front page."

The policeman came promptly out of the paper's interior. "I'll trade fair. You get the paper, I get the news."

After that I had to loosen up enough to tell him what had happened to Mr. Kistler. He was disappointed but still hopeful.

"If it turns out he croaked her, I oughta get a promotion," he urged anxiously. "I bet he did. You take a yarn like that, now— he can't prove it."

"I should think he'd rather die than tell it," I said.

Sitting on the black leather davenport, I looked through the paper for some account of the happenings at Mrs. Garr's house.

"There ain't nothing except in the obituaries," the policeman offered helpfully from his chair.

There wasn't, either. The article was a miracle of inadequacy, on page fourteen. But the second paragraph opened a completely new train of inquiry for me.

MRS. GARR DIES

Harriet Luella Garr, 67, resident of Gilling City since 1884, was found dead at her residence, 593 Trent Street, on Thursday evening. Alarmed by her nonappearance, lodgers called police to search the deceased woman's rooms. She was found there.

Due to a connection with the famous Liberry case of two decades ago, Mrs. Garr was at one time a well-known figure in the city's news. It was at her residence, then on St. Simon Street, that the unfortunate Rose Liberry was found, a suicide. After some years in retirement Mrs. Garr moved to 593 Trent Street, where she has lived quietly. The funeral will be private.

I sat there with my eyes fastened on the paper, but I was thinking, not looking. I should have known. I should have guessed. I should have known there was a story behind the evil in Mrs. Garr's eyes. Keeping a lodging house, suffering all the mean dodges of a penurious life—that alone could not build a face and eyes such as hers. There had been something evil in her life to leave that evil behind. But what, exactly? At what did that last paragraph hint?

I spoke abruptly to the policeman.

"What business was Mrs. Garr in before she retired?"

He coughed and looked embarrassed.

"I ain't supposed to do much talkin'."

"But it's right here in the paper. It's written as if people would know to what it referred, but didn't want to come out in plain words."

"It's a long time ago now. The old folks would remember; the young ones wouldn't. Let bygones be bygones, I say."

"You mean I shouldn't be allowed to know something I'd know anyway if I were ten years older?"

He laughed a little. "Well, no. Put it that way, I guess there ain't no harm tellin'. Lots of people does know. We had her on the records for years. She kept a house."

"You mean she kept a—a *house*?" I gasped.

"Yep, that's what she had, all right. Down on St. Simon Street. Had it from about 1900 to 1919, we figured. Quite a joint, too, I heard—all red plush. Them was the red-plush days. I was just a kid most of that time, but I can remember the stories the boys used to tell. Why, I wouldn't be surprised this black leather chair I'm sittin' in didn't come out of that house."

I got off the black leather davenport as if it burned me.

"Well, I certainly didn't know what I was getting when I took an apartment in this house!"

"Oh, you don't have to worry about that, lady. S'far's we've found out, she never did a thing in her old line of business in this house. Thirteen years, too."

Fascinated, I hovered in the hall, not able to tear myself away.

"The Liberry case, what was that?"

He stalled. "Well, I don't know much about that."

"But this makes everything different! Someone from back there—someone who had reason to hate Mrs. Garr for something she'd done—would have been a reason for murdering her. Think how many there must be! Have you thought of that?"

"I've heard it mentioned," he admitted cautiously.

But I couldn't get another bit of information out of him.

I went into my own part of the house and barricaded my doors.

There went my previous ideas—such as they were—all upset! This put a new slant on everything. Maybe the motive wasn't hidden money. The Hallorans were undoubtedly mistaken as to the amount of money Mrs. Garr had hidden. Maybe the motive was hate—revenge! Girls have relatives. If Mrs. Garr had run a big establishment, there might be scores who hated her, fathers and mothers, brothers and sisters and sweethearts of the girls she'd kept. Wives of men who'd gone there. The girls themselves. The men themselves. You couldn't tell. It might be anyone.

Of course it was a long time ago. The person would have to be past thirty-five, at least. Nineteen nineteen was eighteen years ago. Hodge Kistler was a little young for that, not much over thirty. But the Hallorans, in their forties. Could Mrs. Garr have debauched her own niece? It seemed impossible—but maybe they weren't related. Perhaps the hold the Hallorans had on Mrs. Garr was other than blood. Perhaps that was why they came to her for money. But the lectures had been very "auntly"; she hadn't sounded as if she were being blackmailed.

The others. Mr. Grant. Mr. Grant was almost as old as Mrs. Garr. Mr. Buffingham. The Wallers. Mrs. Tewman. They were all in their forties or early fifties. They were all the right age.

It took me back to the beginning again. They could all be suspected. And again, Mr. Kistler seemed the least likely. Judging by the results I'd had when I'd thought that before, I was probably due to find out he had been born in Mrs. Garr's house of vice. Or that Mrs. Garr had ruined his father.

The problem of who had killed Mrs. Garr had once seemed fairly simple: a prowler caught in his prowling had been such an obvious explanation. But how complicated this business of Mrs. Garr's past made it! Now the possibilities were almost endless.

I'd read enough detective stories to know it was always the least likely person who went in for murder.

That made Mr. Kistler it.

Well, I didn't care if he was it. A man who amused himself as

Mr. Kistler did—a chaser, a sleeper-around! And I'd once actually thought I liked him! He was frightfully amusing. That time he . . .

I quit smiling, to bite into my thoughts again. If Mr. Kistler's story about Friday night was true, then he had an alibi for the time when Mrs. Garr probably came back to the house. But it meant he was an extremely worthless character.

If his story wasn't true, then he must have had something to do with Mrs. Garr's death. Hiding that ticket couldn't mean much else. It would also mean that, for certain, Mrs. Garr had been murdered. I couldn't think of any way her railroad ticket could have come into Mr. Kistler's possession if she had died a natural death.

If he had murdered her, then his story about the girl wasn't true—just a faked-up alibi, made awful to sound more convincing—and then I wouldn't have so much reason to think his character worthless. He might have had a lovely motive, such as revenging a sister.

I caught myself hoping he had murdered Mrs. Garr.

It made me so disgusted with logic I almost decided I'd give it up forever.

I GAVE UP PUZZLING over Mrs. Garr for the time being anyway; I went to bed.

I was glad there was a policeman in the house. Just before I dropped asleep I opened one eye. I'd suddenly thought who the other officer must be and why he'd ducked. He didn't want me to *see* him. I was being shadowed. He was watching me.

11

I WOKE TO THE telephone's ringing, and Mrs. Tewman in the hall, yelling:

"Mr. Kistler, Mr. Kistler!"

"He don't answer," she shouted into the phone. She added crossly, after an interval, "All ri', I'll knock."

Probably, I thought sleepily, I was the only person in the house who knew where Mr. Kistler was—unless the lean-faced policeman was still on duty. No, Mr. Kistler would not answer the knock on his door. What did it matter who called him? Yes, it might matter. It might be that girl. Toots.

I realized it was up to me to be noble. I wrapped my negligee around me in the yellow sunshine and went out into the hall.

Sure enough, the policeman who knew Mr. Kistler's whereabouts *was* gone. We had a new guard. This one sat on the davenport because he probably couldn't get into the chair. He was a fat lump; he didn't say a word, he was just there, staring with his round blue eyes. We were having a wonderful opportunity to look over the Gilling City police force.

Mrs. Tewman, upstairs, was pounding on a door. I picked up the dangling receiver.

"Hello, this is Mrs. Dacres. I—"

"Oh, hello," a young man's voice replied cordially. "I've heard about you. Where's Hodge?"

"Who're you?"

"I'm Les Trowbridge. You know. His partner. The *Guide*. What's he doing—celebrating the murder?"

"Wildly. In jail."

"Oh, my God! Oh, my—God. What's he want to get himself in there for on a day like this?"

"He doesn't. It wasn't voluntary."

"You mean he had the nerve to go out and get drunk and bust up the town last night?"

"Oh no. It was the murder."

"Now listen, Mrs. Dacres. You can't tell me they've pinched Hodge for *murder*!"

"Oh no. They're just holding him. For investigation or something. Because he had a ticket. A Memorial Day excursion ticket to Chicago. That's the ticket Mrs. Garr was going to use to go to Chicago on, but couldn't find. It was a little hard for Mr. Kistler to explain."

"Oh, for cripes sake! Where does he say he got it?"

"Mr. Kistler's darling little story is that a girl gave it to him. One of the girls you and he were out with a week ago last night."

"Well, say—say! Maybe she did! Say, the girl I was with had one, too. They were passing 'em around the table. They said— Say, I'll bet that's where he did get it!"

"I'm hearing you," I said.

"But for gosh sake, he can't stay in jail loafing today! Doesn't he know we've got that advertising manager from the P-X stores coming in today? He's got him half sold on a big advertising contract. And we need that dough. Sister, how we need it!"

"He never goes down till noon anyway," I pointed out.

"Say, woman, do you ever check on when he comes down Wednesday and Thursday mornings? Say, sometimes he doesn't have to come down—he *is* here!"

I didn't realize Mr. Kistler went in so heavily for labor; he'd always spoken of his work as a joke. But he would.

"Then it looks to me as if you'll have to sell your advertising manager yourself," I said.

A loud groan. "But I can't! I don't know the facts. I don't know the figures. I'm no salesman. Hodge handles all that. Do you realize what'll happen if we don't get that dough? Do you realize we got a press right now that breaks—Hey, wait a minute!"

A loud rumbling at the other end of the wire.

"I've got to go," he yelled. "Do something! Get Hodge here!"

"Do something yourself," I retorted, but it didn't do any good. He'd hung up.

Mrs. Tewman, when I replaced the receiver, was behind me, taking the conversation glumly in.

"So they got him locked up now."

"Why, hello, Mrs. Tewman! Where've you been?"

"I was over to my husband's brother's house."

"I suppose you've heard?"

"Oh yeah, I heard." Fury was burning in her. "They kep' me and my husband over at his brother's house all day yesterday, askin' and askin' and askin'. I never heard so much askin'. And Jim, he had to work again last night. Hardly one hour sleep he had. He's downstairs sleepin' now, so dead he might just as well of been murdered hisself. They make me sick."

It appeared, however, that after being questioned through most of the day before, the Tewmans' alibi of the beer party during the evening and night of the Friday in question had been substantiated; people had noticed them because they were so seldom able to get away. Jim had hired a man to replace him at frying hamburgers that night.

"So then they wanted to know why I moved out of here this week, so I told 'em. It was the smell. They said why didn't I tell somebody there was a smell."

"You mean you did notice—Well, for heaven's sake, why didn't you tell someone?"

She shrugged. "It wasn't none of my business. Who should I go tellin' to? Mrs. Garr wasn't here, was she? I went over to my husband's brother's house. I stayed there. Now they told me I gotta come back and stay here. But I ain't goin' to stay in that cellar. I ain't goin' to do no cleanin', neither," she ended doggedly and went to sit in Mrs. Garr's front room. Just sit, doing nothing.

As Mrs. Garr had so often sat. It was shuddery to see her there.

I went about my own concerns, but my thoughts kept veering back to Mr. Trowbridge. I didn't, however, get far with either my concerns or my thoughts. I'd no sooner begun breakfast than quick knocks sounded on my door. I opened to Mrs. Halloran.

"My, you must be feelin' good this morning," she cried spitefully.

"Not especially. I'm sorry it turned out to be your husband, but of course I had to tell."

"Well, I come to tell you somethin'! And you can just put this in your pipe and eat it! Mr. Halloran's out, see. He wasn't nowheres around this house Friday, see? He's got an alibi, see? And they can't prove he don't!" Her voice rose on every word until she had a fine scream at the end.

"I'm glad to hear it. Was that all?"

"No, that ain't all! This house is mine now, see? I heired this prop'ty. The police read it to me in the will. I'm a heiress. And I'll thank you to get out of my house!"

She drew herself up grandly, her little eyes black over cheeks for once naturally red. For the first time I saw the resemblance in her to Mrs. Garr. I understood then, too, the reason for the elation I'd glimpsed on her face and on her husband's face the evening before when they'd been emerging from Lieutenant Strom's office. They'd come into property. I thought fast.

"Why, of course I'll move. Anytime you say. If the police will let me."

"Let you! Huh! Nobody's going to tell me who I can keep in my house. You come here!"

She marched out to the policeman in the hall with me close at her heels.

"I demand this woman get out of my house!" She pointed a theatric finger at me.

The fat lump placidly shook his head.

"You mean I can't tell her to get out of my house?" she shrieked.

Another shake.

"I heired this prop'ty! I'm goin' to live in it! I won't have this woman in it!"

Another shake.

She collapsed, a grounded parachute. "If that don't beat all," she whined, turning to me. "Right in my own house!"

I suppressed my grin.

"That's the way it is—these policemen," I sympathized.

"You'll get out as soon as they says you can, though," she warned, trying to work herself up again.

Now was the time to strike.

"Of course I will, Mrs. Halloran. Do you think your aunt was murdered?"

"I wouldn't be surprised if you did it." She kept viciously to her own track.

"Oh, don't be cross with me," I wheedled. "I'm just interested. Did you know the police are holding Mr. Kistler?"

"I'm glad t' hear it. I don't like him, neither."

"But it wasn't Mr. Kistler who murdered Mrs. Garr, if she was murdered. I'm quite sure of that. It wasn't me. And I don't like being suspected. So I'm trying to find out who did it. If you're going to live here—How many children did I hear you have?"

"Seven. Seven dear little chillern. I always say being a mother is the nobles' work of Gawd, and I don't care who knows it."

"Just think, Mrs. Halloran, if you brought those dear little children here, and there was an unsolved mystery in the house. A murderer walking around!"

"Oh my, and I living right here! Oh my, he won't, either. I'll tell 'em all to move out, right now."

"Oh, but you can't do that. The police, you know . . ." I waved a hand at the fat lump, who had been an interested listener to the conversation, but who hadn't moved to enter it. It was like having a Dictaphone in the hall. But I didn't care. The police already knew the information I wanted to worm out of Mrs. Halloran, and I didn't mind their knowing that I knew it, too.

"What I say is that you and I should get our heads together," I proposed to Mrs. Halloran, "and see what we can think up."

She followed like a lamb into my sitting room, the fat lump blinking after us and moving where he could hear, too. Mrs. Halloran sat stiffly upright on the studio couch, her fingers tangling in the inevitable pearl beads around her neck.

"The reason Mr. Kistler was held was because he had a Memorial Day excursion ticket to Chicago," I began.

"Oh my, you mean he killed my aunt Hattie for that?"

"He says he got it from someone else. Now, if we can prove he did or did not get it from Mrs. Garr, we'll be one step along. Where did you buy your tickets? Railroad tickets, you know, have the time and place they were bought, stamped on the back."

"I dunno. I didn't buy 'em. Aunt Hattie bought 'em."

"You don't know where?"

"No, ma'am. I mean, no, I didn't. I said so once."

"Do you know what day she bought them?"

"No, I dunno."

"What day did she give you yours?"

"It was a while before. Because I know I took it home and showed it to the children. It was on Thursday, that's when it was. I come over here that afternoon."

"Why, that's a wonderful help, Mrs. Halloran! If we can find out the ticket Mr. Kistler has was bought after Thursday. Mrs. Garr must have bought both her tickets at the same time."

"I dunno. I never seen hers."

"Oh," I said, thinking. I was thinking that to get anywhere with Lieutenant Strom, I'd need to have something definite to go on. I wondered what chance there was of finding the person who had sold Mrs. Garr her tickets. If I was going into that, I was going to have a busy day. But I still wanted more from Mrs. Halloran.

"I think it's wonderful you're going to have the house."

"My, yes, I'm going to do a lot of things to this house. You won't know it when I get done. All over, I'm going to do it. Spanish, I think. I think pink stucco on the outside. Like that four-plex across the street. My, I always admired that house."

"Won't that be lovely. Are you going to have money, too?"

"Five hun'erd a year! It's a lot o' money, ain't it? Five hun'erd dollars. A trust fund, she left it in, for me and the children. Halloran says you got to put a lot o' money in a trust fund to make five hun'erd a year. He says maybe we can get it all out. My, that would be a lot o' money."

She was almost crowing.

"Yes, it must be a lot. It must be ten or twelve thousand dollars, at least." My new knowledge of Mrs. Garr's past kept me from being surprised at the amount. "It must be all the money she had."

"No, it—" A halted look came on her mouth.

"Then she left something to someone else, too?" This was what I was getting at—who benefited by the death?

"She left it to—" Mrs. Halloran leaned forward as if she were telling an obscene story. "She left it to a home for animals." She swallowed, with difficulty. "She left it to the dog and them there cats. Them pets o' hers. There was a whole piece in the will, a long piece. About how they was the best friends she ever had, the only true friends, and she wanted they should have a happy home so long as they lived even if she was gone because there ain't no friends like your dog and your cat."

The last words I could barely make out. Her face was shaken, too. Even she couldn't escape the unholy irony of a thing like that.

12

BEYOND THAT, MRS. HALLORAN had little to tell me of the will. The house and five hundred a year from an already established trust to Mrs. Halloran; all the residue for the establishment of a home for animals, the honored patrons of which were to be Mrs. Garr's own four pets.

I wondered what had become of those animals.

And how much that residue was.

One thing was proved. Except for the Hallorans, no individual stood to benefit by the will!

But I had something else to do before I went into that. As politely as possible, I shooed Mrs. Halloran into the parlor to tell her triumphs to Mrs. Tewman. Five minutes after, I was outside the house.

The curiosity seekers were gone now. Two or three men lounged around the corner; one detached himself as I walked away, I noticed, but I didn't see him after that; he was a good shadow.

What I was bent on doing was, if possible, to find out where and when Mrs. Garr had bought her tickets. I wished I'd taken a look at the back of the ticket Mr. Kistler had; then I'd know better how good my chances were of proving Mrs. Garr hadn't bought it. For a moment, I considered calling Lieutenant Strom's office to ask if I might be given the important information stamped on the back of the ticket they held, but I decided against it. They'd never tell me.

The places in Gilling City where tickets were sold would turn out to be few, I hoped. I could think of only two, offhand: the regular ticket windows at the Union Station, and the branch ticket offices, which the different railroads had established around town.

And of those, to which would an old woman—inexperienced in traveling, especially in recent traveling—go?

She'd go to the station.

So did I.

Gilling City's Union Station is one of its joys and prides. It was built in 1918 when railroads were riding high. It's almost the size of the state capitol, and six times as pontifical. The handful of passengers who trickle through it are lost in its cavernous spaces. Twenty-four ticket windows, with their numbers over them in little lights, stretch along the west wall of the huge, seatless entrance lobby.

Fortunately for me, sixteen of the windows were black and barred; I took a deep breath and tackled the other eight.

Every face behind every window was masculine, tired, bored. Ticket sellers, I suppose, must develop immunity to questions. If they didn't feel like answering, they just didn't answer.

"I'm trying to find out if a woman whom we suspect was murdered"—I tried to be as brisk and official as possible—"bought an excursion ticket to Chicago here last week. You might have noticed that she had lovely white hair; beautiful white hair like sleek, shining feathers on a goose. She'd be wearing a horrible draped black chiffon turban on top of it, with withered violets to the front." Mrs. Garr had but one hat, that I'd seen. "And she had eyes like little black coals, set deep in her head."

I tried it on windows one, two, three, four. I didn't even get an admission that the seller sold tickets. Just:

"No . . . no . . . no . . . no."

The seller at window five was even more indifferent than the others, if that was possible. Bored enough to talk.

"Lady, how many people do you think I sold those tickets to? I told the police—" He halted, and an almost human look came over his face. "What did you say she looked like?"

I eagerly repeated, adding every detail I could think of.

"Say, the picture the police had didn't look like her."

"You mean the police were here asking the same thing?"

"Sure. This morning. Just a couple hours ago. Didn't you know? What're you—a reporter?"

"Sort of," I lied. "I'm on my own, though."

"Well, I'm glad to give a girl a hand. The police were in with this picture, see, but I couldn't remember any dame like that buying a ticket. They said she was older, had white hair, but jeez! I didn't remember anybody had that face. But that hair the way you say it. I lived on a farm once. We had geese on it. That's just the same white her hair was, just like you said it; you sure said it. I noticed hair like that. Would she have a lot of pennies and nickels?"

"I wouldn't know, but it's very likely."

"Well, it's like this, see. I'd just got back from lunch, and this old dame stepped up and asked for an excursion ticket to Chicago. I told her $8.42. She says she heard it was going to be $8.00 even. And she asked was there any place she could get it for

$8.00. So I told her not unless she went a couple stations down the line, and it would cost $1.76 to get there. She hauled out a ratty black bag and begun counting out the money; I never saw such a mess of pennies and nickels come into this window all the eight years I've been here."

"Sixteen dollars and eighty-four cents in pennies and nickels?"

"No, lady, $8.42."

"But she bought two tickets, didn't she?"

"Not from me. Eight dollars and forty-two cents. One ticket."

That stopped me. I stared at him, my mind whirling at the implication.

"Could you possibly remember what day that was?"

"What day it—it must have been Wednesday, or perhaps Tuesday. Because by Thursday we were beginning to have a lot of people. And it wasn't a rush day. It was right after lunch."

"You're sure no later than Wednesday?"

"I'm awfully mistaken if it was."

"How long are you on duty here?"

"Go to lunch at twelve thirty."

"I'll be back."

I sped across the lobby to the telephone booths.

"Could I speak to Lieutenant Strom, please?"

"Who's calling?"

"Mrs. Dacres. In connection with Mrs. Garr's death."

"Wait a minute." A pause. "He isn't in his office, but I think I can locate him." Another pause.

"Hello?"

"Lieutenant Strom, this is Mrs. Dacres. I think I've found something."

"That's nice."

"About that ticket. The one Mr. Kistler had. I thought if I could find out when Mrs. Garr bought hers, and then the ticket

Mr. Kistler had was stamped for some other time and place, it would help prove his ticket wasn't Mrs. Garr's."

"What've you been up to—reading that flatfoot's mind?"

"I haven't been reading anybody's mind. But I think I've found the ticket seller. The one Mrs. Garr bought a ticket from."

Interest sharpened his voice.

"You have? Where?"

"Union Station."

"Where're you now?"

"There."

"Stay there until I get there."

It wasn't five minutes before he came striding across the lobby with another officer at his heels.

"Mother's little helper," he said wryly at me. "What window?"

"Five."

He thrust his face at window five.

"Didn't one of my men ask you about selling tickets to Mrs. Garr this morning?"

"Yes, sir. He showed me a picture. I hadn't seen anyone like that."

"Hand that picture over," the lieutenant ordered the man at his heels. The man hauled a flat photographer's picture out of his pocket, handed it over. I craned my neck to see it; it was a much-handled, cracked picture of a stout, sequined woman in her forties, hard face, waved hair, sporting. Mrs. Garr, twenty years before, when she hadn't fallen apart with age.

"This the picture you saw?"

"Yes, sir."

The lieutenant turned to me.

"This look much like Mrs. Garr as you know her?"

"Hardly at all." I repeated my description of Mrs. Garr as she had last looked.

"Oh, for God's sake! You—you—" He turned wrathfully on his underling. "Where'd you get this picture?"

"The *Comet*, chief. It was the last one they had. You know, from when they was playin' up the Liberry case. There wasn't a single picture in the house."

"If you weren't at the bottom now I'd have you demoted."

"Yes, sir."

"And you." He turned to the ticket seller again. "When did you say you sold this old white-haired woman a ticket?"

Window five repeated his story. Not later than Wednesday.

"Give me that ticket."

The flatfoot produced an envelope and from it picked the familiar Memorial Day excursion ticket.

The lieutenant turned it over on its face.

On the back was a square stamp in purple ink.

It had been sold at the Union Station on May twenty-eighth, three forty-five p.m.!

May twenty-eighth! Friday! Three forty-five p.m.! If I'd only known that! Then . . .

"There's another check you could make," I offered eagerly. "Someone at the house might know where Mrs. Garr was at three forty-five on Friday afternoon. Mrs. Halloran. She may still be at the house; she was there when I left."

Lieutenant Strom turned to the man in attendance.

"You do that yet, Bill?"

"No, sir. I was still trying to prove she did buy it, not she didn't buy it. I hadn't got around to that yet."

"Oh, shut up!"

Lieutenant Strom, in turn, left for the phone booths. He was gone quite a while.

"That's that," he said when he came back. He thanked the ticket seller.

"There's one thing more," I put in. "This man says he sold Mrs. Garr only one ticket."

Lieutenant Strom had the man repeat that part of his story, then turned his hooded eyes on me.

"By heaven, if you weren't a suspect yourself, Mrs. Dacres, I'd hire you. What else have you got on your mind?"

"Will Mr. Kistler—"

"Mr. Kistler is even now being removed from durance vile."

"Then Mrs. Halloran did remember—"

"Yep. She swears up and down she was with Auntie at Auntie's house Friday afternoon from two o'clock on. Helping her get ready for the trip. And Mrs. Waller backs her up. She was around, too."

"Oh, thanks! I mean, they needed Mr. Kistler at his paper."

"Kistler ought to pay you a lawyer's fee. And what, if I may ask as I asked before, are you intent on doing next?"

"That part about Mrs. Garr buying only one ticket."

"Well, that may not be important. One person. One ticket. Probably Mrs. Halloran bought her own."

"But she didn't. She says Mrs. Garr gave her her ticket. Gave it to her on Thursday afternoon. That would mean—"

"By God, she never meant to go to Chicago!"

"Exactly! You can't think anything else. The whole thing sounds that way. She bought only one ticket. She wouldn't have made two trips to buy two tickets; she was slow getting around. And then the way she acted when she was waiting for the train with Mrs. Halloran—she wasn't used to traveling; she'd have had her ticket out and ready just as early as Mrs. Halloran, if she'd intended to go. No, she just meant to get Mrs. Halloran off!"

He took me by the elbow. People coming up for tickets were bumping me right and left; I'd been too absorbed in what I was saying to notice. But I looked up now and saw stares.

"Let's go out in the car and talk this over."

He propelled me out, the uniformed officer following. The police car was parked halfway down the half-moon drive in front of the station.

"Where to, sir?" the driver asked as we got in.

"Stay here awhile."

"It wasn't like Mrs. Garr to go to Chicago in the first place," I began.

"Sh-sh-sh. Be quiet a minute. I want to think this over. I see you can talk and think, but I think much better not listening."

He sat quiet for a time, his hands clasped between his knees, his face forward. Then he turned to me.

"All right. It fits with everything I know so far. I'll agree she never intended to go to Chicago. Let's have your version of why she pulled off this Chicago hoax."

He hadn't any more than asked it than I had the answer.

"She wanted to catch someone prowling in her house. Probably Mr. Halloran."

"Repeat your evidence on what Mrs. Garr said when you told her of the prowler incident. And what she did."

I repeated. As I looked back, it seemed obvious that Mrs. Garr had recognized my description of the prowler as Mr. Halloran. Afterward she had had that long talk with Mrs. Halloran in the parlor; had broken with her. Then, after weeks had passed, she had suddenly phoned Mrs. Halloran, had proposed this trip to Chicago. Had she done that just to catch Mr. Halloran at his pilfering?

"You're building up a strong theory in your mind, Mrs. Dacres. Pretty contemptuous of Halloran, aren't you?"

"Yes, I am."

"You'd rather, if this was a murder, that it would turn out he did it—rather Halloran than anyone else?"

"Well, I—"

He laughed. "Just a little Sympathetic Susie. Well, I don't admire Halloran myself. But that doesn't prove to me he murdered
the old lady. There's a second point to consider. Mrs. Garr may
have arranged that Chicago trip for the reason you suggest. But
she may have hoped to catch someone entirely different."

"I can see that."

"Now I'll carry your reasoning a little further. If Mrs. Garr
was so intensely afraid of pilferers, snoopers, or what have you,
one might argue that she was just a timorous old woman. On the
other hand, perhaps she had something she didn't want found or
stolen."

"That's exactly what I've been thinking! She might—"

"Sh-sh-sh. Don't you know lieutenants of police are important people and shouldn't be interrupted? Now look. We gave
Mrs. Garr's rooms a cursory search Thursday night. The only
important things we found were two safety-deposit keys. We had
the box opened. In it were her will, the papers for the Halloran
trust fund, the deed to her house—a few things like that. No
stocks, no bonds, no money. So when we read the will we saw
she'd left the residue of her estate . . ." He paused to glance at me
uncertainly.

"Mrs. Halloran told me."

"Didn't that jolt you?"

"It did, rather."

"Well, I've come across a few things in my time, but that . . . !
What a combination of circumstances! Where was I?"

"She'd left the residue of her estate."

"Yeah. So that sounded as if there ought to be a residue. And
how did we spend Friday, while you were snoozing so peace-
fully? We went over her rooms with a comb. A damn good job
we did, too."

"Did you . . . ?"

"Yep. Five hundred and eighty-six dollars. In bills. Mostly in little bills. Stuck in the God damnedest places you ever saw. I skinned my fingers picking dollar bills from down under the strings of that doggone grand piano. Look at 'em. We found the biggest wad under the bottom drawer of that chest in the room at the top of the basement stairs." He stopped.

"It doesn't sound like a lot. Not compared to the trust fund."

"No, it doesn't. But if there's any more I'll eat it. And we can't locate a bank account. On the other hand," he went on ruminatively, "it might not be money at all some guy was hunting; the old lady was mixed up in some funny things in her day."

He stopped, became brisk.

"Now, Mrs. Dacres, do you believe the police can handle this?"

"Yes. Oh, of course, but—"

"But what?"

"I would like to know for sure. Was she murdered or did she just die?"

He became heavily jocose. "Mrs. Dacres, you have hit on one of the most embarrassing spots in a long and honorable career. I have to admit it—I don't know. She wasn't shot. She wasn't poisoned." He laughed uproariously. "Lady, if you want to hear some stirring language, you ought to hear a police surgeon when he has to autopsy a cat—with kittens!"

"Oh, so that's—"

"Yeah. What did you think? We were going to give 'em away to kids for pets?"

I shuddered. "No, I'm glad they're gone. Then there wasn't anything to tell if it was murder or not?"

"You can't tell much from a mess like that. There wasn't anything else out of place in the kitchen except a glass jar of dry macaroni spilled on the table. Can I drop you anywhere?"

His dismissal was as abrupt as usual.

"No. I'm going home. I'll take the streetcar. But—"

"Another but."

"I'd like to ask something."

He grinned. "I wouldn't doubt it. Ask away."

"Would you mind if I looked around?"

"Hell no. You keep out of that back basement, of course. It's sealed. But if you can get Mrs. Halloran's consent, look ahead in the rest of Mrs. Garr's rooms. Remember, you haven't any right to look through the other lodgers' possessions, though. Here." He wrote a few words on a sheet torn from his notebook. "Hand that to the guy in the hall. Let me know what you turn up. Good-bye."

From the sidewalk beside the driver, I watched him streak away. Friendly, wasn't he? The friendship of an armed truce, waiting to jump on me the minute I made a slip. Generous with his information. Certainly. I might contribute something more.

What of it? I caught my streetcar and knew I was having a perfectly glorious time. I hadn't had so much fun and excitement in years.

MRS. HALLORAN, IT SEEMED, had asked Mrs. Tewman to leave her house, too. When I got back the two women were sitting, each at one end of the davenport, and figuratively—and I'm not sure not literally—spitting at each other.

I told Mrs. Halloran of my project for searching Mrs. Garr's house for anything that might shed light on the death, and saw excitement come into her eyes.

"Oh, my goodness, here I been wasting all this time! I got a right to look into everything there is now, don't I?"

"Of course. And Lieutenant Strom wants me to work with you." I carried on cheerfully my bent for lying.

Craftiness crept back of her eyes.

"I don't need no help."

"Oh, I'm sure Lieutenant Strom would object to your doing it alone," I said. I showed her the lieutenant's note, which read

> *Jack, let Mrs. Dacres make a further search of Mrs. Garr's rooms. But keep an eye on her.*

Mrs. Halloran struggled; I saw her vast dismay. She might have discovered money! But she had to give up.

"The police have already searched everything thoroughly."

I was impatient. "All I'm interested in is clues."

With Mrs. Tewman dismissed to the basement, and the lumpy policeman regarding us solemnly, we started on the parlor, Mrs. Halloran jumping to snatch first anything that I moved to pick up.

"Let's start on the drawer of this table," I said. It was the drawer in which I thought Mr. Grant had been hunting, on that afternoon long ago.

The drawer was full of a litter of papers. Trembling with feverish energy and suspicion, Mrs. Halloran pushed me aside to paw through the papers. She found nothing save paper.

"There ain't nothing here!"

"Mind if I look?"

I sorted the papers carefully. Meager grocery lists: bread, 8¢; 1/2 lb. hamburger, 9¢; 1/2 lb. butter, 20¢; cornflakes, 10¢. Added columns of figures: taxes, $138.72; water, $6.48; fire insurance, $19.64; doorbell batteries, $1.00. Laundry bills. Gas and electric bills, stamped **PAID**. A receipt book.

I picked that up, thumbed through it from the back. Stubs of receipts: to me, for $4.00; to Mr. Kistler, $6.00; to Mr. Grant, $2.00; to Miss Sands, $5.00; to Mr. Buffingham, $9.00.

My eyes were halted, incredulous, by those last two figures.

Miss Sands paid more for her one tiny room with a two-burner gas plate than I did! And Mr. Buffingham paid more than twice what I did!

Rapidly, then, I went through the book. It went back for months. One receipt to each person for each week. Each week a receipt to Miss Sands, $5.00. Each week a receipt to Mr. Buffingham, $9.00.

Carefully, I checked. The sums never varied. Mr. Grant's room was small and its comforts probably provided by himself; $2.00 was about right for that. Mr. Kistler had two nice front rooms and shared a private lavatory. Six dollars was about right for that. But Miss Sands, $5.00 for a room scarcely larger than Mr. Grant's! And Mr. Buffingham, $9.00 a week for a room with one window!

I couldn't make it out. If it were the Wallers' apartment, now . . .

The Wallers! Again I went through the receipt book, every last single stub.

There wasn't one to indicate the Wallers had ever paid anything!

13

I SAT DOWN, THE better to think.

Mrs. Halloran grabbed the receipt book, hunted through it, looked from me to it and back again.

"There ain't nothing you can get anything out of here," she said. "They're all paid up. My aunt Hattie wouldn't never have let anybody stay if they weren't paid up."

What would I gain by keeping my discovery about the Wallers secret? It would be a lot easier and more natural for Mrs. Halloran to tackle the Wallers about their rent than for me to do so. And anything Mrs. Halloran found out I could soon know.

I took the book back from her nervous hands; she gave it to me bottom side up. The cardboard back had been scribbled over with spidery figures, some of them almost erased with handling, the others fresher. The freshest of all was a row of figures added up in a straggling column:

$ 5
$ 9
$ 2
$ 6
$ 4
———
$26

And underneath, in Mrs. Garr's old-fashioned script, were two words:

Not enough.

That decided me. There they were, all the weekly rents for which she had given receipts. And here, too, there was no sum included for rent from the Wallers!

Mrs. Garr was scarcely the person to give people free houseroom—not for nothing. And the Wallers themselves said they had been here for years.

But before seeking an explanation I moved to verify the facts.

"Look," I said to the twittering Mrs. Halloran. "Doesn't this seem queer to you? Not a single receipt for rent to the Wallers!"

She grabbed the book from me again.

"No, there ain't! That's right, there ain't! Well, they're going to pay rent to me, I can tell you that much!"

As I had expected, she didn't wait for more; she hurried out and upstairs.

I went on with the search. In turn, I took each piece of furniture, going over it carefully. When I was halfway through the room Mrs. Halloran was back, half subdued, one quarter suspicious, and one quarter belligerent.

"They says she owed 'em money. They said my aunt Harriet

owed 'em two thousand dollars, and they had a note for it. They says she let 'em live here instead of payin' 'em interest. Well, I ain't goin' to do it. They can't live here on me! And I ain't going to pay that money, either. They can just go to law for it. They'll see! Before they can get any money out of me I'll spend it. I'll spend every penny!"

"Mmmmmmm . . ." I said. "If they can prove Mrs. Garr owed them money, that'll probably be paid before you get yours at all."

She immediately screamed and fell back on the davenport, kicking her heels like an overgrown four-year-old. I gathered, from her comments, that the Wallers were thieves and robbers, I was a thief and a robber, and the sooner I got out of there the better, the police were all thieves and robbers, and she'd get the G-men, that's who she'd get, they'd "pertect" her, they'd shoot us all down!

There wasn't anything to do but let her scream; the lumpy fat policeman, who had wandered out into the hall in boredom at my unsuccessful hunting, returned to the doorway, where he stood contemplating her histrionics with calm round eyes.

I went on searching. Nothing.

Until I got to the overstuffed armchair. That contributed nothing above, but when I upended it I noticed that three tacks, holding one corner of the bottom lining, looked loose. They worked out easily; I poked among the springs with my fingers.

Mrs. Halloran, smelling money, stopped screaming, dashed forward, jerked my hands away, and scrambled inside with her own.

Bills came out in her hands. Ones and fives.

She tore madly at the upholstery with one hand, clutching the money to her bosom with the other, uttering beastly little noises to warn me off. Excelsior, horsehair, wisps of cloth scattered over the floor, but there was only the one cache.

She arose from her couch, glaring at me, breathless, at bay.

The policeman placidly advanced.

"I'll have to take that in charge, ma'am."

"No, you ain't going to take it! You thief! You robber!"

As the officer advanced upon her, she thrust the money into the front of her dress; he caught her two hands easily behind her back in one fat fist, reached down with the other, drew the money forth.

"You wouldn't rob them poor animals, would you?"

She kicked and clawed at him; he fended her off, holding out the money to me.

"Count it, lady."

I did.

One hundred and twenty dollars, even.

He took it back.

"I call you both to witness the amount." With that he stowed the bills away in a big wallet, strolled back to the door, Mrs. Halloran shrieking after him in helpless fury.

After that the searching was out of my hands. Mrs. Halloran sped ruthlessly from one article to another, grabbing picture frames from the walls, ripping them apart, casting the shattered remnants on the floor. Between the back and the photograph in one frame, she found two five-dollar bills. Sewed into an old quilted robe she found in the room under the stairs were seven twenties. From deep down in a mess of buttons, hooks, eyes, nails, and hairpins in a two-pound coffee tin, she drew a neat roll of ones—twenty-eight of them.

The search was on her like a fever; the policeman claimed each new find; she quarreled and sought bitterly on.

The cellar produced nothing. The furnace room had little to search; the storage-room junk was just junk.

It was after six o'clock when, dusty, disheveled, and cross, she gave up. The parts of the house Mrs. Garr had lived in were a rubbish-strewn wreck. And my only satisfaction, as I looked on, was in thinking of the moment when Lieutenant Strom would have to eat, as he had promised, the uncovered money.

Of what I had wanted to find, of one clue that would point to why Mrs. Garr had died, and how, there wasn't a trace. Not one thing to link Mrs. Garr to her past life. I hadn't seen anything anyone would possibly commit murder to get—certainly the trifling sums of money would hardly be cause for murder. Hold it, though. What Mrs. Halloran had found, added to what Lieutenant Strom had found, made over a thousand dollars. Would that be enough to be tempting?

Tired of watching Mrs. Halloran mess around with the contents of the storage room, I lit the heater for a bath and went upstairs to my own apartment. From the floor just inside my door I picked up an envelope. The notice inside instructed me to be present at an inquest into the death of Harriet Luella Garr, to be held Monday afternoon, two thirty o'clock.

An inquest! Of course there'd be an inquest. There, at least, I should find out if Mrs. Garr had been murdered or not.

I bathed, dressed, went out to eat, came home again, thinking solidly all the while. The more I thought on it, the more certain I was that the Hallorans must be at the bottom of the mystery. It was a certainty that struck snags, swung aside, and swam easily on.

The Hallorans were the only ones that really benefited by the death. They were the greedy kind; they couldn't wait to get their hands on money if they knew there was any to be had.

The Hallorans were frightfully stupid.

Yes, but it was a stupid crime, wasn't it? A sneak thief, caught. He'd struck at her, choked her. Then rushed out, locking the door behind him. Run, trembling and afraid, home to his seven dear little children.

But the cats! The dog! The kitchen door opened, they'd have run out, too. And would Mr. Halloran, that sniveling little coward, have dared to run about in that house, in which he ran such risks of being seen, dared to run about catching those animals one by one, thrusting them back into the kitchen? Had he still been in the house when I came home that Friday night, lurking somewhere, hiding in the bathroom, perhaps? Had he stayed there until late, then sneaked down, gone to the back of the house to see the results of his work in the basement kitchen if he could, attacked me when I'd heard him?

If so, wouldn't someone have seen him in the house?

Mr. Buffingham!

Mr. Buffingham had been on his way downstairs when one of the cats was still loose in the house; I had talked to him. If anyone had seen Mr. Halloran lurking, he would be the one.

Rapidly I considered. Mr. Buffingham hadn't been about while I had been in Mr. Kistler's rooms the night before, I was sure; his room had been quiet.

The fat lump had been replaced by the lantern-jawed policeman of the night before. For the second time I approached him with news of a call.

"I'd like to run up and see if Mr. Buffingham's in. That all right?"

"Have your own way!" He waved a cordial hand. "Remember I'm here if you turn up anything on him."

Thus encouraged, I went up to knock at Mr. Buffingham's door.

There was a stir in the room, then silence. I knocked again. The door opened slowly; as it did so a subdued whir sounded in the room somewhere. I looked my surprise up at Mr. Buffingham's usual dark, intent gaze.

"Why, what's that?"

"Burglar alarm," he replied laconically, without smiling. As a burglar alarm, it was effective; I sensed before I saw Mr. Grant's door open and his head appear momentarily around the edge of it.

Well, Mr. Buffingham wasn't having anyone search his room! Then I thought of my own doors and laughed with sympathy.

"Good idea! You should see the way I barricade my own doors!"

"That so?"

Potatoes and hamburgers were frying in a pan on the gas plate standing on the table against his left wall; a coffeepot covered the second flame.

"I don't want to keep you from your dinner," I said hastily. "I just wanted to ask you a question. That night, that Friday night, you know, I came in around ten, and one of the cats ran under the bookcase. Then you came downstairs. You didn't happen to have seen a strange man around the house about that time, did you?"

He stared at me in silence awhile.

"No, I didn't."

"I've identified that prowler I saw in the house once—it was Mr. Halloran. The husband of Mrs. Garr's niece. I thought he might have come around again that Friday."

"I know Halloran—seen him around."

"But not that Friday?"

"Ain't seen him for months. Used to be around a lot."

"You didn't hear anything strange? Going down cellar, for instance? After all, that cat must have been put back in the cellar sometime between ten o'clock, when I saw her, and two o'clock, when the house was searched. She wasn't around then."

"How would I know? I don't spend all my time listening around—I got my own business to tend to. And if I had seen anything I'd of said so to the police, wouldn't I?"

"Yes, of course," I said. "Thanks. Sorry if I've bothered you."

He slammed his door; the buzzing stopped.

That hadn't been very fruitful. I'd had my nose so close to my idea that I'd forgotten that he, as well as everyone else in the house, had been asked just those questions by the police, not only after the discovery of Mrs. Garr's body, but on the very night, after the attack on me.

And on that throttling business—it must surely have been the murderer. It would be stretching coincidence too far to have two criminals attacking in the same house on the same night. No, the murderer must have hung around. In that case, he must have waited somewhere. Outside or inside?

As long as I was upstairs I might as well ask the other lodgers my questions, useless or not. It would serve to find out how they felt about the crime, too. I might be able to tell something from attitudes.

No answer to my knock on Mr. Kistler's door.

Mr. Grant answered so quickly, I suspected him of listening.

"No, no one," he answered me. "Nothing unusual."

Miss Sands, in curlers and kimono over a cheap rayon slip, was pressing a black dress; her room was full of the ethery scent of dry-cleaning fluid.

"No, I'd of remembered it after you got choked, wouldn't I, dearie?" she contributed wearily, turning the iron back on its rest and rubbing at the neck of the dress with a reeking rag. "Did you get a notice to go to that inquest? So did I, and I'll have to go, too, I suppose, though what Mr. Tully's going to say when I ask to get off at two o'clock, right in the busiest time, I hate to think."

"Poor Mrs. Garr," I said. "She didn't make it pleasant for anyone, dying. Except maybe the Hallorans."

"That old leech! I'm glad she's dead!" There was hate in the words. "Now maybe I'll—" She stopped there, stamped sullenly down with the iron. She wouldn't say more; I got no bites on my casts.

The Wallers, too, were uncommunicative. I got the effect, when they opened their door, that they had retired to their apartment as to a fort, to hide there until forays were past. Mrs. Waller opened the door only a crack, didn't ask me in.

"No, we didn't see anyone. No, we didn't hear anything," she answered, and shut her door. I heard it lock.

What did they do? What did they talk about, all day behind that locked door? Going downstairs, I thought about them; they seemed normal people in so many respects, yet what a life they lived. Mr. Waller did odd jobs; I'd pieced that out. Yet he was a retired policeman. Appearance and apparent character would place him above an odd-job man. Was it all to be blamed on the depression, that sausage machine for turning out economic alibis?

What possible reason could Mrs. Garr have had for borrowing two thousand dollars from them? Especially when she had ten thousand to invest in a trust fund for the Hallorans? Or why was she paying them two thousand dollars, if that was the way of it? For the first time, it struck me that this might be a link to her past, the first one I'd found. Two thousand dollars. The interest on two thousand dollars, even at six percent, would be only a hundred and twenty dollars a year. That would mean she let the Wallers have one of the best apartments in the house—their rooms were small, but there were three of them—for only ten dollars a month, less than two-fifty a week!

It didn't seem like Mrs. Garr at all.

The policeman with the Wilsonian jaw said he was surprised to see me come down with empty hands, but I ignored that. I retired to a pencil and paper in my rooms. I think better with a pencil in my hands, and I needed support.

I'd just picked up the pencil when loud, peremptory knocks sounded on my door.

It was Hodge Kistler.

He closed my doors behind him and stood with his arms wide, the corners of his funny mouth almost hitting his eyes.

"Aw, funny face," he said. "So you do love me."

I wished I were the freezing unit of an electric refrigerator.

"Only you could have an idea as ridiculous as that!" I put venom into it.

"Well, baby, you got me out of jail, didn't you? That's a sign of true love, isn't it? Look in any movie from here to Dallas, Texas."

"That was just a by-product. I was really out hunting for facts, and I happened to turn up one that cleared you."

"Madam, for that by-product I thank you." He bowed like a courtier, but the impudence was still on his face. "Jail is a nasty place. My first time in, too. Who knows what vicious habits I might have picked up if I'd been in longer?"

"A rather suitable place, I thought."

"Oh, now, sister! Look, baby, you sit there on the couch, so. I'll sit way over here, so. And I'll tell you about the facts of life. It was facts you were out hunting, wasn't it? We'll consider men first. Particularly unmarried men. I'm not married, am I?"

"I wouldn't be surprised."

"A nasty, suspicious nature. No, I am not married. I am a bachelor. I am thirty-four years old. Now let us consider bachelors. At twenty, say, one may be a bachelor because Mama has not yet untied the apron strings, or because one has a consuming passion for basketball, ice-cream sodas, communism, or the higher life. At thirty-four, not so. At thirty-four, there are only three types of bachelors. In group one, we have the bachelors who, in their carefree way, prefer a chorus to a solo. In group two, we have those who cannot make the economic grade—you will find those down by the railroad tracks if you would like a sample of the genus at its best. And then, we have group three, whose members were not very well equipped by God. Now, you wouldn't want me to belong to either of the last two groups, would you?"

He ended with a plaintive mournfulness which was completely ridiculous.

"So you prefer a chorus," I said coldly.

"I like 'em all." He spread his hands. "I like practically any girl, except the kind with minds like half-cold kettles of tar. They're too hard to stir up."

"What, no brief for beauty?"

"Why, afraid you'd be left out?"

"You forget I'm not competing."

"Sorry. No, no brief for beauty. Did you ever notice what insignificant little twerps get the beauties? Natural-born bachelors from group three. I've got it all figured out. Here we have a guy with not much natural ability, and what does he hunt for? He hunts for a woman that'll have other men saying, 'What a guy, to get a girl like that!' Or he hunts for a girl that packs enough sex appeal to strike sparks even out of him. But a man that's good, and knows he's good, doesn't give a damn what the other fellows think about his girl. And he doesn't go hunting for soul-stirring beauty, either. He just likes 'em all. They're women."

"No charge for these lectures?"

"No." He turned, and I could see that he was serious, under cover. "I'm explaining, in my own roundabout and unrighteous way. Still mad?"

"Mad? I had nothing to be angry about, personally." I tried to keep up the remoteness, but my anger seemed to have evaporated more quickly than I had intended it should, and it was hard to whip it up again. "Not to change the subject or anything, but I don't suppose you've learned anything more about the murder?"

He leaned across the couch to kiss me enthusiastically but nicely.

"So we do kiss and make up? You're a nice kid."

"You're an insufferable advantage taker."

He retired decorously to his end of the couch.

"From now on I commit all my crimes in impenetrable secret. God help me from ever having you on my trail. Relentless, you are. But no, I have heard nothing more of the murder. No, I have just tucked a stray advertising manager of the P-X stores safely under a table. Never, never, so help me God, ever go into the *Buyers' Guide* business."

"I'll help God out of that. But I have been in the detective business. Listen."

I told him, then, everything I'd discovered during the day, with particular emphasis on the case against the Hallorans.

"Nothing new against me?"

"I'm sorry, no. But there are a few things I wondered if you'd find out; they'd be a little hard for me to dig into."

"Ah, now we get the reason for this rush of confidence."

"Exactly. I wish you'd find out about Mr. Halloran's alibi. So we'd know how good it really is."

"Why not wait until after the inquest? Isn't that supposed to reveal all?"

"Even if he has to tell where he was that's not proof. I leave things I forget out of evidence myself, and if I had anything to hide I'd certainly do a little plain and fancy lying."

"Well, an inquest's pretty limited. What about the funeral?"

"Mrs. Halloran says a cremation. She isn't even going herself."

"There's love and gratitude. What does Halloran say he was doing that Friday night?"

"That's virgin territory."

"Well, I'm against territory being virgin, on principle. I've got a proofreader who won't be doing anything Monday. Maybe he'll be a good detective; he's a lousy proofreader. I'll sic him on Halloran. Anything else?"

"Then there are the Tewmans. They've been gone an awful lot. And Mrs. Tewman—her I.Q. is just enough to get her by in a big crowd—admits she suspected, or knew, that something was wrong in that kitchen. That's why she left. Mrs. Garr was always snarling at Mrs. Tewman, and even worms turn. How about their alibis?"

"Phooey. The police have done that."

"The police looked into Halloran's alibi, too."

"But he has a motive. I'd rather put in the time on him."

"There's Mrs. Halloran, too. What if she didn't go to Chicago?"

"That's so easy to find out, even the police couldn't muff it. Wait for the inquest on that one."

"If they don't take it up I'd like to check it."

"Let it ride. But say, how about Buffingham? He'd be my pick if I was going to pick a murderer out of this bunch."

"The only thing I have on him is that he paid nine dollars a week for his room—I saw it on the receipt stubs."

"Whew! Nine dollars a week for that hole? That's robbery! Mrs. Garr could have been jugged for that—why murder her?"

"Miss Sands, too. Miss Sands pays five dollars a week. And the Wallers don't pay anything! They said they hold a note of Mrs. Garr's for two thousand dollars, and she let them have the interest in rent."

"Good God! What a ferret you turned out to be! Who'd have thought this old house was so seamy with mysteries? You certainly have everyone in the house lined up for this job. Somebody stupid, you say? The Hallorans and the Tewmans race neck and neck for that distinction. Good old Buffingham, papa of criminals, runs third. Mr. Grant, dark horse. Miss Sands, not any too bright. Wallers, ditto. Who's left? Only us. I am much, much too gallant to place you, my sweet."

"I hope you're gallant enough to say good night," I said. "I'm tired."

He stood up to say good night with solemnity, shaking hands.

"God bless and keep you from ever falling into the hands of bachelors from groups two or three," he said.

"You, I suppose, have a great deal for which to thank heaven?" I said, because it was practically irresistible.

"Demonstrations on request," he said. "Merely drop a postcard."

14

MRS. HALLORAN KNOCKED ME up bright and early the next morning, which was Sunday. She stood in my doorway with bills in one hand, a pen and Mrs. Garr's receipt book in the other.

"I guess nobody can't take this money away from me," she crowed triumphantly. "I'll thank you for your rent money, Mrs. Dacres."

"But I'm paying in advance, you know. Are you sure you'll want me to stay out my week?"

She struggled, but four dollars in hand beat getting rid of me, in the bush.

"I guess I can't get you out of here in less'n a week, anyhow. You go ahead and pay."

Except for two one-dollar bills, I had only a ten in my handbag; I offered that to her.

She gave me a five and a one in change; sat down with a fine air of business to write out my receipt.

I thumbed my change idly while I waited; my little finger caught in a tear. It was in the five-dollar bill, right in the lateral crease.

The bill was as familiar to me as a read newspaper. It was the same bill I had taken down to the cellar to pay my rent on the day before Mrs. Garr was to have gone to Chicago.

I thought I had the Hallorans then. I debated with myself, wildly, whether I should call for the man in the hall, but the pleasure of facing Mrs. Halloran myself was too great. I spoke softly.

"So you did find some of Mrs. Garr's money."

She looked up, startled; my words had had intensity enough to make them noticeable.

"No, I never did. Only what I found yesterday and the policeman took."

"Oh, I suppose Mrs. Garr gave you the money!" I made it insulting enough so she'd want to deny it.

"Not a cent she didn't give me for almost a month. Mr. Halloran give me the money to go to Chicago, except the ticket. He got his gov'ment money right on that Friday. His June money."

I wasn't interested in her Chicago money; I couldn't imagine her bringing back any she'd taken along. I laid the torn bill on the table before her; she stared at it with bewildered, frightened eyes.

"I recognize this bill. It's the bill with which I paid my rent last week. To Mrs. Garr."

"Oh my," she whispered tremulously. "I must of got it offen somebody in the house. I didn't bring no five-dollar bills with me when I come. All I had was my car tokens, and fifty cents, and two one-dollar bills. And maybe some nickels. All the rest I got goin' around and askin' everybody for their rent."

So that was it! Or was she lying? If her husband had given her the bill, she'd be as frightened as this, too. And she'd lie, of course. I tried again.

"Can you remember who gave it to you?"

"Lemme think. Mr. Kistler come down early wearin' his fishin' clo'es. A five and a one he give me. So then I waited till Miss Sands went down to light the heater; she give me a five, even. I had to go back up with her. So then I knocked for Mr. Grant, and I gave him three dollars change for his five. So then I went to the Wallers, but they said they wouldn't, on account of the estate owed them money, so I said I would get the G-men, and I will, too; they can't do me that way. I knocked a long time for Mr. Buffingham, I guess he was in bed yet, he's got a funny alarm clock. He wouldn't pay me nine dollars like it said in the book, he said it was just three dollars a week; I bet he owed her money; I'm going to look in her papers for that. All he had was a five, but I went to the Wallers and they changed it, and I gave Mr. Buffingham two dollars change. You was the last one."

After that, how much of a story did that torn bill tell? If it had been found by ransacking that kitchen downstairs, then any one of the people who had paid Mrs. Halloran with five-dollar bills would be suspect: Mr. Kistler, Miss Sands, Mr. Grant, Mr. Buffingham. It seemed to clear the Wallers.

But I had paid that bill to Mrs. Garr on Thursday. She was in the house for most of two days after that. She might have paid out the bill in change to any one of the lodgers.

It was maddening. Every time I thought I had a clue, it petered out like that. Anyone and everyone still suspect.

I picked up the receipt book. Mr. Kistler normally paid on Mondays. Mr. Grant and Miss Sands normally paid on Tuesdays, Mr. Buffingham on Wednesdays. Yes, the bill was a clue. If any one of those four had paid it in, it was incriminating.

"Can't you remember? Think. Close your eyes. Imagine Miss

Sands is paying you her rent again. She unclasps her handbag, she takes out money. She gives it to you. A five-dollar bill. You look at it. Is it whole and new, or ragged and torn?"

"Well, it might be." Mrs. Halloran was infuriatingly uncertain.

I tried it for every one of the four, but all I emerged with was limpness and perspiration on the part of Mrs. Halloran. I still wasn't sure she wasn't lying; I tried again to suggest Mr. Halloran had given her the bill sometime during the past week. Denying that was the one thing she was certain about.

From then on, whenever she saw me, Mrs. Halloran would shut her eyes, look blank for a moment, and then open them brightly on me, in indication that no, she couldn't remember about that note—yet. But to all intents and purposes she really did try.

I spent a peaceful day and night. I remember them very well.

Hodge Kistler called me up just before twelve o'clock on Monday.

"Well, here's one more *Guide* started on its earthward journey," he said. "And that proofreader has come across. The lazy bum. I knew he wasn't putting himself into his job. I could buy you some lunch if you promise not to go over thirty cents. We could prepare for the inquest together. Meet me in the Wetmore Grill, one o'clock?"

The cheapest lunch in the Wetmore Grill is eighty-five cents, so I set about the question of armament. I walked in looking blank and raised around the eyebrows, which is as snooty as I can look.

"If you turn into one of those cold-tar girls," Hodge Kistler said, meeting me, "you'll eat lunch alone."

I lasted being snooty until we were sitting kitty-corner on the beige leather seats in one of the booths; we got a corner one.

"What'd your proofreader find out?"

"Wait until I get us something to eat, please, Mrs. Holmes."

He ordered pickled pigs' feet, which I thought was a queer choice, but when they came they were jellied, in slices, with awfully good salads, and he told me how he'd been a reporter on a stockyards paper, once, and all the big meat men said pickled pigs' feet were the biggest delicacy there was, in meats. He talked about stockyards for twenty minutes before he'd come around to Mr. Halloran's alibi.

"Okay, hold everything. This proofreader arrived at the Halloran ménage bright but not early; ten thirty to be exact. Mr. Halloran was still recumbent."

"As I'd expect."

"Sh-sh-sh. Am I telling this? So the proofreader told the little girl who opens the door that he is an American Legion buddy and he is working to get every veteran paid ten thousand dollars spot cash, and he would like to know could he get Mr. Halloran's support. That brought him out like a shot."

"I can imagine."

"They sat in the parlor and communed. Halloran was wearing two-thirds of a pajama and bare feet. Little Hallorans scurried around the house, dashing their heads around doors, staring, and sort of whinnying. Entranced, my proofreader was."

"I've wondered how Mrs. Halloran kept her house. She isn't there much."

"Kept, my dear lady? No, no, unkept, I gathered."

"Ugh."

"So then," went on Mr. Kistler blithely, "the talk sort of shifted. To the trials and tribulations poor veterans suffered. To Mr. Halloran's having been held by the police one night, and why. To how Mr. Halloran knew he didn't murder Mrs. Garr. Did you ever ask Mrs. Halloran how many children she had?"

"Why, yes. Seven, she said."

"Did you ever ask Mr. Halloran ditto?"

"No."

"Ah, my proofreader did. And there, as one might say, was the rub. Or not, to be exact. Sorry, couldn't help it. Opportunity knocked. Anyhow, Mr. Halloran, questioned, says five."

"Five? But—"

"And he was out Friday night getting even."

"I see. A brother of yours."

Mr. Kistler shook his head sadly. "It dismays me to view my attitude toward Mr. Halloran. My proofreader—what the hell, his name's Anderson—did better. He admired. And Mr. Halloran, sniggering, gave name and place. Which Anderson immediately checked, and sure enough, the proprietor says he can almost answer this question in his sleep—he is prepared to say Halloran, in company with a strawberry blonde, was at his place from nine o'clock that Friday night until four a.m., when they dumped him out, and that during practically all of that time, he was too drunk to commit murder or anything else."

"But it's just got to be Mr. Halloran! Why would anyone else?"

"Well, the only chance is that the proprietor is squared. Anderson's out now, hunting the strawberry and two more gents the proprietor remembers having been present. But just remember, those hands on your neck weren't drunk."

"Pooey, pooey, double pooey, and a couple of extra-super pooeys," I said. "I'm disgusted."

"Cheer up. Who knows what the inquest will bring forth? And speaking of inquests, my darling, the hour is come. We're late. It's after two thirty now." We hurried, almost running the two blocks to the city hall where the inquest was to be held. But when we got there, breathing hard, the coroner hadn't even arrived.

Information told us room 223 for the Garr inquest. Room 223

smelled hot and dry, yet woolly, as if a lot of damp winter clothes had dried in there. It was barer than any schoolroom, with Teacher's desk on a raised platform, and rows of folding chairs facing the desk. One row of chairs at right angles to the others was up by the desk; it was filled; the jury, I guessed.

Most of the folding chairs were full, too. All the residents of the Garr house. The Hallorans. The Tewmans. The ticket seller. A scattering of other people. And at the back, bedraggled hangers-on, with a reporter or two. A few policemen stood about the room.

We sat down next to Mr. Grant and whispered about how long we'd have to wait. We waited a good long time. Long enough to take in the flyspecks on the light globes, and the general hopelessness of everyone who straggled past the door. I felt, as I always feel when I've been in the courthouse, that I needed to be fumigated before I'd really be clean again.

The coroner came in briskly when he did come, with Lieutenant Strom and a couple of more men in tow. The coroner—he was the florid politician to the life—sat down behind the desk and went through the preliminaries quickly. Lieutenant Strom sat beside him.

"First witness," the coroner said. "Mrs. Halloran, please take the chair."

I shan't give the whole inquest; you'd find most of it repetition. But there were a few high spots.

Mrs. Halloran's testimony dealt with the Chicago trip. After her came the ticket seller. Then a Mr. Banks was called; he was new to me, a railway employee.

"You examined the tickets for the Great Western's Chicago excursion at eight-five on Friday, May twenty-eighth, Mr. Banks?"

"Yes, sir."

"Do you recall any incident involving Mrs. Halloran, the woman who just testified, and another woman?"

"Yes, sir."

"Describe the other woman."

"She was older, sir. White hair. Very pretty white hair. Old-fashioned hat high on her head. Violets in front. Black dress."

"What attracted your notice to her?"

"Well, sir, this crowd was milling around me. The gate wasn't open yet. And these two women"—he pointed back at Mrs. Halloran—"her and the older one, kept jamming up against me. This one here, Mrs. Halloran, kept waving a ticket in my face and yelling, 'Can't we get through now? We want a good seat.' I get people like that all the time. When the gates opened I began punching tickets as fast as I could and letting 'em through, but these two women got in my way all the time. The old one couldn't find her ticket. The younger one got hers punched but stayed back holding on to the old one. They were getting pushed around. Finally the old one said, 'You go on, get a good seat. I'll come as soon as I find my ticket; I know I got it right here.' And the younger one went."

"To the best of your recollection, did the older woman find her ticket?"

"No, sir. I noticed. She didn't even seem to look for it anymore. Just faded in the crowd. She didn't go by me; I was sort of looking out for her."

"You did not see her again?"

"No, sir."

"Thank you. Stand down."

The next witness was a conductor, who testified he had taken up Mrs. Halloran's ticket and seen her on the train near Chicago. So she had gone, all right.

"Next witness, Mrs. Gwynne Dacres."

My heart beat fast. I got past Mr. Kistler's knees, up to the armchair, was sworn. Then I became so immersed in answering questions I forgot to be frightened. I was asked in detail about coming home that Friday night, the cat in the hall, the noises I'd heard, the attack on me. Then I was told to stand down.

It was obvious they were trying to get the facts as chronologically as possible.

Obvious, too, as the questioning went on, that the whole thing was merely a process of law. To the police, all the evidence elicited was known before. Of course, it would be; they'd gotten the witnesses together and questioned them all before. But I heard a few things which were as useful to me, later, as keys in the hand.

Mr. Kistler was called after me, to tell of finding me that Friday night.

Then Officer Foster was called. He turned out to be the policeman I'd known as Jerry. He told of the search that Friday night.

One after the other, Mrs. Garr's lodgers were then called, to give their testimony up to that point. Especial emphasis was laid on Mr. Grant's testimony that he had seen Mrs. Garr coming home around eight thirty.

The discovery of the death was then taken up, in exactly the same manner. I'll give Foster's evidence.

"Now, Foster, we come to the search of the basement room in which Mrs. Garr's remains were found. You assisted that search?"

"Yes, sir."

"You say the remains, the clothes, and the hair were scattered about the floor, but mostly near the door."

"Yes, sir."

"Was there any sign of a gun having been fired in that room?"

"No, sir."

"Any other implement or thing which showed signs of having been used as a weapon?"

"No, sir. There were knives in the table drawer. But they were all clean. Pretty clean, I mean. Anyhow, they didn't show any signs of havin' been used to stab her."

"No hammers or axes?"

"We found tools in a box in the furnace room. Under test, they show they've been used in the usual ways, nothing more."

"To sum up, then, no weapon for murder was in your estimation present in the kitchen?"

"No, sir."

"Was there any sign of disorder in the room? Of a struggle, for instance?"

"Well, sir, it wasn't in very nice shape, as you can imagine. But there wasn't any furniture overturned, nothing like that. The only sign of disturbance was that glass jar of macaroni. Dry macaroni. It was half spilled out on the table."

"The electric light was not on?"

"No, sir."

"The room was tested for fingerprints?"

"Yes, sir. But we didn't get any good ones, except a couple of the old lady's on the stove and places like that. None on the glass jar. Most of the fingerprints weren't good, surfaces not right. Cement and weathered wood."

"I see. Now the location of the key, Foster. Where was it found?"

I leaned forward, intent. The key! This was the first time I had heard it mentioned.

"The key was lying on the kitchen table, just a little way from the jar of spilled macaroni."

"You are sure the key was there when you broke the lock?"

"Well, sir, we didn't let anyone in that room from the time we broke the lock until the time we searched it. Mr. Waller and Mr. Kistler went to the door and looked in, but they looked over Officer Harlan's shoulder. I don't think they could have thrown a key all the way across that room to the table from the door. Certainly not without Red—without Officer Harlan knowing it."

"You are certain the key found on that table was the key to that room?"

"Yes, sir. We tried it."

"Is it possible that another key could be used in that lock?"

"I don't believe so, sir. We'd splintered out the door to get in, but we hadn't hurt the lock much. We tried a bunch of other keys, skeletons, everything. We gave it the works. None of them even budged the lock. It was a funny old lock, handmade, I wouldn't be surprised. Besides, it didn't show any signs of having been tampered with. It did when we was through."

"You also aided in the search of the rest of the basement?"

"Yes, sir."

"Any yield there?"

"Well, sir, in the storage room. On the rocking chair in there was a black coat, not a heavy coat, just sort of dropped there. And a pocketbook, a black pocketbook, under it. There was a hat dropped down behind a box alongside."

"A moment, please."

Lieutenant Strom here spoke to one of his men, who hurried out, to return with a bundle. It was opened on the desk; the errand runner held up the contents.

"These the clothes found in that storage room, Foster?"

"Yes, sir."

He was told to stand down, while Mrs. Halloran and Mr. Banks identified the clothing as having been worn by Mrs. Garr at the station. Officer Foster was then recalled.

"Did you also assist Lieutenant Strom in his search of the other rooms occupied by Mrs. Garr?"

"Yes, sir."

"Of what do they consist?"

"One parlor, one small room under the stairs, and one hall, sir."

I almost squealed out loud. Mrs. Halloran and I had forgotten that Mrs. Garr occupied the hall. She did, of course. But it seemed so public. Bookcase. Black leather chair and davenport. Phone. Rug. Once searched by the police, could they still conceal anything? I doubted it, but I imagined Mrs. Halloran would soon know for certain! My mind went back to the coroner.

"Where were the deposit-box keys found?"

"In the handbag."

"You considered your search of the rooms thorough?"

"Yes, sir," said Officer Foster fervently. "It sure was a surprise to me when those dames dug up some more dough!"

There was laughter at this, and a general craning of necks in my direction, as if I hadn't had the search taken out of my hands; Lieutenant Strom favored me with an extremely peevish look. It was nice for him, I could see that, having his thoroughness shown up.

"Well, we can't all be women," the coroner said, and there was another wave of laughter. "Now, Foster, it has been suggested that Mrs. Garr believed her house had been infested by a prowler, or prowlers, searching either for money or something else of value. When you searched Mrs. Garr's possessions after the discovery of her death, which we know was almost a week after she had come by her death, did you see any signs that those possessions had been previously searched?"

Officer Foster made a dramatic pause before answering.

"That's a hard question to answer, sir, me not knowing the old lady, whether she was neat or not. But it was my impression at the time, sir, and it's my impression now, that someone had."

15

THERE WAS A SENSATION in the room at this. Mrs. Halloran leaped to her feet, yelling:

"I knew somebody was a-robbin' me! You just tell me who it was and I'll get the G-men on 'em!"

Mr. Halloran, also on his feet, joined in.

"We'll get the G-men anyhow," he screamed. "You ain't a-goin' to get away with stealin' from us. The G-men'll show you!"

Two policemen were called to silence them and get them back in their chairs. The coroner called coldly for order and went back to Jerry.

"Now, Foster, why did you think Mrs. Garr's possessions had been searched by someone before you?"

"Well, for instance, there was a lot of pictures on the walls, and they were almost all crooked, as if someone had jerked them around to look behind them. One of the cushions on the davenport had a tear sewed up on one side; that tear had been slit open with a knife, and the slit side turned down."

I'd thought the police themselves guilty of that, Saturday.

"Then the drawers in the bureau in that room under the stairs were messed around a good deal. That was where we found the biggest wad; we took the bottom drawer clear out."

Was someone, right there in that room, being moved to fury because he, or she, had missed that wad? I looked along the line: the Wallers, Miss Sands, Mr. Buffingham, Mr. Grant; every face showed intent interest, nothing more. The Hallorans showed only thwarted greed, the Tewmans wistfulness. Mr. Kistler's funny face just looked eager and thoughtful.

I was thoughtful myself. This prowling was another thing I should have suspected. Of course the murderer, knowing Mrs. Garr dead, had had from that Friday until the next Thursday to go on his quiet hunt.

The rest of the testimony gave me nothing new. One after the other, all that interminable afternoon, we were called and re-called, until we felt dulled and apathetic. Alibis were gone over, Mrs. Halloran maintaining a straight face through the account of her husband's Friday night. No, none of us thought Mr. Waller or Mr. Kistler could have thrown the key into that kitchen on Thursday evening when the door was broken in. No, we had not seen or heard anything of Mrs. Garr after eight thirty of that Friday. Yes, the attack on Mrs. Dacres was discovered shortly after midnight. On and on, over and over. I could see the jurors' faces stiffen in an agony of weariness.

It was like a breath of fresh air in the room when the coroner closed the testimony and turned to address the jury. He picked up several sheets of typed paper from the desk.

"Ladies and gentlemen, the purpose of this inquest is to determine whether Mrs. Garr died a natural death or whether she was murdered.

"In order to lift the facts of the case for you from out the welter of testimony you have just heard, I shall summarize the known activities of Mrs. Garr during the time under question, drawing only those deductions which seem inevitable.

"We know, then, that Mrs. Garr purchased, on Tuesday or Wednesday afternoon of the week preceding Memorial Day, one ticket to Chicago on a train leaving at 8:05 p.m. on Friday, May twenty-eighth. She presented one such ticket to Mrs. Halloran. Mrs. Halloran and Mrs. Garr left 593 Trent Street to start on this trip to Chicago at approximately seven twenty p.m. of that Friday. At the train gate, Mrs. Garr made an apparent search for her ticket, did not find it, sent Mrs. Halloran on, saying she would follow. Instead of following, however, she left the group at the train gate.

"Now, the deduction which has been drawn from these facts is that Mrs. Garr did not intend to go to Chicago; that the projected trip was only a ruse on her part, either to get Mrs. Halloran out of the way or to induce in someone the belief that she, Mrs. Garr, was to be absent from her house over the weekend.

"Strength is given this deduction by the testimony of Mrs. Dacres, who tells us of Mrs. Garr's suspicion of prowlers. Mrs. Halloran also admits Mrs. Garr accused Mr. Halloran of prowling in her basement on a certain specified occasion.

"You, ladies and gentlemen, will have to test the strength of this deduction in your minds. Against it you must place the probability that Mrs. Garr did intend to go to Chicago, that she bought a second ticket, mislaid or had it stolen from her, and missed the train. A second ticket, indeed, turned up in the house, although good proof has been given that that ticket had never belonged to Mrs. Garr. It has not actually been proved that the trip was a ruse on Mrs. Garr's part.

"At any rate, we are certain Mrs. Garr did not go to Chicago. She may have been seen near the 593 Trent Street house around

eight thirty by Mr. Grant. This is a likely time for her return.
What happened to her from then on, we can only conjecture.

"We do know that at some time before ten o'clock the door of
Mrs. Garr's basement kitchen was opened, and one or all of the
animals shut in there escaped. If they all escaped, the dog and
two of the cats may have been returned to the kitchen or held
captive in some other room before Mrs. Dacres returned at ten
o'clock, but we have the evidence of two people that one animal,
the female cat, was loose in the house at ten o'clock. We are also
sure that no animals at all were loose in the house when Officer
Foster searched the house shortly after midnight.

"We know, too, that at some time Mrs. Garr's hat, coat, and
handbag were left in the storage room, either by herself or some
other person. Whether this was before or after the search on
Friday night, we cannot be certain. The room was looked over
that time, but Officer Foster was looking for a person, not a few
clothes on a chair.

"I will now enter more closely into whether Mrs. Garr was or
was not murdered. Nothing, you remember, is known of her activities from eighty thirty p.m. of that Friday. I will first consider
the possibility of murder.

"Here a variety of occurrences is possible.

"We know, from the police surgeon's testimony, that the
body was probably placed in the room in which it was found not
later than Saturday. Sometime, then, during Friday night, since
such a thing would be extremely difficult to do during the day.

"Could Mrs. Garr have been murdered outside the house?

"This would entail bringing her to the house, carrying her
either through the one front-entrance door and the front hall, or
through the rear door and Mrs. Dacres' apartment." (You can
imagine yourself how that one tensed me!) "There is a door with
stairs to the basement in Mrs. Dacres' kitchen, but that door has

a rusted bolt on Mrs. Dacres' side and is nailed shut on the other. Heavy dust on those stairs was undisturbed. The body, therefore, would have to have been brought in through the front. Extremely risky, but it may have been done. Why? We are not here entering into motives, though I may just as well interpolate here as later that motives may have been plentiful. Mrs. Garr was a woman with whose infamous past you have been tersely acquainted. And she was given to secreting small sums of money around the house. Such money was found.

"To return to our outside murder. If Mrs. Garr was thus returned to the house, dead or alive, by her murderer, it may have been between eight-five and ten, between ten and midnight, between the finish of the search and daylight. Which time we do not know. We only know, from the cat, that the kitchen door had been opened before ten o'clock and was opened again to receive the cat between ten and midnight. It is very unlikely that these activities could have been carried on by anyone not well acquainted with the house.

"We shall now consider the likelier possibility of Mrs. Garr's having been murdered inside the house.

"In that case, she may have returned to the house by herself anytime between eight-five and ten, anytime between ten and midnight, anytime after the search. At any rate, she meets or is met by the murderer within the house and is killed and locked in the kitchen with her pets. One witness in particular has shown a strong belief that Mrs. Garr surprised a prowler at work and was killed by them willfully or in self-defense. It is also suggested that this same prowler, since there could scarcely be two, is the one who attacked Mrs. Dacres later. We know this prowler did not break into the house through Mrs. Dacres' apartment, because her chairs were still hooked under the doorknobs of her front doors when she recovered.

"No evidence has shown how this possible murderer locked the animals and the remains in the kitchen, and left the one key inside.

"You must also bear in mind that the fact that Mrs. Garr's possessions may have been searched in her absence does not prove that such a thief committed murder.

"Nor must you be influenced by merely the strong belief some of the witnesses have shown that Mrs. Garr was murdered.

"I shall now consider the case of natural death. In that case, the simple course of events would seem to be this.

"Mrs. Garr descended into her basement on her return to the house around eight thirty. She may have sat in the storage room on her accustomed chair. She has left her wraps and handbag in the storage room. Sometime before ten o'clock, she has opened the door of the basement kitchen, and the cat escapes. She may have been down there when Mrs. Dacres returned at ten. No one in the house will admit having gone to the cellar that evening, at any time before the search. At some time between ten and midnight Mrs. Garr recaptures the cat, returns it to the kitchen with the others. She may have been listening for prowlers; at any rate, she sits in the kitchen in the dark. She is subject to heart attacks. She suffers, then, such an attack and is overcome by apoplexy or any sudden illness. She dies. This may have been before or after the search of the house; it may even have been the sounds of the attack on Mrs. Dacres and the subsequent tumult that brought on her illness.

"It is extremely regrettable that the basement kitchen was not searched with the rest of the house that night; there is great possibility she was still living; at any rate the cause of death could then have been easily ascertained.

"The foregoing is all conjecture, I repeat. All that is known is that the remains of Mrs. Garr were found late the next Thursday

evening, in such condition that it has proved impossible to determine the cause or exact time of her death.

"Circumstantiating evidence for a natural death is the key to
the room in which Mrs. Garr was found. The door was locked,
and the key inside. Fiction to the contrary, this is very difficult
to effect, for any murderer.

"Ladies and gentlemen, you have been given exact accounts of
the admitted activities of all persons well acquainted with the
house at 593 Trent Street. If your verdict is murder you may, if you
have determined by whom it was committed, name that person."

He stopped talking.

The jury stood up, in a dazed, blundering way, and straggled
out of the room by a side door.

I looked back to the coroner. He was sitting expansively back,
his hands patting his sides. Lieutenant Strom, next to him, was
smiling slightly. I started—was he smiling at me? I had only an
instant to wonder in—he turned immediately to speak to the
coroner.

Hodge Kistler, beside me, made the whisper of a whistle.

"What'll the answer be?"

"Murder. I'm sure it's murder," I whispered back.

"You had your mind made up beforehand."

"Didn't you?"

"M-m-m-m."

"How long do you think it'll take?"

"Any time, up to and including hours."

"F'heaven's sake! Then let's take up our legs and walk!"

We both got up, stretched, walked around the room. The others, when they saw we weren't stopped, got up to do likewise,
pausing in little groups of three and four to whisper and talk. The
atmosphere around the audience was heavy with suspense; only
the policemen walked in lighter air. They huddled to talk, too,

though; I waited until Lieutenant Strom was momentarily detached, and went to speak to him. Mr. Kistler followed.

"Excellently well reasoned, Lieutenant Strom."

"Why aren't you congratulating the coroner on that?" He glinted at me, smiling with his lower lip.

"I recognized the style."

"Nice to be appreciated."

"Oh, I did. I was thinking I couldn't have done better myself."

The lieutenant howled.

"Of all the conceited little minxes!" And to Mr. Kistler: "How do you ever stand a girl like that?"

"She thinks I haven't any, so she hasn't started judging my mental output yet," Mr. Kistler said.

"Surprised?" the lieutenant asked me.

"No. Why?"

"You mean you haven't changed your mind about anything?"

"No. Why should I?"

"How'd you like to have me pass judgment on your mental processes?" He laughed again.

"Go ahead."

"Spare the child," Hodge Kistler broke in. "What's the verdict going to be?"

"Ask me, with all these powerful intellects around?"

"Don't you know yourself?" I put that one in; it was the worst I thought up on the spur of the moment.

"Sure, I know. But do I tell? Just this much—there won't be any detective in your front hall tonight. You haven't had a tail all day. There. Think that one out."

He laughed at me again and went back to his coroner.

"What does he mean?" I asked Hodge Kistler excitedly. "Does he mean they have it all solved? They have the murderer?"

"Maybe." Mr. Kistler's eyes showed thinking, too. "Or maybe

they think the whole thing's just a washout. Just an insignificant old woman, better dead, dying of the infirmities of age."

"It's just got to be murder! I know it's murder!"

I was in a fever of impatience. We went out to get chocolate bars at the stand; I kept running back, thinking I heard sounds of the jury returning. The others were nervous, too. Mrs. Halloran flounced away from her husband and stood twisting her hands. Mr. Grant sat without moving in his chair, his face thinner than it had been, curiously empty. Mr. Buffingham strode back and forth along the side of the room, tapping his eternal cigarette ashes on the floor, fixing his eyes moodily downward, or darting quick glances at one group or another. Miss Sands whispered to the Wallers in a corner. The Tewmans wandered to the door, looking at passersby, standing where everyone bumped them going in or out.

It was after six when the jurors went out. When seven came and they hadn't returned, I asked Mr. Kistler: "What's it usually mean when the jury takes a long time?"

He shrugged. "Someone's a holder-outer."

If there was just one holder-outer, he was a passing good one. It was nearly eight before we saw the doorknob of the door behind which the jury had retired turning, and the widening space between door and frame.

We all scrambled for our seats; the jury filed portentously into theirs.

There was one of those solemn hushes.

The coroner, speaking in ordinary tones, asked the question.

One juryman had remained standing; he was the one that replied.

"We find that Mrs. Garr died a natural death, from cause or causes unknown."

I couldn't believe it. I swung my eyes quickly to Lieutenant

Strom. This time there wasn't any doubt of it. His hooded eyes were directly on me, and his lips smiled triumphantly, sardonically.

I felt as if I had been sailing away up in the sky under a parachute, and the parachute had suddenly folded.

So that was the answer. That was the end.

"Do you mean to say," I asked Mr. Kistler as he hustled me out, "that that's all there is? The police won't do any more?"

"Sure. Your mystery's exploded—there wasn't any mystery. All there was was a poor old lady dying off by herself, in the wrong company. That's what the police department thinks. As far as they're concerned, it's settled. There won't be another detective in that house from now until its last brick is dust in a pedestrian's eye."

Oh, how mistaken he was about *that*!

But I didn't know that then. Not knowing, I enjoyed my hamburgers very much. That's what we had for dinner. Reversal to type, Mr. Kistler said, after our fancy lunch.

Mr. Kistler took the inquest calmly, but I—there's no second way of diagnosing my emotions—was furious.

"To think a man is capable of handling facts and ideas as beautifully as Lieutenant Strom did in his summing up of the case, and then this is the conclusion he draws! Of all the idiots!"

"Did the thought ever trickle into your sweet little head that Lieutenant Strom might be right? After all, he's had experience with murders. You haven't. All you have is a feeling for drama. You feel nothing but murder would fit the particularly nasty circumstances, and so you keep plugging for death by violence."

"Strom can't be right. I know he's wrong."

Mr. Kistler waved the hand holding the hamburger.

"Let's hear you prove it. You wouldn't want to send anyone to the electric chair on feelings, would you?"

I couldn't prove it, of course.

"All right, that laughs you down. Now forget it. This is a holiday. Anytime I take you out is always a holiday. Let's go to a movie and otherwise dissipate. Did you ever send any rum down your intellectual neck? I thought not. Tonight sees the beginning of a new life for you. Not too literally, I hope, of course."

We had fun. I had my first rum sling and saw a movie through it, and we danced. All that hasn't a lot to do with the death that lived and walked in Mrs. Garr's house, so I'll leave it with this honorable mention.

It was perhaps three o'clock when we went home, groping in the dark, quiet, unpoliced hall, pausing to say good night at my door. I unlocked my door, took a swift look to see that all was well—I did this every time, now, knowing how many skeleton keys might unlock my door when I was gone—and reported all okay before Hodge Kistler went upstairs.

I felt good; I was happy, the rum was still a sweet fire inside me. I got ready for bed happy, but not too happy not to hook my chairs under the knobs as usual. I felt awfully safe in the security of those chairs; I smiled back at the evening; I forgot Mrs. Garr entirely, and slept.

I HAVEN'T ANY IDEA how much later it was when I woke.

I woke thinking, *How dark it is!* and lay there, puzzling about the dark. Even if the moon doesn't shine, the streetlamp on the corner always makes my room full of that yellow haze in which objects are perfectly visible.

There wasn't any light there now. Only blackness.

I moved my face slowly, enough so I could see where the windows usually were. Blackness. But no. A thread-thin line of light.

My shades were down.

That was the last moment I breathed.

As surely as if I saw it then with my eyes, I saw myself letting those shades up that night, as usual.

There was sound and movement in the room now. Air, shaken, flowed over my stiffened face. Sound of movement—stealthy, purposeful, deadly. Death. The death that lived in Mrs. Garr's house. Death walking slowly, quietly, surely in my room.

My body was iron, my throat was an empty tube; I opened my mouth to scream and no sound came out of me. An inch at a time I moved my stiffened, weak right arm toward the side of the bed.

The tips of my fingers touched cloth.

I DON'T HAVE TO guess what will go on in my mind when my life is over. I got ready to have it end then. Somewhere in the quiet inside me my lost voice said, "Oh, God, I prepare to die."

The same instant a stunning blow came at me out of the darkness.

16

PEOPLE IN GOOD HEALTH sometimes take a ghoulish enjoyment out of talking about death. I've heard them, so that means I've listened.

But from now on, anyone is going to have a hard time to make me believe dying is pleasant. The place where you go when you die is black; it's a pit, and there isn't even quiet there, no rest, there's terrible pain; you have to break before there's rest, you have to break and stop being. There's terrible pain cracking your weakness, tearing you apart, shredding you, pulling you out thinner and thinner like faint elastic, pulling you out, until the thread of your life is so tenuous it isn't there at all; you're gone; you aren't anymore, here or in heaven or even in death's black pit.

I was almost there.

I was so close that all I had to do was just that final letting go, and then I could have been quiet, because there was no more of me.

It was frightful, coming back. I had to call my substance back, re-create it out of the black pit, and I was so weak. I'd flag, and flow away from myself again, and start anew.

I came back, of course. You know, or I wouldn't be writing this.

I came back into white light, white heat, white pain.

Compared to it, even the black was better. I wanted to slip back, but THEY wouldn't let me. THEY kept doing things to me. Peculiar things; I couldn't distinguish what. It wasn't for a long while that THEY began to break down into people. A man in shirtsleeves, working so hard. Hodge Kistler. White face. Mr. Waller. Lieutenant Strom. Funny. Lieutenant Strom. Not another detective . . . until dust in your eye. I tried to get away from them, but they wouldn't let me. They slapped me and stuck me with pins and poured things down my throat. I was more and more awake. Much against my will. I could locate one worst pain now. My head. Appendicitis in my head. Rum. Did rum do that to me? No, not rum. The THING by the bed. Death.

I almost went out again.

But this time it was easier to come back.

I looked up at the face over me. Hodge Kistler's face. White. Sweating.

"It hit me." That was my voice. I must have left most of it back in the pit.

"Take it easy, but try not to drop off again. Try, try, will you?"

"My head."

A river of air ran back and forth across his face with the smile on it.

"You're still wearing it. It'll fit again."

He stood back, and his voice from away on the other side of the room said, "How's she doing, Doc?"

"Fine," another oceangoing voice boomed back. "Who's going

to be the nurse around here? Fine. Just don't let her drop off to sleep before noon."

It was quiet after that except for the noon whistles in my head. Sometimes Mrs. Waller and sometimes Mr. Kistler was beside my bed. Every time I closed my eyes, they slapped me, which didn't seem kind when I felt so badly. So I found a way to sleep with my eyes open. They didn't object to that.

Finally they really let me sleep. When I woke up, the light was on in the middle of my ceiling, with a paper bag tied around it. People do such ridiculous things. But I was better. My head had decided to run locomotives instead of whistles. Locomotives jar, but they're nicer than whistles. My body was detached from me, but there I was inside it, even if I was loose. I reached up and turned my mind on, like a radio dial. Nice to think again, even if there was a lot of static. Hodge Kistler was sitting beside the bed, his legs stuck out in front of him and his hands in his pants pockets, looking grimmer than I'd ever thought he could look.

"Hello," I said.

He jumped.

"Why, hello! Look who's back in town!" He brought his face down close to me; he was smiling all over it.

"Who did it?"

"If you won't be slithering away again I'll tell you. We don't know."

"You mean you didn't catch them?"

"Gwynne, it's as much a mystery as all the rest."

I wasn't too weak for malice.

"Do the police—does Lieutenant Strom say it was a natural dea—say I fell out of bed on my head?"

He smiled with tight lips.

"If you want to crow, you can. You could buy two of Lieutenant Strom today for one mildewed Chinese yen."

"My head—is it broken?"

"Say, your head can't be broken."

"Then why do I feel so awful?"

"Listen, Gwynne. Smell."

I smelled. "Funny. Like—"

"Like ether?"

"Yes."

"Well, whoever it was went one better than ether. It was an ether dry cleaner. You've got a right to feel rotten."

"I do. You don't have to worry about that."

"Aw, Gwynee." He took my hand. "I'm awfully, awfully sorry."

"I should have taken you up on your invitation."

"Don't."

"You aren't going to leave me here tonight, are you?"

"Don't worry. I've stayed up all night before."

That was a peaceful thought. I went to sleep on it, and this time I really slept. When I woke again, the light was still going inside the paper bag on the ceiling, but sunlight was flowing in the windows, too. Hodge Kistler was sitting fast asleep in the armchair jammed close to my couch, his head almost down to his shoulder, his feet up on another chair, his hands limp and open at his sides, with the palms outward.

It was the only time I'd ever seen him look pathetic.

Clearly I heard a step in the hall; startled, I turned my head. The face of the Wilson-chinned policeman appeared briefly around the door casing, turned owlish eyes on me, disappeared again.

I lifted my head cautiously from the pillow; it didn't fall apart. In fact it was quite a decent head. It was sore when I touched it, but outside of a feeling that I ought to hold on to it with my hands to keep it in place on my neck, it didn't bother me.

I slid down the couch, hoping not to disturb Mr. Kistler in the armchair. I wasn't successful. At the first slide his eyes popped wide open.

"Hey, what're you doing?"

"I'm hungry." I was, too.

"Hungry?" he asked incredulously.

"Of course I'm hungry."

"You can't be hungry. Your stomach's upset."

"I can too be. I should know."

He stood up, yawned, shook himself.

"All you get is orange juice. The doctor said so. Nothing yesterday. Orange juice today."

That was all I did get, too, all day long. We fought about whether I was to get up, too; he called the doctor by phone and came back disgruntled.

"The doc says all right, get up, if you're so damn healthy. Go back to bed the minute you feel weak. I don't see why you don't feel weak; I do. And oh, gosh, I've got to go to work. It's Wednesday, do you know that? Wednesday. I'm going to tell that cop to keep an eye on you."

The first thing I did when I got on my feet was to turn off the ceiling light. I stood in the middle of my bed-living-dining-room floor, reorienting myself.

Heavens, things were in a mess. Newspapers, magazines, books strewn on the floor. The drawers of the buffet yawning, their contents tumbled and spilling over. The lower drawer was entirely out; it stood on the floor. Dishes were pushed about in the cabinet above.

I didn't get it. Even if the people who'd dragged me back to life had needed to find things in a hurry, they needn't have made a mess like this. It was willful, malicious!

I walked toward the passageway to my kitchen. Here, too, on

the right of the little hall, drawers had been pulled out, their contents jumbled. Heartsick, I looked into my closet—all my clothes off their hangers, lying in tumbled heaps on the floor; my trunk was open and its contents thrown to right and left.

The kitchen was in the same state. Mrs. Garr's closet was worst.

I got it then.

And stood there thinking what a fool I was.

I hadn't told the police about the closet Mrs. Garr retained in my kitchen. I hadn't even thought of it.

Coming and going in that kitchen, I hadn't even thought of it as a place to search. It seemed incredible, now, that I hadn't. When I'd first moved into the place I'd been annoyed at Mrs. Garr's holding this corner of my domain. But, except for one time, she hadn't bothered me to get into it. I'd forgotten it was there. I no more thought of it as existing than I did the unused basement stairs beside it. I bent (careful, my head) to pick up an old-fashioned, mothbally mink jacket from the floor; it was torn, slashed. I picked up other garments. A musty hat, torn savagely. A faded, padded sachet, ripped. Boxes and small keepsakes lay together in the heap.

I had it, all right, then. Someone had been ransacking my apartment. On purpose.

I had proof now. There was a prowler. He hadn't found what he wanted in Mrs. Garr's part of the house. So now he had searched mine.

That was why I'd been attacked. He had to get me out of the way.

What was he hunting? What, in heaven's name, could arouse this frenzied seeking? Had he found what he wanted? Found it, here in this closet?

I got dizzy, standing there, and staggered back to bed.

I drank more of the orange juice Hodge had left on the table there. It didn't help much. Orange juice may be full of vitamins, but bacon and eggs keep a body upright. My body rested on the couch but my mind kept working.

What was this insatiable marauder hunting? Money? More money? He must already have found some, between that Friday and the Thursday when the death was discovered; the police, Mrs. Halloran, and I had found the well-hidden caches; these were probably only part of the whole. Suddenly I knew why the macaroni had been spilled on the table below; there had been money hidden there, deep within. I had proof that some of Mrs. Garr's money had been found, perhaps—that torn five-dollar bill. Someone must want money desperately.

Mr. Buffingham with his son in jail, needing lawyers, needing bought witnesses. Mr. Grant, living there, old, not working, liking luxury. What did he live on? Miss Sands. Aging. Hating her job and afraid of losing it. The Wallers, living there on odd jobs, rent-free. The greedy Hallorans. The poor Tewmans.

And, to be consistent, Mr. Kistler, struggling to keep his *Guide* alive. And for the matter of that, Mrs. Dacres. Jobless.

Who didn't want money?

No, I thought. *If it's money, it must be a lot of money.*

Someone knows there's one big pile somewhere. A big pile, that Mrs. Garr would hide best of all, of course. She was shrewd. The ransacker had taken what money he found. There never had been any left among the things ransacked.

Did that prove it was money he was after? No, that just showed he took what he found. What else could there be? Some record out of Mrs. Garr's lurid past? Some incriminating record? Who could be seeking such a thing?

Ever since I'd seen that rent-receipt book on Saturday afternoon, I'd suspected Mrs. Garr was probably blackmailing two boarders. Miss Sands. Why would an aging saleswoman pay blackmail? Yet how else explain five dollars a week for that room? And Mr. Buffingham. Well, some escapade of his son's was the best guess there.

I might know, too, of two who were potentially blackmailing Mrs. Garr. The Wallers. Even if they did produce a note, for what did she owe them that two thousand dollars? No, the rent they didn't pay made them suspect.

The Hallorans. It wasn't unlikely Mrs. Garr held notes of theirs for money she'd given them. Was there a record of some debt that was being sought? And whatever it was, had the end come now? Was the attack on me, the pillage of my rooms, the last link in the chain? Had the prowler found there, at last, what he hunted?

The answer was right there in my living room.

No, it hadn't been found.

No one would have been too stupid not to search Mrs. Garr's closet first. If what was hunted had been found there, the search would have ended.

But it hadn't.

It had gone on through my entire apartment. The disorder here was no red herring. I could have done a neater job, but not a more thorough one.

I knew well enough that there was nothing hidden among my things.

There was only one conclusion to draw. The hunter was still unsatisfied.

I closed my eyes and wondered if I'd be able to live through what was bound to come.

Right there, I quit the Garr case as fun. I went into it as battle: I get the murderer before he gets me.

Skirmishes began with the doorbell's ring, the door's opening, heavy feet in the hall. Lieutenant Strom, flanked by two men, stood beside my bed.

"Well, coming around?"

"I'm practically bursting with health."

"That's one gray hair less on my head. I regret very much that this has happened, Mrs. Dacres. If you want to light into me, go right ahead."

"You still think Mrs. Garr's death wasn't murder?"

He sat down in the armchair and sighed.

"Mrs. Dacres, did you ever spend any thought at all on why society makes such a hue and cry about murder? After all, by and large, I've found out that a good many people who get murdered leave the world better off for their absence. Now, this is the way I look at it. One person kills another, willfully or accidentally. Society feels, naturally, that such a crime should be punished.

"But look at that punishment. It usually consists, or is supposed to, of removal from society—complete excision—either by life imprisonment or death. Why—punishment? Vengeance? Retribution? Not entirely. To cure the murderer of murdering? We haven't found that murder is curable. To stop other people from murdering in their turn? It doesn't work that way; new murderers spring up under the harshest laws.

"No. It's because a person who has killed once, and gotten away with it, is so likely to kill again. It's to remove a menace from people still living.

"Now, you take Mrs. Garr. We can't prove she didn't die a natural death. The simplest explanation, and the one that takes in everything that happened, is that she died naturally. And if she was assisted to die, what's the likelihood that she was pushed over by some surprised prowler? She had a bad heart. Now, few sneak thieves intend murder. He's out for small stuff. No gun on him; he didn't shoot her. No poison administered. The thief's scared, runs. We catch and punish him if we can, but if we can't, then what? *He isn't the type to murder again.* Come along with me so far?"

"I see your argument."

"That's the way things looked up until Monday night. We meant to keep an eye on things here, sure. Officers were ordered to patrol this block."

"It's nice to be so well protected."

"Have your sarcasm. Oh, what a different tale you've made out of this!"

"What do you mean?"

"I mean that it's become attempted murder. Good, solid, tangible attempted murder, with clues. I'm out to get someone now. Oh, yes, indeed. A deliberate attack! Now we know the guy's dangerous. Now we know he's the type that kills again. Now we've got to pick him off society like a flea off a dog, and see he doesn't get back. We can't have him killing off perfectly good, healthy young women"—he smiled slowly down—"damn nice young women, in their own peculiar way."

"Norwegians shouldn't kiss the blarney stone," I said. "It isn't in character. I'm glad to know I'm so important."

"You're going to have all the importance you can stand today. Because I'm going to get every person who was or could have been under this roof for chloroforming purposes that night come in here and repeat the stories they told me yesterday. I'll catch any discrepancies, and you catch any false note, any surprising emotion, anything you think is significant. Fortunately we're confined to people who could have known about Mrs. Garr's keeping things in that closet in your kitchen. By the way, isn't that another item you forgot to tell me?"

"I'm sorry."

"You're suffering for it yourself. Will that teach you to tell the police everything?"

"Yes, sir."

"Think you can stand having me start on witnesses today?"

"Oh my, yes." I sat up in bed, had pillows piled behind me, and almost forgot I'd had no food. "But I want to know what happened, first! I haven't been told one word!"

He laughed. "I can imagine the rapacious state of your mind. Okay, here goes, as testified. You celebrated the inquest with Mr. Kistler, imbibing well and on the whole wisely. Correct?"

"Correct."

"You come home at three a.m. or thereabouts, handling yourself ably. You say good night to Mr. Kistler at your door, after having turned on your light, looked the apartment over, and reported all okay."

"Right."

"Mr. Kistler's testimony. That is all we know of you for some time. Tuesday morning comes. Six o'clock. The telephone rings. It rings and rings. It finally awakens Miss Sands, upstairs. She comes down, answers. It is for Mr. Kistler. She goes up, knocks at his door until he answers. Mr. Kistler, furious, comes downstairs. It turns out the call is from Mr. Trowbridge, who, it seems, is out celebrating because the *Guide* has secured a big advertising contract—"

"Oh, and Hodge didn't tell me! That must be the one he was after Saturday!"

"Yep. Guy came through on Monday. Mr. Trowbridge, it seems, celebrates neither well nor wisely, and has suddenly been stricken with a desire to know how the inquest came out. It is the very shank of the evening, to him. Mr. Kistler hangs up, starts back to bed.

"A thought hits him and he stops on the first step. Why did Miss Sands answer the phone?

"Her room is upstairs, far from the phone. Your bed, on the contrary, is right on the other side of the wall. You are in the habit of rushing out to answer. He decides it is because of the evening before, and turns to the stairs again, when something else hits him.

"A smell.

"He walks over to your doors, sniffs, and then sniffs under the doors. He gets it strong there—ether and naphtha. Why would you be dry-cleaning, coming home at three a.m.? Before six a.m.? He knocks softly, you don't answer. He calls, you don't answer. He takes a run and tries to break the doors down, but they're reinforced by those chairs under the knobs and won't give an inch."

"Oh, my goodness," I said.

"What?"

"The chairs. The chairs were still under the knobs?"

"I'll say they were."

I sat up straight and felt the blood draining out of my face.

"Then how did he—it—get in?"

Lieutenant Strom shook his head at me soberly.

"I've gone over this damn apartment inch by inch. I can't find one way anyone could have got in. Or out."

I stared at him, horror gripping me. What had been there in that room?

17

"LISTEN," I SAID, "I can't stand this. Not without something to eat. Can't I have something to eat?"

"Go call the doc, Van."

Van phoned, came back.

"Nothing but fruit juice till tomorrow, miss."

I used to like orange juice, too.

"I want to be shown," I said when I'd had it. "I want to be shown how no one got out or in."

"Okay, I'll fix it up just like it was before the doors were broken down. I was going to go over that anyway. So you can just as well see it at the same time."

"First tell me the rest."

"The rest was hard labor. Kistler got Waller down, and the two of them busted the lock; the chairs fell when the doors pushed open; your key was still in one of the locks. They rushed in, pulled up the shades, and there you were, with a big wad of cotton batting covering your face, still sopping with the God

damn dry cleaner. Kistler did a lot of work on you, young lady.
If you're glad to be alive yet, you can thank him for it."

"He is nice, isn't he?"

"Sure. Even men think he's nice."

"That proves it. I'll do a nice job of thanks. No sign of where
the ether came from?"

"Oh, sure. Empty can by the couch. Kleenfine."

A picture flashed back into my mind.

"Oh, my goodness! Miss Sands!"

"What's that?"

"Miss Sands. I was upstairs to ask her a question. She was
pressing clothes. And cleaning spots off them with a dry cleaner
on a rag. I saw the can."

"Kleenfine?"

"Yes."

"Well, I brought that out yesterday, in a way. Asked them all
if they had a can. She admitted it. She and Mrs. Waller both did.
It's a common home cleaner. They both showed me their can,
partially full. You can't base much of a case on that alone. Anyone can buy it."

He was eyeing me narrowly.

"It's the sort of plan a woman would think of," I began slowly.

"Um. Before we go into that, there's something I want to go
into with you. What did you go upstairs to ask Miss Sands?"

"Oh. Well, I was hot on the trail of Mr. Halloran then. And I
was thinking about the cat in the hall at ten o'clock. Someone
caught it and put it back in the kitchen before midnight. So I
went up to ask if anyone had seen or heard anyone who might
have done so."

His eyes were hard on my face.

"Who'd you ask?"

"Why, Mr. Buffingham first, and then Mr. Grant, Miss Sands, the Wallers. Mr. Kistler wasn't home either time, of course. None of them had heard anything."

Lieutenant Strom sat forward impressively.

"Has it penetrated your little noodle that a lot worse things happened to you night before last than were necessary to keep you out of the way of a little ransacking? If you'd been found two hours later than you were, probably only one hour later, you would have been dead. Whoever came here that night came with deliberate intent to murder. To murder you."

"Oh my," I said as if I were Mrs. Halloran. "It sounds awfully bloodthirsty when you put it that way."

He snorted. "That isn't what you should be saying. You should be asking a question."

"Why, you mean?"

"Exactly."

"Well, I was in the way. And then I have sort of been nosing around, you know."

He snorted again. "Do I know!"

"But it doesn't do me any good to pull in my horns now," I pointed out. "Because whatever I've done to make someone want to murder me, I've already done. Or if it's something I know, I already know it. I can't undo it or unknow it. The only thing I can do is go ahead and get him before he gets me."

"Dacres the lionhearted. You might acquaint me with a few of your hidden secrets."

"Well, of course it's too late to tell you about the closet in my kitchen. I really forgot that myself."

"Former comment repeated."

"Then there's the receipt book. I found that on Saturday when you gave me permission to look through Mrs. Garr's things,

and Mrs. Halloran and I found the money. I haven't seen you
since, you know. I don't suppose your fat detective told you how
much time I spent looking at that receipt book?"

"No!"

I told him all about it then. He was very much interested in
my theory that the high rents paid by Miss Sands and Mr. Buffingham represented blackmail, and that the Wallers in turn had
been blackmailing Mrs. Garr. Then I told him what I'd deduced
that morning from the state my rooms were in, but he only listened with half his mind to that, and said yes, he'd thought the
same thing.

He got up briskly when I ended, and said he was going to
work on how my would-be murderer had gotten in and out of my
apartment. I got out of bed and into my negligee and slippers. I
showed him how I fixed the doors at night; the metal lock of my
double doors hung by a shred now, but when we forced the doors
together and hooked the chairs under the knobs they were still
tight, even without the lock.

With his two flanking detectives, he spent a good half hour
on those doors, examining the hinges, the casings, the knobs.
Van got on the outside to force the doors; the chairs fell with a
clatter that would have waked me a dozen times over even if I'd
been drunk, which I wasn't.

"That's the way Kistler says they fell in when he and Waller
broke in here Tuesday morning," said the lieutenant.

"No one could go out through those doors, lock them, leave
the key inside, and hook the chairs under the knobs after himself," I said. "That's flat."

"We'd sort of figured that, too," the lieutenant replied dryly.

"Are you sure he—it—wasn't still in here when the door was
broken in yesterday morning?"

"Well, the first thing Waller says he did was to look around, and Kistler saw him do it. I guess he even took some time off from you to look around himself, being a little mad. They both swear there couldn't a soul have escaped 'em. After we got here we looked again, and there wasn't a trace. This place isn't so big anyone could have hid out on Waller or Kistler, either."

After that he went on to the windows. I'd had the windows open, of course. From the top. But they were screened. Well screened, being on the ground floor. One screen was new—the one the policemen had gone through to capture Buffingham's son. Every screen was held on the outside by those little gadgets that turn, and on the inside by hooks. They went over those screens with magnifying glasses, for the least fresh sign of a screwdriver or hammer. But even if they had found any, it would have been impossible for anyone to come and go by any of those windows, leaving the screens fastened both inside and out.

The kitchen window and the kitchen door were given thorough attention next. The kitchen door had once fitted loosely, but it had been weatherstripped; the men figured for an hour before they gave up, to admit the bolt couldn't possibly have been pulled by any contrivance from the outside, however ingenious.

"Besides," I said from my watchtower on the kitchen table, "I've decided that whoever's doing this is someone stupid. You have to look for something easy."

I'll skip the answers I got.

They passed on to the unused door to the unused staircase. Its bolt was rusted as stiffly as ever; the lieutenant worked at it until the veins bulged on his forehead; couldn't budge it.

They tapped the walls, took the rugs up off the floors, and examined the ceilings. Not a chance.

They stood in the living room, then, looking at each other in gloomy defeat. Lieutenant Strom rallied.

"Now, men, I don't believe in ghosts. Not ghosts wielding

hammers and anything as modern as Kleenfine. This was a human being, and maybe even a dumb one at that, if we're going to
go by Mrs. Dacres. Just dumb enough to wear gloves. What I
wouldn't give for a fingerprint on that Kleenfine can! We've gone
over all this stuff, and there's isn't a clue in it. All you can say for
the methods used on Mrs. Dacres is that they were thorough,
except for a lucky chance, but not expert. Our best bet is tracking him down by how he got in or out. That's what we've got to
do, concentrate on those two questions. How'd he get in? How'd
he get out?"

"He might of been in here, hiding, when Mrs. Dacres came in
that night," offered Van hopefully.

"Oh no!" That was me, appalled. "He couldn't have been! I
was all through the rooms."

"Sure of that?"

"Oh yes!"

"In the kitchen?"

"Yes."

"Lavatory?"

"Yes."

"Closet?"

"Yes. I hung my dress away. I don't have so much in my closet
anyone could hide in there."

"How about that closet of Mrs. Garr's?"

"Before all its contents got thrown out it was so full I don't
think anyone could have squeezed in. Besides, look how the lock
on it was broken. I'd certainly have noticed that."

Again the three men walked through the two rooms, looking
for hiding places. My studio couch came low to the floor. My
steamer trunk was tightly against the wall. There just wasn't any
hiding place.

"Now let's snap out of this." The lieutenant was exasperated.

"What if he did hide here? That wouldn't tell us how he got out. There's just one more place I can think of to give the works, and that's those cellar stairs. We'll get at 'em from below. Come on."

The order was to his two men, but I came, too.

"Why, the door's open!" I cried at the foot of the cellar stairs.

The lieutenant turned his hooded eyes on me.

"Sure, it was opened Monday afternoon, by the last cop before he left. Why not? We were through with it."

He went on into the room in which all that was left of Mrs. Garr had been found.

I swallowed hard, but pattered right after.

It was the first time, really, that I had been in that kitchen. Before, I'd just seen it from the furnace room; sometimes the door had stood open, but usually it had been closed. Now I saw it closely. All trace of the nightmare once dwelling there had been removed. The floor was empty, clean. But it was an unappetizing kitchen, for all that. Lavatory to the right, under mine. A door, which Van opened on a flight of stairs going up toward my kitchen. At the left, a grimy, hooded gas stove. A dust-gray cupboard. Against the wall ahead, a table.

My blood quickened.

A kitchen table. One table. The only table. It stood against the back wall, midway between the two basement windows at the back, just about under where my back porch was. It stood four feet under and about three feet to the left of the basement window that was open an inch.

The lieutenant had halted at the foot of the stairs.

"Wait!" I called.

He turned around. "What?"

"The table. Is that the table where the key was found?"

"Sure."

"Then Mrs. Garr was murdered," a loud, clear voice was saying. Mine. "And I know how the murderer got out of this room after he killed her."

The two policemen, already halfway up the stairs, came tumbling back. The three men advanced on me, almost like an army; there was something threatening in the way they stood over me.

"Okay, talk."

"It's awfully simple. The murderer walked out the door and locked it behind him. He probably caught the animals one by one, shoved them in, and locked the door behind them."

"Yeah, he shoved the key in and locked the door behind that, I suppose."

"Oh no. He waited until the house was quiet. Then he walked around to the back of the house, outside, and threw the key in through that partially opened window. It landed on the table. That was the sound I had heard down here. *Plink*, it said."

"By God, Lieutenant, I believe she's right!" Van was excited, staring up at the slit the window was open. "I bet it would make it! Wait. I'll go up and throw my keys in."

He dashed out.

The lieutenant was viewing me sourly.

"Don't mind me," he said bitterly. "Don't tell me anything. I'm the last person to tell things to. Did you ever tell me one word about things falling into the cellar?"

I was mournful about it myself. "I can't help it. I forget things. Then I see something, like the relation between that table and the window, and some remembrance flashes back."

"I wish to God they'd flash sooner. If they had, you might have spent a more comfortable day yesterday." He was definitely cross. But he was abashed, too; I knew he thought he should have thought that out about the window himself. But knowing how he felt about Mrs. Garr's death, I could imagine how perfunctorily he had gone over the room, after his squad of fingerprinters and photographers had finished that night.

By that time, Van was evidently outside, because a key sailed through the window. It hit the edge of the table, then fell to the floor.

"Throw more to the right," the lieutenant called.

The second key came in with a nice curve and landed on the table with a little metallic clink; the lieutenant flourished a handkerchief over his face.

"Not three inches from where that other damn key was. That's enough, Van."

He sat down on the edge of the table to think, juggling the keys in his hands, until Van came back.

"Okay." The lieutenant's eyes were now bright beneath their hoods. "Someone has guilty knowledge of Mrs. Garr's death. Guilty, because why, if it wasn't, would he throw in the key? And now, Mrs. Dacres, you know another little reason why you've had your two little experiences. You are suspected of having heard that key land, and the murderer's suspicions on that point are only too well confirmed. When I think how he grieves now over not having done a complete job on you, I could almost feel sorry for him. By heaven, if I'd ever lapsed from virtue anywhere near you, I'd want you murdered, too!"

He turned to the staircase from which I'd recalled him.

"Now I'm going back to where I was before you jerked me off it. And boy, was I in a whale of a place."

He took me by the shoulders, pulled me to the first step, played his flashlight ahead up the stairs.

"See those steps?"

"Yes, sir."

"Notice anything about 'em?"

"They look like ordinary steps to me."

"That all?"

"The paint's almost worn off."

"Not that. Notice anything about 'em that should be remarked, taking in mind something that was brought out at the inquest?"

He gave me time to think; I thought hard, too. The two detectives were staring over my head. I gave up.

"Okay." There was soothed satisfaction in the word. "Well, I didn't put two and two together, either, when I looked at 'em yesterday. But the minute I stepped foot to 'em this morning it hit me. One of those flashes you talk about. Remember now?"

I couldn't. The other two men were as unknowing as I was.

Greater satisfaction lit the lieutenant's voice.

"Well, I'll just repeat a few words we brought out in Jerry Foster's evidence. This is what those words were: *'The dust of those stairs was undisturbed.'*"

We got it then.

"And now what?" the lieutenant went on triumphantly, over our exclamations. *"Those stairs have been swept!* Swept! Who swept 'em? Not Tewman. She beat it out of here right after the inquest. Swears she wouldn't stay in the house. Not Halloran. Says she hasn't been near the place except when we dragged her over for questioning yesterday afternoon. We got her out of bed at three in the afternoon, Tuesday. Not my squad when I told 'em to clean up here. I was in here after they'd finished and I remember thinking how like the lazy bums it was not to sweep the stairs. No, there's only one person who would have had an interest in sweeping those stairs. And that's the guy who wanted to chloroform Mrs. Dacres. He needed those stairs. He didn't want footsteps to show. He knew fresh footsteps on dust couldn't get by. But there was a chance we wouldn't notice swept stairs. *He got through that door up there somehow!*"

He charged up.

We followed as far as the landing. He was working at the door, playing his light on the four screws in the door casing, with their heads tight against the door.

"We tested the knob for fingerprints last night. Clean. That's suspicious, too. Clean, after all the time this door hasn't been used. But I can't budge it."

Again his flash played up and down the door by the screw-heads. He gave an exclamation of delight. I could see it, too.

In the old gray paint of the door, a tiny, fresh scratch!

"A scratch! See that? A scratch! Bolt or no bolt, I'm taking these screws out of here and seeing what happens."

He took a knife from his pocket, worked at one screw with a flat-end blade that worked like a screwdriver. The screw turned tightly for the first four or five turns, then came with surprising ease the rest of the way. It wasn't five minutes before he had all four screws out.

"Golly, that was easy!"

He took the doorknob in his hand, turned it, pulled back hard.

I reached out a hand to keep him from falling backward on us.

The door had come open!

It sprang open at his first touch! As easily, as freely as any door, it flew open to reveal my everyday kitchen beyond.

It was so sudden, I couldn't think what it meant for a while.

Then I looked at the bolt.

The bolt had parted neatly, right at the edge of the door.

We all stepped through to the kitchen but stood clustering around the door, the men swearing excitedly under their breath. Both ends of the bolt were rusted solidly in their sockets; when the door was closed again both ends met; it was impossible to *see* the break with the door closed.

"Sawed!" Lieutenant Strom repeated for the tenth time, admiringly.

I was considering, startled, what I could sleep through.

"Wouldn't you think I'd wake up? It must have made some noise."

"You didn't get home until three a.m., did you?" The lieutenant decried my lack of imagination. "Plenty of time between midnight and three a.m. for anyone to saw a dozen bolts."

"You mean when I came home, he—it—was waiting down here, maybe listening just on the other side of that door—"

"That's it, all right."

"I don't think I'll ever sleep again!"

He laughed. "Sure you will."

"How can I? Thinking of that, that *something* down there, waiting for me to sleep so he could come and kill me in the dark!"

"It won't happen again," the lieutenant gave reassurance. "I'll post a man down there every night until we get this cleared up. And I'm having a locksmith in to put good new locks on all three of your doors. That satisfy you?"

"I'll never feel safe again! When I think how I *trusted* those chairs under my doorknobs . . ."

Lieutenant Strom winked at the other two men.

"The only advice I can give you is, get married. Nothing's as safe as a husband." He laughed and turned his attention back to the door.

"What a saw that took! Who's an old jailbird in this house?"

"No one that I know of. But of course you know Buffingham's son—"

"I've got that in mind."

Another thought had crossed my mind. "Would it be all right if you told me how much the Buffingham boy's bail is set for?"

"You can't get bail if you're a murderer."

"Any amount goes toward paying a lawyer, though. In a spot like that they'd have to pay cash in advance, I suppose. I wonder, do lawyers ever get a man out on the chance he can rob another bank afterward, and pay them?"

"We aren't getting anywhere talking." The lieutenant was impatient. "I've found out how this friend of yours got out and in, that's something. Right after we've had lunch, Mrs. Dacres, I'm going to begin getting those people together, and you listen to what they told me."

They went out to eat; I had orange juice, a half hour's rest, and dressed. The Hallorans must have been ordered to put in an appearance, because I heard Mrs. Halloran's voice in the front of the house while I was dressing.

Lieutenant Strom, returning, set up an impromptu court in my living room: he in my armchair with the gateleg table before him, I on the couch as both audience and jury.

The Hallorans were called. Nine of them trooped in. Mr. and Mrs. Halloran first, completely detached from their following. Seven children; I counted them. Six sly, snickering children as wild as rabbits, and one girl of perhaps eleven, the oldest, small, pinched, overworked, efficient, who pushed and slapped them into what semblance of order there was.

Mrs. Halloran did the answering to the lieutenant's questions.

"Sure, I know where we was Monday night. We was celebrating, that's where we was. Celebrating our money we come into. I'd like to know who's got a better right—"

"No one's questioning your rights. Will you repeat where you went, and when, please."

"Right home we went from that inquest and got all our dear little chillern." She waved a vague hand at the pack. "So then we went on down to El Lago restaurant like I said yesterday, my, that's a swell restaurant, and we all ordered exactly what we had a mind to, too, on account we got an advance from our lawyers." She preened herself importantly, not loath, I could see, to tell the tale of the evening's pleasures. So they had "got an advance from our lawyers"! I could see Mrs. Garr's house evaporating, dirty bricks and all.

"So then we ate. My, that El Lago certainly has got swell food. After that, the next place we went to was the Red Bubble."

A nightclub! Those children! I gasped and, taking the comment for admiration, Mrs. Halloran went blithely on.

"The best, I always say, is what chillern should get acquainted with. Some of the chillern never saw it before. My, they thought it was swell. We had tables right up to the dance floor, and me and Halloran danced; a couple of the kids went to sleep but we woke 'em up because we had met a couple and we were going on. We went to a beer parlor on Main Street, and then we went and had some hamburgers in a White House, and then we went to another beer parlor on Hampstead Street, and we all got in with a party of folks there, and my, we sure had a swell time."

"Was Mr. Halloran in the party all along?" I asked.

She tossed a coquettish head back at Mr. Halloran, who hovered on her outskirts. "Sure he was with us all the time. You don't think he'd run out on me, I hope."

Mr. Halloran replied to this sally with a silly grin. I could well imagine he wouldn't—not as long as she was an heiress. There was admiration as well as amazement in my look at the small hellions now. Whatever else they weren't, you had to say they could take it.

"Yeah." The lieutenant put a period to Mrs. Halloran. "And what's worse, we've checked it all along the line, and it works. They got home at sunup. At three a.m. they were reported far too far gone to do any delicate chloroforming. I can't see anything more in them, can you?"

The Hallorans appeared impervious to objective insult.

"No." I hated to give them up as suspects, but surely an alibi such as this could be checked thoroughly for holes. With those children, anyone present would have kept them under observation.

"That's all now." So Lieutenant Strom said to the Hallorans. They pushed and clattered out; we heard them in various stages of vociferation all through the house the rest of the afternoon. It was the first time the family had visited, en masse, their new possession. I rather wondered that they hadn't moved in. But it was less than a week, after all, since Mrs. Garr's death had become known. Less than a week! How much had happened in that time! How much must still happen!

If the Hallorans did move in . . . I shuddered. I'd have to move out. But not before this mystery was cleared up. No one was going to nine-tenths murder me and go scot-free, if I could help it.

"Call the Tewmans, Van."

Mrs. Tewman and the rabbity man came in. They, too, must have been in the hall, waiting for this.

"Now, Mr. Tewman, I want to ask you a question. Can you use the same saw on steel you can on wood?"

"Saw?"

"Yes, saw."

"I dunno. I guess so."

"Ever see any saws around this house?"

"Saws? Yeah, I guess so. Saw in the toolbox. Under the washtubs."

"Oh hell, I'll never get anywhere this way. You go ahead and repeat your story about where you were Monday night."

"Well, chief, I was at the inquest, see?" The man was trembling a little. "I'm on nights at my hamburger house, see, because my brother's on daytimes and I'm on nights. So my wife comes back to this house here to get our stuff, and I go right on down to my business. My brother is there, and we talk over this inquest, see, until he goes home around nine o'clock. And it's like I said, chief, I can prove I didn't leave my business one minute because, why, the place it's in, there wouldn't be one stick left in it when I come back if I'd went away. And it's still all there."

"That's a damn good piece of logic," the lieutenant said to me. "That story checks, too. We hunted up a couple customers. Now for you, Mrs. Tewman."

"I come right on back to the house." Her sullen voice held anger. "And I wasn't going to stay in it a minute I didn't have to, either, with that Mrs. Halloran bossing around. So the minute I seen there wasn't a cop in the hall, I went down and packed up quick. I took our stuff over to Jim's brother's house and stayed there. You ain't going to get me back here, either."

"No, Mrs. Tewman, I think we'll let you stay away. You left your key?"

"Right on top of the bookcase in the hall."

"You see?" To me. "The key was there. Of course it's possible for the Tewmans or the Hallorans to have had a duplicate key made, or to have sent someone else here Monday night. But I doubt it. Such a person wouldn't know enough about the house."

To the Tewmans he added, "You may go now."

They went with alacrity.

"I called those four witnesses first for a reason, Mrs. Dacres. I'm convinced that they had nothing whatever to do with the attack on you, and therefore, since we think the two are related, with the attack on Mrs. Garr. For my part, I intend to eliminate them in my further search for the criminal. But it's different with the rest of the people I'm interviewing. It's my best opinion that every one of them is strongly to be suspected!"

MY MIND RANGED RAPIDLY over the rest of the people who were connected with Mrs. Garr's house.

"What do you mean?" I asked flatly.

"Well, look at this thing. Was it someone outside the house? No. It was someone who had access, easy access, to the cellar. Who knew the house and the habits of its inmates thoroughly. If the murderer isn't one of the residents here I'll eat all my notes."

He gave me a side glance.

"After I had to eat that money you and Mrs. Halloran dug up I'm not taking chances with any more paper diets, either. Who do we have as possibilities, then? First, Kistler. Plenty easy for him to have sneaked downstairs again after three a.m., Mrs. Dacres?" He grinned. "Somehow you don't seem the suicide type, and it's very difficult to bat yourself on the head first and then chloroform yourself second."

"By the way"—I was curious—"did you ever find what hit me?"

"Sure. Didn't I tell you? Hammer from the toolbox downstairs. Not a print on that, either. That's another argument it was someone in the house. Knew where the tools were."

I shuddered.

"All right. Where were we? Kistler. Buffingham. Grant. Miss Sands. The Wallers. Six people. If it isn't one of those six people I'll eat—no, I guess I better quit eating."

"I don't think it was a woman. I think it was a man. Except that Miss Sands does have that can—"

"Sure. Except. Except. And if it was the Wallers they must both be in on it. They stick together on their story, anyhow. So that really makes just five possibilities."

"Too bad you can't just put all six in jail."

"You don't know how I wish I could. Innocent till proved guilty, pooey. Let's have Buffingham down, Van."

Van came back alone.

"Gone to work. Gus in the hall here says Johnson's tailing him."

"Hell, what's the matter with me? He would be. Have to wait for him, then. I'll take Grant."

Poor old Mr. Grant came in blinking as usual. Again I thought that he had aged, shriveled in this one week, as if something had gone out of him. He was patently nervous, baked as if he hadn't slept much.

The lieutenant explained the reasons for this second questioning.

"As I told you yesterday, sir"—Mr. Grant sat well forward on his dinette chair, his hands on his knees—"I was upset by the inquest. I kept thinking about—well, thinking. I dined downtown. I walked home from town. I went up to my room and endeavored to read, but my attention wandered. That was how I spent the entire evening."

"You read all evening?"

"Well, I looked over a few old keepsakes in my trunk for a time."

"How late was it when you went out?"

"About eleven, I think." Apologetically.

"You in the habit of walking so late at night?"

"I have been this past week." He smiled faintly. "You should know. I have seen one of your men following me."

Lieutenant Strom grunted. "Okay."

"I walked down the steps to Water Street and wandered about down there. I was nervous. A great many things had come up at the inquest which disturbed me."

"Yeah? What things?"

"The provisions of the will. Irony. A wicked woman, coming to her just deserts."

The lieutenant's voice was low.

"So you think Mrs. Garr got no more than was coming to her."

Mr. Grant straightened, and his words left no doubt of what he thought.

"I could not have wished her a more fitting death," he said quietly.

18

WE ALL STARED AT Mr. Grant. Meek, quiet little Mr. Grant!

The lieutenant snorted, half rose, sat down again.

"You didn't bring this up yesterday! What reason, may I ask, did you have for wishing Mrs. Garr any kind of death?"

Mr. Grant contemplated him passively.

"The inquest reminded us all of the evil in Mrs. Garr's past, did it not? She was a woman who had brought sorrow of the most—the most agonizing kind. On hundreds. On mothers of innocent girls, mothers who died crying aloud—" He pinched his lips together, paused a moment before he continued. "Surely it is just that such a woman should meet a horrible end."

The lieutenant's voice was as quiet.

"And what does this mean to you, to you personally, Mr. Grant?"

Mr. Grant's hands fell listlessly between his knees.

"Oh, nothing, nothing. I merely saw in it the workings of an awful Providence."

"You didn't help Providence?"

"No, I"—he turned his hands outward—"I didn't help."

"Well!" The lieutenant took a deep breath, settled back in his chair. There was something strange in Mr. Grant's attitude. When he said he had not helped Providence, it was almost as if he were defending himself; as if he should have helped Providence and hadn't. I could see the lieutenant tearing at that, then deciding to be jocose but watchful.

"You don't have to feel bad because Providence got along without you. Now go back to your walk."

"I came up the steps, to Adams again. I idled down past Elliott House until a man came up from the opposite way. I recognized Mr. Buffingham. He was returning from work. We came back to the house together, separated in the hall upstairs. I was awakened by the disturbance yesterday morning."

"You ever do any sawing, Mr. Grant?"

Mr. Grant looked blank surprise. "Why, as a boy on my father's farm, I occasionally assisted with the sawing of the winter wood supply."

"What's a steel saw look like?"

"Why, I don't know. I never saw—"

"What do you think it would look like?"

"Why, quite a bit like a wood saw, I should think. Finer, perhaps. And stronger, of course. I didn't suppose steel could be— but yes, yes, I suppose it can. Even diamonds can be cut."

He peered at us over his heavy glasses, obviously at a loss over the last questions.

"That'll do. You can go."

"Food for thought in that guy," the lieutenant said after Mr. Grant had left. "If we could prove he had some connection with Mrs. Garr in the past—but we can't. I had two men working on his past for two days last week. Didn't know I went into things so thoroughly, did you? We can't find any record he was in the city until four years ago; he turned up then in a downtown hotel. His own evidence is he came from Detroit. Retired bookkeeper. Plenty of Grants in old Detroit directories, but, my God—we can't follow them all up! Moved to this house soon after he came in town, lived here since. Lives off a bunch of US bonds, he says. I wish I could find out if Mrs. Garr ever put anything across on him. He isn't the type to murder for a few cents, but he could well enough murder to get even with an old hate."

"He doesn't have an old hate against me, though," I pointed out. "I can't imagine Mr. Grant coming—coming—"

"Don't forget you're the only one heard that key fall. And you'd been upstairs asking some mighty leading questions."

"That would mean he wanted to kill me to protect himself. He looks as if he wouldn't much care what happened to him. Apathetic."

"You psychology fiends." Lieutenant Strom sounded apathetic himself. "Let's see. Kistler. Still at work, I suppose. What time's it getting to be? Four? Well, we'll have to wait for Sands, then, too. Let's have the Wallers down."

My heart beat fast as the Wallers came in. Was the lieutenant going to throw the word "blackmail" at them? I wondered why they hadn't been down to see me before today; I was certain that, when I first regained consciousness the day before, Mrs. Waller had been working over me. Mr. Waller had helped break down the door, too. But if they had been back since to inquire how I was, I hadn't heard of it. If they noticed me at all now as they walked in, it was only a quick glance.

They stood before Lieutenant Strom; he had chairs placed for them; they sat. The expressions on their faces were oddly similar. Poker faces. But behind the masks was apprehension.

"Waller," the lieutenant began in a friendly way, "would you repeat everything you know of what happened Monday night, for Mrs. Dacres' benefit?"

Mr. Waller told of returning from the inquest with his wife and Miss Sands, of having dinner downtown, of talking in their apartment, of sleeping until wakened by Mr. Kistler's call up the stairs about six o'clock on Tuesday morning. He and Mrs. Waller had both stayed to help the doctor. For the first time I heard some of the gorier details.

I thanked them as nicely as I knew how.

When they had both given their stories the lieutenant sat quiet for two ticking seconds before he spoke again.

"Now, Waller, I'm going into something that may be a purely personal matter." He dropped politeness. "Why in hell didn't you include in your previous evidence that you held a note of Mrs. Garr's?"

Mr. Waller stiffened, and I saw Mrs. Waller's fat pink hands clasp in her lap until they were white along the knuckles. She began trembling slightly; I could see the black lace of her revers shake. Mr. Waller's eyes avoided the lieutenant's.

"It didn't have anything to do with Mrs. Garr dying. It was just a private matter."

"It would have been a God damn good reason for a fight with Mrs. Garr that might have ended in her death."

"I didn't fight with Mrs. Garr."

"That's your story. I've heard from others that she asked you to move out of her house. Now let's have your story on why Mrs. Garr owed you money."

"I loaned her the money a good many years ago."

"What for?"

"What for?" He moistened his lips. "I guess she needed some money."

"Hm. Waller, Mrs. Dacres says that when Mrs. Halloran came

back from asking you why you paid no rent, she said she saw the note."

Mr. Waller was silent.

"Why haven't you presented that note to the estate for collection?"

"I didn't want to be hasty. I thought I'd wait." His eyes were focused on a point just over the lieutenant's head.

"Thought you'd wait until the police were out of it, eh?"

"Oh no. I thought I'd just wait until—until it would seem more decent."

"I see, just being considerate. Just being considerate about two thousand bucks. Mrs. Halloran, you see, was impressed by the amount." He leaned forward. "Would you mind telling me when that money was borrowed?"

Mr. Waller swallowed, paused. "That—that has no connection. No connection at all."

The lieutenant thundered in his strongest voice. "You've got that note on you, Waller. I ask to see it."

"It's purely personal. I'm not going to hand it over." Mr. Waller fought back desperately.

"We'll see about that. Van and Bill, do your stuff."

The lieutenant's two huge henchmen advanced on Mr. Waller, no doubt of their intentions and abilities in their stride.

Mr. Waller stared at their advance for a frozen second.

"No! Wait! I—it isn't important enough to make a fuss over, Lieutenant Strom. I'll let you see the note."

The two henchmen fell back. Mr. Waller got to his feet, swaying a little; he took a wallet from his inside coat pocket, fumbled inside it, took from it a dirty piece of paper, folded once, which he laid before the lieutenant.

We waited while Lieutenant Strom, his face impassive, stared at the paper, folded it carefully away in his own wallet. But his eyes when he lifted them were alight, and his voice rang.

"You'll get it back. It's evidence now. Waller, that note is dated July 8, 1919! July 8, 1919! Will you please tell me what dealings you had with Mrs. Garr in the year Mrs. Garr went to jail?"

The excitement in his words was unmistakable. July 8, 1919, the lieutenant had said, as if that date were of surpassing importance, as if the key, the start of all this mystery, might have been that day, that month, that year; as if, stumbling in the dark, he had suddenly had a lamp thrust in his hand, and the lamp's light had illuminated that date.

Mr. Waller backed to his chair, lowered himself into it with a careful, steadying hand on its back. His face was white, hard white.

"She came to me. Came to me for money."

"Why to you?"

"I'd been to the house. I'd been there—selling. She knew I'd made some money."

"Selling what?"

"Liquor."

"Bootlegging?"

"No. Prohibition wasn't—was it in yet? I sold on commission."

"I see. So she just hunted you up. Said she needed money."

"That was it."

"Ever find out why she needed money?"

"Oh yes, it came out. It was in the papers."

"You're referring to the Liberry case?"

"I—yes."

"So you financed her trial."

"Oh, it must have cost her more than what she borrowed from me."

"This two thousand dollars the entire sum you lent her?"

"No, there was more. Three thousand more. She paid that back."

"But not the two thousand. She didn't pay the two thousand back, while she was what I'd call squandering twelve thousand bucks on a trust fund for the Hallorans. That's more generous than I'd have said she was. Ever say why she didn't pay off this note?"

"She wouldn't. Said we could take the interest out in living here."

"Mrs. Dacres testified to hearing Mrs. Garr quarrel with you. She wanted you to leave the house."

"Yes, that's true. She was getting old. Old and, I think, queer." He was answering quickly, desperately, as if this were at once uncertain and rehearsed. "She seemed to believe that the note wasn't good anymore, because it was so old. She said she wasn't going to pay it."

"That sound reasonable to you, Mrs. Dacres?"

"It sounds characteristic," I said.

"Waller, that's absolutely all there is to this note?"

He moistened his lips again. "That's all."

For what seemed like five minutes the lieutenant sat completely silent, to stare at them. If it had been me he stared at so, I should have wanted to break and scream; I wanted to cry aloud to break the silence as it was, yet something held me from it. Mr. Waller's eyes were still on the spot over Lieutenant Strom's shoulder; Mrs. Waller's gaze stayed where it had been, on her clenched hands.

"You can go."

One of the lieutenant's abrupt dismissals.

Mr. Waller put out a blind hand for his wife's elbow; the two of them walked as if leaning on each other for support. We heard their heavy steps go up the stairs, sound over our heads in the hallway above. A door opened, closed. We heard no voices.

Lieutenant Strom leaped to his feet, to walk up and down with long, hungry strides.

"By God, I'm getting something. Did you *see* how scared they were? Why should they be so scared? There's something there. I could feel it, even if I didn't know it. July 8, 1919!"

"But what could it be—what's July 8, 1919? Why's that so important?"

The lieutenant whirled for another trip.

"Important! What happened in July 1919? Why, nothing at all, nothing at all. Except that in July 1919 a girl named Rose Liberry was found dead in Mrs. Garr's house. Suicide. In July 1919, Mrs. Garr's business blew up, and it very nearly blew up the police department. By November of 1919, there wasn't enough left of the police force that had been running the town since the turn of the century to patrol a square block. Old Chief Hartigan's dead now. I never knew the ins and outs. But I do know there was a smell that reached to both coasts. Protection, get me? The city government was reformed so sweepingly that the whole town was done over. It's never been the same again. And this was an old lumber city, remember that, that ran wide open up to the last ditch, and that last ditch was July 1919, when everything was blown to bits."

"I don't see where it gets you in this case, though," I put in practically. "Perfectly reasonable for Mrs. Garr to run to a man she'd been doing business with, in a pinch. That's funny, though, about his being a liquor salesman," I went on, remembering something. "It must have been before he got on the police force. Or else after he retired. But you'd hardly have thought he could have retired even before that."

If I'd thrown a bomb directly at Lieutenant Strom's wide nose, I don't think I'd have gotten as big a reaction. He stopped dead, stared at me so stunned he almost looked weak. Then he walked toward me; if I hadn't known it was impossible, I'd have said he was quivering.

"Would you say that again?" He asked it gently.

I said it again.

Silence.

"Do you recall where you heard that Mr. Waller was ever on the police force?"

"Why, certainly. Mrs. Garr told me. She said he was retired. A retired policeman."

"Mrs. Garr told you. And do you remember bringing out this interesting little fact in your evidence?"

"Why, no. Why should I? You didn't ask me if I knew anything about anyone's past, Miss Sands' or Mr. Kistler's or Mr. Buffingham's . . ."

"Perfectly true. Why should you? Do you remember its having been brought out at the inquest in Mr. Waller's testimony?"

I cast my thoughts wildly back to the inquest; with surprising ease I could remember Mr. Waller talking, Mrs. Waller talking. Nothing about the period when Mr. Waller had been a policeman. But why should they say so? It was perhaps a long time ago. Perhaps for just a short time. Why should that fact have any bearing on Mrs. Garr's death? "No, I don't think Mr. Waller brought it up, either. Why should he? But he knows it well enough. I mentioned it to him once. I said how odd it was he retired so young."

The lieutenant groaned. "I don't see how you've kept alive this long. As far as I can see, you know everything that everyone wants kept secret. As a finder-outer, Mrs. Dacres, you are tops. As a putter-togetherer, Mrs. Dacres, you are bottoms. I don't suppose"—

his sarcasm took on an exaggerated pathos—"you can now recall any more such little facts tucked away?"

"They'll probably come out in time." I said it brightly and carelessly; he wasn't going to step on me; he wasn't my employer. "You ought to be glad I'm here for you to find things out of."

"Oh, I am," he said. "I'm profoundly grateful." He dropped me. He wasn't interested in me anymore. "Gad! Waller was on the force! He has a note signed July 8, 1919. Practically an entire police force retired in 1919. If he was on the force then . . . That entire police force didn't hold notes signed by Harriet Luella Garr! There's something in this somewhere! If there isn't, I'll eat my—I'll eat a suit of winter woolen underwear!"

He shot me a defiant glance on that one; continued to walk in high excitement, turned to me again.

"Mrs. Dacres! I could use you on this. Not today. What time is it? After five. Tomorrow. You've got the background, as I find out bit by bit. Do you want a job? You should be well enough to tackle it by tomorrow. Tonight I'm going to start going through the police records on the Liberry case again. It'll take me a while. I'm using a fine comb this time. And you—know what you can do? You go down to the *Comet* office. Get their old files, beginning about May 1919. Look through every inch until you get the reports on the Liberry case. Read every word. Copy down the headlines and the first paragraph of every account for me. If there's anything that the papers have that the court records haven't, I want to know it. The papers played it up big. We've got pictures, but they've got pictures we mightn't have—social pictures. Get me?"

"I'll get there if I have to crawl," I said.

We were still discussing our plans when Mr. Kistler walked in.

"What! Still alive?" he asked. He looked a little bit worn, but he was grinning as usual. "I've got to get back down to the paper tonight—we distribute tomorrow, you know. But I thought I'd come around and count the latest corpses."

"You don't have to worry. I'm here, Kistler." The lieutenant.

"That's what does worry me."

"There's been some excitement," I said.

"Hush," said the lieutenant. "Secrets."

What didn't he want me to tell? About the note? I turned the subject by thanking Mr. Kistler for saving my life, which he said was a small matter; he did things like that every day. Then the lieutenant put Mr. Kistler through his grilling.

Mr. Kistler told a factual story of our activities Monday evening and until three a.m., then the now-familiar tale of his rescue on Tuesday morning.

"Anything in that, Mrs. Dacres?" asked Lieutenant Strom when he had finished.

"Nothing that I could hear."

"That's a compliment." From Mr. Kistler.

"Cut it, you two. I think I heard Miss Sands come in while Kistler was talking; find out, Van."

"Want me to go?"

"Suit yourself, Kistler. It won't make any difference on this next one."

"Thanks."

Miss Sands came down looking rumpled, as if now, thank heaven, work was over for the day and she didn't have to be so everlastingly neat. Perhaps that was why she looked, as she walked in the door, better and more peaceful than I had ever seen her. It almost seemed as if her face were less lined, as if some care had slipped from her.

"Sit down there, Miss Sands. I'm having each person repeat his story about Monday night so Mrs. Dacres can hear it. But before you begin telling yours, I'd like to have you answer one question, please." He paused impressively, stood up, leaned forward, thundered:

"Why were you being blackmailed by Mrs. Garr?"

I have seldom seen a question produce a greater change in a person. First, the peace fled Miss Sands, and then she crumpled. She cowered back, her eyes fixed on Strom, helpless, at bay.

There was a long silence. She moved her lips to speak once. The lieutenant waited. She moved her lips again; this time we heard a whisper.

"How did you know?"

"So she was blackmailing you!" Triumph.

"No, oh no."

"Oh, she wasn't? Then why were you paying five dollars a week for your one little room when Mrs. Dacres is paying only four for these? When you could get a better room than you've got for three dollars a week anytime?"

"I—I felt sorry for her."

"Sorry for her. Who?"

"Mrs. Garr."

"I see. Charity, eh?"

"Yes. And then, she asked that much. She raised me."

"Miss Sands, how much do you make a week? Remember, I can check on it."

A hesitation. "We sign a slip we aren't supposed to tell."

"Don't let that bother you."

Another hesitation. "Well. Thirteen twenty-five."

I winced at the brutal department-store wage.

"Thirteen dollars and twenty-five cents?"

She nodded helplessly, her eyes fixed on him.

"Five dollars from thirteen twenty-five leaves eight twenty-five a week. Eight twenty-five for twenty-one meals a week. For car fare. For doctor and dentist bills. For clothes. Have to dress

pretty well in a store, too, don't you? Weren't you a bit overgen-
erous?"

Poor thing. She sat with her forlorn poverty naked before our
eyes. Cringing.

"Miss Sands, perhaps you'd like a day or two of quiet to re-
fresh your memory?"

"Don't!" I cried, and Mr. Kistler made a defensive gesture,
too. Lieutenant Strom gave us only black looks for our softness.

A new fright came into Miss Sands' eyes. Quiet—what did
that mean—jail? Her job lost. Her hands flew over her face, and
she began sobbing into them, long, dry, accustomed sobs.

I'd had enough of it. Lieutenant Strom or no Lieutenant
Strom, I stood up to walk over within touching distance.

"Whatever it is, it's over now," I said. "She's dead. Mrs. Garr's
dead. And whatever it was, I don't think you killed her."

Miss Sands let her hands fall as quickly as she'd lifted them;
the face they'd hidden was bitter with hate.

"She's dead! She's dead! I'm glad she's dead!" Her words rang
defiantly in the room. "She's dead, but she goes right on living
for me. Oh, I might have known it'd come out. I knew it'd come
out, but I kept on fooling myself. Maybe, I told myself. Maybe.
That's how big a fool I was. She's got me, living or dead. She's got
me until I kill myself. She's got me, ever since she first got me
into—that house."

There wasn't any mistaking the meaning of those last two
words. Miss Sands didn't mean this house. Not 593 Trent Street.
I was aghast, and even the lieutenant looked startled. I tightened
my grip on her shoulder, but she jerked away from me.

"Sure! Now you know. Now one of you can start blackmailing me. Now you can all blackmail me! Well, see if I care. I'm not
so fond of working in that store. I'm not so fond of living anymore. Seventeen I was when I came to this town. Out of the

country. I got a job in a store. And a man talked to me at a lunch counter one night and invited me to a party a friend of his was giving. Mrs. Garr's house, that's where he took me. It was two years before I could get out of there. Broke, she kept us. One night, a soldier boy going away to war slipped me twenty dollars. I got out. I hid. I did housework. I got a job in a store again. And then, one day, *she* came along. 'I heard you was working here, dearie,' she said, purring like a cat. 'I wonder how the nice people running this store would feel if they knew what kind of a girl was working for 'em? I've got a new house,' she said, 'a nice respectable rooming house. Why don't you come and see one of my rooms you might like to live in?' What could I do? What could I do? The store'd let me go like a shot if they knew. Debutantes from our best families, that's what they want working for 'em. So I went. I came here. She showed me the room upstairs and said I could live there for five dollars a week. What could I do? I couldn't save up money enough to go away and keep me until I could get a new job, on six dollars a week—that's what I used to get before N.R.A.—eleven dollars a week. Twelve years. What could I do?"

Abruptly her stormy sobbing began again.

Hodge Kistler was swearing, steady and low, his face almost dark blue. The two detectives sat stony, their eyes on the lieutenant. His voice was gentle when he spoke.

"Miss Sands."

"Yes."

"Did you kill Mrs. Garr?"

"No, I didn't. I often wished I would have, though. Long ago."

"Just the same, we're glad you didn't."

There was silence in the room for a time, except for Miss Sands' heavy, sobbing breaths. Lieutenant Strom appeared to be thinking deeply.

"Miss Sands, did you know a girl named Rose Liberry at Mrs. Garr's house?"

"No, that was soon after I got out. I saw about it in the papers."

The lieutenant seemed to shake his thought off, return to briskness.

"Now, Miss Sands, what you have just told us is over. You may be certain no one here will let a word of this escape him or her. If anyone ever tries to blackmail you again, and you let me know, I can promise you that you won't be bothered long. Nor will it become public."

She again dropped her hands from her ravaged face.

"I don't trust nobody," she said wearily. "Okay, what's the difference? I've stood plenty before."

"You can go in a moment, Miss Sands. I wonder if you'd repeat your story of events this last Monday night, before you go."

"Sure. I left the inquest with the Wallers. We ate before we came home. We talked awhile in their rooms. Then I went to bed, early. I was still sleeping when I began to hear a ringing somewhere. It was the phone. I answered it, then went up to wake Mr. Kistler. I went back to bed, but I didn't get to sleep again before I heard Mr. Kistler yelling for Mr. Waller. I was along helping work on her for a while. Then I had to leave for the store."

"Don't think I don't appreciate your helping me," I said warmly. "I won't forget it if I can ever do anything for you."

"The best you can do for me is not know me. Can I go now?"

"Thank you, Miss Sands. That's all I wanted."

Mr. Kistler was on his feet, pacing back and forth.

"If you find out she killed Mrs. Garr I hope you get her a reward for it."

"Would you be as generous as that concerning the attack on Mrs. Dacres, too?"

Mr. Kistler stopped short. "No, I wouldn't. Hell, I'd forgotten. I suppose we've got to get your murderer, baby, even if we're sorry for her."

"You're leaping too far ahead," I said. "We've had other things turn up this afternoon more incriminating than this. Miss Sands' story doesn't prove she's a murderer. It proves she's weak. A stronger person would have escaped from Mrs. Garr long ago."

"Remember about the can of Kleenfine she was using? Or have you decided to ignore that?"

"No, I'm not forgetting. But her whole story, if it's true, isn't the story of a person who would make a planned attack on me or anyone else. She hasn't acted on life; she's let life act on her. Look at what she said. She was enticed into Mrs. Garr's establishment in the first place. There must have been ways in which a girl forced into such a house could have escaped, run away, reached the police, and slapped Mrs. Garr's ears with her dirty business. But she doesn't. She just stays there until chance lets her out. And even then she doesn't try retribution."

"Your story's all right for this year," argued the lieutenant, "but her story isn't this year's. It's 1917 or 1918, maybe. Public opinion toward a girl leading that life isn't very lenient even yet. Back then, it was likely assumed that she wouldn't be leading it if her character was all it should be. Mrs. Garr's business wasn't so unusual in those days."

"What Lieutenant Strom so carefully avoids saying," Mr. Kistler put in blandly, "is that Mrs. Garr was undoubtedly protected. Miss Sands could have wept at the official doors until the gaslights were drowned, but all she'd have gotten for her pains would have been the lifted eyebrow, the averted nose, and a reputation that wouldn't get her a job in the whole town."

"Far be it from me to hint the police of this city were ever corrupt." Lieutenant Strom said it lightly.

"Just the same"—I stuck to my line—"think of this attack on me. That was a planned attack. Someone swept those stairs and provided himself with a saw—they must be fairly difficult to get, too. Someone timed the job for the first night we were without a guard. Someone provided himself with a hammer and a can of Kleenfine. Oh, it was all thought out beforehand."

"Different from the murder of Mrs. Garr, wasn't it?" Lieutenant Strom brought out the analogy. "That has all the earmarks of being unpremeditated."

"Yes, but it doesn't necessarily alter the psychology of the murderer. That first crime may have just happened. It was a sort of self-defense, maybe, if you can call it self-defense when a burglar defends his right to burgle. Miss Sands might have committed that kind of crime. But I don't think she'd have had the brains—I don't think she'd have had the *character*—to think up the attack on me."

They all laughed; men can be so infuriating. I was being perfectly logical, too.

"Well, even worms turn; remember that." The platitude was from Lieutenant Strom. "You can rule Miss Sands out if you want to, but she's still a good strong suspect to me. Remember, we said Mrs. Garr's murder was as likely to have its roots in her past as in any small sums of money she might have hidden around. All right, now we've found someone linked to that past. And one with a good strong motive, too. Miss Sands wasn't trying to hide her hatred. And besides that, she had a present reason, too. How'd you feel, if you made thirteen twenty-five a week, and were blackmailed out of two dollars of it?"

I thought it over. "I'd have watched until I knew where some of the little piles of money were. Then I'd have grabbed my chance to get my own back, and left for sunnier climes."

"She admits she's an honest girl."

"I don't mind being a stooge for a laugh."

"Laugh nothing. Don't you realize that's exactly what Miss Sands may have done? She was caught hunting Mrs. Garr's money and killed her."

19

THERE WAS STILL ONE more interview that Wednesday: Buffingham's. The lieutenant had Van call the Elite Drugstore where Mr. Buffingham worked, and order him to return to the house during his supper hour. He came to the house shortly after six; the lieutenant called him in impatiently. Strom was all keyed up by that time, anxious to get at the Liberry case records, anxious to go over them completely, now there was the possibility between Mr. Waller and Miss Sands of a connection with that old case.

Mr. Buffingham slouched in, haggard as he always was; his eyes traveled aloofly from one to the other of us, as unfriendly and as unexpecting of friendliness as if he were of one kind, we of another; as if there never was and never would be much kinship in his life, never anything except the world's hand against him.

He had a son.

I suppose there isn't any tragedy in the world more heart-rending, I thought, looking at him, than being the father of a baby that turns out wrong. Of waiting and thinking about the baby that's coming, afraid and secret and proud; of having the baby be born and going in to *see* it with its mother, glad and tender. Of wondering all the years as the baby grew whether he should say yes, he could go to all the movies he wanted to, or no, no more movies, too exciting; or yes, an allowance, or no, learn to earn; or yes, I'll get you a baseball, or no, I wish you wouldn't play with the Smith boy. Mr. Buffingham was worn with the grief of having made the wrong decisions.

The lieutenant was looking at him, too. As if idly, while he told the reason for this second questioning.

Mr. Buffingham's story was simple. Worked until midnight. Walked home. Car in garage for repairs. Met Mr. Grant near Elliott House. Walked in with him. Wakened by racket Tuesday morning.

"A new bit of information has come to hand," said the lieutenant as Mr. Buffingham finished. There was bite under his carelessness. "Enjoy being blackmailed, Buffingham?"

Mr. Buffingham's dark eyes made a quick swing from face to face, but his mouth was imperturbable.

"Who, me?"

"Yes, you."

"What're you talking about?"

"You, Buffingham, paying blackmail."

"You're kidding."

"Oh no, I'm not."

"What've I done to be blackmailed for?" Mr. Buffingham's eyes were very careful.

"That's what I want to know."

I saw it, we all saw it. It couldn't be concealed.

Relief.

Mr. Buffingham was relieved when the lieutenant said he'd like to know what for. He was still worn, still harried, but the new fear that had crept back of his eyes when the lieutenant first said "blackmail" had crept away again.

"What could anybody blackmail me for?" he demanded now, truculently. "I ain't done nothin'. Just because my boy got in a little trouble, here, you're going to try to hang something on me, too, huh?"

"How much you getting at the Elite, Buffingham?"

"Eighteen per. It's a lousy joint."

"Eighteen dollars a week?"

"That's it."

"You insist on that?"

"Sure, that's what I'm getting. Ask the old man if you don't believe me."

Soft and smooth. "Nine dollars a week is a lot for your room upstairs, Buffingham."

Again Mr. Buffingham's eyes made their darting round.

"Yeah," he said. "Oh, you mean what I been paying old lady Garr recently?" He threw back his head to laugh loudly. "So that's where you got your blackmail, huh? She would leave the receipt stubs around, wouldn't she? Old lady Garr! That's good!" He stopped laughing as if it were turned off by a spigot. "I owed her some back rent, see. No job for a while. And the old lady staked me to the room, see? But jeez, blackmail wasn't so far off, at that. I been paying three times over for that room ever since I got a job again. I'll bet she had me set to pay three times till the walls fell in. Me, I was thinking about moving to get out from under."

If he was lying it was a good job; he was as easy as if there were no judgment at stake, no trial, no life.

The lieutenant tried the methods he had used on Miss Sands.

"Nine from eighteen leaves nine dollars a week. And you drive a car."

Mr. Buffingham waved a weary, careless hand. "Oh, I've got

a couple little sidelines on. You know, Lieutenant. It ain't so hard in a drugstore. You can see why I got to. You wouldn't crack down on me for that, would you?"

He was doing better than Miss Sands.

The lieutenant tried another tack.

"So your boy's going to try a break, eh?"

"Huh?"

"You heard me."

"I don't know what you're trying to put over on me, but—"

"Oh yes, you do. That's how you happened to have that saw."

"Saw?"

"Acting dumb, eh?"

"I don't know what you mean." He was alert and easy, increasingly sardonic as he became more sure of his ability to parry the thrusts of his questioner.

"Wisecracker, huh? Where'd you get that saw?"

"I ain't had any saw."

"Must have quite a little tool kit. What'd you use on the screws?"

"I ain't got no screws to turn."

"Oh, so you're thinking about turning screws. So you were turning screws on that cellar door!"

"Cellar door? There ain't any cellar door."

It was, undoubtedly, the answer anyone in the house would have made—anyone who was not thinking of the door in my kitchen. Because there was no door at the top of the main cellar stairs. How crafty was Mr. Buffingham? If he were guilty, did he have brains enough to make that subtly innocent answer? I could see the possibilities being weighed in the lieutenant's mind. Then he veered again.

"You ever know Rose Liberry, Buffingham?"

"Who?"

"You heard me this time, too."

"Rose, you said? Liberry? Can't say I have. Who's she?"

"No one. Now."

The lieutenant let him go.

He was thoughtful as Mr. Buffingham hurried out.

"Why don't you turn on your psychology now, Mrs. Dacres?"

"On Mr. Buffingham, you mean?"

"On Mr. Buffingham. God! What a name!"

"Well . . ."

"Is he the type that could have done it?"

"Yes," I said. "Yes, I think he might have done it, psychologically speaking. But why should he? We can't know for sure about Mrs. Garr, but why should he attack me? I haven't anything on him."

"Sure of that?"

"Of course I am. I know him less than anyone else in the house."

Mr. Kistler stood up to stretch.

"Yes, he's sort of past your age."

I ignored that, but Lieutenant Strom didn't.

"I can see where Kistler here would have greater charms," he said.

They both stood grinning at me like a couple of apes.

"I thought you were intent only in finding out who started me on that long dark journey from which there is almost no returning," I said witheringly.

"Reproof received," the lieutenant returned. He stretched, too. "Well, Buffingham takes a neat place in the list of suspects, too. He's crooked. Admits it. His boy is in trouble. Needs dough. Tells a good tale to explain the nine bucks a week, but is it good enough? No connection with Mrs. Garr in the past as far as we know. But he moved in here right after Mrs. Garr took the house—did you get that? His testimony at the inquest said he'd lived here twelve years. Looks like Mrs. Garr might have roped him in the same way she roped in Miss Sands. He pays heavier, too—get that. If she was blackmailing him she had him good."

"It might have been for some of his sideline rackets, the ones he admitted," Mr. Kistler said.

"Yeah, it might. But I'm not letting that guy out of my mind. Not by a long shot. Come on, you two, I'm hungry. Don't forget your little job tomorrow, Mrs. Dacres."

He waved his cohorts to him, left.

Mr. Kistler and I were alone. I was dazed after listening to the testimonies, inexpressibly tired.

"I'm hungry, too," I said.

"Oh, the poor baby. She's tired. She's hungry. Papa fix the orange juice?" Mr. Kistler went kitchenward to fix my supper. I pined for tomorrow. The doctor said I could have toast, eggs, milk, mashed potatoes, and fruit tomorrow. I intended to have all of that.

"It's just like having an operation, and I haven't even had the operation to talk about," I moaned over the orange juice.

"What we've got to do is prevent you from being operated on twice." Mr. Kistler viewed the future. "What the hell are we going to do with you tonight?"

"I think I'll manage on my own."

"A poor little sick girl doesn't want extra protection?"

"I'm not sick."

"In that case—"

"No, thanks. I'll sleep with the policeman."

"You mean you prefer a policeman to me?"

"Absolutely. I'll sleep here, the policeman in the chair."

"You'd trust the policeman to sleep in the chair?"

"They should be domesticated by this time."

"Trust me to sleep in the chair?"

"Certainly not."

"I'd think you were a nitwit if you did," he said. "Now, before returning to my labors, I am going out to dine. On steak, medium rare, smothered in onions. New peas. Lettuce with Roquefort dressing. Hot biscuits—"

I moaned into my pillow, and he went out laughing like a Boucicault villain at the end of the second act.

THE NIGHT PASSED WITHOUT a hitch. I slept, the policeman slept, and all was serene in the morning, except that I was so weak I could hardly get my clothes on. I tiptoed past the policeman; he woke with a jump, which I was glad to see, because what is the use of having a guard if he sleeps through having someone tiptoe past him? He wiped his hand across his face and went out into the hall, so I had a free hand for dressing.

My clock said six fifteen, which was the earliest I'd been up for years. I managed to get the coffee on, made toast, cooked three eggs. After I'd eaten that I started over on three more eggs.

It's wonderful what a little food can do for your spine, your character, and your intelligence. I wondered for a bit if I had overdone things, but my interior settled down after a while. I started putting things back into drawers; I knew I couldn't make much headway, but I pushed Mrs. Garr's things back into her closet; I had hung my clothes before going to bed the night before.

I was out of the house about seven; I didn't want an argument with Hodge Kistler about going to the *Comet* office.

It was one of those what-is-so-rare-as-a-day-in-June days, but I had to take a streetcar; my legs hadn't solidified enough for a long walk. I picked up a newspaper on the corner before I got on the car. There wasn't a word in it about me, and I wondered if there had been in yesterday's paper.

The *Comet* building is down on the riverfront, a decrepit hag of a building that holds up mainly, I think, because it is rusted together. It looks rusted; heaven knows what it's made from, under the crust. The crust on the outside is reddish; the crust on the inside is black and looks, if anything, thicker. I'm fairly familiar with the *Comet* offices; in pinches, I'd acted as office boy and taken layouts and copy there from Tellier's.

The board over the *Comet* doorway says:

GILLING CITY COMET
The Biggest Newspaper of Its Size in the World

No one much was around at that hour, but I hunted out a lanky, sleepy youngster sweeping papers back and forth in a big room full of tumbledown desks and typewriters. I asked him if he could show me to their archives.

After long thought he said sure, he didn't know why not, and led me past hundreds of cubbyholes to a dark inside room.

Here he switched on a light, looked blankly around at the overflowing files, and left.

I thought it hopeless trying to figure out where the 1919 files would be. I poked through some huge tomes, full newspaper size, on the open-front shelves that covered the entire back wall of the library, but the rubbed white letters on the back of one volume would say Aug. 17 to Nov. 3, 1924, the one under it Feb. 22 to Apr. 9, 1907, and the one above it Jan. 27 to Mar. 25, 1913.

A wizened little man came in around eight. He poked around as helplessly as I did, seemingly, but I caught him slipping a picture into a file.

"How do you do? I've been waiting for the librarian," I explained to him.

"I'm the librarian," he admitted sadly, as if he hated to be found out.

"Lieutenant Strom of the police force suggested I come to you. He'd like to have me go over the papers for May, June, July, and perhaps August of 1919. Would you let me see them?"

"That's a lot of papers, miss."

"I won't mind."

"It's probable someone has 'em out."

"Someone in the building?"

"Well, I don't know. They might be out or they might be here."

"Would you tell me where they'd be if they were here?"

"They'd be there if they aren't anywhere else." He waved a gloomy hand at the stacks.

I gathered it was useless waiting for help from him; I tackled the stacks in earnest myself. My hands were soon as black as a coal deliverer's; when I shook my skirt after kneeling to look at the bottom shelf the dust flew out in puffs. The librarian stood behind me peering helplessly at the shelves through thick glasses; I wondered if he could even see the white markings.

Halfway through, I found my volume: May 2 to Jul. 28, 1919.

I raised a small dust storm by shaking myself and retired with my find to a corner desk, where I leveled off the piles of newspapers it held enough to let the book lie flat. I was elatedly expectant; hunting those stacks and finding what you wanted there was something like coming on a long-sought treasure island in an uncharted sea.

Beginning with May 2, 1919, I went through the papers item by item. If minutes and hours ticked by, I didn't know it. But it wasn't before I reached the *Comet* for May 24, 1919, that I came on my first news of Rose Liberry. That was a small item on page three. An item so insignificantly placed near the bottom of a column that I almost skipped over it.

AUNT REPORTS GIRL MISSING OVERNIGHT

Miss Rachel Staines, 1128 Cleveland Avenue, called police at eleven o'clock yesterday evening to report the unexplained absence of her niece, Miss Rose Liberry, of Cincinnati, who has been visiting Miss Staines for the past week.

According to Miss Staines, the missing girl left her aunt's home at approximately three o'clock yesterday afternoon for a little shopping. When the girl did not return for dinner, Miss Staines was not alarmed, as Miss Liberry had said she might call an acquaintance of hers and visit a moving picture theater. When Miss Liberry had not returned by ten o'clock, however, Miss Staines became anxious. She waited for some time longer before calling the residence of Miss Liberry's friend, where it was reported that Miss Liberry had not called and that the friend had been at home the entire evening. Miss Staines then called the police.

No trace has yet been found of the missing girl.

It was easy not to miss the account of the mystery on the following day. It was on page one, in the middle of the page.

GIRL STILL MISSING

No Trace of Young Visitor
Yet Unearthed by Police

The whereabouts of Miss Rose Liberry, who left the home of her aunt, Miss Rachel Staines, at 1128 Cleveland Avenue on the afternoon of May 23, are still a mystery to police and Miss Staines. Miss Staines, alarmed that some harm has come to the girl, has notified the girl's parents of the continued absence.

The parents, Mr. and Mrs. J. G. Liberry, of Cincinnati, have telegraphed that they will be in the city this evening to continue the search. No news whatever has come from the missing girl.

Miss Liberry is reported by her aunt to have left the house at three p.m. . . .

I skimmed over the rest of it, but it was all repetition of the previous day's item. I took out my notebook, copied down the two items I'd found so far.

Lieutenant Strom knew what he was doing when he'd said it would do if I copied down the headlines and first paragraphs.

On the *Comet* for May twenty-sixth, the story I sought was plastered all over the front page. It held first place, with a page headline, the right-hand column—and a picture.

I looked at that picture a long time.

I looked at the picture and thought with anger that the girl was dead.

She was lovely. She was lovely in the way that pulls the heart-strings most: a child, and so grave. She was sixteen perhaps; she wore a dark taffeta dress with georgette sleeves; a fashion I could just recall, the fashion of 1919. Her hair was dark, brushed sim-ply back from her face; the widely spaced dark eyes looked lev-elly from the picture into yours, inquiring, holding back a smile of friendliness. It was the mouth I liked best, the lips held so seriously, so wonderingly, so consideringly.

Sixteen, wondering what life had for her.

That was when the Liberry case stopped being something dead, something past. It wasn't dead, couldn't be dead; this wasn't a girl who could die foully and no ripples remain, no anger be held, no deep hatred stirred. This girl's death would leave grief; the manner of her death would leave bitter hate.

Excitement quickened me; my eyes leaped to the day's report.

PARENTS BELIEVE GIRL KIDNAPPED

FATHER ARRIVES TO HUNT MISSING ROSE LIBERRY

GIRL LEAVES AUNT'S HOME MAY 23; NO CLUES FOUND

The theory that his daughter had been kidnapped was offered to reporters today by John G. Liberry, of Cincinnati, who arrived in Gulling City today to direct the hunt for his missing daughter, Miss Rose Liberry. Miss Liberry, 16, disappeared on the afternoon of May 23 from the home of her aunt, Miss Rachel Staines, 1128 Cleveland Avenue.

Mr. Liberry, who is a prominent Cincinnati accountant, is hourly expecting that the kidnappers will approach him for ransom payments, he said today. Police Chief Hartigan counters this theory with a belief that the girl left of her own accord; has perhaps married and left the city.

Anxiety over the girl's absence was first aroused when . . .

There was a long recapitulation of the previous facts; the account ended with a description of the missing girl, and asked anyone seeing her to call police.

On May twenty-seventh the Liberry case took up even more of page one. A two-decked headline flared across the page:

GIRL IN HANDS OF HUMAN TRAFFICKERS?
AUNT ASKS

The middle columns were filled with photographs. Pictures of Rose Liberry at fifteen, at eleven, at three; Rose Liberry, dark eyed and serious at three as she was at sixteen. Pictures of the girl's father and mother, snapped leaving Chief Hartigan's office, the mother short, plump, shielding her face with her handbag; the father short, slight, staring straight at the camera with ravaged eyes.

A picture of Chief Hartigan was captioned "Girl Will Turn Up, Says Police Chief Hartigan."

Chief Hartigan, well-fed, thinking more of his dinner; it wasn't his daughter.

A picture, a camera study, of Miss Rachel Staines, forty, blonde and fairly worldly. Captioned "Aunt Fears Human Traffickers."

Father, mother, aunt. I looked at the pictured faces carefully. I thought over the people concerned in Mrs. Garr's death. I couldn't see any trace of resemblance anywhere. But 1919 was eighteen years ago; a face could change with age and grief by that time. Father, mother, aunt—was one of them living in Mrs. Garr's house now—a murderer?

The story had two columns on the right.

ROSE LIBERRY NOW MISSING FOUR DAYS

Mother in State of Collapse;
Father Pushes Hunt for
Daughter; Attacks Police

Miss Rachel Staines, 1128 Cleveland Avenue, aunt of the missing Rose Liberry, created a sensation in Police Chief Hartigan's office today when, in ringing tones, she stated her belief that her niece was being held in some house of vice for immoral purposes.

Chief Hartigan, holding to his theory that the girl left her aunt's residence for purposes of her own, pointed out the greater likelihood of his elopement theory.

"Gilling City is a clean city," Chief Hartigan declared to reporters during the interview. "Statistics show that a certain number of girls are always reported missing each year. Great numbers of those girls are quietly found. Usually it is discovered that some man is involved. Miss Liberry is sixteen, a romantic age, and I think it will be found the usual thing has happened."

On hearing this statement, John G. Liberry, father of the missing girl, appeared greatly enraged. "It is like Chief Hartigan to cast reflections on my daughter's character," he said. "I have found the police of this city not only incompetent but curiously unwilling to make any but the most routine search. The police force of this city is rotten from the heart out, and you're the heart, Chief Hartigan."

CHIEF REPLIES TO ATTACK

Chief Hartigan greeted Mr. Liberry's attack with a tolerant laugh. "Just like a father," he said. "Parents always know their own children less than anyone else. I can't stand having my administration maligned; every citizen of this city knows how well-policed Gilling City has been under my rule. I respect order, but I also respect liberty. In Gilling we have both. You may quote me."

"Uh-huh. Exactly as I thought!" A voice, a living voice, said loudly in my ear.

I jumped and turned.

Hodge Kistler.

"What're you doing here?" I asked stupidly, still in the past. I would rather have expected Chief Hartigan to appear beside me than Hodge Kistler.

"Me? I'm the Good Samaritan; you just don't recognize me in

this snappy American getup. Have you, might I ask, had enough
regard for your own well-being to get yourself a little lunch?"

"Lunch? My goodness, it isn't—"

"Just as I thought again. It is one thirty. Perhaps a bit after.
You come with me."

"But she's lost. Rose Liberry's missing, and I haven't found
out yet what—"

"She'll keep. Come on along."

I went, resisting, my mind still hitched to the past.

"You're too dirty to eat with me or anyone else. Here, go in
here and wash up. I'll wait."

I was turned neatly into a washroom. Even the washroom was
inky, I noticed, beginning to become perceptive again, under the
influence of water and soap.

"You certainly know your way around!" I commented, re-
joining Mr. Kistler in the corridor outside.

"Didn't I serve my term of purgatory in this joint? Let's go to
the Dutch Moon."

Tucked into a corner booth—Hodge always picks out
corners—I found I was trembling with weakness and excitement.
Hot soup helped the first; I allayed the second by pouring out the
morning's discoveries.

Mr. Kistler listened soberly.

"One thing you can certainly say for this case," he said. "The
more you look into it, the worse it smells. Well, I have a little
incident to relate, myself."

"Don't tell me anything more has happened!"

"Nothing much, but I noticed it. Me, you understand, not the
detective in the hall. Though of course, what with his being so
occupied with you—"

"Don't meander. What was it?"

"Oh, nothing, really; just a bit more of the same. It seems that,

after you, I was the third one up this morning, I having to fore-
gather with the carriers for a few last parting instructions. Mr. B.
was in our joint possession, so I toddled down the hall to the
bathroom. During my occupancy it strikes me I am slightly dizzy.
Looking into the matter, I find I am not dizzy, but the floor is. You
know how the floor is—black-and-white tile pattern, half the tiles
loose. Probably was saving money when she had it done. I investigate, on my knees, and it is immediately apparent that someone
has taken out the loose tiles and then did not put them back in the
right pattern. What do you think of that for sleuthing?"

"You're wonderful."

"Thank you. The gentleman in the hall below was not so honest, but he whistled and phoned Strom."

"I wonder if he's found it now."

"Oh, sure, he called me to say he'd been out, but couldn't
make anything of it."

"What're you talking about?"

"Why, Strom. He went out to look at the bathroom—"

"Silly, I wasn't thinking about him. I mean the prowler. Did
he find what he was after under the tiles, do you think?"

"Not if I'm a good guesser. Nothing under 'em but the old
worn-out board flooring and crumbly cement."

"Then he doesn't have it yet. He'll still be hunting. Wouldn't
you think, when there's a detective in the house all the time, that
he'd sometime get caught at it?"

"God help us every one," Hodge prayed cheerfully. "I think
I'll petition for a cop in every room."

"I know what I'm going to do. Go back to those newspaper
accounts. And if there's anything in 'em to find, I'll find it!"

"Like any help?"

"No, thanks. I work faster and better alone."

He took me back to the *Comet* building.

20

IN THE *COMET* LIBRARY, I found, as I should have known, that my book had disappeared. I had to hunt for it all over again. I found it, finally, on a chair under a pile of papers. The librarian was so startled by my finding it again that he stood blinking at me in admiration for as long as I noticed him.

I went back to where I'd left off: May twenty-eighth. So far, the news accounts had been burgeoning; now they shrank.

The May twenty-eighth *Comet* relegated the story to column one on the left, though it was still a big story.

MOTHER FEARS MISSING GIRL DEAD

ROSE LIBERRY NOW MISSING FIVE DAYS; HUNT CONTINUES

The account below was one of continued, hopeless searching, the parents anguished, the police indifferent, but taking all the publicity they could get.

The story stayed that way. For two entire weeks the Liberry missing girl mystery held a place, slipping from column one to the middle of page one; going back to column one again after a false report that the girl had been found in a carnival. Then it slipped to page two, to page five. Like all mysteries, the accounts became more and more meager, the refrain left unchanging: Rose Liberry still missing.

The *Comet* for June twenty-first was the first one to hold no news of the story. During that whole ensuing week the paper was bare of the references I sought.

I stood up to ease the cricks in my back. Ruefully I looked at my hands; they were blacker than ever. The librarian behind me wandered aimlessly to and fro; occasionally a lanky boy came in with a pile of pictures or clippings.

But I was too hungry for what I sought to pay attention to the workings of the library. Quickly I thumbed through the papers for the remaining days of June 1919. My excitement grew as I took up the paper for July 1, 1919.

July. That was the month Mr. Waller's note was dated for. The date that had aroused Lieutenant Strom. Swiftly but carefully I went over the pages. Nothing. Nothing. Nothing. One complete paper after another. Daily editions. Sunday editions with the same comics as today.

Then, at the bottom of a column on a first page, my eye caught a tiny item.

GIRL KILLS SELF

Miss Ethel Smith, residing at 417 St. Simon Street, was found dead in her room this morning by a fellow lodger. It was reported to police that Miss Smith had committed suicide by hanging.

Was that nothing, too? I looked to the date at the top of the page.

July 8, 1919. The day for which Mr. Waller's note was dated!

Hands trembling, I lifted over that entire paper to expose the *Comet* for July ninth.

I'd been expecting it; I'd known it. But even then, it came at me with some of the sick shock the residents of Gilling City, the state, and the whole country must have felt eighteen years ago, when that story broke. Again Rose Liberry's grave face looked out at me from the page; the picture was thrice the size it had been in the *Comet* of May twenty-sixth. The headline flared, black and heavy:

FATHER IDENTIFIES SUICIDE AS MISSING ROSE LIBERRY

GIRL DEAD UNDER MYSTERIOUS CIRCUMSTANCES

POLICE PUSH INVESTIGATION

Mr. John G. Liberry, of Cincinnati, has found his daughter Rose, for whom he has been searching ever since she disappeared on May 23.

He found her this morning in the city morgue.

She was dead. A suicide.

Ever since that fateful day when she disappeared seven weeks ago, Mr. Liberry has sought her relentlessly. Every day he has visited the hospitals, the jails, the hotels, the morgue.

Detectives in his pay have fine-combed the city.

This morning word came to him that the body of a dark-haired young girl had been brought into the morgue. In pursuance of his search, now a hopeless routine, he went to see her face.

It was his Rose at last. His long-lost Rose.

Dead.

A suicide.

FATHER BREAKS DOWN

For the first time since her disappearance, the father broke. He was seen by reporters in the morgue office, sobbing incoherently, crying for his Rose.

Word was immediately taken to Miss Rachel Staines, aunt of the unfortunate girl. She appeared stunned. It was from her home, 1128 Cleveland Avenue, that the girl disappeared.

It was not possible to inform the mother, who has been confined to a hospital for the past three weeks as a result of the prolonged anxiety over her missing daughter. Hospital attendants say the mother's condition is serious.

HARTIGAN TENDERS SYMPATHY

Upon being informed of the identification, Chief of Police Hartigan expressed his great surprise at the turn events have taken. "My sympathy goes out to the grief-stricken father and mother of Rose Liberry," he said. "I realize what a heavy additional grief the manner and circumstances of her death must be to them."

INVESTIGATION PROMISED

Chief Hartigan then outlined plans for investigating the suicide. "Every effort will be made," he said, "and you may quote my exact words, to find out if Miss Liberry committed suicide of her own free will, or whether any person or circumstances induced her to do so. An investigation will be made of the lodgings at 417 St. Simon Street, in which Miss Liberry's body was found. I understand Miss Liberry has been living there as Miss Ethel Smith, though her reason for taking the alias is not known. I understand the proprietress of this lodging house is a Mrs. Garr. You may rest assured charges will be brought against anyone whom we find culpable in the matter."

REPORTER VISITS SUICIDE SCENE

With only thirty minutes to go before press time, a Comet *reporter was hurried to 417 St. Simon Street. There he was met by Mrs. Harriet Garr, proprietress, who stated that the house was a respectable lodging house, which she had maintained for the past twenty years. She says that the girl came to the house three weeks ago, carrying a small suitcase, and applied for a room, which she rented to her. She said the girl was quiet, kept to her room, went out seldom. When asked if she had not noticed the girl's resemblance to pictures of Rose Liberry recently appearing in the* Comet, *Mrs. Garr stated that she had not noticed the girl particularly; she had so many people coming and going. She was completely at sea, she indicated, as to why the girl had taken her life.*

At the end of the column were three boldface lines:

WATCH TOMORROW'S COMET FOR
NEW DEVELOPMENTS IN THIS THRILLING
REAL-LIFE TRAGEDY!

In the *Comet* for July tenth, the Rose Liberry case took up every inch of the front page. The three-line headline screamed across the top of the page, in the biggest type any newspaper owns:

LIBERRY ACCUSES POLICE OF PROTECTING HUMAN TRAFFICKING RING IN CITY!

SUICIDE SCENE OF ROSE LIBERRY FOUND TO BE VICE PALACE

GOVERNOR TAKES HAND; ORDERS INVESTIGATION OF CITY POLICE AND VICE CONDITIONS HERE

Mr. John G. Liberry, father of the Rose Liberry whose disappearance caused a sensation here seven weeks ago and whose dead body was found at 417 St. Simon Street on July 8 in circumstances suggesting suicide, today went before Governor David Lamson to bring explicit charges of protecting a human trafficking ring in Gilling City.

The charges uncover one of the greatest scandals in the history of Gilling City and of the state, and are based on the work of a Comet *reporter, who today gained entrance to the house at 417 St. Simon Street, where the girl's body was found.*

Disguised as a city water-meter repairman, the Comet *reporter was admitted at the rear entrance of 417 St. Simon Street by a frightened cook and housemaid. From them he wrung the admission that the house, under the proprietorship of a Mrs. Harriet Garr, was being run, wide open, as a palace of vice.*

POLICE CHIEF ACCUSED OF FREQUENTING VICE PALACE

Leaving the servants in the kitchen under promises of silence as to his entry, the Comet *reporter proceeded to the second floor, where he succeeded in entering one of the rooms. In this room were two young girls, also badly frightened, who readily admitted the character of the place. The house was crowded with men nightly, the girls declared. Liquor flowed freely. One of the girls stated that many city officials were frequenters of the house, and added particulars of her own intimacy with Chief Hartigan, who visited the house often, she said, and whom she had seen receive money from Mrs. Garr.*

Gaming Tables Seen

Dazed and unbelieving, the Comet *reporter paid the girls to conduct him to the third floor of the establishment, where he saw with his own eyes a luxurious gambling salon, with tables for roulette, dicing, Canfield, chemin de fer. The entire third story was in one room, richly furnished with deep leather chairs and davenports, oriental rugs, fine tables and lamps; at one end was a complete bar, handsomely appointed.*

Liberry Told of Character of House

At the time of the reporter's visit, Mrs. Garr was absent from the house. It was later learned that she was being interviewed at police headquarters, but was released without charge, the police not knowing at the time the discoveries made by the Comet *reporter. Having assembled his evidence, the reporter hastened to 1128 Cleveland Avenue, residence of Miss Rachel Staines, aunt of the unfortunate Rose Liberry. Here, he found the father of the dead girl and informed him of the discoveries. Greatly excited, Mr. Liberry immediately telephoned for an audience with the governor, whose aid he had several times attempted to attain during his search for the missing girl. The governor granted the interview at once.*

GOVERNOR PROMISES AID

Governor Lamson was deeply moved by the evidence presented to him. "If this evidence is true, and you may quote me," he said, "I promise Gilling City a political shake-up such as no city has seen before. It is a blot on the fair escutcheon of this state, that a lovely young visitor from a sister state should be here inducted, whether willingly or unwillingly, into a house of vice. It is a crime that such conditions should exist."

HARTIGAN TO GO BEFORE INVESTIGATING COMMITTEE

The governor immediately set in motion an investigation into the conduct of the police department under Chief Hartigan. First witness before the committee, the governor indicated, would be Police Chief Hartigan himself. Mrs. Garr, proprietress of the house at 417 St. Simon Street, would also come under scrutiny, he indicated.

My eyes flew over the other headlines on the page. They were blazingly sensational. One:

I FOUND HER DEAD

SHE SPEAKS—THE GIRL WHO FOUND ROSE LIBERRY!

This is the story of the girl, the woman, who found Rose Liberry dead. She prefers to be unnamed except for her first name, Leah.

"It was eight o'clock in the morning." Leah's tear-wet brown eyes closed with pain as she haltingly told her story to a Comet reporter. *"I woke up. There was a girl in the room next to mine. A funny kid. She didn't seem very chummy. But I just thought I'd slip in for a minute and talk while I waited for the bathroom. So I knocked at her door but she didn't answer. I opened her door. None of our doors have keys. Mrs. Garr doesn't care at all if we visit. Only the outside doors are locked because she doesn't like girls slipping out on her without her knowing it. You can't blame her, because where would she be if she had a lot of business and all the girls gone to a movie? So, as I said, I opened the door and walked in."*

Walks in on Death Scene

"I walked in, and there was that poor kid hanging to a hook on the inside of the closet door. With a torn-up bedsheet. I run out of there and downstairs because the first thing I thought was that we ought to have a cop, and I screamed at Fancy—that's the housemaid—that there was a girl killed herself and we had to have a cop. The cops were always awful nice whenever we had anything go wrong at our place. So she unlocked the doors. She has keys, too. I pushed right past her and out into the street in my sleeping clothes, if you can imagine how excited I was, and there I ran into a cop, a young fella.

"He came right back with me into the room. I stood in the door, and I guess the racket of us running upstairs must of woke Mrs. Garr because she came out into the hall yelling.

"'What's going on here?' And she went into the room with the cop and slammed the door. That's all I know."

Another account was headed:

MRS. GARR WON'T TALK

VICE PALACE KEEPER REFUSES TO COMMENT

Another was headed:

CHIEF HARTIGAN CLOSETED
WITH PARTY LEADERS

Another:

AUNT WAS FIRST TO SUSPECT
HUMAN TRAFFICKING IN CASE

Another:

VICE LORDS OF CITY
TREMBLE AS NET CLOSES

Another:

WILL PROMINENT MEN BE NAMED
AS FREQUENTERS OF PALACE OF VICE?

A two-line streamer at the bottom of the page ran:

**THE LIFE STORY OF ROSE LIBERRY FROM BABYHOOD TO
HER APPALLING END IN A DEN OF VICE; STORY ON PAGE 2**

My fingers ached. I'd thought of Lieutenant Strom's request
for headlines and first paragraphs as modest, but I'd discovered

otherwise. My handwriting began to look as if I'd never decipher it. But I got everything on the page. I ran through the rest of the paper, too, gathering all the angles the *Comet* hadn't found room for on page one. Then I turned back to page one to check for anything I'd missed.

The pictures.

I studied them.

Mr. Liberry and the governor, snapped together, the governor smiling genially, the father's face deeply furrowed with tragedy. Another picture of Rose Liberry. A studio photograph of the mother, serene and happy; grim irony now. A snapshot of the aunt behind a flowering rosebush, another grim reminder of unharrowed days. A smiling picture of Chief Hartigan, "Chief Called to Questioning." A picture of a young policeman, Patrolman Walters, "Called by Screaming Girl to Discover Scene of Tragedy in Vice Palace."

My eyes slid over that last picture, and then, as if recalled by intuition, returned. Intent, now, I bent over the pictured face. Young. But add eighteen years to it. Add creases in the forehead, blur the clean chin line with fat. Noses don't change much. Add a lost look to the eyes. Patrolman Walters.

No! Mr. Waller!

21

I WAS QUIVERING WITH excitement.

Mr. Waller! Mr. Waller! How sure could I be? No, I couldn't be sure. If only Mr. Kistler were here! If only Lieutenant Strom were here!

I whirled on the librarian.

"Where can I find a phone? Don't let anyone touch that book. It's important. It's important in a case of murder! Don't let anyone come near it! Where's the nearest phone?"

The librarian, who had backed into the nearest corner, pointed down the other side of the room, to a laden desk. I dashed at it.

"Police headquarters, please." To the girl at the switchboard. "Lieutenant Strom, please . . . Yes, it's important. The Garr case . . . Mrs. Dacres . . . Oh, Lieutenant Strom, I think I've found something!"

"What?"

"I'm not sure. I'm not even sure I've found anything. But I

think so. And if it is so, it may be frightfully important. Can you come over?"

"Where?"

"The *Comet* library."

"Five minutes."

He hung up.

The librarian stayed in his corner; he was still there when Lieutenant Strom stalked in, the omnipresent Van in tow.

"Hello, Mrs. Dacres, let's see what you've got."

My shaking finger pointed out the picture. I didn't say anything; if he didn't get it by himself I was just all wet.

Lieutenant Strom bent over the picture. Then he straightened to stare at me.

"Waller, by God!"

I felt almost faint.

WHILE I WAS DRIVING to the station with Lieutenant Strom there wasn't a doubt in my mind that the case was settled.

Together we'd run quickly through the multitudinous publicity the Liberry case had had in the *Comet* through the rest of July, through August and September of 1919. The investigation of the police department. The volcanic cleaning out. The lurid details of daily life in Mrs. Garr's Palace of Vice, at least forty percent of which was certainly fiction. The revulsion of the ministry. The shrieks to heaven of the women's clubs. The beginnings of Mrs. Garr's trial. The continuous attempts by Rose Liberry's father to uncover evidence that his daughter had been forcibly held in Mrs. Garr's house, that she was forced to suicide as her only escape. The success of Mrs. Garr's attorneys in upholding Mrs. Garr's contention that Rose Liberry had come to the house with a young man for a party, and that she had stayed because she enjoyed the excitement and did not want to go back to her parents.

Not even a suicide note had been found. Again and again, the Liberry attorneys had grilled the girl named Leah, Patrolman Walters, and Mrs. Garr. No suicide note.

Then the *Comet* headlines carried the news that Mrs. Garr had been sentenced to five years at Waterford.

FROM VICE PALACE TO PENITENTIARY— MRS. GARR'S LIFE AT WATERFORD

The Liberry case, as far as the *Comet* was concerned, had been drained to its last drop.

It had been drained to its last drop for Lieutenant Strom, too. We left the library to the librarian. Van was dispatched to bring the Wallers in for questioning. The lieutenant let me wander restlessly around his office while he waited for them to come.

"Can you prove it—can you prove from this that they murdered Mrs. Garr?" I asked, with variations.

The lieutenant merely grunted. He was sitting quietly at his desk, gazing thoughtfully down at the pencil in his hands. He stayed that way until Van brought the Wallers in.

They had been frightened yesterday; they were twice as frightened now. They looked as if they had long seen catastrophe coming, and now it had come.

"Sit down," the lieutenant ordered. He looked at the two, then, with level eyes, let silence frighten them still further.

"Waller," he said, even and low, "Mrs. Dacres has been helping me today by looking over the *Comet* files of the Liberry case. On July 10, 1919, the *Comet* ran the picture of a young patrolman. On the morning of July eighth that patrolman had been

called into a house at 417 St. Simon Street by a woman who came
out in her nightclothes screaming that a girl had hung herself in
a bedroom upstairs. The name of that patrolman was Walters."

Silence.

"Mrs. Dacres has a quick eye. But she didn't trust it. She called
me. I looked, too."

Silence.

"Waller, why didn't you tell me you were once on the force?"

Mr. Waller wasn't looking at him. He was looking at me. With
tired eyes. Mrs. Waller was looking at me, too. With hating eyes.

"I knew she'd bring it up sooner or later." He talked as if he
spoke in a vacuum. "Ever since she said Mrs. Garr told her."

"Yes, you knew!" Strom exploded into a shattering bellow.
"You knew, all right! And you tried to kill her to quiet her!"

Mr. Waller, still leaden, shook his head.

"No."

"Your wife got you the Kleenfine!"

"No."

"She used it!"

"For cleaning. Only for cleaning."

"You went home from the inquest. You waited until the house
was quiet. You went into the basement. You swept the back cellar
stairs. You took out the screws and sawed the bolt of the door
going into Mrs. Dacres' kitchen. You lurked there in the dark
stairway, waiting until Mrs. Dacres came home, waited while she
undressed and went to bed and slept, waited like the coward you
are until it was safe for you to do your beastly work. Until you
could come out in the dark—in the dark—and kill her!"

The Wallers were trembling. I was shaking, myself.

The lieutenant's voice dropped then, and he spoke in cold
little tones like ice.

"What were you looking for in that closet?"

"I wasn't, I swear to God I wasn't."

"Then what were you doing there?"

"Nothing. I wasn't there."

Silence.

The lieutenant whispered.

"Waller, I'm going to have your rooms searched."

Silence.

"No objection?"

Silence.

"So it isn't there, eh? Well, Waller, maybe there's more than one road to town. Waller, I have a note in my safe. That note is dated July 8, 1919. On July eight Patrolman Walters—that was you, Waller—went into a house at 417 St. Simon Street. You found something there. *Something Mrs. Garr paid you two thousand dollars for!*

"Walters, there's only one thing you could have found in that room that Mrs. Garr would have paid you that much money for. No amount of money could have saved her from getting into some trouble, and she knew it. But one thing could have made her trouble a lot worse.

"Walters, all during the Liberry trial, the Liberry attorneys tried to get evidence of a suicide note. They tried to get it from Mrs. Garr. They tried to get it from the girl who found the body. They tried to get it from you, Walters, from the policeman who was really the first person to examine the room.

"But they didn't get it. Because you were lying, Walters. You were lying your soul to hell, and they couldn't prove it.

"But I know something those attorneys didn't know. Something that girl's father would have paid—God, I wonder how much—to know.

"I know about that note you hold, dated July 8, 1919."

Nothing in the room, except the vibration of two people trembling in the silence.

A simple question, simply asked.

Dully Mr. Waller looked at him. And then, as simply as if this were not an answer withheld through eighteen years, he spoke: "Mrs. Garr burned it."

Softly, on an expended breath: "She burned it."

Mr. Waller nodded silently.

Mrs. Waller's head moved, the faint echo of a nod.

I felt like crying. The lieutenant's voice was so still and small it sounded in the small room as if he spoke in a great hall.

"You found the suicide note."

"Yes, I found it."

"Mrs. Garr paid you two thousand dollars to keep silent about it."

"Yes."

"Only the two of you knew."

"Yes."

"Walters, did you read that note?"

The man he was questioning made a sound like a sigh. He didn't answer directly; he said, whispering:

"Paper."

Lieutenant Strom pushed paper and pencil across the desk.

Mr. Waller stared at the pencil and the paper at the edge of the desk for a long moment; then he got to his feet, staggering as if he were drunk. He walked to the desk, bent above it, picked up the pencil.

His fingers were shaking, I saw, but the shaking fingers began writing almost automatically, as if this were an exercise performed many times before. Then he pushed the paper across the desk toward the lieutenant and stood, staring at the floor.

Hardness swept into Lieutenant Strom's face. I moved to read over his shoulder.

Odd handwriting to be a man's. It wasn't a man's writing; it was almost a woman's writing; a writing remembered so exactly in a man's mind that he could almost reproduce it.

> *Father, Mother, I've tried and tried to get out. I can't, the house is locked. The things they make me do are horrible, horrible. Oh, Father and Mother, forgive me. I love you, and I know you would so much rather your Rose were dead.*

I kept my eyes on that paper. I would not, I could not, look at the Wallers. But my ears heard Mr. Waller saying woodenly:

"Now maybe I can forget it. I was new on the force. I owed a lot. We were going to have a baby. It died. That note's eaten the heart out of me ever since."

The lieutenant said, still quietly, "Two thousand dollars was your entire payment for surrendering this note?"

Mr. Waller answered as if now his shame were full, there could be no more.

"She gave me all the money she had in the house, too. That was about three thousand dollars."

"God, Waller!"

Suddenly Mr. Waller stumbled backward to his chair; his head dropped to his hands and he began sobbing, the broken, wrenching way a man sobs. I didn't look, but I could feel Mrs. Waller patting his shoulder.

"Did you kill Mrs. Garr, Waller?" The lieutenant's voice was as even as if he'd been asking about the weather.

"Before God, no."

"Did you make the attack on Mrs. Dacres Monday night?"

"No."

The lieutenant shrugged weary shoulders, turned to me.

"Why don't you go on along home, Mrs. Dacres? The rest of this is just going to be the same reel, over and over until he breaks the rest of the way. I think I might get along better without you. I'll let you know when I get where I'm going. Thanks for what you did."

I went out, down the corridor, past the desk, out into June sunshine. I was tense with excitement. But I was glad to go. I'd had enough of seeing the Wallers bludgeoned. Questions were worse than knives. Worse than clubs. Questions carefully hunt out the vital spot. Then strike! Strike! Strike!

Odd that I should feel any pity at all for the Wallers. Incomprehensible that I should pity Mr. Waller, who had let Rose Liberry's father and mother suffer more terribly because the world was made to think their daughter vicious. Vicious at sixteen. Girls were vicious, sometimes, at sixteen. But not their daughter. Not Rose. Not Rose with the grave eyes.

I called Hodge Kistler from a corner drugstore; over dinner, I told him what the afternoon had brought out.

"It is awful," Hodge agreed soberly when I had finished. "The whole thing's awful. That nice kid, getting into that sort of thing. And then letting her parents think she was rotten. Letting that God-awful oldish-bitch off with five years. Waller ought to be shot."

"That's the trouble," I said. "I think he wishes he was. He looks as if he wouldn't mind if he were shot. I can't hate him as I should."

"Hate him? Why should you? Hate's personal."

"Is it? Then what about Mr. Grant? He hated Mrs. Garr. His reasons were impersonal."

"The reasons he gave were impersonal. You don't know what his real reasons were—or are."

"No, that's true. Well, whatever they were, it doesn't look now as if they had anything to do with what we're interested in. The lieutenant is sure Waller is the one. They have personal enough reasons for wanting to bump Mrs. Garr off, goodness knows. I'd hate anyone who'd led me into doing anything that nasty."

"Mean to say you'd let yourself be led?"

"How do I know? I'm feeling very humble tonight. I only know I was there in the room when Mr. Waller told. And I could feel what he was feeling. I can't get away from it. He was feeling exactly as I would have if it had been me."

"Honest. Now, if it was me, I'm certain I should have run from the house, waving the note on high. Heck, think how I could have rocked the world with that suicide note in 1919! Even 1920! The only thing that could have made that story bigger than it was, and that was big enough. Well, Rose Liberry died to give Gilling City a clean government; she accomplished that much. Lots of men have lived longer and done less."

"Now that note wouldn't mean anything, would it?"

"Not to anyone who didn't know the girl. Oh, a few old-timers might remember the case well enough to be mildly interested. But the lieutenant ought to make an effort to find the girl's relatives, if there are any, and let them know."

"It's meaning something to Mr. Waller," I said grimly.

We went to my apartment then; if the lieutenant called, he would call there. I thought about the Wallers as we waited; I couldn't get them out of my mind. Mr. Kistler was restless and uncommunicative, too. I thought about Mr. Waller, young, in debt. His wife heavy with a baby. Crying about what it was going to cost. Mr. Waller, young, walking along his beat and thinking about his wife crying over where they'd get the money for the baby. A girl running to him in her nightgown, screaming. I thought about Mr. Waller running into the red-plush house and up the richly carpeted stairs, accustomed to the feet of Gilling City's Prominent Men. Waller running, forgetting his crying wife now, running quickly down a hall and into a bedroom where a girl hung by a sheet.

Mr. Waller working fast, taking the girl down and laying her on the bed, but knowing she was dead. Grabbing up the note and reading it. I thought about how Mrs. Garr would run in screaming, offering him money, a thousand dollars, two thousand, three thousand, five—anything, to help keep her out of bad trouble; it wasn't any of her fault, and the law would get her; the law would get her, and she had plenty of money.

"See," she would cry, running out and coming back, "money, money, money!" She would give him all this, her hands full, she would give him more, she would pay him money the rest of his life. The girl was dead. Not taking money wouldn't make her live again.

I thought about Mr. Waller testifying in the court, with Mrs. Garr's frantic little black eyes on him, promising, promising. I thought about Mrs. Garr's hair whitening in prison to that lovely, pure white. And of Mr. Waller, thrown out with the rest of his fellows, to destroy himself on his own slow poison of memory.

We talked fitfully, expecting every moment to hear the phone ring and the lieutenant's triumphant voice announcing a confession.

Hours went by. Then slow feet came into the hall; heavy, leaden feet that lifted someone slowly up the stairs. Just one pair of feet.

"I'm sure that was Mrs. Waller," I whispered. "Alone."

Still we waited. We heard Mr. Grant go out. We heard him return.

We grew even more restless as the evening wore on. Hodge

began making out a time sheet to keep his mind busy, a time sheet covering the Friday Mrs. Garr must have died.

Excursion train due to leave . . . 8:05

Mrs. Garr leaves station . . . 8:07

Mrs. Garr seen by Mr. Grant . . . 8:25

Mrs. Garr waits in storage room . . . 8:27 to 9:10

Mr. Waller goes to cellar kitchen . . . 9:08

Mrs. Garr confronts him . . . 9:10

Murder . . . 9:12

Mr. Waller searches kitchen, puts dog and two cats back in . . . 9:13 to 10:00

Mrs. Dacres returns, sees one cat still out . . . 10:00

Waller returns cat to kitchen . . . 10:55

W. throws key in cellar window . . . 11:00

Waller attacks Mrs. Dacres . . . 11:02

"It's lovely, and very logical, I'm sure," I said. "But it doesn't prove anything."

"Pooey to you, always yelping about proof."

"You can't electrocute Mr. Waller for making away with a suicide note."

"Bigger crimes have been committed in the name of justice."

"I wish Lieutenant Strom would call up. Anyway, what was Waller hunting for in that basement kitchen?"

"Maybe Mrs. Garr didn't destroy that note as she said. How did he know she burned it? Maybe she was holding it over him."

"But why would he want it?"

"Maybe Mrs. Garr was threatening to make it public."

"But what could she do with it after all these years? And anyway, it would be more dangerous to her than to him. Of course, maybe he thought that if she didn't have it, he could force her to pay that two-thousand-dollar note—"

"Exactly, my friend."

"Anyway, I wish we'd get that call."

The doorbell rang then; we stopped talking to listen. The man on duty in the hall answered.

The voice in the hall was Lieutenant Strom's. I ran for my doors.

"Has he confessed? Do you know now for sure?"

Lieutenant Strom looked inexpressibly tired; he flopped into my big chair as if starch had left his muscles forever.

"He's sitting as tight as a wood tick," he said disgustedly. "I can't get another thing out of him."

"What does that mean? Does that mean he isn't guilty?"

"Hell, I don't know."

I made coffee and sandwiches; the lieutenant revived somewhat on those, but he was still thoroughly out of sorts.

"If he did it he's doing a damn good job of holding out."

"I take it few hold out on you?" asked Hodge.

"Damn few," replied the lieutenant arrogantly. "I get 'em."

He told us, then, about other cases he'd handled. One about a man who'd been picked up by a roadside, riddled by bullets. About how he'd gone out himself and picked up hitchhikers: one, two, three. And how he'd turned on the fourth with, "How much dough you pick off that guy whose car you stole after you shot him?" And the boy had screamed with telltale fear.

One triumphant case followed another in his recital; past success poured confidence into him as he talked.

"I tell you frankly, I'm good at getting confessions. I know I'm good. I'm not too good, though. I don't make 'em confess crimes they didn't do. If this Waller croaked Mrs. Garr and tried to croak you, Mrs. Dacres, he's good. The trouble is, I've got to get a confession or else. I haven't enough evidence to pin the thing on him—or on anyone else."

"Good motives for Waller, though," Hodge said. "Mrs. Garr refusing to pay that note and threatening to turn them out. And I understand he admits Mrs. Dacres told him she knew he'd been on the force. One thing awfully dangerous for him to have come out."

"God, don't think I haven't been over that ground. As far as Waller is concerned, there isn't any ground I haven't been over."

"If you tip back any farther in that chair," I told Hodge, "you're going to have to put in a new buffet door for Mrs. Garr's estate. You know what I think we should do? Take our minds off Mr. Waller for a minute, go back to the facts of the murder, and see what else we see."

"So what?" Hodge.

"No, wait a minute. Not a bad idea." The lieutenant. "Where would you begin?"

"Begin where you began with those hitchhikers. How did you know it was the fourth one? Something that came out when you talked, probably."

"Okay, lady. Who would you say it was, forgetting Waller but taking into consideration everything else we know up to now?"

"I can't help it," I said. "When I begin to ask myself who killed Mrs. Garr, I forget the Rose Liberry business. After all, we haven't one single thing to prove that old case is actually concerned in the death. Nothing that counts, except that Mrs. Garr was a principal figure in both. I go right back to where I started. Who benefited by the death? The Hallorans."

The lieutenant and Hodge groaned in unison.

"Now look here," the lieutenant instructed me. "Does an alibi mean anything to you? The Hallorans aren't bright enough to fake alibis like theirs. They couldn't have made that pass at you Monday night."

"What proof have you that was the same person who killed Mrs. Garr?"

They groaned again.

"Didn't we have that all argued out once?"

"Yes, but there's nothing has as many holes as an argument."

"Well, I'll be cremated and eat my own ashes before I'll start again that far back. You, Kistler, is your idea as bright as hers?"

"Not unlikely."

"Shoot it."

"Dark horse. The same dark horse I've quietly ridden from the beginning. Buffingham."

"Aw, a guy with a name like that couldn't commit murder."

"He didn't do it with his name. Name didn't keep his son from robbing banks and doing a little shooting."

"Reasons—any new ones?"

"Just the old ones. Plus my feeling when I have the whole household in one room, which has happened on divers occasions lately, Lieutenant. I look about me and say to myself, 'Who done it?' And my forefinger practically lifts of itself to point out Buffingham."

"Hm."

"Desperate for money, too."

"A couple of Cs wouldn't do his boy any good."

"He looks grief-stricken, too," I put in.

"Mrs. Sorry-for-the-Underdog speaks up from her corner. She's sorriest of all when the underdog chloroforms her."

"It was ether. A dry cleaner."

"Well, you never heard of anyone being ethered, did you? Or dry-cleaned, did you? There isn't any verb for that. It doesn't sound lethal enough."

"Cut it out." From the lieutenant. "Now, if you'd ask me, I'd say this murderer has to be one of two things. Either he's smarter than anyone else I've ever come up against, so smart he can hide what he's feeling and thinking. Or else he's so dumb and tough he doesn't have anything to show. I've had that kind before."

"The first description fits Mr. Kistler perfectly."

"Okay, baby, the second fits you."

"Does it? What I was really thinking was that it might be someone who kept his mind fastened so tightly on something else that it completely covers up what you're trying to get at."

"Say, that would do for Buffingham, wouldn't it? Nice work!"

"A few other people, too," the lieutenant broke in again. "Well, I'm going to have Buffingham down here and take another crack at him."

He ordered the detective in the hall to bring Mr. Buffingham down. Mr. Buffingham returned with him immediately.

"Something's come up that makes me have another go at you, Buffingham." The lieutenant's manner held its usual smooth threat. "I've been going into the records of the Liberry case. You didn't come into that case directly, Buffingham, but I'll stake plenty that you were connected with Mrs. Garr in that old business some way. What were you—a come-on?"

"I never saw Mrs. Garr before I came to this house."

"How about knowing the Wallers?"

"Know 'em? Sure. They been here a long time. Seen 'em around."

"Ever know Waller was once on the force?"

Buffingham hesitated. "I don't know. Had a vague idea he was."

"Know him at the time of the Liberry case?"

"No."

"Oh, you're sure. So you know when the Liberry case was?"

"I remember the story in the papers. Big story."

"Yeah. Big story. What were you doing in those days?"

"Oh, I was workin', I guess."

"Where?"

"Drugstore, it must of been. That's all the jobs I ever had. Mostly jerking sodas."

Lieutenant Strom paused before his next question. The only movement in the room was the flicker of Mr. Buffingham's restless dark eyes.

"Did you ever work in the Stacy Drugstore at the corner of Cleveland and St. Simon Street?"

Again, as on Wednesday, something came and went behind Mr. Buffingham's eyes.

"Yeah, I worked there once." He laughed. "I worked in half the drugstores in town."

"When did you work there?" Sharply.

"When—Let's see. That was a while ago. Twelve years. Fifteen years. I don't know. Hell, I worked in too many places. You know. You get took on for a rush season. Christmas. Or summer at the fountain. Then you get laid off."

"Stacy's still running that drugstore, Buffingham. I can find out."

Mr. Buffingham's shoulders shrugged.

"Sure you weren't working there the summer of 1919?"

"Might of. I wouldn't remember."

"There's something to make you remember. Cleveland at St. Simon Street is only two blocks below 417 St. Simon. And there was plenty of hell popping at 417 St. Simon Street that summer."

"It didn't have nothing to do with me. I wouldn't know."

Was he tense, answering carefully? Or were his answers as casual as they sounded on the surface?

The lieutenant appeared to have gone as far as he could see to go up that alley. He switched to another.

"Now let's get going on last Monday night, when Mrs. Dacres

had this party we've heard so much about. You came in with Mr. Grant just after midnight. You go upstairs. You sleep. Now, Buffingham, you know doggone well there were noises going on in this house that night. It's impossible to go downstairs, even carpeted stairs, in a house this age, without making some creaks. Mrs. Dacres heard 'em, the night Mrs. Garr was done in. You can't—"

He turned abruptly, called:

"You, Jones out there, steal silently upstairs, will you?"

"Say, what is this?" From Jones.

"Do what you're told!"

"Okay."

Jones stealing upstairs was so evident I giggled.

"Swell burglar Jones'd make," the lieutenant interrupted himself further before going back to Buffingham. "Hear that, Buffingham? We know that kind of noise was going on in this house Monday night. Not as loud as that, but some noise. And you can't saw a bolt without a whine. Not quick, the way this guy had to do it. Little Quick Ears here was out. So was Kistler. Sands and the Wallers said they had been in bed a long time; they might have been sleeping hard, if it wasn't one of them that was up and about. But, by God, I'd like to hear your reason for not hearing things. Your room's right at the head of the stairs. You'd just got in. If you didn't hear anything, Buffingham, it sounds doggone suspicious to me."

Mr. Buffingham hadn't smoked this time. But now he took out a cigarette and began revolving it rapidly with both hands, his eyes fixed on it.

"I wouldn't want to get nobody in trouble," he said at last.

"Let me worry about that. You can't get anyone in trouble he didn't get himself into. What'd you hear?"

"Creaks, you know. In the hall. Going down the stairs. Like them he made. Jones. Only not so loud."

"Where'd they start—other end of the hall?"

The cigarette revolved more slowly.

"I guess not. My end. I guess they went past my door."

"Past your door. From Grant's or Kistler's rooms?"

"He"—Mr. Buffingham motioned with his head toward Hodge—"he wasn't in yet. I don't think. I hadn't gone to sleep yet."

"Grant, then!"

No reply.

"Grant," said Hodge. "Baloney."

"Or someone hiding in your rooms, Hodge," I said.

"Grant!" the lieutenant repeated briskly, his eyes alight. "I'm always getting around to that guy. He hated her, too. Said he did. I'm going to have him down. No, Buffingham, you stay here. Grant!"

22

THE OBLIGING JONES WENT upstairs for Mr. Grant. While we waited, Hodge laughingly showed Lieutenant Strom the timetable he had worked out. The lieutenant, not laughing, added the paper to a bunch for his pocket.

"Nice evidence if it turns out you did it," he said.

When he came in Mr. Grant looked so old and frail that Hodge automatically offered him a chair. Mr. Buffingham, without being asked, dropped into one, too.

The lieutenant opened fire at once.

"Walk in your sleep, Mr. Grant?"

"I? No, certainly not."

"Sure?"

"I am certain."

"Mr. Buffingham here has had one of those sudden memory attacks always affecting people in this case. Didn't bring it up before out of not wanting to get anyone in trouble. Says he heard someone walking Monday night, the night Mrs. Dacres was attacked. *Someone who started at your door, walked down the hall and down the stairs."*

Mr. Grant turned his mild proud eyes on Mr. Buffingham; he appeared to ponder his answer before making it.

"That is perfectly true," he said finally, quietly.

The lieutenant made a startled exclamation; whatever he'd expected, it couldn't have been that quiet admission. I was dumbfounded, and I could see Hodge was the same. Mr. Grant talked on.

"I did walk down the hall. I walked along the upstairs hall, down the stairs, and then on down the cellar stairs. I did not say so the other day because it was entirely irrelevant. Nothing came of it."

"You could have let me judge that," barked the lieutenant. "Mind letting me in on why you took this stroll?"

"Not at all. It was something I heard."

"So you heard things, too!"

"Well, I thought I did. Something rather peculiar. You'll be amused, I know. I couldn't imagine why anyone should be doing so at that time of night." He spread his hands. "It was an extremely odd sound for that time of night. A brushing sound. The only thing I could liken it to is—sweeping."

"Oh, so you heard sweeping." The lieutenant's voice bristled with withheld meanings.

"Impossible, of course, but that is the best description I can give."

"You heard sweeping, and you didn't say one word Tuesday, you didn't say a word Wednesday!"

Mr. Grant blinked. "But it couldn't have been important."

"Couldn't have been—couldn't have been! *When we know the person who attacked Mrs. Dacres swept the back cellar stairs that night!"*

Surprise flitted across Mr. Grant's face, and, I thought, mild gratification.

"Someone was sweeping? Then I was right!"

"Right? I'll say you were right! Why, I ask again, didn't you say so before?"

"This is the first time I have heard of back stairs being swept," Mr. Grant pointed out, still mildly.

He had Lieutenant Strom. We all—I mean the lieutenant, Hodge, and I—opened our mouths to speak—and then shut them.

What, after all, was the use? There was every likelihood that Mr. Grant hadn't heard. Certainly it hadn't been brought out at his questioning yesterday, and Mr. Grant wasn't given to gossiping with the others.

Mr. Buffingham just looked blank. He hadn't looked surprised when the lieutenant had outlined the noises there must have been in the house Monday night—had he known before? And Mr. Waller. My mind sped back to the afternoon. He hadn't shown surprise at the lieutenant's reconstruction of the attack, either!

"I'll be fried for an oyster," the lieutenant said helplessly, while he got himself together. Step by step, then, he explained his theory of my attacker's probable movements.

Mr. Grant nodded. "That fits in very nicely. I heard, as I say, this brushing sound. My interest, in view of the strange happenings in the house lately, was piqued. I would like to know who— but no matter. So I investigated. I walked to the cellar, very quietly, but could see nothing out of the way in the furnace room or in Mrs. Garr's kitchen beyond, although I did not turn on the light there. As soon as I had left my room there was absolute stillness in the house. I then returned upstairs, thinking I must have been mistaken."

"You didn't think it your duty to warn the other inhabitants—Mrs. Dacres, for example?"

"Why, no. I—I thought her adequately protected. Chairs under doorknobs are excellent—"

"How do you know about the chairs under the doorknobs?"

"Why, I heard it."

"You *heard* it?"

"Yes. I have neglected to state, perhaps, that it was while I was in the cellar that Mrs. Dacres and one other person—Mr. Kistler, of course—returned to the house. I heard the good-byes in the hall, and her report that everything was—er—okay was the expression, I believe. I heard the doors being locked, chairs being dragged and hooked under the knobs. Not concealed actions at all."

He blinked at me, and I blushed for the rum, but he smiled kindly.

"Very evident. Very evident. Very normal, too. Naturally, I did not wish to be seen. I waited a few minutes before returning upstairs."

He looked at the lieutenant's suspicion as if he did not sense it. The lieutenant stared from Mr. Grant to Hodge, and then to me and around again, trying to form some judgment on this bewildering evidence.

"Sounds screwy to me," he said; then strongly, as if he took his cue from himself, "Yes, and it is screwy, too! You'll have to do a lot more explaining to get out of this, Grant. So you were around at three o'clock, eh?"

"I had no idea of the time."

"But that's when these folks came in!" He turned to Buffingham. "That doesn't square with your story that you'd just come in."

"I only said what it seemed like to me," Mr. Buffingham replied thoughtfully. "I might have been reading a little longer. I might of laid awake a little longer. I wouldn't know."

"Nobody knows anything in this case," the lieutenant snorted. "Grant, you didn't go into that cellar because you heard a noise. You made that noise. *That was you, sweeping those cellar stairs.*"

I began to wonder if the lieutenant hadn't left out a few details in his story of the murdering hitchhiker. I began to guess he had accused the first three hitchhikers, too, and struck pay dirt in the fourth. Certainly, his methods in this case had depended strongly on accusation of everyone who came under suspicion.

He didn't strike pay dirt in Mr. Grant. He threatened, he cajoled, he made the same accusations over and over; Mr. Grant was firm. Mr. Grant became whiter, weaker, frailer, but no less firm.

It was the lieutenant who cried quits.

"Oh, for God's sake," he cried as a finale. "I'm God damned sick of the whole case! You can all get murdered for all I care. I'm going home to bed."

He flung out, growled something at the detective in the passage, slammed the door after himself.

The four of us left in my living room looked bleakly at each other. We'd been pretty well drained of emotion. I know I'd been wrung by pity for Mr. Grant.

I said so.

Looking back, I'm glad I did.

I said, "I don't think it was you that attacked me, Mr. Grant. I'd never in the world believe it."

"You'd be right," he said gently.

"To hell with the police," Mr. Buffingham said. "I'm going to bed." He lurched wearily out and upstairs.

Mr. Grant and Hodge stood up, too.

"I won't say, 'Must go so soon?'" I said, trying to be light. "I know you're desperately tired. I am."

I walked forward to be at the door when they left, walked

past the chair where the lieutenant had sat. Automatically I stooped to pick up a sheet of paper fallen to the floor.

"I hope you both get a good night's sleep; I feel I can sleep safely with that detective—Why, look, Hodge, this is the copy of Rose Liberry's suicide note! Lieutenant Strom must have dropped it when he put your timetable away!"

Hodge leaned over me to read. Mr. Grant grew interested, too; when I looked up he stood beside me, reading.

Without a word or a sign he slipped to the floor.

"He's fainted!" cried Hodge. "Here, let me get him on the couch."

He was curiously light when we lifted him. The detective in the hall came in; together the three of us worked to bring Mr. Grant back to consciousness.

He came back quickly, lay quiet for a while, his face sunken and white but his eyes bright.

"So many questions," he murmured.

He closed his eyes, seemed to doze a little.

"I knew Lieutenant Strom was being too hard on him." I felt indignant at the lieutenant. "Let him stay here awhile. There's no hurry for him to get upstairs."

The detective, instead of going back to the hall, hovered near the windows, watching. I sat by the couch. Presently Mr. Grant's eyes opened; he smiled at me faintly.

"What was I looking at? Oh yes. The paper. What was it you called it?"

"It was something we turned up this morning. I don't suppose you'd remember, but there was a big scandal in Gilling City years ago. A girl named Rose Liberry committed suicide. Her suicide note was very dangerous to someone, and it was destroyed. But the one man living who saw it remembered it very clearly. That was his copy."

To my surprise he nodded.

"I remember. The Liberry case. A great scandal. I remember very well. I—knew the family. But there wasn't any suicide note. I remember very well. No note."

"We just found out about it today," I repeated.

I hesitated, but he was obviously interested, waiting. There was no one else who could hear except Hodge and the detective. Why shouldn't I tell him? Here *was* someone who at least remembered. A friend of the family. One of those who ought to know. But I didn't want to bring Mr. Waller in.

"We tracked down the policeman who was the first official at the scene of the suicide. We were able to prove Mrs. Garr had been paying him money. So Lieutenant Strom forced him to confess he had found a suicide note and that the money was a bribe Mrs. Garr had paid to let her destroy it."

"Destroy? But the note—"

"Mr.—the policeman remembered it perfectly. He couldn't forget. It had been eating at his mind ever since. He wrote it down for Lieutenant Strom just as it was, just as he found it."

Mr. Grant closed his eyes; he was so pale I called out to Hodge, but he hadn't fainted again. He opened his eyes after a few minutes.

"Very interesting. Very interesting," he murmured.

He sat up in another few moments; Hodge and the detective moved to help him upstairs. When he was on his feet, he turned to me absently, as if his thoughts were far away.

"Very interesting. I remember the case well. The girl's parents—I remember them well. Great blow, the girl's death was. The—the circumstances. This makes such a change. The note— would you mind if I studied it? I would return it to the lieutenant in the morning, of course. Very interesting."

I hesitated again. Lieutenant Strom might be furious. But it wasn't an original; if the note were lost, couldn't Mr. Waller be forced to make another copy? I looked at Mr. Grant. A faint pink was coming into his face now; he looked, somehow, like a lost, pathetic old child, asking a favor.

"I don't see why not," I said gently and gave it to him.

He took it in his right hand, carefully; I didn't think he'd lose it. I heard the three pairs of feet slowly going upstairs; Hodge and the detective stayed awhile in Mr. Grant's room before they came down again.

"Something funny about that." Jones followed Hodge into my living room. "I think he had the wind up about that note."

"It was strange how interested he was, wasn't it? He was worn out before, though. It must have been the strain of the questioning that made him faint." I was still puzzling over the request to study the note that night. What did he mean, "study it"?

"I disagree with you," Hodge said thoughtfully. "I was thinking how well he stood up under the questioning. The lieutenant's barbs didn't seem to penetrate. He beat Strom out. No, I think Jones here is right. It was the note that knocked him cold."

"But what could that mean?"

"A lot or nothing," Hodge said. "He said he knew the family. To friends of the family that scandal must have been a world-shaker. They'd remember. Then this note. It's so obvious it makes the girl all right. A victim. It was probably the surprise, coming on top of all the questioning."

"The questioning tonight—Mr. Grant's, I mean—didn't go into the Liberry case at all, did it? It was when he was talking to Mr. Buffingham that Lieutenant Strom went into that."

"I think maybe I ought to call the chief," Jones offered. "But you saw the way he slammed out of here. He ought to be asleep by now. I'd get my head bitten off at the neck."

"Tomorrow's another day," Hodge agreed.

"Especially with you on guard in the hall," I reminded Mr. Jones. "Mr. Grant will still be here in the morning, with you to keep him here."

So Lieutenant Strom wasn't called.

I wonder if it would have made any difference if he had been.

In the end, I am sure, there would have been no difference.

I WAS RESTLESS THAT night.

It was hard to pin my restlessness down to any one thing.

Mr. Waller didn't come home. He was still being held, then. We were safe from him, if he was the marauder.

If he was not, then there was the detective in the hall to keep us safe from whoever it was.

I had left my hall doors open again, and I could hear the rattle of Jones' paper, and his movements as he twisted in his chair.

I finally pinned my restlessness to Mr. Grant. I couldn't figure out his attitude. "Very interesting. Very. I remember the case well. I was a friend of the family." His voice murmured in my ears as I tried vainly to sleep. I tried to put myself in Mr. Grant's mind, to see and feel as he would.

Mr. Grant twenty years younger. Fifty, perhaps. A friend of Mr. Liberry. An acquaintance of Miss Rachel Staines, the aunt. Of course they would have friends. There must be others, still living.

The first thing I should do in the morning must be to hurry Lieutenant Strom into finding the friends and relatives of Rose Liberry, if he hadn't already started doing so. They would like to know.

The girl's father and mother might still live out of town. But the aunt had lived in town. I'd look in the phone book. Staines, Rachel, 1128 Cleveland Avenue. Would the name still be there?

"Miss Staines, this is Mrs. Dacres. You won't know me, but I have good news for you . . . Your niece, Rose Liberry—the one that died so sadly—her suicide note has been found at last."

I'd never sleep, thinking about all this. Mr. Grant, a friend of the family. Worried and kindly when the first news of the disappearance came. Helping with money, perhaps. Horrified when the end came. A friend of the family.

I slept at last, but I had nightmares in which Rose Liberry's family cried to me: "Hurry, hurry, hurry!"

When I woke, it was bright morning, but I was still heavily tired. I dragged myself out of bed and yawned my breakfast ready; funny—the day before yesterday, I'd been starving on orange juice, and now I'd already forgotten that hunger. The top of my head was still sore; that was the only remnant of Monday's attack. It was Friday. About time, I thought sardonically, for me to have another.

After I'd eaten I wandered out into the hall. Mr. Grant was back on my mind. Jones was still there, sleepy and cross.

"Good morning!"

"Morning."

"Everything normal? No murders?"

"Naw."

"Seen Mr. Grant this morning?"

"He ain't been down yet."

"Poor old man," I said. "He's probably all in. I think I'll make fresh coffee and take him a cup."

"Okay, sister. I could use one myself."

So I made coffee, left a cup with the grateful Jones, and went upstairs with the other. The hall upstairs was dark and silent. Hodge was probably gone. Mr. Buffingham would still be sleeping. Miss Sands at work. Mrs. Waller—Mrs. Waller would be alone.

I'd seldom seen either of the Wallers alone. I thought about their life, knit so closely by shared shame. For better, for worse. Mrs. Waller had taken her full share of the shame.

It was really the Wallers I was thinking of as I knocked softly on Mr. Grant's door.

There wasn't any answer.

I knocked again.

The door gave a little as I knocked. Mr. Grant, then, as I had, had left his door unlocked last night. He hadn't even caught the lock. Probably he had been afraid he might be sick in the night and need help.

He was an old man. Surely, he wouldn't mind if I came in to see how he was.

I swung the door open.

He slept on the bed, his face turned to the open window. The light fell strongly on his sleeping face; he looked rested, serene, all the weariness of last night gone.

The room was very bright. I looked upward.

The electric light in the ceiling was still on.

I think I knew then.

Softly I set the cup and saucer on the dresser top. Lightly I touched the man's arm.

Dead.

I knew, too, what to look for.

On the table by the bed were two slips of paper, one laid neatly over the other. The top one was familiar. Rose Liberry's suicide note.

Under it was a shorter note:

> *I am John Grant Liberry. I am very happy tonight;*
> *I cannot wait to go to her.*

23

I WENT QUIETLY DOWNSTAIRS to tell Jones.

He woke up thoroughly then, gave a startled exclamation, ran upstairs, came charging back. I sat down on the black leather davenport to cry; Jones called Strom and paced the floor, anxious.

"Gosh, what'll he say? With me right here!" was his refrain.

Lieutenant Strom appeared with his usual promptness; if he left abruptly, he came abruptly, too. It didn't seem five minutes before he was there in the hall, Van and Bill behind him.

"What's eating you?" he said to me before he spoke to Jones.

"I'm glad he saw the note," I sobbed.

"What note?"

"You dropped Rose Liberry's suicide note. Mr. Grant—he's her father."

"For crying out loud! Come along, Jones!"

They tramped upstairs, all four. Within a few minutes, I was continually interrupted by new arrivals. I didn't know who they were. Police officers, coroner's men, probably. They came in officiously, asked, "Where is it?" and went upstairs.

After a while Mrs. Waller came down, her face mottled and red, her eyes anxious and frightened.

"What is it?" she asked hoarsely.

"It's Mr. Grant. He's dead."

"Dead? He's dead?"

"Yes. I found him. I went up with some coffee for him, and he was—gone."

"What did he die from?" she whispered stiffly, terror beginning on her face.

"I don't know. But he—he did it himself. He left a note."

I hadn't yet thought what the implications might be. Then I did, with a shock, as I watched hope burst into Mrs. Waller's face. I knew immediately what she meant when she cried:

"Did he confess he'd done it?"

"Oh no. No. It doesn't mean he had anything to do with Mrs. Garr's death. It was something entirely different. It was—"

The realization of how directly the Wallers were concerned in both Mr. Grant's life and his death hit me. The realization of the eighteen years of agony they had built him. I turned my eyes away.

"When Lieutenant Strom was here last night he dropped on the floor the copy of Rose Liberry's suicide note, the one your husband wrote. Mr. Grant saw it."

I paused. Culpable as I felt the Wallers to be, I could hardly tell her the rest. I could feel her fear growing around me, pressing against me, but there was compulsion in it, too. Compulsion to tell. I went on.

"Mr. Grant saw the note after Lieutenant Strom had left. He fainted. He—his name wasn't Grant. It was John Grant Liberry. He was her father."

Mrs. Waller held her breath so long I was frightened into looking at her. Then she began sobbing horribly.

She wasn't an imaginative woman. I think that was the first

time she really understood what their withholding of the note
had meant.

I couldn't be sympathetic, but you have to do what you can
for another human being. I went into my kitchen, reheated the
second batch of coffee, and made her drink a cup. Mr. Buffingham came down while she was drinking it.

"What's going on now?"

I explained shortly.

"Jeez!" he exclaimed excitedly. "You mean he's murdered?"

"No. He left a note."

"Cripes! Suicide!"

"It looked that way."

He began pacing up and down the hall with long, fast steps.
It was curious: Mrs. Garr's death had left him imperturbable, as
had, so far as I could see, the attacks on me. But Mr. Grant's death
excited him wildly. He ran upstairs after a bit; I heard his voice
now and again talking to the men upstairs.

Lieutenant Strom came down to tell Mrs. Waller and me to go
into my apartment and shut the door.

We did; there was a shuffling of feet on the stairs, then com-
parative quiet.

Lieutenant Strom knocked on my door; came in alone. He was
genially elated.

"God, what a finale! This beats anything I ever had!"

I caught at one word with blank amazement.

"Finale? What do you mean, finale?"

"Well, everything's answered now, isn't it?"

I just stared at him, my lower jaw hanging. He laughed at me.

"Don't tell me your supercolossal mind hasn't tumbled, Mrs.
Dacres. Do you mean you didn't get it? Why, it's as plain as the nose
on Kistler's face! John Grant Liberry! Gosh, what a melodrama!

Girl's father waits until the woman who brought about his daughter's downfall is out of jail. He never believed the willing-victim business. He knew the girl. He considers Mrs. Garr her murderer. So when she gets out, he comes here to find her. Changes his name, breaks loose from his past. That alone shows he was out for her. We don't know when he begins his hunt, but he finds her eventually, and luck's with him—she's running a rooming house. He takes a room with her. He probably has that suicide note on the brain; he hunts in the house for that or some other clue to Mrs. Garr's guilt. He can afford to take his time. Maybe he finds something, maybe he doesn't. I think he doesn't. But she comes back from that Chicago trip too early, catches him hunting in the kitchen. There's some kind of a scrap, and she hits the floor. Everything fits. Why, *he even said he'd seen her that night*! Golly, I should have caught on, right there. That slipped out, that did. So he tries to pass it off by saying he'd seen her out the window. And who was it raised the hue and cry about Mrs. Garr being gone in the first place? Mr. Grant! The girl's father! Boy, here's one place this story can hit the papers, anyway." He stopped, insufferably satisfied.

"But the attacks on me," I objected. "Do you think he did those, too?"

"Sure, why not? Why, I almost had him last night on one of them! He actually admitted he'd been in the cellar that night. Had to cook up a story to meet Buffingham's evidence that he'd heard him prowling around. Admitted he'd heard you hooking your chairs under the doorknobs! Just you think about that. Standing with his ear to your kitchen door, that's where he was. Why, I must have been off my feed, not hanging it on him last night. I knew it the first thing I woke up this morning. I was just going to start for here when Jones called. Oh, he knew I had him, all right. Well, he saved the city the expense of a trial."

I stared at his cocksure face.

If he was as sure as that, he must be right. He had experience with solving murders; I hadn't.

"What did he——?"

"Sleeping powders. Nice quiet way. I don't blame him. He knew he was through. I don't blame him for much of the rest of it, either, except that he was a little hard on you. Probably didn't realize how hard he was being. The girl's father! Golly, what a story!"

I looked away from his self-satisfaction to Mrs. Waller; hope was blazing in her face again; she was drinking hope.

I asked the question she trembled to ask.

"I suppose Mr. Waller will be home soon, now."

"Oh, sure. Sure." He paused, thought. "God, that was a dirty deal, but I don't see what I can do about it after all these years. Mrs. Garr dead, too. As far as I can see the whole thing's washed up."

"If you make a Roman holiday for the newspapers out of this, I'll be mad at you forever. Poor Mr. Grant," I said.

His manner took on more reserve after that.

He went out into the hall where five or six men were still buzzing around. They turned out to be reporters; some of them, at least. Strom talked to them a long time. Mrs. Waller escaped through them with her apron over her head. I had men knocking on my door to ask me questions, too, but I was careful what I said. The lieutenant's sins against Mr. Grant could all be on his own head.

All day, I never knew when a reporter would knock on my door. Mrs. Halloran arrived in midmorning; she took it on herself to answer questions, which was lovely, because she didn't know of a thing that had happened since Wednesday.

One of the few half hours the hall was empty I called Hodge

at the *Buyers' Guide* to tell him. He was stunned, too. Not at the suicide—we both thought that natural enough under the circumstances. But that Mr. Grant should be a murderer.

"I can't get it," Hodge repeated, "but I guess you never can tell."

"He had reason enough to hate her. I suppose it has to be true. I can imagine murdering Mrs. Garr with very little compunction if it had been my daughter."

"So can I."

"Now I'm furious at Lieutenant Strom. He's a publicity grabber, that's what he is. Wouldn't you think the poor old man had had enough trouble in his life, without being branded for this when he died?"

Hodge agreed with me then, but he came bounding into the house at noon with a *Comet* extra he'd picked up downtown.

"Read that and eat your words about Strom."

I did. Lieutenant Strom had been awfully, awfully decent. That was when I was glad I'd been careful about what I'd said to the reporters.

OLD MYSTERY CLEARS AS
JOHN LIBERRY DIES

LONG-LOST SUICIDE NOTE OF
FAMOUS ROSE LIBERRY TRAGEDY
FOUND BY POLICE

Two decades ago the Rose Liberry tragedy stirred Gilling City and the world; today, its last echo sounded in a small room of a house at 593 Trent Street, where lay John Grant Liberry, dead by his own hand, happy.

On the day before, police, while following the lucky clue of a $2,000 note which had turned up in the estate of the late

Harriet Luella Garr, forced confession from the holder that the money was due him in payment for concealing the discovery of Rose Liberry's suicide note.

TRAGEDY RECALLED

Long-time residents of the city will recall the Rose Liberry tragedy clearly. The unfortunate girl, then only sixteen, left the home of her aunt, Miss Rachel Staines, then residing at 1128 Cleveland Avenue, on the afternoon of May 23, 1919. She was never again seen alive by relatives or friends.

The girl's parents, Mr. & Mrs. John Grant Liberry, of Cincinnati, pushed the search to the utmost but were hampered by the notorious Hartigan political regime, then in power. The tragedy burst forth as world news when the body of a suicide in an infamous house on St. Simon Street, run by Harriet Luella Garr, was identified as the missing Rose Liberry.

Every effort was made to prove the unhappy girl had been led to and kept in the house by force, but no proof could be brought against the claim of Mrs. Garr that the girl had stayed at the house willingly. No suicide note was found, nor could evidence of one be obtained, although the Liberry attorneys expended every effort at this point. The case resulted in the political cleanup, pushed by David L. Lamson, then governor of the state, which resulted in our present clean political setup.

STROM ENGINEERS COUP

The discovery of the missing suicide note is entirely due to the excellent work of Lieutenant Peter Strom, in charge of the homicide squad, Gilling City police.

In investigating the death of Mrs. Garr on May 28 of this year, a death found to be due to natural causes by a coroner's jury on Monday, Lieutenant Strom found that a lodger in Mrs. Garr's house had paid no rent for years. Under pressure, the lodger produced a note signed by Mrs. Garr and dated July 8, 1919, the day the dead body of Rose Liberry was found. Struck by the date, Lieutenant Strom began investigating old court records and the Comet *files.*

Comet Picture Is Clue

One investigator noted a resemblance between a picture of the young patrolman, who was the first one called to the scene of Rose Liberry's suicide, and the lodger in question. Lieutenant Strom confirmed the likeness. Armed with the information, Lieutenant Strom faced the lodger with the inescapable deduction that the only thing for which Mrs. Garr would have paid $2,000 to the policeman first called to the suicide scene was the destruction of the suicide note.

Note Destroyer Confesses

The lodger then confessed. According to his own story, the note was worded as follows:

"Father, Mother, I've tried and tried to get out. I can't, the house is locked. The things they make me do are horrible, horrible. Oh, Father and Mother, forgive me. I love you, and I know you would so much rather your Rose were dead."

Note Clears Girl's Character

The overwhelming importance of the note is obvious at a glance. It proves beyond question that the girl was a victim, and demonstrates the fearful tragedy of her position. With it, the Liberry attorneys could unquestionably have gained a much heavier penalty than the five-year sentence which was meted to Mrs. Garr.

FATHER CONTINUES SEARCH

It now appears that after the death of the girl's mother and aunt, hastened by the family tragedy, the girl's father, John Grant Liberry, did not abandon his fight to clear his daughter's name . . . Appearing as John Grant, he traced Mrs. Garr's movements after her release from Waterford, until he found her as the keeper of a now-respectable lodging house. Altered in appearance by his sufferings, he evidently was not recognized by Mrs. Garr. He took rooms in her house, and there it is probable that he kept up his search, hoping he might find some clue to his daughter's death.

FATHER SEES NOTE

Lieutenant Strom, while questioning the lodgers in the house relative to the death of Mrs. Garr, accidently dropped a copy of the Rose Liberry suicide note, as reproduced by the former patrolman, on the floor. It was seen by Mr. Liberry. He fainted, but on revival manifested an interest in the note so normal that no great mark was taken of it.

At approximately nine o'clock this morning, however, a young woman lodging in the 593 Trent Street house, made anxious by his nonappearance, knocked at Mr. Liberry's door. The door swung open. The ceiling light was on. Mr. Liberry, even to her inexperienced eyes, was dead. Lieutenant Strom, called immediately, found a note—the last words

*of an old news story that ranks as the most sensation Gilling
City has ever given to the world. This was the note:*

> *I am John Grant Liberry. I am very happy tonight; I
> cannot wait to go to her.*

Down the middle of the page, the *Comet* ran the old pictures—
the one of Rose Liberry I had seen in the *Comet* of May 26, 1919.
John G. Liberry and the governor of the day. Miss Rachel Staines,
now deceased, her death hastened by family tragedy. Mrs. John
G. Liberry, too, plump and dark. A broken sentence Mr. Grant
had once spoken sounded in my ears:

"Girls whose mothers died crying aloud—"

"I am very glad Mrs. Garr is dead," I said, blowing my nose.
"Lieutenant Strom was decent, wasn't he?"

"I like to see you change your mind; you do it so seldom.
Lady, lady, what a story. If they'd break like that often, I'd be
willing to give up my beggar's independence and go back to
prowling streets for the *Comet*. But it doesn't happen often, re-
gretfully."

"You're hateful! You don't care what awful things happen,
just so there's a good story!"

"Is that fair, when I've forsworn reporting? Ye gods! Me with
two dumb repairmen working on my press! See you tonight!"

He hurtled out again.

MR. GRANT'S FUNERAL WAS on Monday. It was on Tuesday that
Mrs. Halloran knocked to say the phone was for me.

The voice on the other end of the wire had me clutching the
receiver with surprise. It had been so final that last time I'd
heard it that I'd taken it for granted I'd never hear it again.

"Hello! Been reading the papers?" Genially.

"Yes, I have."

"Mad at me?"

"No, I'm not. I think you were awfully decent."

"I had that in mind. Nice not to be a suspect anymore?"

"That's right! I'm not, am I? I feel almost forlorn."

"I pay my debts. Would an ex-investigator like the best dinner in town tonight?"

"An ex-investigator and who else?"

"No one else."

"You mean I should go out to dinner with a married man? Why, Lieutenant Strom!"

"What makes you think I'm married?"

"You look married."

He swore fluently; the telephone rules say it's not permitted, and he was an officer of the law, too.

"You'll get your telephone taken away from you," I said.

"Now I know what keeps Hodge Kistler where he is," he said. "I know it isn't your face. I'll be around at seven o'clock."

I put on my best bib and tucker, and spent all afternoon dressing. When I came downstairs from taking my bath, Mr. Waller was in the hall; he'd started upstairs but stepped back when he heard me coming; he stood half turned away with his head bent.

It's sad to see a man as broken as that, even if he's done an evil thing.

"Good afternoon, Mr. Waller."

He mumbled something, dragged himself upstairs.

Lieutenant Strom came smack on the dot of seven; he was all shining and pressed, and set to do the town. He took me to the Athletic Club for dinner, which, he explained kindly, only big shots could afford to belong to; after that he took me to the Orchid Room at the Plaza, which has the best dance floor and the best bartender in town. I'd never been either place before, which shows how much money the men I know have. It was fun, but most of the fun was the fighting.

We fought over every detail of the case from beginning to end; on his solution with Mr. Grant as the murderer, we did a pitched battle that lasted well into dawn.

He had an awfully good case, of course, such a good one I was really beaten down. He began illustrating his logic with other cases he'd handled; by that time I was so contrary, I questioned the handling of those, too. The more he talked and drank, the more furious he was; we'd be dancing, and he'd push me off to roar in my face some new argument he'd thought up.

It was wonderful.

He drove me home in the good old police car.

"The Foreign Legion ought to import you," he said. "Anytime they couldn't scare up a war, you could always give 'em a little excitement."

"Battles on request," I said. "Or I could charge fifty cents a battle."

"You couldn't keep yourself from giving 'em away," he said grumpily, but he laughed.

When we came into the hall at 593 Trent Street, Hodge Kistler was sprawled asleep in the black leather armchair. He woke up right away.

"Where the hell have you been?" he wanted to know crossly. "If Miss Sands hadn't sworn up and down you'd gone out with Lieutenant Strom and weren't home yet, I'd have busted in your new lock."

"I was out," I said. "With Lieutenant Strom. Celebrating the triumphal conclusion of a case."

Hodge hauled his watch out of his pocket.

"Look at that."

I focused on it.

"Four thirty."

"Is that a nice time to come home, with a death in the house only a couple days ago?"

"Well, I came home with you at three once, and that was too early. Think of what happened to me after that."

"That's one thing you don't have to worry about," Lieutenant Strom pointed out largely. "You don't have to keep tabs on the lady anymore, Kistler. She's as safe as if she was locked up in a cell."

"That's what you think," Mr. Kistler said shortly.

24

———————————

AT ANY RATE, I was safe that night. Nothing happened to me after four thirty except sleep.

It was after that night that Hodge Kistler began acting differently toward me. He still knocked at my door when he came in at night, still kidded me about my master mind. But he didn't ask me out anymore. He often seemed to be thinking about something, but he wouldn't let me in on it. I thought it was just silly. Why should he mind if the lieutenant took me out? When the lieutenant asked me again, I went. Hodge didn't say anything.

Of the things that I had expected to happen then in Mrs. Garr's house, some did, some didn't. Mrs. Halloran moved over some of her belongings that week after Mr. Grant's death. She was there all day every day, but she didn't stay at night. And none of the rest of her family moved in.

"Aren't you moving over?" I asked her.

She looked at me portentously.

"Didn't you ever hear about deaths coming in threes?" she

asked in tones of sepulchral gloom. "If it'd been just Aunt Hattie died out of this house, I wouldn't of minded. But two deaths! I ain't going to move in here until another one dies."

Nice.

Mr. Halloran was around occasionally. Usually in company with burly, shifty men; the lesser grade of contractors, I gathered. They knocked at my door and tracked through my rooms, staring speculatively around at the walls. Mr. Halloran was desperately important, of course.

Money to spend.

Mrs. Halloran told me they were getting a mortgage on the house.

The Tewmans never came back.

But the rest of the tenants didn't make the exodus I'd expected at all. Miss Sands was the only one to tell me she was leaving.

"Mrs. Halloran wants me to go on paying five dollars for that measly room, can you imagine that?" She paused and flushed. "It's nice you aren't telling. I can just see those Hallorans playing the same game on me Mrs. Garr did."

"So can I," I said. "You don't have to worry."

Hodge, when I asked him, said, "Why should I move? I like an eventful life. This house has developed charms I never expected. Besides, think of the company!"

Mr. Buffingham, after Miss Sands had given notice, had a fight with Mrs. Halloran right outside my door; he won with a weekly rental of three dollars.

Most surprising of all, the Wallers didn't move. Mrs. Halloran reported that they were paying six dollars for their rooms now, without a murmur.

"I'm still thinking who could of give me that five-dollar bill," she reminded me. "You know, the one that was tore. It doesn't seem to come to me that it was Mr. Grant. But it wouldn't surprise me if it come to me sometime. I got an awful good memory."

She repeated not one word of her previous request to me to move.

I didn't think of moving.

I admit now why I didn't, but you couldn't have made me, then. Then, I laid it to something I felt when I went to bed at night.

The house wasn't at rest yet.

The house still listened.

It wasn't logical at all. If Mrs. Garr had been the evil spirit of that house, as I fully believed she had been, then surely the house should have been quiet now. If Mr. Grant had precipitated the horrors of the weeks just past, as Lieutenant Strom believed, then surely the house should have been quiet now.

It wasn't.

We had no more detectives around, of course.

I blamed it all on my imagination, as I lay awake, hearing the stir and groan of the walls and floors, feeling the stare of eyes open on the dark, hearing the strain of ears tense in the night. When I told Lieutenant Strom about it, on our second date, he laughed loud and long. Hodge Kistler, when I told him, didn't.

The next Friday, a week after Mr. Grant's death, and the day Hodge is freest from his duties on the paper, I saw his car scoot up Trent Street toward the house with an extra passenger in it. The extra passenger was Mr. Waller.

When I mentioned it, Hodge said, "Waller? Sure. Saw him on the street. Gave him a lift."

I thought no more of it then, but that next Sunday, not having anything else to do, I baked cookies. I took a plate of them up to Hodge. When he opened his door, Mr. Waller was in his sitting room. I thought that was queer.

Mr. Waller looked almost like his old self when the door opened, but when he saw me he collapsed into humiliation again. He didn't go, though. I did. I left the cookies and went downstairs.

That day Mrs. Halloran had ads in the papers for renting Miss Sands' and Mr. Liberry's rooms. She had people tracking in and out of the house all day. Curiosity seekers; she didn't rent.

Poor Mr. Grant. His death had kindled one bright flare, and then he was forgotten. I heard from Lieutenant Strom that he'd left his money to an orphanage; as far as he could find, there were no Liberry relatives left.

"In all the world there are probably only you and me and the Wallers to whom the name Rose Liberry still means anything," I said sadly, thinking of the lovely pictured girl.

It was another Friday evening when I had that talk with Lieutenant Strom about Rose Liberry; the Friday two weeks after Mr. Grant's death. It's funny how so many things in Mrs. Garr's house did happen on Fridays; except for that second attack on me, almost all the big happenings did.

For the second time, Hodge had completely ignored me on his freest evening, so when Lieutenant Strom had called me to suggest a movie and a drink, I'd gone willingly.

But I wasn't awfully happy. At ten, I said I was tired and wanted to go home. I didn't like the way things were turning out; Lieutenant Strom was acting as if he rather liked me, and I wasn't particularly anxious to have him. I felt uneasy with him that night, as if I were trying to ward off something.

He took me home right away and said good night without any fuss. I knew I had him to think about.

I picked up a book to read. I didn't get much meaning out of the words; my mind would slip to Lieutenant Strom and then to Hodge Kistler and his irritating lack of interest in me lately.

I heard Mr. Buffingham come in. Then, after him, Hodge.

Peculiarly, I thought the man with Hodge was Mr. Waller; I knew the footsteps quite well by this time.

I was too keyed up to sleep if I did go to bed; I hated trying to sleep when all I did was listen to that house. I wished I had a private bathtub so I could take a hot bath to make me sleepier. Mrs. Halloran was proving as economical as Mrs. Garr in the matter of hot water. There was sure not to be any; I'd have to turn on the heater if I wanted a bath.

It was nonsense to be so lazy. I finally padded down to the basement as a lesson in moral stiffening, and turned the heater on. It was a rusty old heater; I'd have to wait fully thirty minutes for enough hot water.

I poked around my room those thirty minutes. I got my bed ready, climbed into pajamas and negligee. When I went down to turn the heater off, the hot water still came only a foot and a half down at the top of the tank. I waited around down there five or ten minutes for it to get a little hotter. I was infuriated with the inefficiency of the house; imagine all that trouble for a bath!

I started up the basement stairs, the stairs near whose foot Mrs. Garr had sat so many days, in her curious listening; the stairs where Jerry the policeman had cringed back when a cat's eyes shone at him from the top; the stairs which my attacker, three weeks ago, had stolen down, perhaps at this very time of night, to lurk below until he knew me home and sleeping.

Old stairs, worn stairs, showing the grain of worn wood through worn gray paint.

A few steps from the top I stopped short. My eyes were on the step next to the top.

It was something about the light. The basement light hung close to the basement ceiling, almost on a level with that step.

In the crack at the back of that step, almost invisible, was the dull gleam of worn metal.

I bent forward to look more closely.

My eyes saw that tiny metallic gleam in the angle between the step and the rise, while my mind saw Mrs. Garr sitting in her rocker below.

Watching.

What?

I didn't have to find out what that bit of metal was. I knew.

It was part of a hinge.

As if it moved of its own accord, my right hand reached out, took hold of the overhanging edge of the step next to the top.

I lifted.

It was as easy as that.

The step lifted as easily as if it were a box cover. Easily. Not a sound. Not a sigh.

There were cleaning rags in the space beneath. Musty. Soiled. Newspaper under them.

Clean, smooth newspaper.

I don't know what I expected to see under that paper; I wasn't expecting, I wasn't thinking. I was acting. Bent over, I lifted that paper.

Money.

Thick stacks of money. New bills, as clean as the day they left the mint, unfolded. I began taking the money up; thick stacks of new bills, bound together by strips of glued paper.

That instant, the darkness in the room ahead of me split, and part of it came down on the back of my neck.

Human darkness smashed down on me. I fought wildly. Fought because the minute the hands touched me, I knew that *this was it*. These were the same hands that had reached for my throat that night Mrs. Garr died. This was the same blackness that had been beside my bed that night my rooms were ransacked. This was the Death I had been hunting and had not found.

I struggled to rise, to get my head back, to glimpse the face; for an instant, I turned my head, but there was only blackness where a face should have been. Again, I fought to get up, but the hand on the back of my neck pressed me down; I fought to scream, but the hand over my mouth only pressed closer. I fought to make a noise, any noise that would awaken the household, awaken Hodge, but I had been forced to my knees, and they seemed soundless on the stairs.

I fought to keep my balance; fought most desperately for that, because it was likely death to fall backward as this Death fought to make me go.

I lost there, too.

A minute, two minutes, perhaps, of struggle.

Then I went hurtling straight downward.

I knew the Death I clutched was falling, too; I was taking it with me, but I was beneath; the night cracked as my head hit the stairs behind me.

I didn't feel the rest of the fall.

When I came to, it was like a door opening on a dim stage.

There was fighting on the stage, men crashing over me. Grunts. Swearing. A yell.

"Look out for Gwynne!"

A man's voice. Recognizable. Hodge.

The fight went farther away from me. I turned my head a little; an arm was there, all crumpled up under my head and shoulder. Whose arm could that be? Not mine. I could never get my arm into a position like that. Cement floor under it. I was in the basement, then. Slowly I got my position. Light over me. I was at the foot of the stairs. The fight must be going on over by the furnace. I looked that way, dizzily. Three fighters. Three men, fighting. Striking, staggering back, surging forward again.

One face bent sidewise as a fist flashed forward. Hodge, that was, his hair all over his face. Blood on it. Was he the Death? Three men, all fighting each other. I couldn't see—was it two against one, or were there three sides? I thought of the stacks of money, lying there in that step as in a box. That was it. They were fighting for the money. I was still puzzling over it when one man went down. For a second the group hung stationary: two men standing bent and spent over one man fallen.

One man turned and bounded at me.

"Watch him!" he yelled. It was Hodge. "I've got to get her upstairs. Get a doctor! Get Strom! Get a doctor first!"

He lifted me quickly, charged upstairs. I noticed that the arm under me, the extra arm, came, too. It must be mine, then.

But my mind wasn't on it. My mind was on the significant group by the furnace. The group of two with one man crouched, panting, over the second lying quiet with his head against the furnace.

One thing more I saw, my head bobbing back over Hodge's shoulder.

Money.

Money strewn far and wide. Money on the basement floor.

The arm didn't seem to hurt much then, with Hodge yelling orders and pushing glasses in my face and people running. But the minute the doctor came and touched it, it hurt, excruciatingly.

I pleased myself very much by fainting again. I came to at intervals after that, always under odd and unexplainable circumstances. Once I was on a bed, but it was moving fast. Once I was on a bed, but it was shooting upward. Once I was on a bed with a blinding light over it; my eyes were quickly covered, and the only air to breathe was sickeningly sweet. Once I was on a bed, but when I moved, knives struck at me from six sides.

The next time I came out of it the circumstances were still odd, but explainable.

I was in a hospital.

I was so bandaged, I couldn't move, but even if I could have moved, I wouldn't have wanted to. I tried wiggling my little finger once, and the result told me that was nothing to do at all.

There was a nurse in bright morning light.

"Hello," I said.

"Good morning," she said with that impersonal cheer nurses use bedside. "And how are we feeling this morning?"

I didn't care how she felt.

"What's the matter with me?"

"Just a few simple fractures," she encouraged. "You fell downstairs."

"Who was it jumped at me?"

"Now, now, just be quiet and rest."

That was all I could get out of her.

All I did that day was sleep and ask questions that weren't answered. I'd sleep, and then the questions would get so insistent, I'd wake up to ask them, but that was all the good it did me. I asked the nurse, the doctor, a woman who came in and swept, a cheekbony intern. I asked Hodge Kistler.

He came in sometime during the afternoon. I woke up as far as I could for the occasion.

"Did you get him?"

"Yes, we got him this time. You won't be jumped at again."

"Who was it?"

"You're not supposed to be excited."

"How can I keep from getting excited when no one will tell me anything? Did he get the money? I found the money. I found a lot of money. It was in the step below the top. Who was it? Was it Mr. Halloran?"

"The patient is getting excited. You will have to go now," the nurse said, and shoved him out.

I hope the look I gave her was nasty, but only one eye was out of the bandages.

"Tomorrow," she told me. "Just be quiet until tomorrow. Tomorrow we'll let Mr. Kistler talk to you for fifteen whole minutes."

She wiped my tongue with a soppy piece of rag.

By the next afternoon, I was still sleepy enough to drop off occasionally, but I didn't drop off when it came near three o'clock. I was burning with impatience, and it's no fun burning when you can't even move, and no one ever answers.

Hodge came promptly at three. He walked in, short and quick, grinning his three-cornered grin; his face looked scrubbed with pleasure and triumph.

"Well, well, so you're going to live," he crowed over me.

"Who said I wasn't?"

"Well, I was sort of doubtful when I saw you hadn't landed on your head. You should always take knocks on your head; it seems to hurt you less."

"I haven't time to be insulted. *Who was it?*"

"Don't you know?"

"No, I don't know. And I'm going to break in a few more places if I don't know pretty soon."

"What did you see in that top step?"

"Money."

"Anything else?"

"No."

"Then you didn't take the money out?"

"I took some money out. I lifted the top of the step, and took the rags out and took up the newspaper, and there it was. Packages of money. I lifted some out. And then it hit me, bang."

"I thought it was like that. He was bending over you at the bottom of the stairs when I got there. Said he'd heard you fall and run down, but he was clutching money in his hand, and when I saw the black scarf in his pocket I reached for his chin."

"He? He! Would you like me crazy?"

"Me? My, no. But I think you deserve the full dramatic impact. You see, in one way you were right. There was money. But there was something else, too. There was a link with the Liberry case. It was there, with the money, hidden in that step. The one last link."

"Can't you tell me? Can't you show me?" I wailed.

"All right. Now this is solemn. This is the moment. I borrowed this document from Lieutenant Strom, and I will probably fry in the electric chair if I lose it. But with what I've got on Lieutenant Strom—well, we'll skip that. This is the incriminating document. And the name at the end is the name of the person who murdered Mrs. Garr, choked you once, and tried twice to kill you. Ready?"

"Hurry up!"

"Okay."

His eyes alight on my face, he reached into his inner coat pocket, brought forth a sheet of letter paper, yellowed and old, unfolded it. I had no hands to use; he held it up in front of my face. It was handwritten in faded black ink, the handwriting irregular, nervous.

> *I confess it was me that got Rose Liberry to go to Mrs.*
> *Garr's house. She come into the drugstore for a soda.*
> *She was a knockout, so I mixed her the right kind of*
> *a drink, and when it'd taken hold, I said I'd take her*

to a place where she could lay down awhile. Like I did
with all the girls I got for Mrs. Garr. She paid me $25
extra.

That was all, except for the signature; the name I'd known the minute my eyes reached the second line.

Charles Buffingham.

25

THE NURSE CHASED HODGE out then.

It wasn't until the next day that I got the explanations. That day, I graduated from having a nurse of my own to being tended by the regular nursing staff. What are a few broken bones? I'd made the doctor tell me how often I'd cracked, too: a fractured collarbone and a left arm broken in three places. The rest were only concussions, bruises, and such.

I was bursting with hows, whats, whens, and whys when Hodge again arrived promptly at three o'clock. I'd found out it was Wednesday, so it was nice of him to come in the daytime. He brought what must have been his seventh bunch of flowers: daisies again, with tall stalks of gladioli.

He was so triumphant, it hurt your eyes to look at him.

"What a bunch of 'I told you so' I bet you're spreading," I told him.

"Sure, why not? It isn't often I'm as right as I was this time."

He's good at taking the curse off himself.

"Tell me everything. Do you realize how long I've waited?"

"Ah, but you know the denouement. Some nice points, though. Guess who got the second-best bit of clinching evidence?"

"I give up right away. Who?"

"Waller."

"You mean he suspected Mr. Buffingham, too?"

"He got around to it. You see, after Grant died, and Waller got let out by Strom, he came around to the *Guide* office to see me. Said now that he'd quit being afraid of being found out, he'd got to thinking. He asked me who I thought the murderer probably was, before it had been pinned on Grant, and I said Buffingham. So he said, 'Funny, I've come around to Buffingham, too.'

"We talked it over, and Waller decided he'd trail Buffingham as much as he could without being seen, because there wasn't much he could do working back over what had happened; that'd all been covered by the police. He trailed Buffingham now and again from then on, and he also hung around the Elite Drugstore on the nights Buffingham was off.

"It wasn't long before he began to get on to something. He noticed an awful lot of men dropped into that drugstore late at night and paid a visit to a back counter. It wasn't hard to get in on. Buffingham and the owner of the store were running a little numbers racket of their own, taking bets on the total livestock receipts at the South Gilling stockyards; the figure's printed in the *Comet* every night.

"He got to know the regulars: shoe salesmen, collectors, carpenters, grocery clerks, punks—it's a low-pay neighborhood. He didn't get anything out of them until one night, he was talking to a guy he'd seen there almost every night. When he asked him what his business was, the guy said 'bank guard.' Get that? Bank guard."

"I don't see what connection that would have."

"Neither did Waller, at first. But he went on chatting, eventually mentioning that he lived in the same house as Buffingham, where an old lady had died, Mrs. Garr, to see if he'd get any reaction. And for the first time, he got one. The bank guard said, 'She died, did she? Who got all her dough?' Waller said, 'Oh, she didn't leave so much.'

"The bank guard said, 'Didn't leave much? I'll never forget the time she come in the bank when we went off the gold standard, carrying an old black reticule my great-grandmother wouldn't of been seen out with. She lugged that reticule up to a cashier's window, took a good swing on it to lift it, and splashed gold all over the counter. That was the biggest lot of gold we ever had turned in by a private individual. "Give me new paper money for it," she says. Forty thousand dollars even, the cashier said it was. She stuck those stacks of bills back in the reticule and walked out like it was forty cents.'

"'I guess she'd been giving a lot to her niece,' Waller said quickly. 'Man, that's a good story. What'd Buffingham say when he heard it?' 'Said he never knew the old bitch had so much dough,' the bank guard said to Waller."

Hodge stopped to let it sink in.

"F'heaven's sake," I said, "and I thought I was a detective."

"Yeah. Waller's got a gift for it. He'd have got along all right as a cop if he hadn't been ruined by what he did for Mrs. Garr."

"Go on, go on."

"So Waller was so excited, he almost bit his pipe in two. But he asked one more question. He got such a shock on that one, he did bite it—right smack through! Showed me the pieces."

"Go on!"

"Want to know what that question was? Well, this is it. Waller says to this bank guard, 'What'd the other guys around here think about that?' And the bank guard said, 'Why, I wouldn't tell a story like that to a bunch of folks. Some of 'em might not be good characters. As a matter of fact,' the bank guard says, looking sort of nervous, 'I wished afterward I hadn't told Buffingham that story. There was one other man heard it. He died, that other man did. But it sure taught me a lesson to look folks over before I talk shop like that. Made me pretty nervous when it came out in the papers.'

"Waller says, 'What story was that?' And the bank guard said, 'About that other man getting killed. Zeitman, his name was. He used to hang around here some before he got killed.'"

"Zeitman!"

"Yep, Zeitman."

"Hodge, you mean that gangster? That man I found in back of the house?"

"I mean the same."

"But why didn't that bank guard tell the police when he read about the killing? Why didn't he say he—?"

"Where do you suppose his job would have been if he had?"

"Oh, my goodness! Zeitman knew about the money in Mrs. Garr's house, too, then! And Mr. Buffingham knew Zeitman!"

"Guess what day this was Waller talked to the bank guard."

"Friday evening, I suppose."

"Not that close. Thursday night, though. We were still arguing about whether to turn in this discovery to Lieutenant Strom or wait until we had something more."

"You didn't have to wait long," I contributed grimly.

"You're a wonderful bean spiller, my sweet."

"Wait. I've got more questions. Why had he ever written that confession, the one you brought in here?"

"Strom got that out of him. Mrs. Garr's lawyers made him write it, back when she was having her trial. The lawyer threatened to have Mrs. Garr testify Buffingham brought the girl to the house and seduced her, left her there with Mrs. Garr. In that case, as the lawyer pointed out, our state would probably have had a lynching to its credit. This town was stirred up about Rose Liberry. Buffingham signed quick. Then the lawyers used the confession to make sure Buffingham wouldn't testify against Mrs. Garr. And when Mrs. Garr got out of jail, she used it for her private pleasure—blackmail. Buffingham never got over being afraid of it."

"That Liberry case is undoubtedly the world's nastiest."

"It's done now."

"Yes, it's done now. Does Buffingham say—does he admit he killed Mrs. Garr?"

"You should have seen your friend the lieutenant making up for lost time when he got hold of Buffingham Friday night. He confessed, all right. We had that part down pat. He was in the kitchen hunting for the forty thousand in new bills when she came in and caught him. He strangled her."

"But that part about that gangster, Zeitman. Where did he—?"

"Strom got that out of him, too, once he had the bank guard's statement and Buffingham knew it was all up, anyway. Buffingham bumped him off, too. And why, do you think?"

"Why?"

"Because of you, baby, *because of you*."

"You're insane."

"No, I'm not, my sweetling. You may look harmless, but because of you, a man died. Zeitman."

"How—?"

"I like this. The day you first came to Mrs. Garr's house to look it over, Buffingham stood on the stairs and heard Mrs. Garr say she kept a closet in that kitchen. He'd only just begun his hunt then. Mrs. Garr stuck so close, Buffingham couldn't search your rooms before you moved in. Then you stuck around too much. Zeitman was getting hard up and wanted to rush things; it was his idea to burgle the joint, tie you up or bump you off so they could look your rooms over. Buffingham objected; he said he never intended any violence, up until he got caught. Probably he wanted to find the dough by himself and double-cross the other guy, too. Zeitman thought so, anyway. They had a fight, sitting in Buffingham's car. Zeitman pulled his gun just for a little threatening, and the next thing he knew he had a pitchfork in his tail. All over you!"

"But how did he get where I found him?"

"Zeitman was killed in the car, out by Lake Maris somewhere, where they'd driven to talk things over. When Zeitman was dead, Buffingham just drove back to town with the body—he said it just looked drunk—calmly drove up in back of 593 Trent, dumped the body over the guardrail, drove back to the side of the house, wiped out the car for fingerprints—all the blood had soaked into Zeitman's own clothes—and went to bed."

"He didn't seem to mind killing when he got started. What about me?"

"He even confessed that."

"But why did he pick on me?"

Hodge's triangular grin came on again. "So thick-witted," he said.

"WHY?"

"It seems that after a certain run-in, he was always afraid you would put two and two together. After all, you caught him hunting for that cat on the night Mrs. Garr was murdered."

If I could have lain back any harder, I'd have lain back harder.

There it was, staring me in the face.

That was what Mr. Buffingham had been doing, that Friday night before Memorial Day, when I'd come into the hall at ten. *He had been chasing the cat!*

I felt so low, I couldn't even climb up close enough to the bottom to ask any more questions.

It's bad enough having another amateur find a murderer you've been hunting yourself, without having it pointed out to you that you should have jolly well known it all along.

THAT'S THE STORY OF the murder of Mrs. Garr.

The rest of this is about what happened since then, in case you'd like to know.

I wasn't lonesome in the hospital after that day. Girls I'd known in offices came to hear all about it, every one agog. Hodge saved the papers for me; I read them all. About how I'd found Mrs. Garr's hidden savings, how Mr. Buffingham had been listening to me because I'd stayed so long in the basement, how he'd crept down to see if I was hunting, too, and seen me make the find.

So I knew who the listener in the house was, after Mrs. Garr was dead.

Mr. Waller and Mr. Kistler got a big hand for their capture of Buffingham, and Mr. Waller was given an extra play for his discovery of the talkative bank guard. There were all sorts of pictures: the house, the one remaining picture of Mrs. Garr—the one I'd seen at the railroad station—Charles Buffingham, Reginald Buffingham, even the black scarf Buffingham had tied over his face.

The papers finally had the story they'd been cheated out of at first.

But reading, you could see the accounts were incomplete. That was when the rumors began to spread. People began wondering about why the police hadn't known Mrs. Garr was murdered. Interest was whipped up as promises were made of sensational disclosures at the trial.

On my ninth day in the hospital, the trial and the newspaper accounts all ended with a bang and a whimper.

Mr. Buffingham hanged himself in his cell.

MISS SANDS CAME IN to see me one evening. I was glad; you can gossip with a woman so much more thoroughly than with a man, and she knew the facts. I'd had to be careful with the girls from the offices.

She seemed pathetically glad because I enjoyed her coming; after the first time, she came every night. She told me Lieutenant Strom had called Mr. Waller in to see him, and after hemming and hawing around said they were taking on a new group of substitutes, and he had been agreeably impressed with Mr. Waller's work on the bank guard. Then he gave him back his two-thousand-dollar note, and Waller tore it into bits and threw it into Strom's wastebasket and walked home with a job. Miss Sands said he went home and cried.

Lieutenant Strom sent flowers but didn't come himself. I wondered what that meant.

The Wallers didn't come, but Mrs. Halloran did. She'd bought herself a forty-dollar black satin dress, the very first of the fall preshowings; she sweated in it proudly all the hot afternoon she visited me.

"My, you'll hardly know the place when you get back," she said. "We got men stuccoing the outside now. Pale green, we decided on. My, it's going to look swell. We're going to raise all the rents."

"You'll want richer people than me, then. This hospital is cleaning me out."

I was willing to move now.

"Why, I wouldn't think of asking you to move, Mrs. Dacres, in your condition and all, but if you could see your way around to, it would be lovely, just lovely." She paused, hinted. "Wasn't it around this time of week you used to pay?"

Hodge had brought my handbag down, with necessities.

I paid her eight dollars for two weeks.

"I'll be very sorry to lose you, Mrs. Dacres, such prompt pay and all, but that's the way it is, some go up in the world, and some go down."

"You're still going up nicely?"

"Oh my, yes." She leaned forward confidentially. "You know that money? All that money you found? We got in touch with some swell lawyers; they come around to see us when the story come out in the papers. They said it was a shame, the way we were the only relatives and all, we shouldn't get the money. They said we had a swell case, in view. In view, you know. They don't think the people who are supposed to start that dog and cat house will fight very hard. And then we'll get all that money! My! Forty thousand dollars! I cer'n'y never knew my aunt Hattie had that much money, the way she lived and all."

"That'll be lovely," I said. "So nice for the children."

"Oh my, yes. For me, too."

"For the lawyers, too?"

"Oh no, they're very reasonable, they said. Dirt cheap, they said. If we win they get half, but if we don't win they only get two thousand dollars. We wouldn't hardly notice two thousand dollars, not out of forty thousand."

I didn't point out the flaw in the logic.

So that was what was to become of the forty thousand dollars, the money Mrs. Garr had watched, rocking below in her chair by day, sleeping on the couch in that room at the head of the stairs by night. That was what was to become of the money Mr. Buffingham had killed for twice, and would have killed for again, and for which he had hanged himself in his cell, and for whose lack, his son would take the punishments his crimes had earned.

The lawyers would get half, Mrs. Halloran would get half, and there would probably be stucco on the inside as well as on the outside of Mrs. Garr's old house.

Just before she left, Mrs. Halloran's face brightened with the brightness of one who remembers something important.

"Oh, Mrs. Dacres, you remember that five-dollar bill, the tore one, the one you was asking about? The minute I took in the paper Sat'd'y and read about the money and how he confessed and all, I remembered it just like it was happening right then. He give me a bill, and it was tore. It was Mr. Buffingham give me that bill, that's who it was."

TWO WEEKS FROM THE day I entered the hospital the doctors said I could leave. That, you'll notice, was a Friday, too.

I still wore the cast, of course. And the left side of my face, where I'd landed, was still a lively purple, with burgundy borders.

Hodge came around in midmorning, to take me home in his car. We drove through residence streets.

"Nice of you to get out of hospitals on Friday, when I have lots of time," he said.

"Nice of you to allow me a Friday. I thought you were being awfully stingy with 'em for a while."

"Suppose I had let you in on what we were doing. You'd have run around to Buffingham's room, asking, 'Now, just tell me everything you've done that's suspicious.'"

"Don't forget I found out about that ticket."

"We'll celebrate that today. In fact I'm thinking of spending the whole day celebrating. I have to stop in here to see a guy first, though. Want to come along?"

"I wouldn't mind," I said. "I haven't been many places lately."

The house was white with a wide porch. Hodge punched the bell.

A mild, white-whiskered old man answered the door.

"You're the young man for eleven o'clock?" he asked. "Come right in."

We went into a horsehair and mahogany parlor; I didn't think any had survived.

The white-whiskered man looked at me doubtfully, but didn't ask me to sit down.

"You have the license?" he asked.

"Right here," Hodge answered and handed him a paper from his pocket. A clean one, folded.

"Has—ah—the young lady been in an accident?" asked the old man.

"Oh no, not at all," Hodge said. "I take 'em by capture. She put up a fight. The methods of my forefathers are good enough for me."

You have to remember I was on my way home from a hospital, and I'd been in bed steadily until two days ago.

"What do you mean, capture?" I asked dizzily.

"Oh, haven't you heard?" Hodge asked me airily. "You're marrying me today."

The old man laughed politely.

"Young people are so lighthearted nowadays," he said.

He scuttled away and came back with two women.

He married us then, with his wife and his maidservant for witnesses.

"I'm doing this as a life-saving measure," Hodge explained kindly, back in the car. "It isn't safe to leave you alone at night. You have too many accidents. And I always did wonder if it was fun to be a philandering husband, too."

"I wonder what Lieutenant Strom will say," I said, which was a silly thing to bring up.

"Strom? Oh, he's already said it. This last time you cracked up, I told him we were engaged. Had been for two months. Sort of surprised him, but he's a philosopher. Swore a little."

I saw where I'd have a struggle to call my soul my own.

We drew up in front of 593 Trent Street with a flourish. It was ringed with piles of sand, boxes of cement, funny iron kettles like big empty iron balls. Men, too. Leaning on shovels and things.

"I've rented us a furnished apartment to live in until you can hunt up what your domestic nature requires." Hodge gave the orders. "I've got my stuff all packed, and most of your stuff. Movers coming at two o'clock. Now we'll go in and quick pack up the rest of your stuff so we can grab a wedding luncheon before the movers get here."

Halloran children scuttled out of the hall when we came in; Mrs. Halloran herself, movie magazine in hand, moved to the parlor door from her chair to smile a genteel but aloof welcome upon me.

My dishes were packed in barrels in the kitchen, my pots and pans, even my groceries. Funny how well Hodge had known what was mine and what Mrs. Garr's—Mrs. Halloran's now. The only thing left to pack were my clothes, bedding, linens.

I directed Hodge while he dragged my trunk and suitcases out of the closet; I was clumsy with one hand, he was clumsy at packing clothes with two. His hair came uncombed and his face red.

"See the pretty bridegroom," I said.

"What nice bride would have her husband of—wait a minute—fifty minutes packing her panties? Answer that one, my bruised beauty."

"Bruised by another man, too."

"When I think how long I have to handle you carefully—oh well, I'll regale you with tales of what's going to happen. Lots worse said than done."

He slammed my trunk shut, knelt to lock it.

"That all? Then I'll run up and lock my trunks before we shoot downtown for that lunch. I've got a few things to throw in, too. Think you can stay here without busting a leg, or do you want to come along? Hell's bells, I see where I take you along to the office, next."

"Thank you," I said with dignity. "I shall be perfectly safe here."

He left me. I could hear the scurryings of the little Hallorans in the house, like heavy mice. I walked through my rooms for that inevitable last look. Studio couch where I'd slept, nearly been killed. Armchair where Strom had held court. Shelves where my dishes had stood. Cavernous icebox where so much ice had melted, and so fast. The twice-bolted cellar door behind which a murderer had lurked. The closet where my clothes had hung; into which, panting, Mrs. Garr had helped me lift the trunk Hodge had so easily lifted out.

It was the last time I would think, in her own house, of that evil woman, sitting below to watch the precious contents of that step. Sitting downstairs listening to me, too, because she had come into my rooms so quickly whenever I did anything unusual. That time I changed the furniture around. That time I took the trunk out for my summer clothes.

I stood there in the little passageway, stock-still.

Why had she listened so to me? Why, when it was that step she guarded? Why had she listened so closely to me? I was thinking hard, my heart racing, the blood pushing against the bruised half of my face.

She came up when I moved furniture. She came up when I moved the trunk. She had helped me carry the trunk into that closet.

The one thing she'd done when I moved in.

She had helped me carry it back there when I'd taken it out.

I stared into the closet. Bare walls, hooks, hanger rod.

Nothing.

Except the little platform for the trunk.

There was a noise in the hall. I nearly fainted.

I darted into the living room; the hall doors were shut but not locked; the key was there; I turned it with my one hand. Quietly I dragged the chairs to go under the knobs.

If Hodge wanted to get in, he could knock.

Quickly I slipped back to the closet, bent over the platform, tugged at its edge.

It didn't budge.

I tugged harder.

No giving.

I stood up to tell myself what a fool I was.

Of course there was nothing there. Why should there be?

But a platform. Why a platform?

She'd said stairs were under here. But stairs weren't under there. They were at the side.

I knelt now; looked the platform over every inch. Not a break, not a suspicious crack.

I tried lifting the top again, tugging with all my one hand's strength. It was immovable.

I sat back on my heels to think again.

The rise. It looked solid. It was solid. The baseboard.

The baseboard ended where the platform began.

The baseboard ended where the platform began!

A box might open from any one of four sides.

If that wasn't the answer, there wasn't any answer. I took the palm of my right hand and pushed downward, hard, on the front edge of the platform.

My throat tightened.

It moved!

I jerked my head to the quiet behind me, expecting that, somehow, something would strike out at me. It was so much like that other night.

Nothing came.

I went back to the kitchen, the living room, looked.

Nothing was there.

Trembling with the excitement, with weakness, I dropped to my knees in front of the platform again. Quickly now, I pressed with the slanted palm of my hand against the platform's outer edge.

The top fitted tightly; it came up slowly, inch by inch.

Then suddenly, free of the back wall, it flew back.

I looked under it, gasped, and clung dizzily to the wood lid I held.

There was no concealment under that platform's top. No cleaning rags. No newspaper. Just money.

Money! Stacks of bills which, at the sides, were four inches thick. I picked out one or two, riffled through them. One stack of fives. One of twenties. Bumpy envelopes.

Shaking, I lifted one package of ten-dollar bills, counted. There were two hundred. I counted the twenties I had taken out before. Two hundred of those. The package of fives was the same size. I looked in a manila paper grocery bag. Fifty-cent pieces. Too many to count. I opened a smaller envelope. Five-dollar gold pieces. Exactly twenty of those. I piled money behind me on the closet floor in disorder as I estimated. Paper bags of silver, dimes, quarters, dollars. I didn't count those. More stacks of bills, ones, fives, tens, twenties, all in the packages of two hundred. One was of hundred-dollar bills. I worked feverishly, awkwardly, bemoaning my useless left hand.

When I was done I settled back on my heels, looking with dazed unbelief at the money strewn about me.

One hundred and thirty thousand dollars. And the silver besides.

All I could do was to stare at it, stupidly.

I stood up, still staring at it. I thought about Rover, Richard, George, and Cecilia—Mrs. Garr's pets. This was their money. This, plus the forty thousand I had found before, was the "residue of my estate." This was the money that had been willed to Rover, Richard, George, and Cecilia.

Rover, Richard, George, and Cecilia, who had not waited to be fed, and so had died.

The money belonged to their heirs now. To men who would fight only moderately over forty thousand dollars, but would fight with more vehemence for the privilege of disbursing this larger sum for the pleasance of dogs, of cats—and of themselves. It belonged to lawyers, who would settle on the Hallorans in buzzing buzzard swarms. Shyster lawyers. It belonged to the Hallorans, if there was anything left after that; enough money, perhaps, so even the baby could get drunk.

I jumped.

Knocking at my door.

My right hand went up to protect my throat before I remembered.

"What's the idea, locking me out? Took me longer than I thought. I'd forgotten—" he began. *"Hey, what's the matter with you?"*

I shook my head at him, locked the doors behind him again.

"Come with me," I said.

I led him with my right hand to the closet.

He gasped, too; gasped and leaned against the closet wall for support.

"Ye gods, ye catfishes, and ye little brass monkeys," he swore softly after a while. "Baby, I'm going to leave you alone often."

THAT WAS THE LAST thing that happened to us before we left Mrs. Garr's house forever.

Since then, rather nice things have happened to some of the people who used to live in Mrs. Garr's house. Almost miraculous, some of them.

One thing is that Mr. Kistler, co-owner of the *Buyers' Guide*, has a new printing press; a press over which he and the other co-owner, a Mr. Lester Trowbridge, croon with pride and joy. The people who have been brought in by physical force to look upon its glory include the cop on the corner and every advertiser the *Guide* begs, buys, borrows, or steals.

Another thing was that a young lawyer, who is a friend of Hodge's, discovered that Miss Sands had been left eighteen thousand dollars by an uncle Hubert she scarcely remembered having. She said a ringing good-bye to the store and went out to live with the Wallers, who have rented a little house on some acres of ground in the country. Mr. Waller drives in to town for work. Miss Sands tells me she is starting a garden—in August.

Me? I am very well, thank you.

I know I am a thief. I know I am dishonest. I think sometimes of the lawyers I am defrauding—but I never *quite* weep over them.

I am redecorating our apartment to match my blue sofa. I have a new linen tablecloth so heavy it blisters my palm to iron it ice-smooth. I have a chest of sterling silver so lovely it's like watching a ballet to look at it.

Husbands are nice to have, too.

One of the most popular American crime writers of the twentieth century, **Mabel Seeley** was known as "The Mistress of Mystery." Critically acclaimed titles like *The Listening House* (1938), *The Crying Sisters* (1939), and the Mystery of the Year–awarded *The Chuckling Fingers* (1941) have placed her stories and characters alongside those of Agatha Christie, Dorothy Sayers, and Sir Arthur Conan Doyle. Among her many accolades and awards, Seeley was most proud of her service as the first director of the Mystery Writers of America. Born on March 25, 1903, in Herman, Minnesota, Mabel Seeley is best known for crime novels featuring female detectives who defied the stereotypes of the time as self-reliant and strong-willed Midwestern heroines.

Ready to find
your next great read?

Let us help.

Visit prh.com/nextread

Penguin
Random
House